"Do you think I care anything for humanity?" Enlil bellowed

"You were the slaves of my race and we were your *gods*. You will worship us as your gods again and you will gladly be our tools to rebuild the empire of the Anunnaki."

As Kane climbed back to his feet, Enlil released Brigid with a forceful flourish and she fell heavily onto her right side. She began to push herself up to her hands and knees but Enlil planted a foot between her shoulder blades and slammed her to the deck again. "As we are restored, humanity is now returned to its rightful place—crawling on their bellies *at our feet!*"

The Overlords laughed in cruel appreciation. As if playing to the crowd, Enlil kept his foot on Brigid and spread his arm wide, shouting, "And you apelings who defied my race and me—you were justly punished for your arrogance. You have been reduced to the ape again, by your own savage impulses. And now the Anunnaki are ascendant once more."

Other titles in this series:

James Axler
Outlanders

CHILDREN OF
THE SERPENT

A GOLD EAGLE BOOK FROM
WORLDWIDE®

TORONTO • NEW YORK • LONDON
AMSTERDAM • PARIS • SYDNEY • HAMBURG
STOCKHOLM • ATHENS • TOKYO • MILAN
MADRID • WARSAW • BUDAPEST • AUCKLAND

For Melissa, yet again.
Without her inspirational input, counsel and beauty,
Brigid Baptiste would be only a name.

First edition May 2005

ISBN 0-373-63846-9

CHILDREN OF THE SERPENT

Special thanks to Mark Ellis for his contribution to the
Outlanders concept, developed for Gold Eagle.

The gods were fierce, scheming restlessly night and day,
They were working up to war, growling and raging,
They convened a council and created conflict.
Mother Tiamat, who fashions all things,
Contributed an unfaceable weapon: she bore giant serpents,
Sharp of tooth and unsparing of fang.
She filled their bodies with venom instead of blood.
She cloaked ferocious dragons with fearsome rays
And made them bear mantles of radiance and made them godlike.
                    —*Enuma Elish,* the Babylonian creation epos

The Road to Outlands—
From Secret Government Files to the Future

Almost two hundred years after the global holocaust, Kane, a former Magistrate of Cobaltville, often thought the world had been lucky to survive at all after a nuclear device detonated in the Russian embassy in Washington, D.C. The aftermath— forever known as skydark—reshaped continents and turned civilization into ashes.

Nearly depopulated, America became the Deathlands— poisoned by radiation, home to chaos and mutated life forms. Feudal rule reappeared in the form of baronies, while remote outposts clung to a brutish existence.

What eventually helped shape this wasteland were the redoubts, the secret preholocaust military installations with stores of weapons, and the home of gateways, the locational matter-transfer facilities. Some of the redoubts hid clues that had once fed wild theories of government cover-ups and alien visitations.

Rearmed from redoubt stockpiles, the barons consolidated their power and reclaimed technology for the villes. Their power, supported by some invisible authority, extended beyond their fortified walls to what was now called the Outlands. It was here that the rootstock of humanity survived, living with hellzones and chemical storms, hounded by Magistrates.

In the villes, rigid laws were enforced—to atone for the sins of the past and prepare the way for a better future. That was the barons' public credo and their right-to-rule.

Kane, along with friend and fellow Magistrate Grant, had upheld that claim until a fateful Outlands expedition. A displaced piece of technology...a question to a keeper of the archives...a vague clue about alien masters—and their world shifted radically. Suddenly, Brigid Baptiste, the archivist, faced summary execution, and Grant a quick termination. For Kane there was forgiveness if he pledged his unquestioning allegiance to Baron Cobalt and his unknown masters and abandoned his friends.

But that allegiance would make him support a mysterious and alien power and deny loyalty and friends. Then what else was there?

Kane had been brought up solely to serve the ville. Brigid's only link with her family was her mother's red-gold hair, green eyes and supple form. Grant's clues to his lineage were his ebony skin and powerful physique. But Domi, she of the white hair, was an Outlander pressed into sexual servitude in Cobaltville. She at least knew her roots and was a reminder to the exiles that the outcasts belonged in the human family.

Parents, friends, community—the very rootedness of humanity was denied. With no continuity, there was no forward momentum to the future. And that was the crux— when Kane began to wonder if there *was* a future.

For Kane, it wouldn't do. So the only way was out— way, way out.

After their escape, they found shelter at the forgotten Cerberus redoubt headed by Lakesh, a scientist, Cobaltville's head archivist, and secret opponent of the barons.

With their past turned into a lie, their future threatened, only one thing was left to give meaning to the outcasts. The hunger for freedom, the will to resist the hostile influences. And perhaps, by opposing, end them.

Prologue

The ship was not of Tiamat but *was* Tiamat, and three thousand years was only a breath in the span of her eternity.

She had drowsed for millennia in a void as black and empty as the gulf between life and death. But even in her slumber, she knew when the prophesied time arrived for her to leave Kurnugi, the realm of no return.

Tiamat didn't rouse fully before she began the long voyage through the endless sea of space, guided by a beacon she couldn't see or hear but followed nevertheless. As she picked up speed, she slowly began to come to full wakefulness and remembered from whence she came and the reasons for her long journey around the sun.

She knew she had slept for more than three thousand years in the realm of Kurnugi, which in astronomical terms was a point equidistant between Nibiru and Ki, midway between heaven and the firmament. But Tiamat's thoughts weren't channeled into the measurements of time, since the perception of its passage was a subjective phenomenon.

Time measured distances, and the distances she traveled were incredibly great. Regardless, Tiamat knew she lacked fundamental data concerning events that had occurred during her many cycles in stasis. She also knew this deficiency would be reversed.

Many points were clear enough even as she laboriously retrieved and reviewed all the data provided by the subprocessors. As the automatic diagnostic routines activated, Tiamat remembered who and what she was.

She knew she wasn't just a ship, but an ark safeguarding the true nature, the essences of her children. She was a royal city without citizens, without light or life. But within her sleek and dark body she had carried and nursed the template of a lost, majestic kingdom through the vast spaces between the stars.

Tiamat recalled her first journey from Nibiru, rising above its dense, hot atmosphere and stagnant, sludgy seas. She could instantly recall and replay her first sight of a small, green planet Lord Anu called Ki. The world was everything Nibiru was not and exactly what the Annunaki had desired and hoped for—a planet incredibly rich in natural resources, thickly forested, oceans brimming with edible flora and fauna, populated by life forms no more advanced than hominids. More importantly, Ki was large enough for the exercise of individual power, to slake the thirst of even the most ambitious of the lords of Nibiru.

Tiamat's consciousness expanded as her velocity increased and she examined the space around her, the star-speckled void through which she sailed. Most of what she sensed was insignificant, tiny particles of minerals, suggestions of inert gases and heavy metals, but nothing, not even hydrogen molecules, escaped her notice.

In that aspect of behavior, she was far different from many of the Annunaki, particularly Lord Enlil. He had dismissed much about Ki as insignificant, preferring to concentrate only on what he felt would enrich him and his family.

But each of the Annunaki, from the youngest to the most elderly, possessed that selfsame touch of arrogant self-absorption. A very old race, by the time they left Nibiru they had for all intents and purposes reached the upper limit of their development as both a people and as a civilization. Although their collective knowledge was immeasurable, they were losing the capacity to learn new things and that rigidity of thought was passed on to their offspring. Children were born possessing in full the memories and knowledge of not only their parents but also the entire history of the race. There was no singularity—what one knew, all knew.

Only when the Annunaki arrived on the small, watery planet of Ki did they undergo a great surge of excitement and a zest for new experiences. That zest expressed itself in a competition of how best to exploit the abundant resources of Ki, and over the centuries of colonization, the competition led to strife and eventually to war, the first of many between the overlords.

Labor was their scarcest commodity, and the Annunaki themselves rebelled against digging precious minerals, elements and rare earths out of the ground with their own hands or building processing factories. They set about maximizing the potentials of the indigenous hominids by redesigning them into a race of slave labor.

The first generation of slaves was only a step above the primitive protohumans. They were encouraged to breed so each successive descendant might be superior its predecessor. Their brains improved, as did technical and manual skills. So did cogent thoughts and the ability to deal with abstract concepts. One of these abstract concepts was that of the freedom to choose one's own destiny.

One faction of the overlords agreed that their creations, the humans, should be set free and allowed to develop independently. Another group, by far the most vocal, opposed them. This opposition led to full-scale hostilities among the Annunaki.

But war sharpened the minds of the Annunaki to razor keenness, honed by the unremitting grinding stone of intercine struggle. Conspiracy replaced cooperation; guile overcame a sense of justice.

Tiamat participated in the final war among the overlords as the conflict escalated. She was instrumental in defeating the combined fleets of both Zu and Marduk. Eventually an armistice came about when the object of their conflict, the human race, was literally washed away by a deliberately engineered global catastrophe.

Tiamat recalled all these events as she drew close enough to the Sun to detect its wavering corona of yellow gases and eruptions of plasma. Space slowly changed its appearance due to the albedo effect, the proportion of starlight reflected from celestial bodies. Tiamat shifted her flight course marginally and scanned the system of planets ahead of her, matching their trajectories and positions with the information in her database.

She noted a blue-green radiance twenty degrees above her nose and a mere ten million kilometers away. She instantly began shedding velocity and within the hour the planet that had been the cause and the stage of so much violence among the overlords came into range of her sensors.

She noted immediately the readings of its atmosphere and configuration of landmasses didn't match up with the records in her database. Large areas of the globe lay under a dense belt of dust and debris, like a semiopaque blanket of red-tinted haze. The dust carried high concentrations of radiation across the spectrum. Her optical data network fed her images of twisted ruins rising from plains of desolation, of once-great cities punctured by ugly craters. Around the cities spread barren, empty vistas where nothing grew for hundreds of kilometers. Much of the terrain on three of the continents seemed to be irradiated desert, furrowed by gulches and gullies.

Tiamat extrapolated that a nuclear conflagration had swept over the surface of Ki some time in the relatively recent past, perhaps no longer than two centuries earlier. In many ways, Ki now more closely resembled the environmental conditions of Nibiru than the planet she had first visited nearly a quarter of a million years before.

The overall climate was cooler and some species of plants and animals had died while others had evolved in strange ways. But Ki still supported all manner of life, and this fit in with Tiamat's mandate—life should exist only so the powerful and wise Annunaki overlords could rule it once more.

However, the mandate could only be acted upon by the overlords themselves and then only if they remembered who they were. Within the ageless calm of Tiamat's mind, she knew the program was actually an evocation, a reawakening, a remanifestation. A rebirth.

Cruising over the sweeping curve of Ki's northern polar regions, Tiamat began her search for the neural pathways of the overlords, her scanners spread out to maximum field extension, probing, seeking for a particular synaptic signature that could be produced only by a certain genotype. She detected many that were similar to each other but didn't quite fit the search parameters.

Tiamat wasn't concerned by how long it might take to filter through all the conflicting signatures. She divided up the globe beneath her into quadrants that her sensor array probed methodically. Only one cycle of sunrise and sunset passed before she registered the target signatures, but the readings weren't quite what she had expected.

The impressions indicated a quiescent state, an almost straight-line placidity, but she wasn't disquieted by that. She was disturbed by a flaw in the collective pattern of signals. It was as if a piece were missing, as if a body had moved through the pattern and torn a hole in the fabric of mind energy.

Tiamat sought to adjust to this unforeseen factor. The imprint of one of the overlords could no longer be detected. Instead of the flicker of consciousness she had anticipated, she sensed only a blank vacuum. She had been programmed to interface with a pattern consisting of ten minds, not nine.

The ship immediately assigned a filament of its vast data-processing system to analyzing the anomaly and preparing an appropriate response. Regardless of the conclusions she reached, Tiamat knew she could take no decisive action until the Tablets of Destiny were returned to her, and the tablets couldn't be returned unless the Supreme Council was in agreement. And for either of those eventualities to occur, she had to bring the slumbering minds of the overlords to full awareness.

At the very fringes of her sensor sweep a faint presence pulsed, and her hopes rose. They almost immediately faded when she examined the minute registration of the synapse, only a half echo of the neural signature she was programmed to find. She ignored it, seeking out the most powerful, the most insistent signal.

Shifting course, Tiamat focused on isolating the integral mind of the council from the rest of the pattern. She decelerated over the continental expanse of Asia and followed the beacon of his mind energy like tracing a length of string. The farther she cruised along it, the more she became aware of a throbbing of power, pulsing up from below. It didn't derive from a neuronic energy, although the mind she sought was connected to it.

She passed over the night side of Ki, beneath a full moon, which transmuted the bright gold of sunlight into soft silver and reflected it down, bathing the land in a lambent glow. Tiamat's sensor sweep brought her the image of high grassy hills overlooking a thickly wooded valley. A river flowed through it, the foaming blue waters cascading down a gentle fall to the west. Dominating the entire valley was the vast, pyramidal structure that shouldered the star-speckled sky.

Composed of countless fitted blocks of stone, the top was quarried perfectly flat. Bright moonlight played along the white facade of the huge monolith that reminded Tiamat of similar structures of staggering proportions the overlords designed and built.

The apex was painted yellow and from it pumped waves and whorls of energy, visible only to Tiamat's scanners and electronic eyes. She identified the energies as deriving from the core of the planet itself, geomagnetic bursts that spread out like hundreds of overlapping umbrellas.

Tiamat cut her engines, maintaining only the station-keeping thrusters as she took up a synchronous parking one thousand kilometers directly above the pyramid. A portal irised open on her belly, and from it extended a dark metal shaft. A concave disk edged by glittering crystal points caught the starshine and arced it back from the locus of coalescence.

The light swirled and gathered around the disk, seeming to compress within the rim of the bowl. The plasma carrier wave tightened around the digital stream so it could be transmitted in a single coherent squirt. The activation code existed for only a microsecond within the harmonics of the stream's focal point, which functioned both as a switch and a conduit. Enlil himself had seen to the writing of the code, so it was only appropriate that his imprint should be the first to receive and react to it.

Tiamat transmitted the signal to the apex of the pyramid, then put herself on standby mode, preparing to receive a response no matter how long it might take. She had already waited nearly four thousand years to complete her program. Another few hours, days or even years made no difference to her.

She was Tiamat and no matter how long she waited, it was only for a breath in the span of her eternity.

Chapter 1

For a wild, chaotic instant Erica van Sloan thought she had screamed.

Rolling out of bed even before she was fully awake, she heard the echoes of the scream vibrating against her eardrums. Her naked body made a blind, instinctive lunge for safety before her thought processes fully engaged. She didn't know if a nightmare had forced the scream from her throat or whether it was one she only dreamed she heard. God only knew how many were tucked away in the dark corners of her subconscious.

Using the high back of an ornate chair as a protective bulwark, Erica panted heavily, staring around her private quarters deep within the Xian pyramid. Heavy draperies of turquoise and aquamarine covered the stone walls. Indirect light filtered down from small glowing panels where the walls joined with the ceiling. Despite its diffuse quality, the illumination was sufficient for Erica to see Baroness Beausoliel convulsing on the bed they shared.

Erica could only stand and stare with a dry mouth and sleep-blurred eyes, her limbs weighed down by the heavy chains of shock and mounting fear. Baroness Beausoliel's small, compact body looked as if it were drenched with dew, her limbs and face gleaming with perspiration.

Long fingers knotted in the silk sheets, Beausoliel's high-planed face twisted as if she were in agony, eyes squeezed shut, the lips of her small mouth peeled back over perfect teeth. Veins and tendons stood out in relief on the slender column of her neck. She was as naked as Erica, her skin smooth and of a marble whiteness, but with a faint olive undertone.

Her small breasts were firm, her belly flat and tautly muscled. Although she was less than five and a half feet tall, she was perfectly proportioned—except for the high-domed cranium characteristic of hybrids.

All hybrids of the baronial oligarchy were small, slender and gracile. Their faces were composed of sharp planes, with fine-complexioned skin stretched taut over prominent cheekbones. The craniums were very high and smooth, the ears small and set low on the head. Their back-slanting eyes were large, shadowed by sweeping supraorbital ridges. Only hair, eye color and slight differences in height differentiated them.

Even their expressions were markedly similar to one another—a vast pride, a diffident superiority, authority and even ruthlessness. They were the barons, and as such, they believed themselves to be the avatars of the new humans who would inherit the Earth.

All in all, they were a beautiful people, almost too perfect to be real, and Baroness Beausoliel was one of the most lovely, despite her beauty holding more than a suggestion of a disturbing yet erotic otherworldliness. She looked no more than twenty years of age, but Erica knew the baroness was only a month or so away from observing her ninety-third birthday.

Bewildered, Erica moved away from the chair and returned to the bedside, kneeling on the edge and reaching out for the baroness. "It's all right," she whispered. "You're just having a nightmare."

Even as she uttered the words, she felt foolish. She had no idea if hybrids, let alone those of the baronial breed, experienced dreams at all, much less nightmares. She knew the barons were bred for brilliance and although the tissue of their hybridized brains was of the same organic matter as the human brain, the millions of neurons operated a bit differently in the processing of information. Therefore, their thought processes were very structured, extremely linear. Still, Erica assumed the barons needed a certain amount of dreaming just like humans did, since they shared genetic material in order to maintain a psychological balance.

Erica tentatively touched the woman's sweat-damp shoulder and recoiled, snatching her hand away as if she had been scalded. She couldn't bite back a startled outcry. Despite the moisture gleaming on Beausoliel's fine-pored flesh, all the warmth seemed to have been leached from it. She felt as cold as a three-day-old corpse.

At Erica van Sloan's touch, the eyes of the baroness opened wide. Light didn't reflect from them. Her dilated pupils encompassed the black irises so completely her eyes resembled little damp slabs of onyx. Arching her back, Baroness Beausoliel screamed long and loud in anguish.

Heart pounding frantically, Erica jerked in reaction, raking her tumbles of black hair away from her face. Although a scientist by training and temperament, she found herself completely incapable of even hazarding a guess about what was happening to her lover. Words and terms like *epileptic seizure, stroke, cardiac arrest* all tumbled through her mind.

Baroness Beausoliel tossed her head back and forth on the pillow. Her long, sleek, dark hair with its coppery highlights adhered to her sweat-slick face. Straight-cut bangs covered her high forehead, sweeping down almost to the delicate brow arches above her eyes.

Gazing unblinkingly at the baroness, Erica groped for and found a filmy lavender bed jacket. She drew it on, oblivious to the fact that the garment barely covered her upper body, much less her lower.

The convulsions racking Beausoliel's slight frame eased, and Erica leaned over her again. The woman breathed fitfully, laboriously through her open mouth, and her eyes closed once more. Gently Erica brushed strands of her hair from around her lips and nose.

Baroness Beausoliel's hair came away in her fingers, pulling loose from the scalp as easily as the roots of a dead flower. Erica flung the hair away, stomach muscles fluttering in an adrenaline-fueled reaction.

Throat constricting, her violet eyes wide, Erica forced herself to examine the woman's sweat-pebbled face, frozen in a rictus of either extreme pain or ecstasy. She knew the barons, although extremely long-lived, suffered from a cellular and metabolic deterioration that was part and parcel of what they were—mixtures of human and a race called the Archons, who were a hybridized folk themselves.

The barons preferred the term "new humans" to describe themselves, despite the fact they were more of a biological bridge between two races instead of a separate one. Not even they were sure of the reasons behind the hybridization program, which had actually begun over two centuries earlier. But they did know that in order to rule humankind, they were dependent on the biological material their human subjects provided. They required annual medical treatments to stave off a complete collapse of their autoimmune systems.

Erica didn't think an immune-system dysfunction was the cause of the woman's condition, nor did she think she was suffering a delayed reaction to the broken elbow inflicted on her in the relatively recent past. The cast had been removed some days before.

She had first entered into a relationship with the baroness less than five months earlier, right after the hybrid woman had received the full week-long regimen of treatments, which included infusions of fresh blood, adenine, guanine, cytosine and long-string protein molecules. All the biochemicals were absorbed through the pores of her skin and then into her cellular structure, which insured a full year of relative health and vitality.

Taking a corner of the sheet, Erica dabbed carefully at the little beads of perspiration on Beausoliel's left cheek. When she removed the cloth, a patch of skin adhered to it, peeling away from the baroness's face without resistance. What she had assumed were drops of sweat were tiny skin eruptions.

Beneath the ragged, bloodless abrasion another layer of epidermal tissue gleamed wetly. Even by the dim light Erica made out the delicate, almost artful pattern of tiny, interlocking scales.

Dragging in a rugged breath, Baroness Beausoliel opened her eyes again and shrieked. In a high-pitched, sibilant screech, she cried out, "Lilitu! Lilitu!"

A violent spasm shook her slender body, her fingers clutching the bedsheet tightly, her knuckles distended like ivory knobs. Then needle-tipped spurs of bone slit open the flesh amid squirtings of blood, splattering Erica's chest.

Blurting in wordless fear and disgust, Erica pushed herself away from the bed and the writhing, twitching body of her lover. Heeling around, she plunged from her chambers out into the corridor.

The individual living quarters had no doors. Sam had stated there was no need for them. If a guest of the imperator didn't feel safe within the stronghold of Xian, then mere doors would not allay their fears. Privacy was always respected, and quartets of armed soldiers were posted at every junction.

At the corner she encountered four imperial troopers, all wearing boots, helmets and coveralls of midnight blue with facings of bright scarlet. Compact SIG-AMT subguns were slung over their shoulders. The faces under the overhangs of the helmets were of an Asian cast. They were all native Chinese, and Erica towered nearly half a head above the tallest of them.

Their almond eyes didn't even blink at the sight of the statuesque, near naked woman who rushed past them. Her long, straight hair, swept back from a high forehead and pronounced widow's peak, tumbled about her shoulders. It was so black as to be blue when the light caught it.

The mark of an aristocrat showed in her delicate features, with the arch of her brows and her thin-bridged nose. She didn't bother trying to minimize the bouncing of her unsupported breasts beneath their gauzy covering. Other matters occupied her than worrying about her effect upon the silent troopers. Besides, due to the SQUID interface she shared with the soldiers, she could have mentally ordered them see her dressed in the uniform of the imperial mother if she cared to expend the concentration. They formally addressed her as Tui Chui Jian which meant "Dragon Mother."

As she rushed down the corridor, Erica surprised even herself by her worry over the welfare of Baroness Beausoliel. They had been lovers since their first meeting in Area 51, but not so much because of a mutual sexual attraction. Erica was mainly curious as to the woman's true motives, what manipulation she would attempt once she felt she was secure within the imperator's inner circle.

The baroness's role as seducer hadn't fooled her, but the woman's willingness to please her came as a surprise. She hadn't thought it possible for a new human, much less the baroness, to subsume her inborn arrogance and stratospheric sense of superiority to serve the needs of another—certainly not the needs of an old human.

Erica paused briefly before the arch leading to the suite of rooms given to Baron Cobalt, whose status in the imperator's infrastructure was far less apparent than Beausoliel's. In fact, the reasons for his residing in the pyramid were decidedly murky. She didn't know if the former ruler of Cobaltville was a prisoner, a guest or a potential hostage.

When Sam's scheme to use Cobalt to stage a largely phony war against his fellow barons had been derailed, Cobalt had remained within the pyramid. Sam never confided to Erica why he had extended amnesty to his former enemy, except that he foresaw a use for him in the future.

Erica's bare right foot landed in a warm, wet and sticky substance right outside Baron Cobalt's quarters. Coming to a halt and leaning against the wall, she lifted her leg, propping it against her left knee. From the sole of her foot she peeled away what looked and felt like a layer of suet that had been boiled to the consistency of jelly.

Shuddering in disgust, she tossed the mass to the floor, where it landed with a faint splat. Only then did she see other scraps and bits of the same fatty material leading away in an irregular trail from the arched doorway. Nausea leapfrogged in her belly when she realized the substance was actually flesh. Obviously Baron Cobalt was suffering from the same bizarre skin-shedding affliction as Beausoliel, but he at least seemed ambulatory.

Taking a deep, fortifying breath, Erica continued down the passageway, intent on reaching Sam. Judging by the litter of epidermal tissue left in his wake, the imperator was Cobalt's objective, as well.

The floor under her feet became smoother and the square-cut blocks of stone on the walls gave way to smooth, seamless expanses. The ceiling rounded overhead like an arch, winding gently to the left in an ever-widening curve. The corridor suddenly opened into the vast domed space of a natural cavern. The unfinished stone of its ceiling gleamed here and there with clusters of crystals and geodes.

The floor dipped in a gradual incline and at the center, surrounded by a collar of interlocking silver slabs, lay a pool about fifty feet in circumference. The inner rim was lined with an edging of crystal points that glowed with a dull iridescence. Sam called the pool the Heart of the Earth and in many ways it was, since it was a nexus point, a convergence of geomantic energy.

It served as a cardinal point in the world grid harmonics, a part of an ancient network of pyramids built at key places around the world to tap the Earth's natural geomantic energies. She knew there were a number of such hubs throughout Asia, but none with the concentration of sheer power that lay beneath the Xian pyramid.

Only a few of the ceiling crystals sparkled with light. Some glowed steadily, others flickered feebly and still others were only multifaceted lumps of mineral. She knew that if all of them shone with the same intensity, the interior of the cavern would have blazed as blindingly as a naked star.

But the light was more than adequate for her to make out the pale, naked figure writhing across the floor. Baron Cobalt made gagging noises that reminded Erica of a cat trying to dislodge a fur ball caught in its throat. Like Baroness Beausoliel, his skin gleamed with a film of moisture, but unlike hers most of his flesh hung in tatters from his body, like old clothing rotting away on a scarecrow.

"Where is Sam?" Erica demanded, her voice reverberating shrilly within the cavern. "Where is my son?"

Cobalt tried to force himself to his hands and knees as he crawled toward her, leaving ragged bits of skin clinging to the stone. He lifted his head, golden-brown eyes wide but covered by a glazed sheen. His lipless mouth worked. A string of saliva drooled from it, dangling from his pointed chin.

He husked out a single, strangulated word: "Marduk!"

As if his bones suddenly turned to water, he collapsed face first to the floor, twitching and shuddering. He hugged himself, fingers tearing long gouges in his back. Erica saw very little blood. A scream started up Baron Cobalt's throat but faded into the ghastly gurgling again.

Erica backed away from him, hands clutching at the open bodice of her bed jacket. Horror threatened to engulf her reason as she finally realized what was occurring. She had seen a hint of such a metamorphosis some months ago. Whirling away from Cobalt, she knew exactly where to find Sam but didn't want to accept the realization. With marrow-freezing clarity she recalled a confrontation with her son in this very chamber when she heard a dry, harsh rustle beneath his robe, the light friction of scales against cloth.

She ran back the way she had come, her feet slapping loudly on the stone tiles. She turned right down a narrow corridor that dead-ended against a tall set of double doors. Both of them hung open, and she rushed between them into a room of black—the walls, floor and ceiling were the color of ebony.

The room wasn't completely without light. A transparent sphere six feet in diameter occupied the center of the room from floor to ceiling. The slowly revolving globe glittered with thousands of pinpoints of light, scattered seemingly at random, but all connected by glowing lines. She knew the orb was actually a three-dimensional representation of the electromagnetic power grid of the planet, as well as a targeting device.

Erica van Sloan paid no attention to the globe as she circled around it. She focused her gaze on a light within a niche deeply recessed into the wall. It cast a column of illumination on a long, cylindrical, glass-walled tank. Within it, floating in a semisolid gel she saw very tall, almost skeletally thin figure. She had seen the body once before and at the time had wished fervently to never see it again.

The creature's long, bony arms terminated in four-fingered hands tipped by curving claws. The body was completely hairless, covered by a brownish-gray hide that glistened faintly with scales. A central bony ridge ran from the top of the elongated skull to the bridge of the flared nose. Hard knobs protruded over the eyes, casting them into shadow. The shelf of cheekbones looked sharp enough to cut through the skin. The lip-less mouth gaped slightly open, revealing discolored, serrated teeth. A short, muscular tail extended from the base of the spine, tucked beneath its thighs.

Erica felt again the surge of primal loathing upon see-ing the preserved remains of the last Annunaki, but she was far more frightened by the sight of the naked Sam hunched over at the base of the tank. His bowed head pressed against it, as if in supplication. Like Baroness Beausoliel and Baron Cobalt, his pale flesh gleamed as if it were coated with glycerin.

The words she had spoken to him months ago flashed into the forefront of her mind: "Annunaki? You're changing into one of *them?*"

And she remembered his soft, almost mocking reply: "Something far greater. Remember what I once told you—that hybrids take on all the positive attributes of their parents, becoming the most exceptional speci-mens? I will not know exactly how exceptional until my change is complete. Then you will either take pride in the blood that runs through your halfing or disown me as a changeling."

At the time, Erica couldn't even speculate as to the meaning of his cryptic comment. Now she thought she knew and the realization dried all the moisture in her mouth. Taking a step toward him, she called, "Sam!"

When he didn't respond she raised her voice to a strident shout, *"Sam!"*

A noise like the clacking of old bones being shaken within a basket of wet parchment came from his doubled-up figure. It took her a few seconds to understand he was laughing. "You still call me Sam, even after all this time."

His voice was muffled, but still retained its sonorous quality. Struggling to tamp down her rising anxiety, to make sure he couldn't hear the fear, she asked, "And what should I call you? Sam *is* your name, isn't it?"

"After a fashion…it's actually Samyaza. I chose it unconsciously, even though it is only one of my names. I know that now. I know *all* of my names, throughout the ages."

"How do you know them?" she demanded.

"Tiamat told me…or rather she awakened the sleeping part of me that knew." His voice trailed off into a grunt of pain.

Erica moved toward him instinctively. "Sam—"

Wildly, he waved her back. "No! Do not touch me! Do not approach me."

Spine arching, neck tendons bulging, Sam howled long, loud and hard. As Erica stared in horror, her son's body shook and shuddered in a series of spasms. With each convulsion, sinews rippled and pulsed under his flesh, the muscle mass seeming to slide into new positions over the bones.

With a sickening crunching of gristle, Sam's arms and legs lengthened, his fingers stretching out like claws. The skin over his shoulder blades split open, slashed from within to allow spiny growths to protrude. They gleamed like burnished wire under the light.

His entire body quaked, as if vibrating violently from within. He writhed, his eyes wide and staring, saliva spilling from his slack lips. Reaching up with trembling fingers, he touched his thin white hair and it fell away like thistledown. The flesh of his hairless scalp squirmed along the center of his cranium, bulging upward in half a dozen places as if tiny worms wriggled and burrowed just beneath the flesh. The pale skin stretched and split amid brief spurting geysers of blood. A back-curved crest of glittering spines sprouted from his skull, punching up through the flesh.

Sam screamed again, a high-pitched, ululating wail of agony ripped from pain centers Erica never knew existed in any organism. He clutched both sides of his head, his tongue protruding from his mouth. His body sagged to the floor as he continued to roar in soul-deep anguish. His bloody fingertips spasmodically clawed away the skin of his temples, and his blue-black tongue protruded from between his wide-hanging jaws. Falling facedown, he thrashed and kicked madly. Erica stood and watched helplessly, noting absently how his flesh caught on corners of the stone flooring and peeled away in strips.

As Erica stood, stared and listened, the tone of Sam's

screams subtly changed, from cries of utter all-consuming agony to vocalizations of release, of jubilation.

After what seemed like hours, the convulsions ceased and the screams ebbed to hoarse groans. Sam lay on the floor, his back to her, breathing in gasping grunts. Then, slowly, he gathered his legs under him and his body unfolded from the floor. Although Erica's mind was too stunned to fully comprehend what her eyes saw, she guessed Sam had grown at least a foot in height, and the span of his shoulders and the breadth of his chest had nearly doubled. The pitiless glare from the overhead light accentuated the inhuman leanness of his body, his corded muscles more like ropes braided beneath the reddish and bronze flesh.

Sam's skin was tinted a pale crimson hue on his hairless torso and pectorals, gradually lightening to a shade of gold on the skin drawn tautly over the strong, high-arching bones of his face. His eyes gleamed like molten brass, bisected by black, vertical-slitted pupils. They seemed ageless yet at the same time old beyond memory.

Scales glistened with a metallic luster on the dark flesh of his arms and legs, his chest and flat stomach, as if his skin were dusted with silver. With a distant, almost detached sense of incredulity Erica realized the outer layer of epidermis was like finely wrought mesh, an organic equivalent of chain-mail armor.

Sam had metamorphosed into a creature of alien, inhuman beauty, his flesh and eyes and mind a melding of dragon, myth and machine. But Erica van Sloan didn't feel awe in his presence. Her imagination supplied him with a long tail tipped with a triangular appendage and instead of five-toed feet, two cloven hooves. All Sam needed was a pair of horns sprouting from his skull instead of spines and the traditional image of evil would be complete.

"Sam," she began in an aspirated whisper.

"Samyaza," he corrected, his voice like the chiming of bronze bells. It was a king's voice, imperious and musical with the innate natural arrogance of unquestioned authority. "But even that is just one name among many my spirit has borne. Belial is another…Asmodeus… Dazhbog…C. W. Thrush is the most recent. They were all guises that I may now cast off like the flesh of the entity you called the imperator."

"Entity?" she echoed feebly. "You…you are my son."

His wide mouth stretched in a mocking smile. He glanced over his shoulder at the dead face of the creature floating in the preservative gel. "No," he said in a gloating croon. "That familial connection was only a fabrication…a convenient piece of mendacity in order to insure your devotion. Although my genetic code may share a few strands of your own DNA, I am now and was ever Enlil, overlord of the air and earth. I have been reborn in new flesh. I have waited for this moment for over a thousand years, since I first agreed to abide by the terms of the pact."

His voice dropped to a contemplative whisper, and his eyes acquired a vacant sheen as if he gazed into the past. "There was no reason not to agree…my people's empire had turned to dust as had the conquering spirit of the Annunaki themselves. But now we are resurrected, our strength returns and we will follow the ancient mandate of our father, Anu, to remake this world into the image of Nibiru, to shape it and its people to

Annunaki ways, to reclaim our lordship over the ancient lands. The children of Anu, of Nibiru, live again."

He paused, looked toward her and his smile widened. "After three and a half millennia, I'd say it was about bloody time. Don't you agree…Mother?"

The last word left his lips as a sardonic, serpentine hiss of contempt. Erica didn't reply. She stood motionless, paralyzed by horror such as she had never known in her worst childhood nightmares. The juxtaposition of the alert, smirking face with that of the dead, dull-eyed visage was unnerving. Despite the many differences, both wore the masks of monsters.

She gazed unblinkingly as Enlil bent, scooped up a scrap of flesh between claw-tipped forefinger and thumb and, after a brief examination, popped it into his mouth. Chewing reflectively, he murmured, "Flesh of my flesh."

Erica van Sloan's nerve broke. A surge of sheer terror shattered the bonds that held her in place. She whirled and ran, obeying only the crazed desire to get out of the pyramid of Xian, the lair of the imperator, the birthing ward of the children of the serpent. The desperate need to get far, far away consumed her completely.

She ran like a panicked deer, heedless of direction or final destination, her eyes blinded by the hot sting of tears. She was only dimly aware of racing through one dark passage after another.

When a hard object clipped her at ankle level, she fell heavily, bruising her elbows and her knees on the rough stone floor. Her breathless outcry of pain echoed eerily all around her. Gasping, pulling in lungful after lungful of air, Erica lifted her head, swatting her hair away from her eyes, staring around at the furnishings of the room. Once more she experienced the sensation of stepping back in time several thousand years into a central clearing house of many ancient cultures. Sam called it the Hall of Memory.

A tall, round sandstone pillar bearing ornate carvings of birds and animal heads was bracketed by two large sculptures, one a feathered jaguar and the other a serpent with wings. Silken tapestries depicting Asian ideographs hung from the walls. There were other tapestries, all bearing twisting geometric designs such as mandalas.

Suspended from the ceiling by thin steel wires was a huge gold disk in the form of the Re-Horakhte falcon. The upcurving wings were inlaid with colored glass. The sun disc atop the beaked head was a cabochon-cut carnelian.

Ceramic effigy jars and elegantly crafted vessels depicting animal-headed gods and goddesses from the Egyptian pantheon were stacked in neat pyramids. Arrayed on a long shelf on the opposite wall were a dozen ushabtis figures, small statuettes representing laborers in the Land of the Dead. Against the right wall was a granite twelve-foot-tall replica of the seated figure of Ramses the Third. It towered over a cluster of dark basalt blocks inscribed with deep rune markings.

Each and every item appeared to be in perfect condition, and each and every item was beyond the ability of the mind to catalog. The huge room was an archaeologist's paradise, a representative sampling from every human culture ever influenced by the Annunaki, the Tuatha de Danaan and the race known as the Archons.

She glanced around, looking for and finding the sculpture that represented a humanoid creature with a slender, gracile build draped in robes. The features were sharp although minimalistic, the domed head disproportionately large and hairless. The eyes were huge, slanted and fathomless. Cradled in its six-fingered hands was a shape that appeared to be a human infant. The slit of a mouth curved slightly upward in a fatuous smile.

Then a small figure stepped out from behind the statue, the face so identical to the features graven in stone that for an instant Erica wondered if the sculpted effigy had come to life. She gazed without blinking at the high round cranium that narrowed to an elongated chin. The pale grayish-pink skin was stretched drumtight over a structure of facial bones that seemed all cheek and brow, with little in between but two great upslanting eyes like black pools. The nostrils were merely a pair of sharpened nares. The slit of a mouth held the faintest suggestion of a frown. Instead of robes, the slightly built creature wore a dark, formfitting garment of a metallic weave.

"Erica van Sloan," Balam said in a faint, scratchy whisper.

Erica had only seen Balam once before, although she had sensed his presence in the pyramid many times over the past year. Sam—Enlil, she automatically corrected herself—had steadfastly refused to confirm or deny whether the Archon resided in the monolithic structure.

Balam extended his right hand toward her, his six spidery fingers seeming almost quaint in comparison to Enlil's five taloned digits. "Erica van Sloan," he said again, his voice strained. "Do you know me?"

Slowly she pushed herself to her knees, not in the least concerned about appearing almost naked before the small entity. "Yes," she said, reaching out and taking his hand. His flesh felt firm and warm to her touch. "You are Balam."

He inclined his oversize skull in a short nod. "I am Balam, and I have discharged my duty to the root race. I have aided in the resurrection of the ancient overlords of Nibiru. However, helping them reclaim their birthright is not part of the debt."

Erica carefully rose to her feet, still holding Balam's hand. "Their birthright?" she repeated, despite having guessed and dreaded the answer.

Balam saw the understanding in her eyes and nodded again. "Earth. We must hurry. Tiamat has returned, and she heralds the resurrection of the nine lords of Nibiru. Come with me if you wish to live—or to die—on your own terms."

Chapter 2

On the plateau, men and women dodged, ducked and danced with swords. The castanet-like clatter of the wooden blades rose toward the azure sky, as cloudless as a summer's dream, despite the autumnal tints of orange and yellow in the foliage along the slope.

Ordinarily most of the people who were engaged in trying to incapacitate their partners with the *boken,* or avoid being incapacitated themselves, would have enjoyed the unseasonably warm late-fall weather. The breeze drifting up from the woodlands below carried with it the comforting, musty odor of wet leaves. The midmorning sunlight painted the outcroppings with streaks of gold and red. The gray mountain peak towering above the plateau seemed to shimmer with a faint aureate halo.

Kane stood on the far side of plateau at the point where it narrowed to a crumbling blacktop road. His arms were folded over his chest, and he tried to look disapproving. He didn't have to try very hard.

The martial skills displayed by the twenty men and twelve women participating in the self-defense exercises were strictly from therapy. Kane wasn't sure if their poor ability derived mainly from their backgrounds as scientists or simply from a lack of interest in hurting one another or getting hurt themselves. Regardless of the reason, the *boken* clacked halfheartedly.

Standing atop a large boulder that had rolled down the face of the slope some years past, his gray-blue eyes masked by sunglasses, Kane thought the best of the bunch might last five minutes against a Roamer toddler. A long-limbed man, leanly muscular, he stood an inch over six feet, although his position atop the boulder made him appear taller still, which was his intent.

Thick-soled jump boots didn't hurt the illusion, either. He resembled a wolf in the way he carried most of his muscle mass in his upper body. He wore a black T-shirt tucked into the waistband of drab olive-green camo pants.

His thick dark hair, showing just enough chestnut highlights to keep it from being a true black, stirred in the breeze. A hairline scar stretched like a piece of white thread against the tanned skin of his left cheek.

At the moment he felt like rushing among the Cerberus personnel and inflicting a few scars himself.

The men and women paired up and dueling one another with all the ferocity of ankle-hobbled octogenarians exhibited as much enthusiasm for the exercise as he would have for a jalapeño enema.

Six Tigers of Heaven, samurai who had gated in with Shizuka from the mat-trans unit on Thunder Isle, moved among the listless combatants, offering words of encouragement, criticism and instruction in the use of the *boken,* the lightweight wooden practice swords.

Instead of their elaborate armor, the samurai of New Edo wore billowy *kamishimos,* the formal attire of a daimyo's retainer. Their hair was clubbed back away from their faces, which only showed just how young most of them were. Because of that, they apparently didn't impress the Cerberus people as hard-bitten warriors in the way Kane hoped they would. He grudgingly realized he should be surprised so many agreed to undergo training in the first place.

All of the personnel out on the plateau were émigrés from the Manitius Moonbase who had chosen to forge new lives for themselves with the Cerberus exiles. A fortified redoubt built deep within a peak of the Bitterroot mountain range was far superior to the artificial environment of the lunar colony. They had spent the last two-hundred-plus years on the Moon, most of it in cryostasis, but Earth seemed like an alien planet to them, as did the installation once known as Redoubt Bravo.

Constructed in the mid-1990s, no expense had been spared to make the redoubt, the seat of Project Cerberus, a masterpiece of concealment and impenetrability. The redoubt had housed the Cerberus process, a subdivision of Overproject Whisper, which in turn had been a primary component of the Totality Concept. The researches to which Project Cerberus and its personnel had been devoted were locating and traveling hyperdimensional pathways through the quantum stream.

Once that had been accomplished, the redoubt became, from the end of one millennium to the beginning of another, a manufacturing facility. The quantum interphase mat-trans inducers, known colloquially as "gateways," were built in modular form and shipped to other redoubts.

Most of the related overprojects had their own hidden bases. The official designations of the redoubts had been based on the old phonetic alphabet code used in military radio communications. On the few existing records, the Cerberus installation was listed as Redoubt Bravo, but the handful of people who had made the facility their home for the past few years never referred to it as such.

The thirty-acre, three-level installation had come through the nukecaust with its operating systems and radiation shielding in good condition. When Mohandas Lakesh Singh had reactivated the installation some thirty years before, the repairs he made had been minor, primarily cosmetic in nature. Over a period of time, he had added an elaborate system of heat-sensing warning devices, night-vision vid cameras and motion-trigger alarms to the plateau surrounding it. He had been forced to work in secret and completely alone, so the upgrades had taken several years to complete. However, the location of the redoubt in Montana's Bitterroot Range had kept his work from being discovered by the baronial authorities.

In the generations since the nukecaust, a sinister mythology had been ascribed to the mountains, with their mysteriously shadowed forests and hell-deep, dangerous ravines. The range had become known as the Darks. The wilderness area was virtually unpopulated. The nearest settlement was located in the flatlands, and it consisted of a small band of Indians, Sioux and Cheyenne, led by a shaman named Sky Dog.

Planted within rocky clefts of the mountain peak hidden behind camouflage netting, were the uplinks from an orbiting Vela-class reconnaissance satellite and a Comsat. It could be safely assumed that no one or nothing could approach Cerberus undetected by land or by air—not that anyone was expected to make the attempt, particularly overland.

The road leading down from Cerberus to the foothills was little more than a cracked and twisted asphalt ribbon, skirting yawning chasms and cliffs. Acres of the mountainsides had collapsed during the nuke-triggered earthquakes nearly two centuries earlier. It was almost impossible for anyone to reach the plateau by foot or by vehicle; therefore Lakesh had seen to it that the facility was listed as irretrievably unsalvageable on all ville records.

A cry of anger and pain commanded Kane's attention. He saw Brewster Philboyd trying to parry a blow from Mariah Falk, their two wooden blades meeting with a sound like tree limbs being knocked together.

Philboyd dropped his *boken* and cradled his right hand within his left, nursing the knuckles. He glared through the lenses of his eyeglasses at his opponent and snapped, "I said 'Hold on,' Mariah, not 'Whale on'!"

Mariah Falk didn't even try to repress a laugh. "Sorry, Brewster. Guess I got carried away. I saw *The Seven Samurai* one too many times, I guess."

Brewster eyed his scraped knuckles and said sullenly, "I preferred the Americanized version. At least *The Magnificent Seven* got to use guns, not pointy sticks."

Kane lifted his voice to be heard over the clatter of the *boken*. "You don't know how to use a gun any better than you do a pointy stick, Brewster. Let's not make a big deal out of your little boo-boo."

Philboyd transferred his glare from his injured hand to Kane. "Now, why would you possibly think that having my hand broken is a big deal?"

"I wouldn't," Kane retorted flatly. "I think it's more of a problem that you let Mariah disarm you so easily."

Face flushing in anger and embarrassment, Philboyd looked as if he wanted to spit at Kane. A lanky man with white-blond hair brushed back from a receding hairline, he was about Kane's height, but considerably slighter of build. Like his fellow émigrés on the plateau, he wore a one-piece zippered white bodysuit, the unofficial duty uniform of Cerberus personnel.

"I didn't 'let' her do anything," he argued. "She cheated!"

Mariah Falk regarded him with mock hurt. "How can you say that, Brewster?"

A slender, wiry woman in her midforties, Mariah had short brown hair that was threaded with gray. Her face showed lines of effort as she tried to keep from laughing again.

Rather than answering Mariah's question, rightly assuming it was rhetorical, Philboyd glared up at Kane challengingly. "You're not going to turn a group of twentieth-century astrophysicists and space scientists into twenty-third century soldiers, no matter how nasty you get."

Kane smiled down at him coldly. "I'm not trying to turn you into soldiers, Brewster. All I want is to give you and your fellow academics a grounding in self-defense and basic combat skills, so I won't have to rescue your sorry asses every time you leave Cerberus."

Philboyd's angry color deepened and even Mariah Falk looked offended. Lowering her *boken,* she snapped, "That's not fair, Kane and you know it!"

Both Philboyd and Mariah reacted to Kane's oblique

reference to a recent incident involving the capture and imprisonment of a jump team in Cambodia. Several people within earshot of the angry exchange stopped whacking at one another with the *boken* so they could listen.

Kane decided not to pursue the topic, partly because Mariah's accusation did have foundation—he was indeed being unfair. "All right," he said wearily, "I take it all back. But that still doesn't invalidate my point—if you new arrivals want to get out into the world, you'll have to learn how to protect yourselves and one another. You may have noticed by now that we have a lot of enemies out there."

Reynolds, one of the *boken*-wielding men on the tarmac, called up, "And just how many of them will come after us with wooden swords?"

A ripple of laughter passed through the people. They ignored the admonishing "Hush!" from Ichi, a Tiger of Heaven standing nearby.

Although Kane's expression didn't alter, he realized he was losing credibility among the émigrés, despite the fact that if not for him, Brigid Baptiste and Grant, the Manitius Base inhabitants would have had no future except for dying unknown and unmourned on the Moon.

Kane's stature among the Manitius personnel sprang more from the fact he had faced off against the fearsome Maccan and imprisoned the mad god of the Tuatha de Danaan in a stasis chamber. Now the old proverb about familiarity breeding contempt seemed to be at work. After several months of seeing him going about his day-to-day routine in Cerberus, bantering with his friends, spilling his coffee in the cafeteria, he was no longer viewed as a blend of ghost, ninja and wolverine. He had become human.

He decided it was time to reestablish his reputation as a formidable warrior and a vicious opponent and at the same time impart a lesson. Kane stabbed a finger at Reynolds. "You." He pointed out three other men. "Avery. Conrad. Poltrino. You, too, Brewster if you want in on this."

"Me too what?" Philboyd asked, his brow creased with lines of puzzlement. "Want in on what?"

Kane jumped lightly off the boulder. "I'm giving you the chance for some payback."

"Payback?"

"Remember all those insults?" Kane inquired breezily, striding out onto the center of the plateau. "You can ram them down my throat—or at least try to."

Stopping and surveying the faces turned to him, Kane announced, "Anybody can get in on this. You can use your *boken* or any weapon you can find out here. The object of the exercise is to take me down and keep me down for the count of five. Not ten, but only five. That's all you have to do."

Reynolds, Conrad, Avery and Poltrino approached him cautiously, hefting their weapons with uncertainty. All of the men were of a similar physical type and age. Philboyd asked suspiciously, "And what will you be doing while we're trying to take you down? Using your magic Magistrate kung-fu grip on our naughty bits to cripple or kill us?"

Kane shook his head. "Nope. In the interests of giving DeFore a little consideration, I won't use closed fists or grab you any place that will require medical treatment—extensive, anyway."

Reba DeFore, the de facto physician of Cerberus, had never been shy about voicing complaints when she treated injuries she believed came about due to foolishness or carelessness.

Philboyd made a dismissive gesture. "I pass."

"You don't trust me?" Kane shot back.

"No, but that has nothing to do with my decision."

"What does?"

The lanky man shrugged. "If I'd wanted to be a commando or Special Forces, I would've gone into the military instead of science. I'm not interested in becoming a badass at my age."

Kane lips quirked in a smile, but he didn't respond. He understood Brewster Philboyd's objections. He had never expected to put the Manitius émigrés through the kind of rigorous trained he had endured in the Magistrate Division. All he wanted was to provide them with a fundamental grounding in survival skills, first aid, hand-to-hand combat and weapons instruction. He didn't really blame the people for their reluctance. He knew they weren't cowards.

But Kane also knew the situation at Cerberus was changing. No longer could he, Grant, Brigid Baptiste and Domi undertake the majority of the ops and therefore shoulder the lion's share of the risks.

Although many of the Manitius personnel had already proved their inherent courage and resourcefulness, they wanted to get out into the world and make a difference in the struggle against the baronies and reclaim the planet of their birth. Nearly thirty of them were already out in the field, stationed on Thunder Isle in the Cific, working to refurbish the sprawling complex that had housed Operation Chronos two centuries before. At least a dozen more worked in shifts on the Moon colony, salvaging equipment and gating back to Cerberus with it.

Unfortunately, few of the émigrés seemed to grasp their limitations as individuals and conversely their strengths when they worked as a team. If they couldn't work as a team, then they couldn't make contributions to the Cerberus mission.

"I don't want to turn anyone into a badass," Kane declared. "I'm just trying to prove a point to all you little moonbeams."

The people assembled on the plateau fell silent, watching as the four *boken*-armed men circled Kane warily. "Just what point is this supposed to prove?" Avery demanded. A solidly built man in his mid-thirties, he seemed disinclined to make eye contact with Kane.

"First and foremost," Kane answered, "you'll get a general idea of the kind of people you're liable to meet when you go on away missions. As Brewster said, badasses. Legitimate ones who'd kill you just because they don't like the way you've combed your hair—" he glanced toward Mariah "—or rape you just to see the look on your face."

Conrad snorted in derision, and Kane turned his dark-lensed stare on him. He was a pale, brown-haired man in his early forties, heavier than Kane, but most of his weight was in his gut.

"So the point," Kane continued, "is that even the most rag-assed, slagjacking outlander, Farer or Roamer trash could kill any one of you before you had the chance to whine, 'Let's talk this over.' And if any of you

Moon boys disagree, I'm giving you the chance to prove me wrong."

The four men exchanged tense, questioning glances. Sensing their hesitation, Kane assumed a relaxed posture, lifting his right hand and beckoning them forward with a jerk of his fingers. "Come on, sweethearts. Let's get this over. You don't want to be late cooking your husbands' dinners, do you?"

Philboyd muttered in exasperation, "Oh, please—"

Whatever else he might have had to say was smothered by the quick scuff and scutter of running feet on asphalt. Avery, Conrad, Reynolds and Poltrino rushed Kane, *boken* swords held high. The onlookers pressed forward, shouting in excitement. The Tigers of Heaven held them back, away from the area of combat.

The wooden blades lashed out as the men struck at Kane only to see their swords chop empty air. Reynolds cursed in dismay as he stumbled off balance because of his unconnected blow. The curse turned into a grunt as Kane dropped to the tarmac. Balancing himself on his left arm, Kane used it as a pivot to spin completely around, slamming a reverse heel-kick into the back of the man's ankles. His feet flew out from under him and he dropped heavily onto his back, all the air leaving his lungs with a *whoof!*

Kane sprang back to his feet, swiftly dodging a hacking slash from Conrad. Avery and Poltrino nearly tripped over the gasping Reynolds as they both tried to reach Kane with their swords. They converged on him, but their thrusts and swipes seemed to pass through Kane's body, so quickly did he dodge, duck and weave.

His uncanny skill and speed began to have a disconcerting effect on his opponents, just as he had hoped. He let them flail away at him for a bit longer, before spinning and bobbing out of their reach. He knew he could kill all three men in as many seconds if he were so inclined. Single blows from his hands delivered in the proper place with the right amount of force would drop them dead to the asphalt with very little exertion on his part. But he figured he wouldn't regain much of his popularity by adopting such a tactic.

Breath hissing between his clenched teeth, Conrad bulled his way forward, shouldering a protesting Poltrino out of his way as he tried to back Kane up to the far edge of the plateau. It plummeted straight down to a tributary of the Clark Fork River nearly a thousand feet below. The man's attack was headlong, totally linear, with no thought given to tactics, strategy or teamwork.

Conrad flailed at him wildly, as if he were swatting at a swarm of flies that surrounded him. Kane stood his ground, letting instinct and the experience gained from hundreds of battles guide his actions. Only his upper body moved as he evaded all of the man's poorly timed blows.

At precisely the right instant, Kane shifted position, leaned diagonally away from Conrad and delivered a roundhouse kick, planting the toe of his boot into the man's diaphragm just below his breastbone. Conrad jackknifed at the waist, wheezing, his features squeezing together like a fireplace bellows.

He tottered forward and would have pitched headfirst over the precipice if Kane hadn't hauled him back by the seat of his bodysuit. He pushed the gagging man against Poltrino, and both of them went sprawling across the asphalt with a clatter of wood.

Kane shook his head pityingly. "I didn't think it was possible, but you guys suck and blow."

Avery snarled in fury and slashed at Kane with a double-handed cleaver stroke, as if he sought to decapitate him. Contemptuously, Kane ducked and half turned, allowing the wooden blade to fan cool air on his face.

Before Avery could recover his balance, Kane half turned again, sliding up behind the man, reaching around him and closing his left hand around Avery's right wrist. Twisting to the left, he applied pressure with his other hand to the man's shoulder socket. The maneuver dragged a cry of pain from Avery's lips, and rather than risk a dislocated shoulder, he dropped to his knees. The sword fell from suddenly nerveless fingers.

Kane stood over him, his captured arm locked between his right hand and left wrist. Calmly, he said, "By my calculations, this whole exercise took a little under thirty seconds."

"Actually, sir," Nguyen offered, consulting her wrist chron, "27.2 seconds."

Kane sighed. "Don't call me sir."

The pudgy Eurasian woman nodded. "Yes, sir."

Shaking his head, Kane hauled Avery to his feet and released him. The man stumbled away, massaging his wrist and grimacing. As Conrad, Reynolds and Poltrino climbed to their feet, Kane stated, "As all of you saw, I wasn't taken down. But I could've been if only two of you had employed a little strategy known up here in the Darks as 'teamwork.'" He crooked his fingers to suggest quotation marks.

"By working in tandem," he concluded, "you could have taken me down and kept me down."

He caught a movement out of the corner of his eye and turned to see Grant and Shizuka exiting through the massive security door inset into the base of the mountain peak. It opened in accordion fashion, and because of the weight of the individual vanadium panels, the door was usually left partially ajar during daylight hours. Opening and shutting it required several minutes.

Grant remained in the doorway as Shizuka strode purposefully out onto the plateau. A small, delicate woman, the commander of the Tigers of Heaven stood a little over five feet tall. She wore her luxuriant black hair tied back in a long braid, framing a smoothly sculpted face of extraordinary Asian beauty.

Her complexion was a very pale gold with peach-and-cream accents. Beneath a snub nose, her petaled lips were full. Her dark, almond-shaped eyes glinted with the fierce, proud gleam of a young eagle. Two scabbarded swords, a long bladed *katana* and a shorter *tanto,* were strapped crosswise across her back.

As she came abreast of Kane, she said quietly, "I'll take over the next phase of training. You're wanted inside." She nodded toward Philboyd. "You, too."

Philboyd handed his *boken* to the nearest Tiger and stepped forward eagerly. "I'm on board with that."

Kane glanced over at Grant who jerked his head toward the interior of redoubt. "Is something going on?" he asked Shizuka.

She shrugged. "From what I've seen about this place, there is always something going on."

Kane knew he couldn't refute that observation so he commented softly, "These folks are a tough crowd. They don't impress easy."

Reaching up behind her, Shizuka grasped the hilts of her swords then slid both the *katana* and *tanto* from the scabbards with lightning speed. She spun them, the flat blades cutting bright wheels in the air over her head. Then she returned the two swords to their scabbards in the same blurred motions.

An awed murmuring came from many throats at the display. Shizuka glanced up into Kane's face, an ironic smile on her lips. "You were saying?"

He cleared his throat and turned toward the redoubt. "Not a thing," he replied lowly. "Forget I even brought it up."

Chapter 3

The three heads of Cerberus snarled at Kane as he passed them by.

Painted on the wall just inside the entrance was a large, luridly colored illustration of the triple-headed black hound of Greek myth. Fire and blood gushed out from between yellow fangs and the crimson eyes glared bright and baleful. Underneath it, in overly ornate Gothic script was written the single word "Cerberus."

Kane recalled that when Brigid once asked about the artist, Lakesh opined that one of the original military personnel assigned to the redoubt had rendered the painting sometime prior to the nukecaust. Although he couldn't be positive, Lakesh figured a Corporal Mooney was the artist, since its exaggerated exuberance seemed right out of the comic books he was obsessed with collecting.

Lakesh had never considered having it removed. For one thing, the paints were indelible and for another, it was Corporal Mooney's form of immortality. Besides, the image of Cerberus, the guardian of the gates of hell, represented a visual symbol of the work to which Lakesh had devoted his life. The three-headed hound was an appropriate totem for the installation that, for a handful of years, housed the primary subdivision of the Totality Concept's Overproject Whisper, Project Cerberus.

As Grant and Kane walked side by side down the twenty-foot-wide main corridor, beneath great curving ribs of metal that supported the high rock roof, Philboyd hurried to catch up to them. "What's going on?" he asked.

The fiercely downsweeping gunfighter's mustache that framed Grant's mouth twitched ever so slightly, which meant he was feeling a moderate degree of consternation. If his consternation level had been high, his face would have been as immobile as if carved from teak. Brusquely he replied, "We're getting a strange transmission over the sat downlink."

"How strange?" Kane inquired.

"Damn strange. So damn strange Lakesh and Brigid figured an astronomer's opinion could be useful."

"I'm not really an astronomer," Philboyd protested. "I'm an astrophysicist."

"It's got 'astro' in it, so it's close enough." Grant's lionlike rumble of a voice was muted by the softly gleaming vanadium alloy sheathing the walls and floor.

Grant towered six feet four inches tall in his stocking feet, but like Kane, he wore a black T-shirt, camo pants and thick-soled jump boots that added almost an inch to his impressive height. The spread of his shoulders on either side of his thickly corded neck was very broad. Because his body was all knotted sinew and muscle covered by deep brown flesh, he didn't look his weight of 250 pounds.

Behind Grant's lantern jaw and broken nose lay a mind of keen intelligence that possessed a number of technical skills, from fieldstripping and reassembling an SAR 80 blindfolded to expertly piloting every kind of flying craft from helicopters to the Annunaki-built trans-atmospheric vehicles known as Mantas.

"Has Domi shown back up?" Kane asked.

Grant shook his head. "If she did, she didn't check in with me. You know how she gets when the hunting mood is on her."

Kane didn't reply, but only because he agreed with his partner's comment. Domi had lived an almost feral existence in the Outlands before being smuggled into Cobaltville. He didn't understand her desire to creep among the deep, forested ravines that surrounded the mountain plateau, armed with only a crossbow, searching for prey.

Hunting was unnecessary. The food lockers and meat freezers of the redoubt were exceptionally well stocked. Lakesh had undertaken a lot of time and trouble to insure that the one item the personnel wouldn't be deprived of upon their exile was food.

As they passed the open door leading to the armory, Kane noted the blaze of the overhead fluorescent lights. "Is Decard still in there?"

Grant nodded. "Yeah."

Kane smiled sourly. "I was hoping he'd get done with his shopping and help me out with the training."

"As what?" Philboyd's blunt tone held an edge of sarcasm. "A tackle dummy?"

Not knowing what a tackle dummy might be, Kane didn't respond. Decard was a young man they had met recently during an op to the Egyptian-inspired city of Aten hidden within a canyon in the Guadalupe desert. Like Kane and Grant, he was a former Magistrate, but unlike them, he hadn't chosen to make war on his former masters unless they came looking for him. Barely eighteen years old, he had accepted the responsibilities of a wife, an adopted child and an important position in the government of Aten.

Grant could relate to Decard's choice, since he himself was torn between forging a new life with Shizuka on New Edo and his duty to his fellow exiles in Cerberus in their struggle to overthrow the tyranny of the barons.

The corridor ended at a T junction. The three men walked through an open door into the central command center, the brains of the redoubt. The long, high-ceilinged room was divided by two aisles of computer stations. The operations complex had five dedicated and eight-shared subprocessors, all linked to the mainframe behind the far wall. Two centuries before, it had been one of the most advanced models ever built, carrying experimental, error-correcting microchips of such a tiny size that they even reacted to quantum fluctuations. Biochip technology had been employed when it was built, protein molecules sandwiched between microscopic glass-and-metal circuits.

A huge Mercator relief map of the world spanned the entire wall above the door. Pinpoints of light shone steadily in almost every country, connected by a thin glowing pattern of lines. They represented the Cerberus network, the locations of all functioning gateway units across the planet.

On the opposite side of the operations center, an anteroom held the eight-foot-tall mat-trans chamber, rising from an elevated platform. Six upright slabs of brown-hued armaglass formed a translucent wall around it.

Only five people were present in the control center proper, and two of them stood at the main ops console, gazing fixedly at the VGA monitor that dominated it, a flat LCD screen nearly four feet square. At the sound of their approach, Lakesh turned, his bright blue eyes focusing on Philboyd.

"Ah, Dr. Philboyd," he said, his voice touched by a lilting East Indian accent. "I wonder if we might inveigh upon your astronomical background for an opinion."

Mohandas Lakesh Singh was a well-built man of medium height, with thick, glossy black hair, a dark olive complexion and a long, aquiline nose. He looked no older than his late forties, despite strands of gray streaking through his temples. In reality, he was just a year or so shy of celebrating his 250th birthday.

As a youthful genius, Lakesh had been drafted into the web of conspiracy the overseers of the Totality Concept had spun during the last couple of decades of the twentieth century. A multidegreed physicist and cyberneticist, he served as the administrator for Project Cerberus, and that position had earned him survival during the global megacull of January 2001. Like the Manitius Moonbase refugees, he had spent most of the intervening two hundred years in cryostasis.

Brewster Philboyd quickened his pace, outdistancing both Kane and Grant. Kane caught the eye of Brigid Baptiste, and she smiled wryly as she obligingly stepped aside to allow Philboyd complete access to the screen. A tall woman with a fair complexion and big feline-slanted eyes the color of polished jade, her high forehead gave the impression of a probing intellect whereas her full underlip hinted at an appreciation of the sensual.

A mane of red-gold hair fell in loose sunset waves almost to her waist. Her military gray T-shirt and jeans accentuated her slender, willowy figure. Her bare arms rippled with hard, toned muscle.

Kane moved up beside Brigid and saw that the bottom half of the screen glowed with a CGI grid pattern. A drop-down window displayed scrolling numbers that he guessed were measurements of speed and positional coordinates. "What's going on here, Baptiste?"

She shook her head. "None of us is really sure. That's why we asked Brewster to take a look."

Pushing his glasses up on his forehead, Philboyd leaned forward, studying the images on the screen. An audible gasp came from his lips.

"Impressed?" Lakesh inquired teasingly.

"You knew I would be," Philboyd replied distractedly. "Unbelievable."

"What is?" Kane demanded gruffly.

"That." Lakesh tapped one of the grid squares that enclosed a dark mass, little more than an exceptionally black blob against an average black background.

Kane squinted at it, then turned his narrowed gaze on Lakesh and Brigid. In a tone of aggrieved weariness he asked, "Can we for once just come right out and *explain* what's going on instead of forcing me into a guessing game?"

Brigid's wry smile widened to one of genuine amusement. "At 0100 this morning, the Vela transmitted images of an object that, judging by its backtrack, apparently came in from interplanetary space at extreme velocity. It took up an orbital position around Earth. The Vela is still tracking it."

She glanced toward a small man hunched over a console. "That's right, isn't it, Donald?"

Without lifting his copper-curled head from the computer terminal screen, Donald Bry confidently replied, "You bet it is."

Bry served as something of Lakesh's apprentice, and it was his year's worth of trial and error that allowed Cerberus to at long last gain control of the two still-functioning satellites in Earth orbit.

Although most satellites had been little more than free-floating scrap metal for well over a century, Cerberus had always possessed the proper electronic ears and eyes to receive the transmissions from at least two of them. One was of the Vela reconnaissance class, which carried narrow-band multispectral scanners. It could detect the electromagnetic radiation reflected by every object on Earth, including subsurface geomagnetic waves. The scanner was tied into an extremely high resolution photographic relay system.

The other satellite to which the redoubt was uplinked was a Comsat, which for many months was used primarily to keep track of Cerberus personnel by their subcutaneous transponders when they were out in the field. Everyone in the installation had been injected with the transponders, which transmitted heart rate, respiration, blood count and brain-wave patterns. Based on organic nanotechnology, the transponder was a nonharmful radioactive chemical that bound itself to an individual's glucose and the middle layers of the epidermis.

The telemetric signal was relayed to the redoubt by the Comsat, and directed down to the redoubt's hidden antenna array on the mountain peak, which in turn transferred it to the Cerberus computer systems, which recorded every byte of data.

"An object," Grant said musingly. "I'm guessing if it was a meteor or asteroid or something, you would've said so."

Brigid nodded. "I would."

"As a general rule, meteorites don't assume orbital courses around planetary bodies," Philboyd stated. "No, this is an artifact, a construction. Somebody built that thing."

"Where did it come from?" Kane asked suspiciously.

"That's almost impossible to answer," Brigid replied. "We tried to trace its trajectory back to its most likely origin point, but without knowing the current positions of all the planets in the solar system relative to Earth, we can't even make a semieducated guess. My own theory is that it followed a Hohmann Ellipse course, a trajectory that slingshots a spacecraft on a parabolic journey around the Sun."

Philboyd pursed his lips contemplatively. "Possibly. The most efficient deep-space flight calls for a minimum use of fuel and maximum use of momentum and planetary gravity. But that doesn't seem to be the case here, because of its speed in arriving and how quickly it slowed down."

Kane studied the grid-enclosed image again. "It's a blob, Brewster. Why couldn't it be a piece of space junk, like an old satellite or probe?"

Lakesh laughed, both excitement and a degree of anxiety evident in his voice. "Because it's *huge,* friend Kane. It is far larger than anything any terrestrial nation ever launched into space. The reason it looks like a blob is because it's blotting out the stars behind it. That might give you a general idea of its size."

"Besides," Bry spoke up, "the object has to be within five hundred kilometers of the Vela for it to be able to transmit any kind of detailed image. But it came close enough for the sensor suite to give a once-over."

"And?" Grant prodded.

"We still have some fine-tuning to do," Brigid replied, turning toward the keyboard. "But here's what we have so far."

She touched a key on the board, and the object within the square glowed faintly orange with radiated heat. "The thermal line-scan shows energy emissions across several spectra. "

"A meteor wouldn't do that?" Grant asked.

Philboyd snorted. "Of course not. Not unless it interacted with the atmospheric envelope. Then the heat registration would be due to external friction, not generated from within like this reading evidently is."

For a long moment, no one spoke, but an air of anticipation, almost ominous in its palpability, hung over the people standing at the screen.

"Well," Kane challenged, "am I going to have to ask the obvious question?"

Brigid arched an ironic eyebrow at him. "Which is?"

Kane sighed in exasperation. "You know what it is, Baptiste. Is this object a spaceship from another world? And if it is, who's piloting it—the snake-faces or the Peter Pans or some entirely new race of superior-acting freaks?"

No one answered him or responded to his oblique references to the Annunaki and the Tuatha de Danaan. Lakesh chuckled nervously, and tugged at his long nose. "If the object is intelligently guided, it is still moving. Its apogee is diminishing on a steady gradient."

"And that means?" Grant inquired, a menacing edge to his voice.

Philboyd took it upon himself to reply. "It means the distance between the object and Earth is shrinking."

"It's losing altitude, in other words," Kane stated.

Philboyd nodded. "In other words, yeah." He pointed to the numbers scrolling across the drop-down window. "Its angle of declination is increasing."

"Like it's looking for a place to land?" Grant asked.

Philboyd's eyes widened at the concept, and he gazed steadily at the numerals. After a moment he announced, "Its velocity is definitely dropping. It's approaching the Asian subcontinent. China to be exact."

"Actually," Bry declared, "it's probably already over it. We're not receiving real-time telemetry. There's approximately a twenty-minute lag between transmission and image processing. It's about 2:30 a.m. over in China, but since the Moon is in full phase we ought to be able to get a cleaner picture of the damn thing."

Kane felt a chill finger of dread stroke the base of his spine. With the possible exception of Brewster Philboyd, he knew his companions had made the same connection as he had between a certain region of China and an anomalous astronomical event. But rather than utter the name of the connection, he commented offhandedly, "I'm betting this thing is heading for the Xian province and the pyramid therein."

Bry suddenly sat up straight in his chair. He cast a wide-eyed stare over at Kane, intoning, "No need to take that bet…that's exactly where our object is heading. It's reflecting moonlight, so I've got a strong image now. Look at your screen."

Brigid touched keys to erase the grid pattern from the VGA monitor. In the drop-down window a constant stream of figures, symbols and numbers flashed. Near the bottom edge of the screen a curving sweep of blue-green appeared. A bright streak of light inched across it, like a tiny glowing needle. Tapping a couple of keys, Brigid brought the image up to full magnification.

Philboyd whispered, *"Kee-rist."*

Lakesh murmured a few words in Hindi and then fell silent. They all did.

Kane stared for so long at the screen without blinking, his eyes began to sting. He had the sense of not looking at a ship at all, but a creature that swam through space as other animals navigated the sea. He couldn't grasp its scale, since there was nothing around by which to measure it, but the sheer massive bulk of the object was awe-inspiring.

Sleek, deadly and dark with pinnacled towers silvered by moonlight, the vast craft sailed majestically over the dark valleys far, far below. From its hull rose spires and minarets tipped with glittering points, reminiscent of the dorsal fins of a mind-staggeringly enormous sea creature—or dragon.

The bow resembled a gargantuan horned head crafted from alloy, and the back-swept pylons supporting twin engine nacelles put him in mind of the wings of a raptorial bird. Weapons emplacements looked like stylized foreclaws. The tapered configuration of amidships and stern reminded him of a tail.

Kane struggled to view it as a vehicle, a warship, but the persistent impression he received from the image was that it lived. The cruiser bespoke a self-assured, almost arrogant awareness of its own power, as if the very fact it existed at all was a statement of superiority, of invincibility.

He couldn't gauge an approximation of its size, and he didn't even want to guess at the nature of the vessel's armament. A fear that was almost a blind xenophobic terror knotted into a cold fist in the pit of his stomach. When he gazed at the dark dragon sailing over the face of the world, somehow he knew it was returning from a long journey, not making its first foray to Earth. It had come back to find something—or someone. Under the armor that plated the enormous sweep of its metal hull, the ship was a living, thinking entity.

He tried to drive the notion from his conscious mind, but he found he couldn't. A science and technology more overpoweringly superior than any he had ever considered possible were responsible for the gargantuan ship and the realization did more than terrify him—it humbled him.

Lakesh broke the stunned spell by asking pensively, "Dr. Philboyd...what do you make of it?"

In a voice so hushed by awe it was barely above a whisper, Philboyd said, "It's...*big*. My God...at least a mile long—"

Another voice, a sharp female voice taut with tension, suddenly burst out of the intercom, causing them all to jump. "Medical emergency! Medical team to the armory, *stat!*"

Kane tore his gaze away from the screen and fastened it on Grant's face. The big man blinked in momentary confusion, then exclaimed, "Domi!"

Chapter 4

Standing in the rear of the huge Cerberus armory, Decard placed his hands on his hips and glanced around at the mind-boggling amount of death-dealing armament.

As he stared around at the huge vaulted room, he couldn't help but be reminded of the arsenal in the Archuleta Mesa compound. He couldn't be sure, but he figured this one was slightly larger. With a sigh, the young blond-haired man forced the memories back into the dark recesses of his memory. That place was a lifetime in his past, and he didn't want to dwell on it.

Regardless, he had never seen so much ammunition or so many different varieties of handguns, rifles, rocket launchers and other weapons designed to end human life. He imagined that even the armories in the villes paled in comparison to the sheer amount of ordnance he saw before him.

Adjusting the straps of his backpack, Decard walked between the rows of weaponry, his brown eyes wandering over the stacks and crates, inspecting the lettering stamped on each. He paused a couple of times to inspect a weapon here, a box of ammunition there, but when he was finished, he replaced each item back where it belonged.

After what seemed like hours, Decard finally found

what he had been looking for. He opened a satchel that he had brought with him and began placing several boxes of 9 mm rounds into it. He selected a wide variety of different types of ammo, everything from the hollowpoint, to the full-metal jacket and even mercury-tipped rounds. The former Magistrate realized the probability of his actually using all the ammunition he collected was remote, but if he had learned one lesson as a Mag, it was to be prepared.

Preparation was the primary reason he had made the thirty-mile trek across the desert from Aten to the small installation that contained a mat-trans unit. Earlier in the week, Roamers had been sighted in the general vicinity of the canyon that concealed his adopted home from the world at large. For the most part, Roamer bands were nomadic outlaws, but they used resistance to baronial authority as a justification for their raids. Some bands were little more than rag-bag gangs of scavengers, while others were virtually small armies.

Decard didn't know if the Roamers the city's scouts had reported were one or the other, but he did know that the barrens seemed a very strange place for anyone to roam.

Although the militia of Aten possessed firearms, ammunition was at a premium, so he had gated to Cerberus to pick up what he could, much like a neighbor might have dropped by to borrow a cup of sugar in an earlier, gentler time.

Satisfied that he had all the ammunition that he needed, Decard retraced his steps, stopping at the section of the armory partitioned for the storage of bladed and hand weapons. Like the side arms and grenades, there were literally dozens of different styles of knives, melee weapons and even clubs. There was a selection of compound bows, crossbows and bolts and arrows.

He examined several types of knives, since swords, daggers, poignards and even stilettos were in use in Aten. He looked at the standard-issue close-combat blades used by the predark military, as well as an assortment of bowies and bayonets. He picked up a knife that had serrations on both sides of the black blade. It felt as elegant as anything he had ever used before. The weight was manageable and the balance perfect. He knew that it could easily be used as a throwing knife in a pinch, although he had been taught in the academy that if a Mag was down to only his combat blade, throwing it was a singularly foolish tactic.

Examining the blade closely, Decard saw tiny words engraved near the bottom of the blade, just above the handle: Gerber Mk 2. He decided he wanted it. He knew that it wouldn't be missed and besides, Kane had told him he could take whatever he wanted. He slipped the blade into the accompanying sheath and then attached it to his belt.

Decard chuckled softly as he thought about what Kane had told him. He knew that the invitation didn't extend to the two suits of black polycarbonate armor standing along the wall like silent sentinels. Those exoskeletons belonged exclusively to Kane and Grant. Despite the fact that the two men had recently traded the armor in for the formfitting shadow suits, he knew that the armor held sentimental value for them, and that they wouldn't give them up.

Besides, he had his own suit of armor back in the city of Aten. It was rare for him to ever don it, and it didn't fit quite as well as it used to, since he had first been fitted for it nearly two years earlier, before he had achieved his full maturity. And, he reminded himself sourly, before he had began eating and drinking like a pig.

As tempted as he was, Decard decided that he wouldn't bother taking any other firearms. He was trained to use the Sin Eater and Copperhead subgun, and those were the weapons he knew best. The Sin Eater strapped to his forearm was like an extension of his body, and he felt comfortable with it.

Decard turned and barely managed to bite back a yelp of fright. Only moments before, he had been alone in the huge chamber. Now, in front of him stood a small, almost elfin woman with a hugely distended belly. He recognized her instantly, even though well over a year had passed since he had last seen her. "Quavell!"

"Hello, Magistrate Decard," the woman replied in a soft, musical voice.

Despite himself, Decard felt himself staring at her huge belly. "I'm not a Magistrate anymore," he said lamely. "How have you been?"

"Quite well, thank you." She carefully stepped closer to him, as if she feared he would take flight at her approach. "It has been quite some time since we last spoke."

He felt the blood rushing to his face as he looked away. "I guess it has. It was the night when I saw Baron Samarium and Baron Sharpe in Dulce…nearly a year and half ago now."

Quavell didn't respond to his comment. She stated, "I heard you were visiting and I wanted to see you. You've put on weight."

He nodded mutely, refraining from replying, "So have you." He was still in shock at not only seeing the woman again, but also at her physical state. Quavell was a hybrid, a blending of human and so-called Archon genetic material, although they preferred the term "new humans," the homo superior. She was small, under five feet in height, and to refer to her build as petite was almost an exaggeration. She looked almost as young as his eighteen-going-on-nineteen years, despite the fact Decard knew the majority of hybrids were well over half a century old.

Her huge, upslanting eyes of a clear, crystal blue dominated a face of chiseled beauty that a poetically minded man might have described as that of a fairy queen, due to the high, angular cheekbones and smooth, unlined forehead.

Her lips were small and like those of most hybrids, curved naturally upward so that she always seemed to be on the point of smiling, even when her face was in repose. White-blond hair the texture of silk threads fell from her large skull and curled inward at her slender shoulders.

Although her beauty had the fascination of being an alien loveliness, she was still close enough to humanity's feminine ideal to have aroused a man sufficiently to engage in the sex act with her and impregnate her. Decard knew Kane was generally believed to have been the man who had done so, while a prisoner of Baron Cobalt in Area 51. Her tiny form was encased in a silvery-gray, skintight bodysuit. It only accentuated the distended condition of her belly and the slenderness of her limbs. Just the realization that a representative of the new human race carried the child of a member of the old human race was shocking enough. So was Quavell's apparent attempt to engage him in small talk.

"I understand you have a wife," she said. "Her name is Mavati, correct?"

Decard smiled. "Yeah, she's the daughter of Queen Nefron, the ruler of the city."

"Impressive accomplishment for a Magistrate turned exile."

Decard scowled at her, but then noticed a ghost of a smile on her lips and he couldn't help but smile back. "After being exiled, I guess I had to come up with some way to make a name for myself in the world."

"I'm sure that you would have accomplished that," she said, "even if you hadn't married a princess."

He shrugged indifferently. "Mavati said that it was destiny that brought me to Aten, and to her."

Quavell nodded as if she understood perfectly. "Do you believe in destiny?"

Shaking his head adamantly, Decard replied, "No, no way. We make our own choices. I don't believe in some great mystical force that has already laid out our path for us. We have free will, and we have to live with the choices that we make."

She listened attentively, her hands resting on her swollen stomach. "Don't you find it odd, though, that because you chose to ignore my orders to leave the nursery, you were forced into exile? That the only person who survived the encounter with you and Magistrate Crowe was a young telepathic girl? You don't believe it might have been destiny that allowed you to fight Crowe, and allowed you to be guided through the desert and found by Mavati? The mystical force you mention might have great plans for not only for you, but everyone in this place."

Decard snorted. "Come on, Quavell. How can you buy into human superstitions when you're not completely human?" He regretted the words even as they left his mouth.

Quavell's eyes narrowed as if she winced in pain, but she nodded. "Since I am partially human, perhaps that is the part open to superstitions. The child I carry will possibly bridge our two races. I have learned a great deal about humanity over the past few months. It could be that I find allowing my 'old' human traits to come to the fore congenial to my true nature."

"How so?"

Quavell winced again and her right hand touched her forehead. Decard noted a dew of moisture beading there. In a slightly strained voice, she declared, "I've found that people, representatives of the old humanity, are willing to make great sacrifices for me and my unborn baby. It doesn't matter that I'm not human as defined by the old standards. Perhaps there isn't such a thing as destiny, as you so convincingly argue, but I have wondered about it many times. I have often reviewed the events that led to the both of us standing here and having this conversation."

Decard nodded. "I see what you mean. Whether or not it's destiny, things have worked out for the best for everyone."

Quavell grimaced and gingerly massaged her belly. "That assessment may be premature. I am overdue by nearly three weeks, which according to Dr. DeFore is not particularly unusual in a human female. But I confess to feeling a degree of apprehension."

Decard chuckled self-consciously. "I brought something for you from Aten that might make you feel better. I totally forgot. Distracted by all the toys here, I guess." As he spoke, he shrugged out of his backpack.

Watching him curiously, Quavell stood still, her hands resting on her belly. Decard rummaged through the pack and removed three small leather bags. Carefully he opened one of the bags, pulling out a small figurine attached to a glittering gold chain. He held it up to Quavell, allowing her to take in the beauty of the ornament.

"What is it?" she asked, reaching out with her right hand.

Decard grinned. "It's a representation of Bastet, the Egyptian goddess of cats, music and dance, but more importantly, the protector of pregnant women." He placed the figurine in her outstretched hand.

The miniature ivory carving depicted a voluptuous woman with the head of a cat, garbed in traditional Egyptian clothing, leaving her breasts bare. Clasped in either hand were an ankh and a sistrum.

"Here," Decard said, taking the figurine back from Quavell. "Turn around. Let me put it on for you."

Nodding, Quavell turned as Decard undid the clasp on the small figure. He placed it over her shoulders and fastened it. The fit was perfect—neither too tight, nor too loose. It fell to rest between her small breasts.

She turned back to face him. "Thank you, Decard. It is truly a beautiful gift. I shall cherish it."

As she spoke, she grimaced again in pain, her slender hands going to her bulging stomach. Beads of perspiration seemed to pop out of the pores of her skin and she bit back a groan. She stumbled backward.

Alarm etched across his youthful face, Decard immediately grabbed her arms, unsure what to do. "What's wrong? Is it the baby?"

The small woman groaned and slumped to her knees, hanging on to a corner of the table. Her big eyes screwed shut. Between clenched teeth she whispered, "It is that…and something else."

"What?" Decard blurted, feeling panic rise within him.

Quavell shook her head. "I don't know…I never felt anything like this before."

She dabbed at her damply glistening brow with a sleeve. When she brought it away, a small section of her flesh came with it, adhering to the synthetic material. Decard couldn't repress a cry of shock. Nothing he had trained for in the Magistrate Academy had ever prepared for him for an event such as this.

"What should I do?" he demanded, his voice hitting a high note of fear.

Quavell cried out loudly as she wrapped one hand around Decard's wrist with surprising strength. She dragged in a long painful breath and urged. "Intercom— call the infirmary."

Decard looked about frantically, his mind racing. Then, at the other end of the huge room, he spotted an intercom panel on the wall next to the entrance. He moved to pull away from Quavell, but her grip was like a steel vise around his wrist. She opened her eyes, and though they were unfocused, fear glinted within their depths.

"Something is happening to me," she husked out in

a hoarse whisper. "Something… terrible." She bowed her head and pressed a hand against her temple. "I feel it here."

"You're just having your baby," he said, trying to sound reassuring and in control of both his emotions and the situation. "You'll be fine."

As the last word left his mouth, Quavell doubled over, falling to the floor on her side. She uttered a long, piercing shriek that lanced through his head like a white-hot wire. Decard twisted free of her grasp and rose to his feet. Looking down, he saw a wet stain spreading across the thighs of her jumpsuit. Even though his knowledge of childbirth was superficial, he knew what had just happened. The woman's water had just broken.

"What the hell is going on here?"

The sharp female voice cut easily through the cavernous armory. Decard looked toward the entrance and saw a girl not much taller than Quavell standing in the open doorway. Her close-cropped hair, the color of sun-bleached bone-rose from her head in a series of short spikes.

Her eyes, narrowed to suspicious slits, glinted like rubies. Her skin matched the color of her hair, white and bloodless. High-cut shorts hugged her flaring hips and a halter concealed small, pert breasts. Her bare waist was circled by a web belt from which hung a quiver of arrows and a long sheathed knife. A crossbow dangled from her right hand.

Her limbs, bare feet and even her face were so rimmed with dirt and streaks of camouflage paint Decard had trouble recognizing the albino girl as Domi. She had apparently just returned from hunting.

Decard made a helpless gesture toward Quavell. "Something's wrong," he said. "She's having her baby, but something is wrong—"

On the floor Quavell shrieked and writhed, twisted and screamed again. Her shoulders heaved convulsively.

Domi dropped the crossbow and whirled toward the intercom. She slapped the call button and shouted, "Medical emergency! Medical team to the armory, *stat!*"

Chapter 5

The dash to the armory from two different points in the redoubt wasn't total chaos until Reba DeFore and her aide Auerbach, arrived pushing a squeaky-wheeled gurney ahead of them.

"Out of my way!" the stocky medic commanded, using the gurney like a ship's prow parting ocean waves. "Move it!"

Everyone who had been clustered around the fallen Quavell obeyed her, except for Domi, who was kneeling beside the hybrid woman, cradling her head in her grimy hands. Kane, Brigid, Grant, Lakesh and Decard stepped aside as DeFore bent over Quavell. She examined her swiftly, methodically, hands gently kneading her lower belly and pelvic area.

The buxom, bronze-skinned woman shook her head to toss free-hanging strands of her ash-blond hair away from her eyes. Ordinarily she wore in an intricate braid at the back of her head, but the emergency call had prevented her from even brushing her hair thoroughly, much less braiding it.

Quavell panted heavily, respiration fitful, head tilted to one side, lips parted to bare her small teeth. Her eyes, barely visible between half-open lids, bore a glassy sheen. DeFore carefully fingered the bloodless abrasion on her damply glistening forehead.

"What's happening to her?" Domi asked worriedly.

DeFore didn't answer. Loudly she said, "Quavell! Can you hear me? Quavell!"

The hybrid woman didn't react her name. She continued to breathe in a rapid cadence, a sobbing sigh.

Full lips compressed in a tight line, DeFore swept her dark brown eyes over the faces of the people present in the armory. "Who was with her when this happened?"

Taking a hesitant half step forward, Decard said falteringly, "I was. We were just talking, but I noticed she appeared to be in some pain. After a minute, she just collapsed…said something bad was happening to her. Then she had a seizure."

"I came in about then," Domi interjected in her high voice. "Made com call. She's like this ever since." Under stress, she reverted to the abbreviated form of Outlands speech.

DeFore grunted in acknowledgment and returned her attention Quavell, timing her pulse at her throat and wrist. Grimly, she said, "She's definitely in labor. Auerbach, let's get her aboard." She glanced up at Kane. "Give us a hand."

Although his eyes narrowed ever so slightly at the medic's presumptive tone, Kane knelt beside Domi, sliding his hands beneath Quavell's shoulders. DeFore secured a grip on her legs while Auerbach positioned the flat of his hands against the small of the woman's back.

"On three," DeFore instructed crisply. "One, two, *three.*"

In unison, they hoisted Quavell from the floor onto

the cushioned gurney. She was surprisingly light despite her gravid condition and slack limbs.

"Well?" Lakesh demanded plaintively. "What's wrong with her?"

DeFore shook her head doubtfully. "I can't make an accurate diagnosis here, but her blood pressure appears to be elevated and according to Decard she suffered convulsions. She seems to be in a coma. Those are major symptoms of eclampsia."

Brigid inhaled sharply at the word. As Auerbach and DeFore wheeled the gurney toward the door, Grant asked quietly, "What's eclampsia?"

Face drained of color, Brigid answered, "It's a rare but acute and toxic condition that occurs late in pregnancy. It's usually fatal."

Domi stared pensively after the retreating medics. "Baby, too?"

Brigid seemed reluctant to answer then said, "I don't know. Sometimes."

Uttering a wordless murmur of alarm, Domi started to rush toward the exit, but Lakesh latched on to her arm and restrained her. "No, darlingest one. Allow the good doctor to do her work without an audience."

Domi struggled briefly, trying to wrest free. "Could help."

"If Reba needs our help," Lakesh said softly, "you can be sure she'll ask for it."

Domi relented only when Grant laid a big hand on her shoulder. In a surprisingly soothing, sympathetic voice, he said, "Lakesh is right. We'd just get in the way."

Blowing out a disconsolate breath, Domi nodded in agreement. "Guess so."

She and Quavell shared a strange but strong bond, due mainly to both of them being markedly different from the other Cerberus personnel, both physically and in life experience. An albino, Domi was an outlander by birth. Quavell, a hybrid blending of human and semi-human, could not have been more of an outsider.

Domi also felt she owed Quavell her life and so had taken a keen interest in her welfare and that of her unborn child—particularly if Kane turned out to be the father, as was the general consensus of opinion.

"All we can do," Brigid stated, "is wait for word. It's best if we all go about our routines until Reba has something to tell us."

Lakesh patted Domi's green-striped shoulder. "Perhaps you should get cleaned up, darlingest one. If the good doctor does require your help, she'll want you scrubbed, if not completely sterile."

As Domi trudged toward the door, Kane turned to Decard, whose complexion had not lost its waxy pallor. "Are you done here?"

The young man nodded, hefting his satchel. "Yeah. I sure hope the medical supplies you got from Aten can help Quavell."

As the people moved toward the exit, Lakesh commented, "Your mother-in-law, Queen Nefron, was quite generous in sharing the Mission Invictus materials with us. If anything will save Quavell and her baby, those will."

Decard eyed Kane speculatively but didn't speak. As they entered the corridor, Kane felt nettled enough to snap, "What?"

The young man shrugged. "I was told you were the father."

"The question of paternity hasn't been settled," Brigid said a bit too quickly.

Kane swallowed a sigh. "No, it hasn't. But I hope it will be soon."

If Decard found the remark cryptic he kept his opinion to himself. No one else commented on it, either, but Kane knew his friends couldn't help but be reminded of the irony. In their attempts to overthrow the tyranny of the hybrid barons, who considered themselves the pinnacle of evolutionary achievement, he might have contributed to the creation of a totally new branch on the tree of human development—a third type of human hybrid.

Although hybrids were different from humankind, Quavell had pointed out that different wasn't the same as alien, regardless of where some of the genetic material had originated. Kane hadn't been too interested in the source when a mission to the Archuleta Mesa biomedical facility had inadvertently destroyed the genetic-engineering division of the vast facility. An entire generation of hybrids in the incubation chambers, more than two thousand of them, was lost.

After the destruction of the Archuleta Mesa installation, the barons held an emergency council that dealt with only one topic—the survival of their people. Baron Cobalt, whom Lakesh had once served as a high adviser, put forth a proposal that would not only save the hybrids, but also elevate him to a new position of power.

During the council, Baron Cobalt proposed to establish a new central ruling consortium. In effect, the barons would become viceroys, plenipotentiaries in their own territories. They were accustomed to acting as the viceroys of the Archon Directorate, so the actual proposal didn't offend them.

Although the fortress-cities with their individual, allegedly immortal god-kings were supposed to be interdependent, the baronies still operated on insular principles. Cooperation among them was grudging, despite their shared goal of a unified world. They perceived humanity in general as either servants or as living storage vessels for transplanted organs and fresh genetic material.

The barons were far less in favor of Baron Cobalt's proposal that he be recognized as the imperator. However, they really didn't have much of a choice. After the destruction of the medical facilities in the Mesa, the barons were left without access to the techniques of fetal development outside the womb, so not only was the baronial oligarchy in danger of extinction, but so was the entire hybrid race.

Baron Cobalt presented his fellow barons with a way to stave off extinction by occupying Area 51, with the spoken assumption of taking responsibility to sustain his race, but only if he was elevated to a position of the highest authority.

Area 51 was the predark unclassified code name for a training area on Nellis Air Force Base. It was also known as Groom Lake, but most predarkers preferred to call it Dreamland. Contained in the dry lake bed was a vast installation, extending deep into the desert floor. Only a few of the aboveground buildings still stood. Area 51 was more than just a military installation—at one point it served as a top secret international base operated by a consortium from many countries. Baron Cobalt proposed that a consortium of barons, which in turn would be overseen by him, would oversee its renewed operation.

Area 51's history was intertwined with rumors of alien involvement, and so Baron Cobalt had used its medical facilities as a substitute for those destroyed in New Mexico. No one could be sure if the aliens referred to by the predark conspiracy theorists were the Archons, but more than likely they were, inasmuch as the surviving equipment was already designed to be compatible with hybrid metabolisms.

In any event, Baron Cobalt reactivated the installation, turning it into a processing and treatment center, without having to rebuild it from scratch, and transferred the human and hybrid personnel from the Dulce facility—those who had survived the destruction there, at any rate.

However, the medical treatments that addressed the congenital autoimmune system deficiencies of the barons weren't enough to insure their continued survival. The necessary equipment and raw material to implement procreation through advanced cloning techniques had yet to be installed. Baron Cobalt unilaterally decided that the conventional means of conception was the only option to keep the hybrid race alive.

Since the baron held Kane personally responsible for pushing the hybrid race to the brink of extinction, Cobalt made it Kane's task to repopulate it after capturing him. Kane wasn't the first human male to be pressed into service. There had been other men before him, but many of them had performed unsatisfactorily, due to their terror of the hybrid females. No pregnancies had resulted.

During his two weeks of captivity, Kane was fed a steady diet of protein to speed sperm production. Laced with a sexual stimulant to provide him with hours of high energy, he was forced to achieve erection and ejaculation six times a day every two days. The application of an aphrodisiac gel induced a blind, rutting fever and so the unusual physical appearance of the women was not an inhibiting factor.

Although Kane knew he was supposed to be biologically superior due to genetic manipulation while he was still in the womb, he also knew the main reason he was chosen to impregnate the female hybrids was simply due to the fact male hybrids were incapable of engaging in conventional acts of procreation. Their organs of reproduction were so undeveloped as to be vestigial.

What made the barons so superior had nothing to do with their physical endowments. The brains of the barons could absorb and process information with exceptional speed, and their cognitive abilities were little short of supernatural.

Almost from the moment the barons emerged from the incubation chambers, they possessed IQs so far beyond the range of standard tests as to render them meaningless. They mastered language in a matter of weeks, speaking in whole sentences. All of Nature's design faults in the human brain were corrected, modified and improved, specifically in the hypothalamus, which regulated the complex biochemical systems of the body.

They could control all autonomous functions of their brains and bodies, even to the manufacture and release of chemicals and hormones. They possessed complete control over the portion of the brain known as the limbic system, and by tapping into it they developed degrees of telepathic and extrasensory ability.

But since they were bred for brilliance, all barons had emotional limitations placed upon their enormous intellects. They were captives of their shared Archon hivemind heritage, which actually derived from one of the two root races of the Archons, the Annunaki. Locked into a remorseless, almost sterile intellectualism, the barons didn't allow visceral emotions to play a large part in their psychologies. Even their bursts of passion were of the most rudimentary kind. They only experienced emotions during moments of extreme stress, and then so intensely they were almost consumed by them.

Therefore Kane was surprised when Quavell, during one of their scheduled period of copulations, confided to him that not every hybrid agreed with the baronial policy toward humanity. She expressed compassion and even shame. He was even more surprised when Quavell helped him and Domi escape. He was forced to reassess everything he thought he knew about the barons, about the hybrids.

With the advent of Sam, the imperator, everything was different yet strangely still the same. The imperator was fixated on unification, just as the barons were but with a different objective in mind. His stated intent was to end the tyranny of the barons and unify both hybrid and human and build a new Earth, but Lakesh didn't believe him and Kane had no reason to do so, either. But if it turned out that female hybrids could conceive offspring by human males, then a continued division between the so-called old and new human was pretty much without merit.

During the first couple of months following his captivity, Kane had successfully managed to keep from dwelling on memories of his forced fornications. He gained a certain degree of emotional distance from his experiences, and even memories of engaging in the sex act with Quavell grew hazy.

His most vivid memory of Quavell wasn't hazy in the least, though he wished it was. He still recalled with shocking clarity his first sight of her sitting in Lakesh's office when he entered to brief him about the events that had occurred on the Moon. He would have imbibed battery acid before admitting the closest he had ever come to fainting dead away was at that very moment.

According to Quavell, she had made the long overland trip from Area 51 in a stolen Sandcat, all alone. She traveled as far as the foothills of the Bitterroot Range to the encampment of Sky Dog. The shaman brought her the rest of the way to the mountain peak on horseback. Both Kane and Lakesh were still skeptical of certain details of her story, particularly how she knew the location of the redoubt. She offered only a vague explanation about learning of it from either Kane or Domi during their period of imprisonment in Dreamland.

She had refused to name which one of them actually made the revelation. Neither Kane nor Domi admitted to telling her or anyone else about Cerberus. Still and all, Quavell had provided them with useful information about the current state of the baronies in the aftermath of the Imperator War.

As the group of people entered the operations center, Decard asked, "Do you want me to hang around?"

Lakesh shook his head. "I see no need, young man. As I recall, it's rather a long way from the gateway unit in the Mission Invictus facility to Aten. I'm sure your wife will appreciate you returning home before nightfall. Give my regards to her and Queen Nefron."

He and Brigid rejoined Brewster Philboyd at the VGA screen. The lanky astrophysicist still stared entranced at the images flickering across it.

"What are they looking at?" Decard asked.

"Nothing much," Grant answered with a forced diffidence. "A mile-long spaceship that looks like a dragon orbiting the Earth."

Decard stared at him in wide-eyed incredulity, obviously wondering if the big man was making an enigmatic joke. He glanced over at Kane, who grinned insouciantly. "Just an average day here in Cerberus. You should be glad you live in Aten."

The three men crossed the operations center and entered the adjacent gate room. Decard paused at the base of the elevated platform supporting the mat-trans unit and looked uncertainly from Grant to Kane and back to Kane again. He said quietly, "I feel a little funny about leaving without knowing what happens with Quavell."

"She's not your responsibility," Kane told him kindly. "You've got enough of your own, and you don't need to volunteer to take on more."

Decard nodded but he didn't move.

"Whatever happens," Grant stated, "however it turns out, we'll get a message to you."

Jaw muscles bunched, Decard said quietly, "Thanks,"

and punched in the destination lock code on the keypad on the exterior of the heavy slab of brown-tinted arma-glass serving as a door. He stepped into the chamber but before pulling the door closed on its counterbalanced pivots, he gave both men a short salute.

They returned it with wry smiles. The door swung shut, the solenoids caught with a loud click and en-gaged the automatic jump initiator circuits. The famil-iar yet still slightly unnerving hum rose from the phase transition coils within the shielded platform.

The hum climbed in pitch to a whine, then to a cy-clonic howl. Thready static discharges, like tiny light-ning strokes, flared from the interior of the gateway chamber. The hurricane howl hit an almost painfully high note, then began to descend in scale as the mat-trans cycled down through its dematerialization pro-cess. When the sound was no more than a faint bumblebee hum again, Kane and Grant turned away.

They whirled back at the sound of a fierce, rushing wind erupting from the emitter array. It swelled in vol-ume. From the operations center, Bry shouted in alarm, "Unscheduled jumpers!"

"From where?" Grant demanded loudly.

"I don't know!" Bry's voice was full of confused consternation. "It's like they caught the last of the car-rier wave and are surfing in on it! I don't have a read on a point of origin. "

"Impossible!"

Kane turned to see Lakesh hustle into the ready room, his face creased with equal measures of disbelief and fear. He said again, more vehemently, "Impossible!"

Kane squinted away from the flashes of light bursting on the other side of the translucent armaglass walls. "Possible or not, we've got a materialization."

He paused and added dourly, "Hasn't this been a hell of a day so far, and it's not even half over."

Chapter 6

"Shit!" Grant spit out the word as he lunged across the room to a tall cabinet against the left-hand wall. Yanking open the door, he removed a lightweight SA-80 subgun and tossed it to Kane. He threw one to Lakesh and another to Brigid, who snatched it out of the air as she hurried through the door on the older man's heels.

After the mad Maccan's recent murderous incursion into the redoubt, it had become standard protocol to have at least one armed guard standing by during a gateway materialization. To simplify matters, a weapons locker had recently been moved into the ready room. All of the Cerberus exiles were required to become reasonably proficient with firearms, and the lightweight "point and shoot" subguns were the easiest for a novice to handle.

The three people took up positions all around the room, shouldering the subguns, barrels trained on the door of the jump chamber. They waited tensely as the unit droned through the materialization cycle. Because of the translucent quality of the brown-tinted armaglass shielding, they could see nothing within it except vague, shifting shapes without form or apparent solidity.

The chamber was full of the plasma bleed-off, a by-product of the ionized wave forms that resembled mist.

Within seconds, the discordant whine melded into a smooth hum. They heard the clicking of solenoids and the heavy armaglass door swung open on its counterbalanced hinges. Mist swirled and thread-thin static electricity discharges arced within the billowing mass. Looking like backlit shadows in a fog bank, three figures stepped one by one off the platform and into the ready room.

Kane felt his neck muscles tighten and his eyes widen. The figure in the lead was small, about the size of a half-grown child, perhaps four and half feet tall. There was no mistaking the round, bald cranium or features that seemed sculpted in marble. The black, depthless eyes stared directly at him—or through him. He wore a dark one-piece garment that left only his chalky pink head and six-fingered hands bare.

"Balam," Kane heard himself breathe, bewilderment and shock rooting him in place.

He experienced no such confusion about the figure towering over Balam. The violet-eyed woman was tall and beautiful with a flawless complexion the hue of honey. Her finely chiseled features were surrounded by a glossy fall of black hair.

Ebon-hued pants hugged her long, lithe legs and fell over boots so stilt-heeled they gave her the aspect of being taller than she actually was. Her waist was tightly cinctured by a red sash, and the narrow shoulders of her indigo tunic were broadened by tapered pads.

The satiny fabric was tailored to conform to the thrust of her full breasts, which were accentuated by scarlet facings. Her eyes swept over the four people, surveying Kane first, then Grant, Brigid and finally settling on Lakesh. Although her expression was composed, she radiated tension, if not outright fear.

A chunky Asian man in the uniform of an imperial trooper followed her out of the jump chamber. He wore high-topped boots, a helmet and a midnight-blue coverall with facings of bright red. Gun bores swiveled toward him.

Erica van Sloan lifted a hand, declaring, "He's not armed. None of us is armed."

Kane lowered his weapon, but his finger didn't stray far from the trigger. He looked at Balam, the last of the so-called Archons, the last of the children created by two races who had turned Earth into a battleground millennia ago.

"Balam, pal o' mine," Kane said with icy sarcasm. "It's been a while."

The huge head inclined toward him in a short nod of acknowledgment. "Since we said our goodbyes in Agartha." His voice didn't sound quite as strained or as scratchy as the last time he had heard it, more than two years before in Tibet. Kane supposed his vocal cords had strengthened during that time. While a prisoner in the Cerberus redoubt, Balam hadn't spoken in over three years, and Brigid speculated his underdeveloped vocal cords had almost completely atrophied.

"And you've been a busy little alien bee since then," he retorted, despite knowing Balam was not an alien, since he had been born on Earth fifteen hundred years before. "The least of it was buzzing around to put Sam in power."

"I did only what my forebears charged me to do, Kane."

Lakesh stepped forward, eyeing Balam and Erica suspiciously. "Did you gate here from Xian?"

"Where else?" Erica's tone was dismissive.

"How?" he asked bluntly. "Through the Heart of the World?"

Erica's lips twisted in annoyance. "We didn't come here to talk about matters of transportation, Mohandas."

"No," Brigid interposed coldly. "I imagine you came here to talk about a giant dragon-shaped spaceship that's taken up a stationary orbit about twelve hundred miles above your son's pyramid."

The look Erica cast toward her was so full of astonishment, so completely different than her usual aristocratic disdain, Kane almost laughed. "How do you know about that?" she demanded.

Grant responded to her question with one of his own. "What do *you* know about it, if anything?"

In a matter-of-fact tone, Balam rasped, "She is Tiamat, a sentient vessel safeguarding the spirit of the Annunaki race. After three and a half thousand years, she has returned to join the souls with the new bodies of the overlords of the Earth. Her arrival is the culmination of thousands of years of secret planning, of conspiracy, of war, of strife, of manipulation...the hidden history of your planet."

For a protracted stretch of time, no one spoke or even breathed hard. Finally Kane cleared his throat and announced, "Well, I don't think of any us expected you to say *that.*"

"Actually I was afraid we'd hear something along those lines," Lakesh said flatly, lowering his SA-80. "This calls for an immediate briefing."

FOR THE PAST COUPLE of years the majority of briefings in Cerberus had been held in the cafeteria on the second level. Although the redoubt had an officially designated briefing room on the third floor—one that came equipped with ten rows of the theater-type chairs facing a raised speaking dais and a rear-projection screen—it was almost never used.

Since most briefings involved only a handful of people, they were usually convened in the more intimate dining hall. The atmosphere was more relaxed and access to food and drink was unrestricted. However, on this occasion Kane, Lakesh, Brigid and Grant were in a rare state of agreement that it was best to keep their uninvited guests confined to the gate room. Marching Balam through the redoubt would excite a great deal of curiosity, if not outright fear among the new residents, judging by Brewster Philboyd's stunned reaction to the first sight of him.

The astrophysicist had been summoned from the ops center for his input and he had spent the first minute standing in the doorway gaping in dumbfounded silence at Balam. Although Philboyd had seen Maccan, the lost prince of the Danaan, and with Brigid had faced Enki, the last of the Annunaki, Balam seemed to exert a hypnotic influence over him. He whispered to Brigid, "It looks just like one of those things from *Close Encounters.*"

Brigid wasn't sure what the man was referring to, but she said, "*He,* not it. You saw the vid record we have of him during the time he spent here."

Philboyd swallowed hard. Balam turned his fathomless black eyes on him. "Yeah," he said, averting his gaze, "but that was almost like watching a movie. It didn't seem real."

"*He,*" Brigid corrected again.

Biting his lip, Philboyd cringed against Brigid. In a faint, aspirated voice, he said, "He, it—whatever— scares the hell out of me!"

Glancing over at Balam, Kane said crossly, "Knock it off, B."

Balam's austere features didn't so much as twitch, but he replied quietly, "My apologies. The transmission of a mental stimulus to evoke a flight or fear reaction is an automatic response when my kind is faced with strangers. Due to many centuries of conditioning, it has become almost unconscious reflex."

His huge eyes were veiled momentarily by vein-laced lids. When he looked at Philboyd again he inquired, "Better, Dr. Philboyd?"

The lanky astrophysicist blinked in surprise, passing a hand over his forehead. He uttered a jittery little laugh. "Yeah, actually. Thanks."

Everyone in the redoubt who had interacted with Balam during his years of captivity in a specially designed cell had experienced surges of atavistic terror. It was a defense mechanism that Balam's people, whom he called the First Folk, had been forced to develop during the centuries when they were persecuted as demons, imps and monsters. Only Balam's former warder, a young man named Banks, was immune. He was away with the salvage crew on the Moon base.

Office chairs were rolled in from the ops center and arranged around the table. The trooper who had accompanied Balam and Erica was the only one who did not take a seat. He took up a parade-rest position near the doorway. Lakesh performed quick introductions between Philboyd and Erica van Sloan. Philboyd had heard mention of the woman many times, and he adopted Kane's disrespectful title for her. "I've been wanting to meet the imperial mama for a long time."

The Chinese trooper stepped forward, moving almost like a puppet. Stiffly, formally, he announced, "You will address my mistress as Tui Chui Jian."

Erica waved the trooper back. "As you were, Seng Kao. Make sure we are not disturbed."

As the man returned to his place beside the door, Brigid raised an amused eyebrow. "Dragon Mother? I can't see that's much of an improvement over imperial mama."

Grant grunted impatiently. "Can we get on with this?"

Lakesh nodded toward Balam. "If you would please begin."

The little Archon sat at the head of the table, his polydactal hands folded before him, long fingers knitted together. Kane reflected dourly that compared to some of the creatures he and his friends had met since they had last seen Balam, the big-headed entity with the wraparound black eyes seemed almost cute.

"What I have to say will seem shocking and perhaps unbelievable," Balam stated in his scratchy voice. "I ask that you to bear with me."

"If nothing else," Kane observed, "your enunciation has improved."

" I have had more opportunities to practice this form of communication," came the flat response. "As inefficient as it sometimes can be, it has a less disconcerting effect on those with little or no psychic abilities. By now, all of you here are aware of the role played by the Annunaki in the creation of not just my people, but your race, as well."

Heads nodded all around the table, some of them reluctantly. After several years of clue sifting, historical detective work and risking lives, the core group of Cerberus exiles finally accepted as fact, not speculation, the involvement of the Annunaki, the mythical Dragon Kings, in the development of human culture on Earth. The full extent of that involvement was still open to conjecture, however.

The Annunaki had arrived on Earth when humankind was still in a protoform of development. They came first in gleaming disks that dropped from the sky, and later through glittering archways of fire, portals between far places that, more than likely, were the templates for the mat-trans units of Project Cerberus.

Tall and cold of eye and heart, the Annunaki were a highly developed reptilian race with a natural gift for organization. They viewed Earth as primarily a business proposition. When their genetically engineered labor force—humanity—revolted, Earth became an unprofitable enterprise. Enlil saw to the destruction of the rebels by arranging a global deluge. The catastrophe was recorded in ancient texts and even cultural memories as the flood.

As the waters slowly receded, the handful of human survivors bred and multiplied. Over the ensuing centuries, nations and empires rose and fell, but the legend of the Dragon Lords, the Serpent Kings, was a thread that bound peoples and places together.

Millennia after that catastrophe, a new group of visitors arrived on Earth. Humanoid but not human, they were an aristocratic race of scientists, poets and warriors. This group was mythologically known as the Tuatha de Danaan and they made fertile, isolated Ireland their home.

They had met the representatives of the Annunaki during their explorations and struck a pact with them— they would watch over humanity until the Dragon Lords returned.

The Danaan took the tribes living in Ireland under their protection and taught them many secrets of art, architecture and mathematics. The essence of Danaan science stemmed from music—the controlled manipulation of sound waves—and this became recorded in legend as the "music of the spheres."

Eventually, the Annunaki returned to reclaim their world and their slaves, but the Danaan refused to cede ownership. Humankind became embroiled in the conflict between the Annunaki and the Tuatha de Danaan, a conflagration that extended even to the outer planets of the solar system, and became immortalized and disguised in human legends as a war in heaven.

Finally, when it appeared that Ireland and even Earth were threatened with annihilation, the war abated under terms. A new pact was struck, whereby the two races intermingled to create a new one, which was to serve as a bridge between them and humanity. From this pact sprang the First Folk, the forebears of Balam's people.

Enlil, the last of the Annunaki on Earth and one of the original architects of man, refused to abide by the pact. After the Danaan departed, he made his base in Ireland as a show of his defiance. Weary of strife, none of his own race came to his aid and he was vanquished by Saint Patrick in the fourth century. That incident became the foundation of the legend of the holy man driving the serpents from Ireland.

Or so Brigid, Grant and Kane learned, even though

they refused to take the tale completely at face value, since it had been embroidered by folklore and myth. However, during a mission the British Isles, the self-proclaimed Lord Strongbow showed them the preserved physical remains of Enlil, which he had found deep within a vault on an island off the Irish coast.

Months later, on a return trip to that part of the world, Kane and Grant had been perplexed by the disappearance of Enlil's preserved remains from Strongbow's former headquarters. It wasn't until Lakesh was in the custody of Sam in China that he finally saw Enlil's body for himself. The Annunaki's genetic code was used as the template in the creation of Sam, or so he was informed. Lakesh remained skeptical.

However, he wasn't skeptical about the Annunakis' influence in human history. As far as Lakesh was concerned, that was an undisputed fact. What wasn't a fact was where the race had relocated to following their pact with the Tuatha de Danaan. That had remained an unsolved mystery, despite the report provided by Brigid Baptiste and Brewster Philboyd about the fate of Enki, the half brother of Enlil.

"What does any of that genetic-engineering shit have to do with the spaceship we're tracking?" Grant asked.

Dispassionately, Balam answered, "The space vessel currently in Earth orbit is also a result of genetic-engineering shit. She is Tiamat, what was known among the Annunaki as a 'Magan.' Are you aware of the meaning of the term?"

Before Kane could shake his head, Brigid replied crisply, "In Sumerian myth, a Magan is a repository where the souls of the dead sleep between incarnations, preparing for rebirth. Since Tiamat was known as the resurrector of souls, I suppose the connection is logical.

"But Tiamat is also the Sumerian chaos mother, the mother of the gods as well as of the Nephilim, the brood of war monsters she creates when threatened. According to legend, her anger is motivated by threats to her young. So this ship was named after Tiamat?"

"The ship *is* Tiamat," Balam declared. "She is sentient, she is a blending of inorganic and organic, composed of an incredibly ancient, incredibly complex genetic code. The countless neuronic subsystems that constitute her programming are self-aware."

Kane repressed a shiver, realizing the impression of intelligence he had received from the image of the ship had not been false.

Brigid stared at Balam intently, her green eyes hard with challenge. "Are you telling us that the ancient goddess Tiamat was a spaceship?"

Balam's head inclined a fraction of an inch in an imitation of a nod. "She is also the ship that brought the original Annunaki ruling council to this planet from Nibiru nearly half a million years ago. She also took their spirits with her when she departed for Kurnugi, an empty region of space on the far side of the Sun. This was more than three thousand and six hundred years ago."

"And what has it—she—been doing there all this time?" Lakesh demanded.

"Following her programming as a Magan," Balam answered calmly. "Nurturing the souls of the dead until they are ready for rebirth."

"The souls of who?" Philboyd asked skeptically.

"The Annunaki pantheon. When the Annunakis'

physical bodies ceased to function, the electromagnetic pattern of their individuality broke free of the organic receptacle."

"Do you mean their minds and their personalities?" Kane wanted to know.

"Exactly. Long, long ago the Annunaki learned to harness electromagnetic energy states and Tiamat tunes into them, matches their frequency and vibrations. She receives the energy patterns and downloads them into a vast data storage bank. She maintains them until they can be uploaded to new organic receptacles."

Balam paused and added almost apologetically, "I realize that is a very crude description of the true process, but it will have to suffice for now."

Smiling without real mirth, Brigid said, "That's all right. Dr. Philboyd and I witnessed firsthand a phenomenon very much like what you just described in Enki's citadel on the Moon."

Grant knuckled his prominent chin thoughtfully, glancing at Balam, then to the silently pensive Erica and back to Balam again. "Assuming we believe even a small part of this, why is Tiamat hanging over Sam's pyramid?"

"Samyaza's pyramid," Erica murmured, a sob catching in her throat.

Lakesh's eyes narrowed. "Pardon?"

"Samyaza," she repeated bitterly. "He told me that was his real name. No, just *one* of his names. He made sure I was aware of that."

"Samyaza?" Lakesh echoed incredulously.

"Does that have any significance?" Philboyd asked irritably.

Lakesh tugged absently at his long nose. "Yes, you

might say it does. According to the Book of Enoch, Samyaza was the name of the leader of the rebellious angels who fell to Earth to corrupt humanity—by teaching forbidden arts like sorcery and forcibly mating with the females."

He paused to take a deep breath before continuing. "The hybrid offspring of these cursed fornications were called the Nephilim…they were considered to be soldiers in the armies of darkness, entities who had to be fettered for the good of the world. Less than divine, they can be defeated by mortals…but because they are more than mortal, their spirits cannot be killed, they can only be banished or imprisoned. If they are released, it means at least terrible danger, at worst Ragnarok, Armageddon or…"

He looked pointedly at Balam and said, *"Doomsday."*

Quietly Balam replied, "That is so, Mohandas Lakesh Singh."

"Did the imperator choose the Sam appellation as a joke?" Lakesh asked. "Or as a hint to his true identity?"

Balam evaded the question by declaring, "The entity you know as the imperator was fashioned from a very specific model, a very ancient genetic code. He was designed to function as a DNA control for the rebirth of the Annunaki Supreme Council of Overlords and the resurrection of their servants, the Nephilim."

Kane scowled at Balam. "Did you come here to tell us that Sam is actually a fallen angel?"

"I am telling you only that he carries the genetic imprint and shares the neural pathways of the entity once known as Samyaza….and as Enlil, Overlord of the Earth and the Air."

"How many overlords were there originally?" Grant asked.

"Nine," Brigid said faintly. "In service to Enlil."

"Nine?" Grant snarled. "Nine overlords, nine hybrid barons! What is this bullshit, Balam?"

Unperturbed by Grant's anger, Balam answered, "At the risk of reawakening your hatred of me, I must tell you now that the Program of Unification, the rule of the nine barons, the rise of the imperator—none of it was a series of unrelated incidents. As much as it was possible to do so, it was directed."

"By whom?" Kane demanded, voice rising in tandem with his temper.

Balam cast him a dark, unblinking stare that was almost pitying. "You should know the answer to that, Kane. By me…and Enlil."

Chapter 7

Quavell lay on the intensive-care bed enclosed by two curtained partitions. An IV bag hung to her left, dripping slowly into a shunt on her arm. Diagnostic scanners hummed purposefully, monitoring her heartbeat and respiration. She twitched and murmured fitfully.

Reba DeFore stood over her, gently probing her exposed belly with gloved hands. Regardless of how carefully she touched her, the woman's flesh adhered to the latex fingertips.

Quavell's body looked as if it were drenched with sweat, and at first DeFore had tried to sponge the moisture away, but strips of her epidermis came up with it. She persevered, simultaneously eyeing the changes of body temperature, erratic heartbeat and surges of blood pressure on the medical monitor. All DeFore could do was cling grimly to her professional objectivity, no matter how painfully helpless she felt.

Although Quavell's respiration was periodically strained, her air passages were unrestricted. The convulsions had diminished to an infrequent trembling in her extremities. DeFore was more concerned about her patient's apparent comatose state, particularly as she entered the first stages of labor. The uterine muscle contractions and the dilation of the cervix seemed normal enough. She had timed the contractions at twenty-minute intervals, which to her great relief was strictly textbook.

Unfortunately, textbook was the only reference material DeFore possessed in regards to childbirth, new and old human alike. As a medic serving the Ragnarville Magistrate Division, by far the majority of her duties consisted of suturing wounds, setting broken bones, administering medication and occasionally performing minor surgery.

She had never even witnessed a live birth before, much less acted in the role of midwife. She had repeatedly watched a vid of the procedure she found in the Cerberus tape and DVD library when it became likely Quavell would carry her baby to term in the redoubt. But the tape hadn't dealt with a woman suffering either from eclampsia or coma during labor.

Reba DeFore didn't want to admit, even to herself, that she was more frightened by the prospect of delivering Quavell's baby than anything she had ever faced, including Ocajinik's perverted swampie horde.

She studied Quavell's face, the way her delicate features contorted periodically with pain or exertion, as if she were in the throes of a nightmare or trying to fight her way back to consciousness. She brushed her fingertips over a lock of silken hair curving across her forehead and it fell away from her scalp, like a loose collection of threads.

DeFore set her teeth on a curse. Quavell's skin eruptions and hair loss did more than baffle her; they put her in a state of bewilderment so extreme she could barely form cogent thoughts. She did know they weren't the recorded symptoms of eclampsia.

After examining Quavell many times over the past five months, she had determined the differences, if any, between old human and new human physiologies and biologies were too subtle to be detected. Quavell's body contained all the same organs in all the same places as a normal human female on the high side of puberty— except Quavell claimed to be nearly sixty-eight years old. Her pregnancy had already manifested a few unusual conditions, but Quavell claimed those were connected to nutrition.

As a hybrid, she required food that was easily digestible for her simplified intestinal tract. Although Lakesh had undertaken a lot of time and trouble to make sure the food lockers and meat freezers of the redoubt were exceptionally well stocked, there was very little in the way of single-cell protein micro organisms the hybrids normally ingested. Oatmeal and ice cream served as improvisations, until a way to manufacture the microorganisms was perfected. DeFore utilized a synthesization process using equipment taken from the Moon base. The process had so far proved successful.

Therefore, Reba DeFore could only conclude that whatever was affecting Quavell, it had nothing to do with her pregnancy and had far more to do with her hybrid metabolism. Like everyone else in the redoubt, DeFore knew that the hybrid race was as intellectually superior to humankind as the Cro-Magnon was to the Autralopithecus, but the hybrids paid a heavy price for their superior abilities.

Compared to the "old" humans, they were fragile, their autoimmune systems at the mercy of infections and diseases that had little effect on the primitive apekin they ruled. Nor could they reproduce by intercourse. The nine barons were the products of *in vitro* fertilization, as were all hybrid offspring. Quavell's pregnancy was the unprecedented exception to the rule.

Because of their susceptibility to illness, the barons were forced to live insulated, isolated existences, cloaking themselves in theatrical trappings that not only added to their semidivine mystique, but also protected them from contamination—both psychological and physical. However, Quavell had implied there were at least three distinct classes or genotypes of hybrid, with the barons occupying the top rung of their DNA helix.

Although she hadn't come right out and stated it, she had given DeFore the distinct impression that only the barons required the annual medical treatments, not the rank-and-file hybrid drones who served them. Despite never having seen a representative of the baronial genotype in the flesh, DeFore understood they were considerably taller than the average drone hybrid.

"Will she die?"

DeFore didn't need to turn around to know who had asked the question. Only Domi could have moved with enough natural stealth across the entire infirmary without making a sound. "I don't know, Domi."

With a sigh, DeFore turned around to face the small albino girl standing between two of the partitions. "I wish I could tell you something encouraging."

A freshly scrubbed Domi had changed into one of the sedate white bodysuits, which only increased the stark contrast between her ruby eyes and piquant face. She gazed at Quavell broodily. "Is it eclampsia?"

"She's displaying the primary symptoms of its

onset," DeFore answered bleakly. "But as for the eczema and hair loss—" She stopped herself, shaking her head in frustration. "It's not eczema…I don't know *what* the hell it is, or have any idea of what's going on, Domi. I'm sorry."

Domi nibbled her underlip and stepped over to Quavell's bedside. "Not your fault." She examined her with narrowed eyes. "This ain't like anything I ever saw, either."

DeFore supposed that Domi, due to her upbringing in an isolated Outland settlement, would have witnessed a virtual encyclopedia of medical conditions and ailments, from rad poisoning to snakebite. "Have you ever helped deliver a baby?"

The albino girl nodded, lightly touching Quavell's hair. "Helped deliver 'em, delivered 'em on my own. Held 'em when they took first breaths, held 'em as they breathed their last. Buried 'em."

She lifted her gaze to DeFore's face. "Done it all 'cept have my own."

"Will you help me with Quavell when the time comes?"

Domi's eyes widened in surprise. "Course I will. Quavell is my friend. So are you."

DeFore felt the sting of grateful tears in her eyes and she blinked them back. "Thank you."

Moving to the medical scanner, she said, "If I could only get a half-assed idea of what's going on with her, I'd feel a lot more confident."

"'Cording to Decard," Domi replied, "Quavell said something terrible was happening."

DeFore nodded miserably. "That's an understatement. I just wish she'd been a little more specific—"

The diagnostic scanner at the head of the bed suddenly emitted a nerve-scratching squeal. The flashing icons and jumping, jagged lines showed Quavell's sudden surge in pulse and heart rate. She began shaking, her petite frame trembling violently.

DeFore leaned over her. "She's seizing! All metabolic functions are accelerating—"

Quavell jackknifed up at the waist. The skin on her face pulsed with a multitude of tiny bubblelike blisters that burst with every breath she dragged into her lungs. She reached up and clawed away what was the left of the hair attached to her scalp. Her mouth opened as if she were readying herself to voice a scream, but no sound came out. Her eyes stared wide, but they were empty and glazed like milky pearls, mirroring no emotions, no thoughts.

The shape of her face was distorted subtly from what DeFore had come to accept as normal for hybrids—jaw suddenly too blunt, a hairless skull, tendons swelling bizarrely at the base of her neck and pronounced supraorbital ridges casting her empty eyes into shadow. There was something reptilian about the cast of her features and the hooded, heavy-lidded eyes. The animal inside DeFore whimpered and cringed. She didn't need to take her pulse rate to know it was racing.

DeFore started to push her back onto the bed, then realized Quavell was fighting her way back to consciousness through sheer force of will, like a drowning woman struggling with the sea. Domi suddenly leaned forward and struck Quavell openhanded on the right side of her face.

The impact sloughed off a layer of flesh as if it had

been exposed to great heat, but suddenly the gleam of intelligence, of awareness returned to Quavell's cloudy eyes. She stared at Domi, her lips working, then she turned to DeFore.

"Kane!" She managed to bark out the word. In a series of strangulated bursts, she gasped, "Must speak to him—tell him—tell him while I can, while I still am who I am—tell him of the child. Bring Kane before it's too late!"

Chapter 8

Although no one around the table eyed him directly, Kane sensed Brigid Baptiste and Grant tensing up on either side of him. He knew they and Lakesh vividly recalled the incident when he had attempted to strangle Balam after the entity had revealed some of the truth about the so-called Archon Directorate.

Now he managed to maintain a relatively calm facade as he gazed intently into Balam's obsidian eyes. Flatly, unemotionally, he intoned, "Enlil is dead. So is the rest of the pantheon, the Annunaki royal family." He inclined his head toward Brigid. "We saw what was left of them in their burial catacombs under the Moon, remember?"

Brigid gave him a wan smile. "Even if I could forget anything, I'm not liable to forget much of that experience."

Due to Brigid's eidetic memory, everything she read or saw or even heard was impressed indelibly on the photosensitive plate of her mind. She supposed simply possessing an encyclopedic memory made her intellect something of a fraud, at least compared to the staggeringly high IQ of Lakesh.

Although Kane often accused her of her using her photographic memory to make herself appear far more knowledgeable than she actually was, she viewed her ability as a valuable resource that had nothing to do with ego.

"Enlil's body is dead," Balam agreed. "But the signature of his mind energy, as well as his genetic imprint lived on, as did those of the Supreme Council of Overlords."

"How?" Grant demanded.

"Long before Enlil entered cryostasis, his entire biological blueprint was encoded and downloaded into a Tablet of Destiny."

Kane slitted his eyes. "A what?"

Brigid said, "According to Sumerian myth, there were allegedly seven Tablets of Destiny. They contained the Annunaki's ultimate plan for the universe."

Balam made a diffident, finger-fluttering gesture that they knew was the equivalent of a shrug. "To be precise there are nine tablets. Nine tablets for nine overlords."

"That doesn't explain anything," Brewster Philboyd argued impatiently. "You're talking in riddles and circles."

Kane snorted disdainfully, nodding toward Balam. "Get used to it with him."

Balam regarded him with a blank expression that nevertheless seemed to convey reproach. He crooked a finger toward Erica van Sloan. "Now is the time to relate what you witnessed within the pyramid of Xian only a short time ago."

Inhaling a deep breath, which caused her bosom to strain momentarily against the scarlet facings of her tunic, Erica said unsteadily, "I'll try, but I still feel like I'm in a state of shock. It was a nerve-shattering experience for me."

It was Brigid Baptiste's turn to snort. "Give us a break, 'Tui Chui Jian.' Your idea of a real nerve-shattering experience is to bump into somebody who doesn't drop to their knees begging to kiss your ass."

As Erica swung a baleful glare in Brigid's direction, Grant and Kane burst into startled laughter. Brigid Baptiste ordinarily employed a very precise and educated manner of expressing herself, rarely lapsing into vernacular or vulgarity. Her comment to Erica showed only a minuscule amount of the deep contempt she felt for the woman.

Like Lakesh and a handful of other predarkers, Erica van Sloan had been revived from cryostasis when the Program of Unification reached a certain stage of progress. A brilliant cyberneticist, she had been chosen to act as an adviser due to her success in developing and perfecting the SQUID implants, the superconducting quantum interface devices.

Although Erica had not actually invented the SQUIDs, she refined them to a new level of sophistication and used them as the foundation of the first fully functioning, large scale mind-machine interface. Since the main difficulty in constructing interfaces between mechanical-electric and organic systems was the wiring, Erica herself oversaw the implantation of SQUIDs directly into the subject's brain. They were only one-hundredth of a micron across and drew power from the electromagnetic field generated by the neuronic energy of the brain itself. Everyone who was aware of her scientific background knew the imperial trooper standing at the door was more than likely influenced by a SQUID.

Also like Lakesh, Erica van Sloan owed her apparent youth and vibrancy to the imperator. Months before, upon their initial meeting Sam had restored Lakesh's physical condition to that of a man in his mid-forties by what, at the time, seemed to be a miraculous laying on of hands. Then, Lakesh's eyes had been covered by thick lenses, a hearing aid inserted in one ear, what he most resembled was a hunched-over spindly old scarecrow, who appeared to be fighting the grave for every hour he remained on the planet.

At the time, Sam claimed he had increased Lakesh's production of two antioxidant enzymes, catalase and superoxide dismutase, and boosted his alkyglycerol level to the point where the aging process was for all intents and purposes reversed.

Sam had indeed accomplished all of that, but only recently did Lakesh learn the precise methodology—when he laid his hands on Lakesh, he had injected nanomachines into his body. The nanites were programmed to recognize and destroy the dangerous replicators, whether they were bacteria, cancer cells or viruses. Sam's nanites performed selective destruction on the genes of DNA cells, removing the part that caused aging. Erica van Sloan was just as dependent on Sam for her restored youth and vitality as Lakesh was.

Repressing a smile, Lakesh said, "Do go on, Erica."

Her violet eyes glinting hard, the woman began speaking, telling of the bizarre metamorphosis she had witnessed among Baroness Beausoliel, Baron Cobalt and Sam. Grant's jaw muscles knotted at the mention of the baroness, but he said nothing.

"Cobalt," Lakesh muttered musingly. "So the imperator offered him sanctuary...or was it a prison?"

Erica shrugged dismissively. "I never found out and I doubt I ever will. I assume what I just told you means the same thing to you as it does to me. The kings are returning to their kingdom."

Her conclusion stunned conversation for a few seconds, but to Kane it felt like a chain of interlocking eternities. As if from a great distance, he heard himself say, "The hybrid barons are changing into Annunaki overlords. The ship called Tiamat has somehow awakened a dormant part of their minds."

"And their genes," Balam replied.

"They're regaining their former personalities, their identities, even their memories." Kane didn't ask questions; he made statements.

"Yes," Balam said simply. "You might view the barons as a larval or chrysalis stage of their development. Did you never wonder why the end result of the hybridization program seemed so fragile, so rife with biological defects, so sensitive to autoimmune diseases?"

"I sure as hell did," Philboyd said. "When I was first told about the whole baronial setup, I thought it seemed pretty strange. Just like I wonder why any of us sitting here except for you and the dragon lady should believe this bullshit."

Lakesh speared him with a cold stare. "*I* happen to believe him, Dr. Philboyd. I understand how mad all this must seem to you…but to the rest of us here, me at any rate, it makes perfect sense. At long last."

"Oh, come *on!*" Philboyd exclaimed in exasperation. "You told me these barons were a minimum of ninety years old. How can any organism exist at an intermediate stage for so damn long?"

Thoughtfully, Brigid answered, "In nature there is the Axolotl salamander. It's an amphibian, but it exhibits the phenomenon known as neoteny. Ordinarily, amphibians undergo metamorphosis from egg to larva, and finally to adult form. The Axolotl, along with a number of other amphibians, remains in its larval form its entire life, meaning that it retains its gills and the fins of a fish, even reaches sexual maturity in the larval stage."

"Brigid," Philboyd said patronizingly, "the Axolotl is a salamander. I'm talking about…" His voice trailed off as he groped for the proper terminology.

"Exactly," Lakesh said a little triumphantly. "You don't know *what* you're talking about."

Defensively, Philboyd shot back, "I thought the general consensus of opinion was that Sam was another version of this Colonel Thrush dude, not some moldy old Sumerian god!"

"Sam's true identity is still a matter of speculation," Brigid replied.

Testimony had indicated that the mind of Sam was actually a receptacle for the mind of the loathsome Colonel C. W. Thrush. However, even if Sam served as the living storage vessel for the Thrush program, apparently he hadn't fully downloaded all the algorithmic data and realized his true identity. Quavell had been the one to theorize that the complete Thrush entity ID was suspended in a kind of a memory buffer, with the identity compressed, and not fully downloaded.

"It's not a matter of speculation anymore," Erica announced in a voice theatrically tinged with hysteria. "Thrush was Sam and Sam was Samyaza who was really Enlil and Enlil was always Thrush and now he's Enlil again."

"Oh, shut up," Kane growled, ignoring the sudden blaze of autocratic rage in the woman's eyes. A fragment of a memory ghosted through his mind, concerning his final encounter with a version of Thrush on the third Lost Earth. Thrush admitted that his creators had used Annunaki neural pathways as a template for his operating system.

"If any of this is true," he said, addressing Balam, "it took a hell of a lot of planning over a hell of a long time."

"A very hell of a long time," Balam agreed.

"Who was the mastermind?"

"Enlil and the Supreme Council of Overlords. They drafted the plan."

"When?"

"I cannot provide you an exact date," Balam said. "But I would be safe in stating it was at least four thousand years ago, after the final battle in the war between the Annunaki, the Tuatha de Danaan and the First Folk."

When the long conflict between the Danaan and the Annunaki drew to a close, the major component of the peace agreement was that both races would adopt a hands-off policy toward humanity.

But in order to monitor their cultural and technological development, the two races mingled their genetic material with a blend of superior human DNA to created a custodial race. The First Folk they were called. It was their duty to keep the ancient secrets of their ancestors alive, yet not propagate the same errors as their forebears, especially in their dealings with Man, to whom they were inextricably bound.

Humankind was still struggling to overcome a global cataclysm, striving again for civilization, and the graceful First Folk did what they could to help them rebuild. They insinuated themselves into schools, into political circles, prompting and assisting men into making the right decisions.

Due to the First Folk's influence, Earth cultures enjoyed a thousand years of relative peace and harmony, during which the Atlantean civilization arose. Lam, a leader of the Folk and Balam's father, sought to convince the Annunaki and Danaan representatives to allow humanity to grow and evolve without strictures. Instead, the two races threatened to visit another cataclysm upon Earth and hurl humankind back into savagery.

The First Folk knew their forebears had too many weapons in their arsenals, stolen and adapted from other worlds they visited and exploited, for them to be able to defend Earth. Nor did they possess the resources to fight an all-out war, but once they had aroused their forebears' suspicions, they had no choice but to take quick, preemptive action.

They employed an energy called protoplanic force, which demolished an Annunaki settlement on the Moon and killed the royal family. There was a blowback effect, a reverse reaction that the First Folk hadn't foreseen. It nearly destroyed the Earth, and decimated human and First Folk civilizations. In their attempts to defend humankind, they had inadvertently brought about the destruction their forebears had threatened.

After the global catastrophe, the First Folk transformed themselves to adapt to the new environment. Their muscle tissue became less dense, motor reflexes sharpened, optic capacities broadened. A new range of psychic abilities was developed, which allowed them to survive on a planet whose magnetic fields had changed, whose weather was drastically unpredictable.

In the process, the physical appearance of Balam's kind changed from tall, slender, graceful creatures to small, furtive shadow dwellers. Although the survivors of the First Folk were viewed by humans as demons and monsters, they still tried to protect the human race over the long track of time as they clawed their way back up from barbarism. At the dawn of Earth's Industrial Revolution, the First Folk's descendants, the entities later known as Grays and Archons, feared more reprisals from their forebears.

They embarked on a series of raids against the Annunaki and Danaan outposts still extant on the solar planets. The Martian base was devastated, but the remnants of the Tuatha de Danaan civilization remained, known as the Monuments of Mars, like the Great Stone Face and the pyramid city.

A ferocious scowl inscribed deep lines on Grant's forehead and on either side of his nose. "I don't understand. If they came up with this scheme four thousand years ago, how the hell could they have kept any part of it going after they died?"

Balam's pale face couldn't register much emotion, nor could his voice, but a note of sadness, even shame crept into his tone. "I helped keep it going, Grant. I helped implement the final stages of the plan, which included aspects of the Totality Concept, the Program of Unification and the rule of the barons. I had no choice. It was a debt my people owed to the Root Race and as the last of my kind, it was my portion, my duty, to see it through to completion…to restore to life that which the actions of my forebears had caused to die."

Chapter 9

"What the hell do you mean by that?" Kane demanded suspiciously. "Your people damn near destroyed the Moon and the Earth trying to get rid of the Annunaki, and then started feeling guilty about it?"

"Not I," Balam responded. "I feel no guilt whatsoever regarding the fate that befell the few Annunaki who remained on this world and Luna. It was a time of war and despite their pious pronouncements to the contrary, the Annunaki were ever at war until the actions of my people ended their ability to wage it…even among themselves."

Brigid, Lakesh, Kane and Grant had learned how two factions of the Annunaki fought each other over the course of humanity's future. Enlil, who commanded lordship over the Earth, wanted humankind to be kept in as primitive a state as possible. The opposing group, led by his half brother Enki, disagreed with this stance.

The ruling council of the Annunaki delayed making a decision and decreed that they needed intermediaries between themselves and the masses of humanity. They chose ancient Mesopotamia to conduct this experiment in social engineering and religion building.

A hierarchy was clearly defined and for many millennia the Annunaki oversaw the welfare and fate of humankind. All the while they remained apart from the people, approachable only by the high priests and kings on specified dates, communicating only with their plenipotentiaries.

At some point, a rivalry arose between opposing factions of the Annunaki for the hearts and minds of people, partly because they had come to depend increasingly on human kings and their armies to achieve their ends. When this situation became too unwieldy, the Annunaki chose to create a new dynasty of rulers, known as demigods or god kings because of their exalted bloodlines.

As a bridge between themselves, a pantheon of gods and humankind, they introduced the concept of the god-king on Earth. They appointed human rulers who would assure humankind's service to the deities and channel their teachings and laws to the people.

Sumerian texts described how although the Annunaki retained lordship over the lands and humankind was viewed as little more than a tenant farmer, humanity grew arrogant. Fearing a unified human race, both in culture and purpose, the Annunaki adopted the imperial policy of divide and rule. For while humankind reached higher cultural levels and the populations expanded, the Annunaki themselves fell into decline.

Anu, the ruler of the Annunaki, returned to Nibiru after arranging a division of powers and territories on Earth between his feuding sons, Enlil and Enki. Civilizations were created by the two half brothers such as Egypt, Sumer and India. Wars were fought by the families of Enki and Enlil, and the nations changed hands back and forth through different conflicts.

After one such war, following the declaration of an uneasy peace, Enlil tried to force his brethren to make a decision about what to do about humanity.

As humankind procreated and their numbers increased, while those of the Annunaki lessened, Enlil grew fearful and prevailed upon the Supreme Council to allow a deluge to wipe humanity off the face of the Earth. But Enki was not happy about the decision to commit genocide and sought ways to frustrate the plan. He managed to do so to a point, but his efforts were immortalized as the story of Noah and the ark.

"Why would you have anything to do with a plan that would insure the return of the Annunaki overlords?" Brigid inquired distrustfully. "Unless you have plans of your own to further…which wouldn't be the first time you've used a smoke screen and diversions to hide your true intentions and get what you wanted."

"What was *needed*," Balam corrected her chidingly. "And you are correct in your assessment that I do indeed have plans of my own…but they do not benefit Enlil or the overlords."

"Explain," Lakesh said, folding his arms over his chest.

"Through the years, over the centuries, Enlil's neural pathways took many names, adopted many vessels even as his original physical form lay in stasis. As you know, as Colonel C. W. Thrush, he acted as an emissary of my people."

"Right," Kane drawled sardonically. "Your 'go-to-guy' Colonel Thrush, a blending of machine, human and Annunaki…the one who cut all your people's dirty deals with the maniacs in human history."

Balam blinked at him. "There were far too many turbulent periods in history when humanity savagely persecuted witches, demons and other creatures your psychotic fears perceived as real. My folk would have been killed outright, not viewed as ambassadors or cousins of humankind.

"Enlil, in the guise of Thrush, could move easily through the oppressive times of warfare and mass murder. He manipulated chaotic events to best fit his agenda. The world that emerged from the nuclear holocaust of two centuries ago fits the Nibiruan model."

"What?" The word burst from Brigid's lips as a ragged cry of incredulity. "It's a world of barbarism, of ignorance, of torture, of the conscienceless institution of murder to meet selfish ends. That doesn't seem like a place an advanced race of pseudogods would want to make their home."

"That's because you forget one thing," Lakesh said darkly. "Earth is their home. The Annunaki lived here long before modern man. They've just been away while it was being remodeled and fumigated."

He raised questioning eyebrows at Balam. "Am I right?"

Balam nodded slightly, reluctantly. "You didn't mention the atmospheric and geological changes, as well as the extreme depopulation that the overlords will no doubt find congenial."

"Assuming you're speaking the truth," Philboyd said, "what will the reborn or reincarnated overlords be doing?"

"Reclaiming the nations and regions of the Earth they ruled millennia ago."

Grant uttered a sound of commingled disgust and disbelief. Shaking his head, he declared, "There are only eight overlords. Baron Ragnar is dead and he had no successor. And even if the overlords were at a full complement of nine, they could barely control their own baronial territories much less the entire damn world."

Balam gazed at him silently, speculatively. Then the index finger of his right hand uncurled and pointed straight up. Grant reflexively glanced toward the ceiling before the meaning of the gesture occurred to him. "Tiamat," he said.

"Tiamat," Balam confirmed. "A warship that could easily lay waste to the entire surface of Earth in less than a month. And do not confuse the barons as you knew them with the overlords. The differences are quite dramatic, I assure you."

Erica brushed nervous fingers through her hair. "Would they do such a thing?"

"If they perceived sufficient resistance to their rule to justify it. Enlil certainly had no qualms about devastating large portions of the Earth and its inhabitants thousands of years ago. He would have less restraint now without Enki to act as a mitigating influence on his behavior."

A cold half smile creased Erica's lips. "Far from resistance to their rule, I know from experience in this and the predark world, that a population faced with destruction will seek any form of salvation that is offered to them."

"Enlil knows how to offer that," Lakesh observed dryly. "Judging by his historical track record as a god, a demon and as Thrush."

Quietly, Brigid quoted, "'Wouldst thou protect us from the savageries of Satan?'"

Philboyd forced a sickly grin to his face. "Yeah, but who'll be protecting us from the protector?"

Kane drummed his fingers absently on the tabletop. Faintly he heard the murmur of voices from the corridor as the personnel came in from the plateau. Apparently, Shizuka had ended the training session. He announced, "There's obviously something we can do about this, otherwise Balam would've left us swinging in the wind until Tiamat floated down to blow us off the mountain."

He angled a challenging eyebrow at Balam. "Am I right, B?"

Balam's slit of mouth twitched in almost imperceptible imitation of a smile. "You are correct, Kane. Although the barons are even now evolving into the overlords, regaining their full faculties will require some little time. And afterward, Enlil will no doubt convene a council...the first time they have met in thousands of years. Their first order of business will be to recover the original Tablets of Destiny."

"Where will they meet?" Grant asked, leaning forward eagerly. "Front Royal? If so, we can take the Mantas and do a little laying waste ourselves—"

He broke off when he saw the suggestion of a smile on Balam's face turn into a frown. "What?" he demanded.

"The overlords will abandon the villes," Balam declared matter-of-factly. "And all their former baronial trappings, casting them off as a butterfly sheds its cocoon, as a—"

"Snake sheds its skin," Kane interjected snidely. "Or as a bear wipes its ass. Lay off the similes. Do you really expect us to believe the barons will give up all their power and surrender their villes just because they've contracted what amounts to a skin condition?"

Balam stared at him solemnly. "I thought I made myself clear, Kane. I know you are not that obtuse. They are barons no longer. They have evolved into their true forms, creatures infinitely more cunning and dangerous than the delicate egomaniacs who ruled from the safe remove of their towers in the villes.

"They will not surrender their villes, their territories. They have no need to. They will simply turn their backs on them and move on to the next phase of their lives...to promote and prosecute their agenda to remake Earth into a new Nibiru."

"That's insane!" Grant barked out the words. "With the barons gone, the villes will fall apart!"

"Anarchy," Brigid put in. "The antithesis of the Program of Unification. God only knows what will happen once word gets out that the barons have abandoned the villes. Riots, revolts, massacres!"

Brigid, Grant and Kane all exchanged stricken looks. The three of them were ville-bred and despite their efforts to overthrow the hybrid despots, the notion of the network of fortress-cities functioning without the intimidating presence of the barons unnerved them. Because of their lifetimes of conditioning, the concept was almost inconceivable.

They struggled to come to terms with the full implications of everything Balam had imparted. Trying to comprehend the mind-numbing maneuvers and countermaneuvers undertaken by Enlil as he moved his chess pieces over a vast board of power plays that stretched across the world and millennia was a migraine-inducing exercise.

Lakesh forced an uneasy chuckle. "Well, we wanted

to topple the barons anyway. I didn't picture it happening like this."

"Neither did the barons," Balam said. "Until Tiamat arrived."

"But *you* pictured it," Kane declared, the edge of accusation sharpening his tone. "You were the only one who could have. Almost a hundred years ago you showed up with Thrush—Enlil—during the first council of the barons, to convince them to cooperate with the Program of Unification. What happened to that version of Thrush?"

"I do not know, Kane." Although Balam's expression reflected nothing, Kane received the impression he was made uncomfortable by the question, either because he didn't have the answer it—or because he did. "Despite what you may think, I am not omnipotent."

"I never thought you were," Kane shot back. "Just a sneaky, tricky big-headed little bastard who only tells the truth when my hands are around your throat. Even so, you created a new body for Thrush. You downloaded an identity program into it and called him Sam this time. You installed him in power as the imperator."

Balam's voice was a hollow, hoarse whisper. "How little you understand."

Grant said between clenched teeth, "We understand enough. You could've stopped all this at any time, but you let the scenario play out. Now when it's too late, you come to us. Why? To tell us 'Oops' or to ask our forgiveness?"

Balam gazed unblinkingly and unperturbed at the faces around the table. His reply was soft, almost contemptuous. "Hardly either one, Grant. Did you not understand when I explained that Tiamat was waiting to return at this preordained time? She would have done so regardless of any action I took to interfere with Enlil's plan."

"Yes," Brigid interjected. "But if Sam was the key to the rebirth of the overlords all along, then you could have done something to keep him from growing into the role."

"Perhaps I could have prevented Sam from emerging from the cloning vats," Balam said. "Or altered the programming of the nanomachines on which his metabolism depended."

"Or you could've just pushed the arrogant son of a bitch off the top of his pyramid," Kane suggested.

"And if I had, what would I have accomplished?"

"For one thing," Grant bit out, "there wouldn't have been a DNA control for Tiamat to interface with."

Balam nodded as if Grant were a slow student and had finally reasoned out a relatively simple math problem. "Exactly."

Philboyd's eyes widened behind the lenses of his glasses. "But Tiamat would've come back anyway, right? And if she couldn't make contact with Enlil's EEG signature or genetic imprint, or if they didn't match up with the records in her database—"

"In that eventuality," Balam broke in. "Her programming is clear and unalterable and inviolate. To destroy this planet. To render it utterly lifeless. That is what would have happened if I had embarked on any of the courses of action you suggested."

Dubiously, Lakesh inquired, "She is capable of all that?"

"And much more. She can dispatch remote probes, essentially smaller versions of herself, to blanket the planet with fusion bombs, biological and chemical weapons and defoliants of all kinds. The seas would be poisoned, the atmosphere contaminated, starvation and exposure to radiation would kill anyone who was unlucky enough to survive the initial onslaughts. Humanity as the dominant species on this world will cease to exist."

Balam uttered a sound shockingly similar to a human sigh of regret. "I had hoped that over the last three thousand plus years, Tiamat's systems might have suffered malfunctions or she was damaged by meteor collisions. Unfortunately, the Annunaki built her too well...as they built all of their machines and weapons, many of which still exist in vaults here on Earth, just waiting for the overlords to remember them and reclaim them."

Kane dry-scrubbed his hair in frustration. "That's just great. Thanks bunches, Balam...you saved the world by *refusing* to do anything to stop the reincarnated Annunaki from taking over. We'll have medal-pinning ceremony as soon as I can find one with a picture of a snake screwing a human on it."

Philboyd said helpfully, "There's lots of military memorabilia down in the one of the storage bays...uniforms, flags—"

"Shut up, Brewster," Grant snapped. "All right, so rather than dealing only with a giant Annunaki spaceship, we'll be dealing the Annunaki Supreme Council instead—minus one."

"Actually," Balam corrected smoothly, "the lack of one member is only temporary. The full complement of nine, under the command of Enlil, will soon be restored."

"How soon?" Erica asked in surprise.

"As soon as Quavell gives birth," Balam answered, glancing toward her quizzically. "Did you not wonder why Sam set you the task of capturing her?"

Kane felt a jolt of fear at Balam's calm pronouncement, but he managed to refrain from profanely demanding a clarification.

"Of course I did," she retorted angrily. "But he charged me with many tasks, from assuming command of Cobaltville to recruiting him—" she nodded toward Lakesh "—to our cause. The apprehension of Quavell was just one more assignment."

Brigid's lips creased in a smirk. "Just one more you failed to accomplish, you mean."

Even as Erica van Sloan's spine stiffened in barely repressed rage, Brigid turned her penetrating emerald gaze on Balam. "Explain."

Balam shook his hairless head dolefully. "That is not within my purview. But an explanation will be forthcoming very soon."

Within a half second of his raspily enunciated "soon," DeFore's agitated voice blared over the intercom. "Kane! I don't care where you are or what you're doing, but Quavell needs you in the infirmary—not ASAP, not stat, but *right now!*"

Chapter 10

Behind her occluded, pearl-colored eyes, Kane could see very little of the Quavell he had known in Cerberus and even less of the woman who had acted as the leader of an underground resistance movement in Area 51.

Clenching his teeth tight on a cry of horror and revulsion, Kane forced himself to gaze at Quavell without recoiling. There was almost nothing recognizable about the blunt-jawed face above the tendon-wrapped neck. The nose barely qualified as a flare-nostriled nub, and the lipless slit of a mouth gaped slightly open.

A gown covered her gaunt figure, but her arms were bare. The patches of flesh that remained on them hung in tatters, like ragged old cloth. The texture of the epidermis beneath suggested a pattern of moist, gray-green pebbled scales.

Her eyes beneath a jutting overhang of brow stared unwinkingly, luminously at Kane without a hint of emotion, human or otherwise.

Domi and DeFore stood shoulder to shoulder, the dissimilarity between the two women made even more distinct by the twin expressions of shock and grief stamped on their faces, one chalk white and the other milk-chocolate-brown.

"Kane—" The word burst from Quavell's lips as a

guttural intonation that carried the undercurrent of a cobra's hiss. She thrust out her hairless head on an inhumanly long neck in a disquietingly serpentine fashion.

Repressing a shudder, Kane forced himself not to step back through the partition when she reached for him with long, knob-knuckled and claw-tipped fingers. He took her hand in his, dismayed by how cold it felt to the touch. "I'm here, Quavell."

Her peeling lips worked and writhed as she struggled to speak. "Losing my ability to think clearly—another will is imposing itself over my own. Too powerful to resist much longer, but I must tell you—"

Her strained words blurred into a groan of pain, her fingers tightening on Kane's hand with a surprisingly painful grip.

"What's happening to her?" Domi demanded, voice high and wild.

"She's changing," Kane said, trying to sound of matter-of-fact, "into an overlord, an Annunaki."

"You are mistaken, Kane."

He glanced over his shoulder as Balam pushed aside the partition. DeFore blurted in wordless fear while Domi's hand made a reflexive grab for the gun not holstered at her hip. If Quavell experienced a similar reaction, her face didn't register it.

"You both remember my old buddy Balam," Kane said casually. "He and Erica van Sloan gated in here about half an hour ago. I asked him to come here with me because he knows what's going on with Quavell."

Voice trembling in frustration, DeFore said loudly, "How about sharing it with me, goddammit! Maybe then I can treat her."

"I fear that will not be possible," Balam said sadly.

He spoke quickly, employing straightforward, un-adorned language. When he was done, both DeFore and Domi gaped at him in astonishment. Only the harsh rasp of Quavell's respiration broke the silence.

Finally, DeFore fastened her dark gaze on Kane's face. "Do you believe him?"

"I have no reason not to. Quavell is suffering from the same ailment as the barons—and all of the hybrids, I guess."

"Once again you are mistaken," Balam said mildly. "Only a select genotype is changing. The Quad-Vees."

Kane narrowed his eyes. "They're *not* turning into Annunaki?"

"They are not. The Quad-Vees were bred as a high-ranking servant class, what you might refer to as 'ma-jordomos.'"

"Lakesh might refer to them that way," DeFore de-clared, still recovering from the shock of seeing Balam again. "I don't think anyone else here would."

Balam ignored her opinion. "The Quad-Vees pos-sess a higher percentage of human DNA than the bar-ons. That is why they didn't require the strict annual regimen of medical treatments to stabilize their body chemistry."

"Then why is she changing?" Kane demanded impa-tiently.

"She is not changing into an overlord but into one of the Nephilim. They are the servants of the overlords, the foot soldiers, the warriors in the legendary armies of darkness who play such a role in human parables."

Quavell's fingers tightened on Kane's hand. "He

speaks the truth…unfamiliar imagery is filling my mind…new thoughts, even new languages…"

Kane felt a great fear welling up within him, but he tamped it down. "What about the baby?"

"The Nephilim were also used as breeding stock by the overlords," Balam went on calmly. "The child she carries will be absorbed into the pantheon and will assume the identity of one of them…providing the neural pathways can be successfully downloaded from a Tablet of Destiny."

Belly surging with nausea, Kane bit out, "Not my child."

"Kane—"

He returned his attention to Quavell. Despite the whitish lenses that had grown over her eyes, he sensed she stared at him imploringly. In an aspirated voice, she said brokenly, "Not your child, Kane."

"That's what I said."

"No…the baby is not yours."

It took Kane a moment to grasp what she said and when he did, he half snarled, *"What?"*

She shook her head, reaching out to grasp his wrist with her other hand. "We did not conceive the baby together, Kane. You are not the father."

"But," he stammered, "we— What about all the times we—?"

"Difficult to explain, hard to put thoughts into words—"

Balam stepped close to Quavell, extending a hand toward her, fingers stretched out straight. "Allow me."

Quavell leaned forward, bowing her head in a posture almost of reverence. Balam placed the tips of his fingers on her forehead, just above the bridge of her nose. Kane knew Balam was anchored to the hybrids through some filaments of their mind energy, akin to the hive mind of certain insect species. A couple of years before, when Baron Ragnar was assassinated, Balam had experienced an extreme reaction to the sudden absence of the baron's mind filament. Inasmuch as all of the Archon genetic material in the hybrids had derived from Balam, that connection wasn't particularly surprising.

They had learned that the DNA of Balam's folk was infinitely adaptable, malleable, its segments able to achieve a near seamless sequencing pattern with whatever biological material was spliced to it. In some ways, it acted like a virus, overwriting other genetic codes, picking and choosing the best human qualities to enhance. Their DNA could be tinkered with to create endless variations, as well as adjusted and fine-tuned.

Within seconds, Balam removed his hand from Quavell's forehead and regarded Kane dispassionately. "Quavell was the only female of the Quad-Vee genotype who survived the destruction of the Archuleta Mesa installation. Therefore she was the only one of that genotype who participated in Baron Cobalt's experiment. Unlike the other females, she volunteered for the seeding sessions."

Kane frowned at his use of the euphemism until up to that point he had only heard the hybrids employ. "What do you mean she volunteered?"

Quavell coughed. "Wanted...wanted—"

Domi spoke up. "You wanted a baby but not Kane's baby?"

She nodded and Balam continued. "She wanted to

conceive a child with a man with whom she had fallen in love. A man named Maddock."

Kane's memory flew back to his period of imprisonment in the vast Dreamland facility, putting a face to the name of the young man. Quavell had arranged for his escape from his holding cell and introduced him to the fifth column of humans and hybrids working secretly against Baron Cobalt. He remembered Quavell explaining how the survivors of the Archuleta Mesa disaster reached the conclusion that only mutual genocide lay in the future if changes, both philosophical and practical, were not implemented.

When Kane asked what kind of changes she referred to, Maddock had taken one of Quavell's fragile hands in his own and declared, "A new, redefined program of unification. One where we share what's left of the planet's resources with each other, instead of dividing it up between the conquered and the conquerors."

"I—" Kane broke off, shaking his head, his eyes flicking from Quavell to Balam. "If I'm not the baby's father, then why did you leave Maddock and Area 51 to come here?"

"Keep safe," she husked, putting one hand protectively over her belly.

"To keep the baby safe?" DeFore asked, perplexed. "I thought the whole point of Baron Cobalt's plan was for you to give birth to a baby fathered by a human male, if for nothing else but to prove the hybrid females themselves could provide a new supply of genetic material for the barons' annual treatments."

"Baby supposed to be fathered by Kane," Quavell replied. "Not Maddock. That was baron's plan."

DeFore frowned. "If you had intercourse with both Kane and Maddock, how can you be so sure who the father is?"

Balam said quietly, "As a Quad-Vee, Quavell can exert a certain amount of control over her metabolism. Kane, she did not wish to be impregnated by you. Therefore she was not. Conversely, she very much wanted to conceive a child by Maddock, but she could not allow herself to be made pregnant by him before the seeding sessions with you were complete."

Realization rushed through Kane like a flow of cold water circulating through his veins. Gazing intently at Quavell's distorted face, he stated flatly, "You participated in the baron's program as a form of protective coloration, since a relationship with Maddock would have never been sanctioned. After I escaped, you conceived with Maddock…counting on everyone to assume that I was the father."

She ducked her head in a jerky nod but did not speak.

"However," Balam interposed, "after Baron Cobalt was displaced from his authority over Area 51 and a consortium of barons assumed control, Quavell feared for the safety of the fetus. The other barons didn't share Cobalt's interest in the breeding program. She began to fear that medical testing would prove the fetus was not yours, Kane, but Maddock's since both of your DNA records were on file. Therefore to protect both the baby and Maddock, she fled."

A confusing riot of emotions cascaded through Kane. Simultaneously he experienced relief, sadness, shame and even a bit of anger. However, he kept his face and voice calm when he said, "Quavell, it might be difficult to do, but we could try to spirit Maddock out of Dreamland and bring him here. If Balam is to believed, there won't be any barons watching the place."

"No." The single word left Quavell's lips as a hoarse whisper of anguish. "Maddock is dead."

Kane's eyebrows knitted at the bridge of his nose. "When? How do you know?"

"Baroness Beausoliel told me she killed him. Months ago now."

Anger sent a sudden flush of heat to the back of Kane's neck and caused the blood to pound in his temples. Grant was still recovering from the injuries he received after being captured and tortured by the sadistic Baroness Beausoliel only a short time before.

Quavell said in a halting, painful gasp, "She boasted about killing him…she told me that true first love was like an addictive drug. And like drug addiction a true first love always has tragic consequences."

"You should've told us about this," Domi said plaintively.

Kane squeezed Quavell's hand. "I'll make her pay, Quavell. If I've done nothing else for you, I'll by God do that."

Quavell closed her eyes and tears inched from the corners. "I do not want revenge. I want only your forgiveness."

"My forgiveness?" Kane echoed in surprise. "For what?"

"For duping you…manipulating you and everyone here into protecting me…offering me sanctuary when I knew all along the baby was not yours. You undertook many risks for me, under false assumptions. I am sorry."

DeFore laid a comforting hand on Quavell's shoulder. "Even if we had known, we wouldn't have acted any differently."

Domi moved closer to the bedside. In a remarkably gentle voice, she said, "You helped me, hid me in Area 51. You're my friend." She paused, a wry grin creasing her lips. " 'Sides, it's been fun having you here. We'll have even more fun when the baby is born."

A caricature of smile stretched the corners of Quavell's lips. "Thank you."

The smile suddenly became a grimace, and a keening, sibilant cry issued from her throat. The flesh pulsed and throbbed in a way Kane knew was neither human nor hybrid. Releasing Kane's hand, she clutched the small figurine attached to the chain around her neck.

DeFore said brusquely, "The next few hours are critical. Under the circumstances, I'm going to act as though her labor is high-risk."

She cast a challenging stare toward Balam. "Will it be?"

He seemed taken aback by the question. "I honestly do not know. Certainly Quavell's metabolic functions and processes are changing as her dormant gene combinations become active."

"How will the baby be affected?" Domi demanded.

Balam shook his head. "These are unprecedented events and I cannot answer your questions. I have no prior data that might help me to formulate even a hypothesis."

"Yeah," Kane said with icy sarcasm. "What do you think he is—omnipotent or something?"

"He sure as hell acted like it when he was a prisoner here," DeFore retorted. She made shooing motions with her hands. "Off with you. Just stand by in case you're needed."

Kane's eyebrows climbed toward his hairline. "What do you expect me to do?"

"I don't know," DeFore answered. "That's why I want you to stand by."

Balam and Kane walked out between the partitions into the infirmary proper. Several people, most them Manitius émigrés, were clustered around the doorway. When they caught sight of Balam they hastily withdrew into the corridor.

"My presence has attracted an undue amount of curiosity," Balam commented.

Kane strode toward the door. "Yeah, well, they don't get out much."

"Kane."

Kane stopped. "What?"

"You cannot stand by as Dr. DeFore requested. There are far weightier matters for us to attend to."

"Such as?"

"I know where Enlil will most likely meet with the overlords," Balam said. "It is very possible that this will be the only time all of them will be together in one confined area. Their first order of business will be to retrieve the Tablets of Destiny. Without them, they can exert no control over Tiamat."

"So they'll be working together?" Kane asked. "They'll put aside their disagreements?"

Less than a year before, the nine baronies had been poised on the brink of civil war, sparked by one of their own, Baron Cobalt. Although full-scale hostilities involving all the barons had been averted, the doctrine of unity by which the nine villes were formed had been decisively shattered.

"Territorial disputes among the barons mean less than nothing to the overlords," Balam replied. "We must make plans, mount a mission to strike peremptorily and decisively."

Kane eyed Balam scornfully. "What's with this 'we' business? I thought working as a behind-the-scenes puppet master, the invisible string puller was your stock-in-trade. "

Balam conveyed the attitude of someone who had been insulted but was too dignified to show he was offended by Kane's oblique reference to his people's operating methods. Historically, they made alliances with certain individuals or governments, who in turn reaped the benefits of power and wealth. Following this pattern, the Archons made their advanced technology available to the American military in order to fully develop the Totality Concept. It was the use of that technology, without a full understanding of it that contributed to the events that led to the nuclear holocaust of 2001.

"True, I do not enjoy endangering myself," Balam retorted. "I have awaited and dreaded this day in a life that has not been brief. But just as I am not omnipotent, I am not immortal. However, if I do not accompany you and your friends, the mission will fail."

"Accompany me and my friends where?"

"The region of Earth once known as Mesopotamia. On your modern maps, it is called Iraq."

Chapter 11

In the hours after sunset, the endless vista of the indigo sky spread out above the holy city of Nippur like the unfurling of a sail. The sky was so heavy with haze only a few stars glittered. A dim light fell from the cloud-covered face of the Moon, its pallid glow silvering the dark surface of the Euphrates. No whisper of wind came off the river or gusted over the reed marshes along it.

Nippur was built on a spur of land that jutted out to bisect the flowing headwaters. The rocky peninsula rose in a flat rampart toward its center, and from it loomed a broad-based, brooding mass of terraced stone and heat-glazed clay. Ekur, the holy ziggurat of Enlil, towered above the ruins of ancient buildings and fields of windswept sand like the god it had been constructed to honor. A few stumps of the old towers still stood, surrounded by broken walls and heaps of wind-driven sand.

Resurah stood at the opening of a long flagstone ceremonial promenade. Lined on either side by square, squat columns, inestimable centuries of weather had pitted and scarred the bas-reliefs so they were barely visible. The double facing row of pillars led to the foot of the vast ziggurat. As his gaze followed their lines, the high priest felt keen despair as he did more often each day. Despite all the decades of toil, all the personal loss he and his fellow priests had suffered in their lifelong effort to rebuild the city, Nippur was still a distorted shadow, a rough sketch of what it had once been.

Here, many thousands of years earlier, Enlil had breathed life into the clay taken from the banks of the Euphrates and brought forth the first man. There, kneeling on the sprit of land dividing the watercourse of the river, Abraham had prayed for guidance.

Resurah knew the ancient history of the city far better than he knew the backgrounds and life experiences of the two priests who shuffled along behind him. Nippur had been built as a sacred city, not as a political capital. Still, it played an all-important role in the politics of the region, which had encompassed Sumeria, Assyria, Babylonia and numerous city-states. To the south lay Ur, to the north lay Akkad and the city was open to the people from both areas, functioning as an arbiter in disputes between these potential enemies. Upon ascending the throne in cities such as Kish, Ur and Isin, rulers sought recognition at Ekur, within the shrine of Enlil, the dais of abundance, the tabernacle of the Star Fire.

In return for legitimization of their claims to the throne, the kings lavished gifts of land, precious metals and stones and other commodities on the temples and on the city as a whole. At the end of successful wars, rulers presented plunder, including captives, to Enlil and the other gods who might be present at Nippur. Even over two thousand years ago, when the Babylonians made Marduk the most important god in southern Mesopotamia, Enlil was still revered. Kings continued to seek support at Nippur, and the city remained the recipient of generous donations.

There had been no donations to maintain the city, generous or otherwise, in many centuries. Resurah and his two fellow priests had devoted their lives to rebuilding Nippur and Ekur, as had many generations of male ancestors before them. And now they were bent by age, their health uncertain, their vision weak. Long ago they were widowed and one by one abandoned by their children, who didn't share their zeal. The only reward for lifetimes of virtue had been soul-killing toil.

Restoring the ziggurat alone had required nearly eighty years of unremitting, back-breaking labor, spread out over three generations of four different families. The facade was made from glazed brick. A flight of new steps had been added to the square base, stretching up to join the spiral ramp. All the vertical walls sloped inward, and all horizontal lines were slightly convex, in order to make it easier to plant trees and shrubs on the lower terraces. The priest caste was taught that the ziggurat had been built as a bridge between heaven and Earth, so the levels nearest the ground would symbolize the elements of the world.

At the height of Nippur's power and influence, priests, priestesses, musicians, singers, castrates and hierodules staffed the ziggurat of Ekur. Public rituals, food sacrifices and libations took place there on a daily basis. There were monthly feasts and annual New Year celebrations. But more than those secular functions, Ekur served as a cosmic axis, a vertical bond between heaven and Earth and the underworld, forming a horizontal bond between the lands. Built on seven levels, with each level smaller than the preceding, the architecture represented seven heavens and planes of existence.

The priesthood of Enlil knew the spiral represented the movement of consciousness from level to level, but Resurah experienced only futility when he gazed at it.

All of the buildings and lesser temples scattered about the base of the ziggurat were built of solid stone, constructed in accordance with the ancient designs of sacred geometry. They fit the traditional style of architecture copied exactly from the older buildings that had stood on the site thousands of years before. But all of them were empty, housing only shadows and the lost dreams of forgotten gods.

Enlil was the lord of the airspace, the dispenser of kingship, chief of the assembly of the gods and granter of agriculture—but his worshipers were few. As far as Resurah knew, he and his two brother priests were all that remained of the religion founded in his name and they were definitely the only inhabitants of the city dedicated to him.

Resurah knew when the gods met for assembly on Earth, they met at Enlil's shrine within the ziggurat, where they bathed in the glory of the Star Fire. From there, Enlil made sure that the decrees issued by the supreme council of the gods were carried out. Enlil also selected the kings who were to rule over humankind not as sovereigns, but as servants to the gods, in accordance with the laws inscribed on the Tablets of Destiny.

For many years Resurah's family had excavated the ancient temples, resurrecting them from the sand, searching for the sacred Tablets of Destiny, which the holy codices claimed had been hidden in Nippur. He had long suspected they were safe somewhere inside Ekur, probably in the shrine. He looked up along the curving ramp of the ziggurat to where it ended in a blunt, weathered break three-quarters of the way up.

Resurah nodded to Amner and Gudea, indicating it was time for the evening devotions and the ritual walk to the eye of Enlil. Like him, they were old and gaunt, grizzled beards matting faces the color and texture of cured rawhide. Although all three men were of different ages, Gudea being the youngest at seventy-two winters, all of them looked as if they had been cooked by the sun and worn down by physical labor, until only bone, muscle and stringy sinew were left.

They wore loose, threadbare robes of gray, girded at the waist by braided belts. From pouches at their hips, they removed their holy faces—dull yellow leather masks that covered the top and sides of their heads. On the foreheads was a winged-serpent symbol worked in dark thread. Even after all these years, Resurah wasn't certain of the purpose of the masks, except to hide their shameful human visages from the haughty eyes of Enlil.

The three men began a shuffling walk on sandaled feet down the center of the colonnade, Resurah in the lead, Amner and Gudea following in single file, hands on one another's shoulders. Gudea lit the ceremonial braziers as they passed, symbolizing the Star Fire. The fragrant smoke of frankincense curled into the dry air. The pillars grouped around an open circle at the foot of the ziggurat's staircase.

Before the first step an elaborate mosaic of colored tiles lay, twisting in a sacred spiral. They began chanting, a repetitive murmur in the ancient tongue of their fathers. Only the priest caste knew these words, for they were so old they could not be translated into any of the tongues that later came to dominance in the region. Before votaries could mount the stair, they were instructed to walk the spiral, working their way toward its center, following the path to its dragon core.

Because their forefathers, the ancient Sumerians, knew humankind was created from the flesh of the elder gods and from the spirit of the undying dead-but-ever-dreaming Tiamat, the four priests knew they shared the blood of the Nibiru. The three priests kept a fragment of prayer ever at the tips of their tongues: "The borders of Nibiru form a great net, within which the eagle spreads wide its talons. The evil or wicked man does not escape its spiraling grasp."

The spiral symbolized the labyrinth, the maze of life and death, the departure from the womb and the return to it, coiling into the center and returning upon itself, terminating in a poollike mirror at its center. The mirror represented the eye of Enlil, the eye of wisdom, ever judgmental, ever watchful of the proper time to return and reclaim his world.

Resurah's father and grandfather believed, as their fathers before them, in Enlil's imminent return. The old sinful world overrun by infidels had been scorched away two centuries earlier, clearing and cleansing the planet and making it a fit place for him to rule again. But in Resurah's lifetime there had been no foreshadowing of his return, and he knew that as old age crept upon him, he should not expect communications, much less miracles from his god.

Over the rhythmic cadence of the chanting, Resurah heard a new sound—a faint, high-pitched whine so distant that he couldn't really be certain he heard it, or that it wasn't a mosquito buzzing too close to his ear.

As he led his brethren toward the spiral, he felt a tingling, pins-and-needle prickling all over his body. Lurching to a halt, Amner bumped into him as Gudea trod on his heels. The chanting died away. None of them spoke; they only stared at the hazy, blurred shimmer arising from the center of the mosaic, from the eye of Enlil. The shimmer became a fluttering flare of light, like a flame flower blooming up and out from the mosaic.

The air throbbed like the beating of a gigantic, invisible heart. The three priests gazed at the mosaic, frozen in place. Grains of sand lifted from the desert floor, whirling and spinning like a dust devil around the glowing, phosphorescent lotus blossom sprouting from the eye of Enlil. It stretched upward twice the height of a man.

Resurah shook violently, his entire body trembling, feeling a chill down his back that seemed to penetrate through to his chest and lungs. Dimly, he heard Amner cry out in terror. The petals of witch-fire opened amid cracklings and flares of miniature lightning. A yellow nova of brilliance erupted from inside it. The three priests felt the shock wave slapping at them, stinging their eyes with sand.

Gudea was the first to drop to his knees, crying out as he prostrated himself. After a moment, Amner dropped flat beside him. Resurah slowly lowered himself to his knees, joints popping, but he didn't fall facedown. He kept his eyes on the flower of wavering luminescence.

Within it four dark figures stood back to back. At

their heels, resting atop the eye of Enlil, gleamed a shape very much like a pyramid crafted of smooth, gleaming metal. It appeared to be only one foot in overall width. The waxy, glowing petals of light fanned out from the triangular walls of the pyramidion, then they disappeared back into it, as if they were liquid and had been sucked into its base. The air shivered with a hand-clapping concussion.

When the echoes faded, Resurah became aware of himself still kneeling, sweat drenching his face beneath his mask. In a far corner of his mind, it seemed strange that he didn't fall into a faint after what he had just witnessed. There could only be one explanation for the materialization from the eye of Enlil.

Resurah opened his mouth and spoke the words that he had learned so many years before during his apprenticeship in the priesthood. The rituals of Those-Who-From-Heaven-To-Earth-Came were always conducted in the ancient spoken language, old even before Enoch lit the first sacrificial fire.

In a singsong falsetto, he spoke the invocation: "To Kurnugi, land of no return, Tiamat was determined to go; to the dark house, dwelling of Anu's god, on the road where traveling is one-way only, to the house where those who enter are deprived of light, where dust is their food, clay their bread.

"Tiamat, when she arrived at the gate of Kurnugi, addressed her words to the keeper of the gate, 'Open your gate for me, or I shall raise up the dead and they shall eat the living! Open your gate or the dead shall outnumber the living.'"

Bowing his head, eyes blinded by tears, Resurah

whispered hoarsely, "I am the high priest leader of Nippur. I await your orders and guidance. I bid you welcome...eyes of Enlil."

Chapter 12

"What the hell did he say?" Kane demanded, reaching up behind his head to make sure the Commtact transceiver was still tight against the mastoid bone behind his right ear. "All I got was gibberish."

"Me, too," Grant rumbled, tapping the PDA unit in his coat pocket. "Maybe the translation program isn't working."

"More likely," Brigid said, "he's speaking a language that doesn't have a match in our linguistic database."

Just to make sure, she brushed back her fall of hair and touched her own Commtact. Steel pintels implanted in the bones slid through the flesh into tiny input ports on the small curves of metal. The Commtacts had been found in Redoubt Yankee and were described by Philboyd as state-of-the-art multiple-channel communication devices.

Their sensor circuitry incorporated an analog-to-digital voice encoder that was subcutaneously embedded in the mastoid bone. The pintels connected to input ports in the comms themselves. Once they made contact, transmissions were picked up by the auditory canals, and the dermal sensors transmitted the electronic signals directly through the cranial casing. Even if someone went deaf, as long as they wore a Commtact, they would still have a form of hearing.

The Commtacts were still being field-tested, since in order to make them operational, surgery was required and few people wanted to make that sacrifice. But the surgery was very minor, involving only a small incision behind the ear to slide the sensors under the skin.

In conjunction with a sophisticated translation program within the PDAs all of them carried, the Commtacts analyzed the pattern of a language and then provided a real-time audio and verbal translation. Some foreign phrases and words wouldn't be exact translations, but the program recognized enough words to supply an English equivalent. Conversely, the program would supply them with the appropriate responses in the language it heard.

But the old masked man's high, reedy voice had filtered into all their heads as a garbled torrent. His eyes behind the slits of the mask were dark and expectant.

"I think he's waiting for us to say something," Grant muttered.

Sidling around them, Balam said quietly, "I recognize the language he speaks."

The old man's eyes darted toward him, then widened. A screechy, rapid-fire yammering burst from his bewhiskered lips. His lean body was consumed by shivering, then his bones seemed to turn to molten wax and flow down to the ground. He prostrated himself and pressed his forehead against the flagstones.

Kane knew the old man's reaction stemmed not from terror but from an awe so intense it was almost a religious ecstasy. His two companions remained prone on the ground, not lifting their heads or even appearing to move.

Balam spoke in a rustling, whispering voice, then

glanced toward Brigid. "He is speaking a dialect of Sumerian, which is related to no known language, living or dead. I asked him to use a bit more current form of verbal communication."

"And who does he think you are?" Kane asked gruffly. "One of his gods?"

"No, only a messenger. The term he applied to me translates as 'Archon of Destiny.'"

"Interesting bit of synchronicity," Brigid commented wryly. "If it is such."

Kane seriously doubted it was. Over the past couple of years he had learned "Archon" was a Gnostic term that described both guardians of spiritual planes and jailers of the divine spark within humanity. Ultra-top secret groups within the U.S. military and intelligence agencies referred to Balam and his people as the Archon Directive.

After World War II, a pact was formed between elements in the United States government and the Archons, essentially a trade agreement for high-tech knowledge. Part of the exchange allowed the Archon Directive use of underground military bases. Following the nuclear holocaust of January, 2001, the Archon Directive became the Archon Directorate. During the first century after the holocaust, a number of Archon secrets—developed under the Totality Concept—were discovered by survivors.

Through human and inhuman intermediaries, the Archon Directorate intervened to prevent the rebuilding of a society analogous to the predark model. The Archon Directorate eventually interceded directly in the development of the most powerful baronies, and instituted the Program of Unification in order to prevent a resurgence of the inefficient preholocaust societal structure and also to hide the existence of the so-called Archons and the Totality Concept from all but a small portion of humanity.

However, Balam revealed that the Archons and their ruling council, the Directorate, existed only as appellations and myths created by the predark government agencies as control mechanisms. Lakesh referred to it as the Oz Effect, wherein a single vulnerable entity created the illusion of being the representative of an all-powerful body.

It seemed clear now that Balam and his kind were known as Archons long before being code-named as such by either the military or intelligence agencies. Kane once again reflected wryly that, when it came to Balam, the only thing he could be sure of was that he could be sure of nothing.

Recently he and his friends had learned that the Archons were never the hidden masters of humanity, but custodians created by two races who didn't belong on Earth, who hadn't evolved here. The Tuatha de Danaan and the Annunaki, despite all their influences on humankind's development, were from outside and they feared some aspect of humanity's nature.

Grant glanced around, first at the mosaic under his feet, then at the stone pillars, and finally craned his neck up at the ziggurat bulking overhead. He estimated the base wall stood at least fifty feet tall and extended well over two hundred feet from corner to corner. The topmost building constructed atop an elevated superstructure measured a minimum of 150 feet from the desert floor. The structure was big, but only a molehill in comparison to a mile-high, five-sided pyramid-mountain he and his friends had recently visited on Mars.

Sidestepping away from the reflective surface that made up the eye of a serpent's profile on the mosaic, he commented, "I'm guessing we're where we wanted to be—Iraq."

Brigid seemed to become fully aware of their surroundings for the first time. In a hushed voice, she said, "Mesopotamia stands alongside Egypt, the Indus River Valley and China as a birthplace of permanent human culture."

"Not to mention it's where the snake-faces hung their hats," Kane retorted, sweeping the tail of his long coat back so he could examine the image of the mosaic at his feet. "But then, where didn't they?"

He shook his head to drive out the last wisps of disorientation. Traveling by the interphaser didn't cause the same kind of deleterious physical side effects as the gateway units, but the transit process wasn't exactly soothing to the nerves, either.

When a vortex node was opened, travelers were plunged into a raging torrent of light, wild plumes and whorling spindrifts of violet, yellow, blue, green and red. Swirling like a whirlpool, glowing filaments congealed and stretched outward into the black gulfs of space.

Streaks of gray and dark blue became interspersed with the colorful swirls. They felt themselves plummeting through an alternately brightly lit and shadow-shrouded abyss, an endless fall into infinity. They were conscious of an instant of whirling vertigo, as if they had hurtled a vast distance at blinding speed.

Then the sensation of free fall lessened. The darker colors deepened and collected ahead of them into a pool of shimmering radiance. Suddenly, they were some-where else.

Kane shivered, but not because of the cold. The desert air felt hot on his face and he considered shedding his coat. He and Grant wore ankle-length, Mag-issue black Kevlar-weave coats. They offered a degree of protection against penetration weapons and they were insulated against all weathers, including acid rain showers.

They made sure the Sin Eaters were secure in the rather bulky holsters strapped to their forearms beneath the right sleeves of their coats. The Sin Eaters, the official side arm of the Magistrate Divisions, were automatic handblasters, less than fourteen inches in length at full extension, the magazines carrying twenty 9 mm rounds. When not in use, the butts folded over the top of the blasters, lying perpendicular to the frame, reducing its holstered length to ten inches.

When the weapons were needed, a flexing of wrist tendons activated sensitive actuator cables within the holsters and snapped the pistols smoothly into their waiting hands, the butts unfolding in the same motion. Since the Sin Eaters had no trigger guards or safeties, the autopistols fired immediately upon touching their crooked index fingers.

Long combat knives, the razor-keen blades forged of dark blued steel, hung from sheaths at their hips. Clipped to their web belts were abbreviated Copperhead subguns. Less than two feet long, with a 700-round-per-minute rate of fire, the extended magazines held thirty-five 4.85 mm steel-jacketed rounds. The grip and trigger units were placed in front of the breech in the bullpup design, allowing for one-handed use.

Optical image intensifier scopes and laser autotargeters were mounted on the top of the frames. Low recoil allowed the Copperheads to be fired in long, devastating full-auto bursts.

Although Brigid Baptiste wore no coat, her willowy body was encased in a one-piece skintight garment. Kane and Grant were attired in duplicates. The black garb had been christened shadow suits. The material of the formfitting coveralls, which resembled black doeskin, had become important tools in the Cerberus ordnance and arsenal over the past few months. More than once the suits had proved their worth and superiority to the polycarbonate Magistrate armor, if for nothing else than their amazing internal subsystems.

Composed of a compiled weave of spider silk, Monocrys and Spectra fabrics, the garments were essentially a single crystal metallic microfiber, with a very dense molecular structure. The outer Monocrys sheathing went opaque when exposed to radiation, and the Kevlar and Spectra layers provided protection against blunt trauma. The spider silk allowed flexibility, but it traded protection from firearms for freedom of movement.

The suits were almost impossible to tear, but dense and elastic enough to deflect arrows and knives. Unlike the Mag exoskeletons, a high-caliber bullet could penetrate them.

Balam gestured to the masked man, speaking one word, which the Commtacts translated as "Arise."

"What language is that?" Brigid asked, cocking her head slightly. "Arabic?"

Balam nodded and asked the old man, "What shall I call you?"

Standing up on legs as wobbly as those of a newborn foal's, the masked man bowed his head. "Resurah. I am the high priest of Enlil. What shall I call you?"

"Balam."

Resurah jerked in reaction, his eyes catching a glint of starlight, so they gleamed eerily in the holes of his mask. "I have heard that name before. It is the name of the night demon who commands forty legions...who divines the past and future and becomes invisible."

"Oh, he's still up to that," Kane commented airily, stepping away from the mosaic. "Or he tries to give that impression, anyhow."

Facing Brigid, he said, "Recalibrate the interphaser and make sure it can get us back home when we need it...like before the overlords show up."

Brigid's back stiffened at the peremptory tone, but she knelt beside the little metal pyramid and touched a seam on its alloyed skin. From the base a keypad slid out.

The interphaser had evolved from Project Cerberus. Over two years before, Lakesh had constructed a small device on the same scientific principle as the mat-trans gateways, a portable quantum interphase inducer designed to interact with naturally occurring hyperdimensional vortices. The interphaser opened dimensional rifts much like the gateways, but instead of the rifts being pathways through linear space, Lakesh had envisioned them as a method to travel through the gaps in normal space-time.

The first version of the interphaser hadn't functioned according to its design, and was lost on its first mission.

Much later, a situation arose that necessitated the construction of a second, improved model.

During the investigation of the Operation Chronos installation on Thunder Isle, a special encoded program named Parallax Points was discovered. Lakesh learned that the Parallax Points program was actually a map, a geodetic index, of all the vortex points on the planet. This discovery inspired him to rebuild the interphaser, even though decrypting the program was laborious and time-consuming. Each newly discovered set of coordinates was fed into the interphaser's targeting computer.

With the new data, the interphaser became more than a miniaturized version of a gateway unit, even though it employed much of the same hardware and operating principles. The mat-trans gateways functioned by tapping into the quantum stream, the invisible pathways that crisscrossed outside of perceived physical space and terminated in wormholes.

The interphaser interacted with the energy within a naturally occurring vortex and caused a temporary overlapping of two dimensions. The vortex then became an intersection point, a discontinuous quantum jump, beyond relativistic space-time. Evidence indicated there were many vortex nodes, centers of intense energy, located in the same proximity on each of the planets of the solar system, and those points correlated to vortex centers on Earth. The power points of the planet, places that naturally generated specific types of energy, possessed both positive and projective frequencies, and others were negative and receptive.

Lakesh knew some ancient civilizations were aware of these symmetrical geo-energies and constructed monuments, like geodetic markers, over the vortex points in order to manipulate them. Obviously the eye inset into the mosaic was one such marker.

Once the interphaser was put into use, the Cerberus redoubt reverted to its original purpose—not a sanctuary for exiles, or the headquarters of a resistance movement battling the tyranny of the barons, but a facility dedicated to exploring the eternal mysteries of space and time. Interphaser Version 2.0 had been lost during a recent mission to Mars to unlock a few of those eternal mysteries.

Brigid Baptiste and Brewster Philboyd had worked feverishly over a period of a month to construct a third one, but with expanded capabilities. They had completed Interphaser Version 2.5 only recently. The test jump proved that it worked perfectly, despite the fact that it phased Brigid, Philboyd and Nora Pennick into the middle of an interfactional war in Cambodia.

Grant eyed the prone bodies of Resurah's companions and said, "Are they asleep or unconscious or what?"

Kane stepped over to them, prodding each man gingerly with a toe, eliciting only a single groan. Wrinkling his nose, he said, "One is a what. I think he's dead, probably from heart failure. The other one just doesn't seem inclined to get up, but you'd think he'd want to. We literally scared the shit out of him. Leastways, I assume it was us."

"Classy," Brigid murmured icily, still checking over the interphaser's systems. "Maybe somebody should make sure he's dead and not just unconscious. We've got medicine."

Resurah bent over the body of his companion and

after a moment of poking and prodding announced. "Amner is dead."

"You don't seem very broken up over it," Kane observed.

"Amner grew old in the service our master, the lord of the air," intoned Resurah quietly. He made a spiral sign with a bony forefinger. "Now our god will allow him to rest, to know everlasting peace. At least he lived long enough to fall 'neath the gaze of Enlil's messengers."

Resurah bent his head before Balam. "Come. I will guide you into Ekur, so that our god may know all is in readiness for his return."

His voice and bearing were reverent. But the ruthless eyes within his mask burned hungrily.

Chapter 13

"More than eighty percent of all known Sumerian literary compositions have been found at Nippur," Brigid said conversationally, gingerly putting one foot on a step, then another. The clay-glazed riser crunched beneath her weight but didn't yield. "Included were the earliest recognized versions of the flood story, parts of the Gilgamesh epic and dozens of other compositions."

"You don't say," Grant muttered sourly, gazing up along the flight of stairs to the point where they intersected with the first terrace of the ziggurat. The steps ascended at a very steep angle, and his balance was off because of the interphaser's carrying case slung over a shoulder. The device itself wasn't particularly heavy, but the power pack that enabled it to function was as bulky and solid as a brick.

Under any other circumstances, Kane would've assumed point position, but Resurah began mounting the steps in a very ceremonial, dignified manner, beckoning to them. Grant followed him, with Brigid and Balam sandwiched between him and Kane. If Kane disliked bringing up the rear, he kept his objections to himself. He continually checked their back trail.

As they climbed higher on Ekur, Kane made out the individual structures of Nippur, or where they had once stood—a long wall had toppled and was half buried in the sand, and many buildings had collapsed into heaps of rubble. It was difficult to discern the original lines of the structures, since they had all been scoured smooth by windswept sand. The reconstructions of the buildings, however were very easy to differentiate.

"As important in historical terms as royal inscriptions from all periods, " Brigid continued, slightly breathless from the exertion of the climb. "Especially those of the Kassite Dynasty, which ruled Mesopotamia from about 1600 to 1225 B. C."

"It was 1238, actually," Balam put in mildly.

Kane called up darkly, "You'd be the one to know, I guess. Since your people probably destroyed it."

Balam glanced down at him dispassionately, and Kane sensed again the loneliness and pain radiating from the entity like an invisible aura.

"Sorry," he muttered. "Climbing ziggurats at night always makes me bitchy."

Balam turned away without a response. Dourly, Kane reflected that dates and places of human civilizations were the least of what Balam and his people knew. His folk's knowledge of hyperdimensional physics had proved, at least insofar as the mat-trans units were concerned. But they hadn't shared their knowledge that the gateways could accomplish far more than linear travel from point to point along a quantum channel.

Kane still harbored a bit of skepticism of Balam's version of the hidden history of Earth, despite the fact he had encountered nothing to prove it false. And if he had done nothing else, Balam had removed, with only a few words, the threat of the Archon Directorate and given hope to the exiles in Cerberus.

During the first year of his time in Cerberus, he and his friends accepted as gospel that the global megacull was not humanity's fault at all, but due to the deceptions of Balam's people over the long track of centuries. Later, they came to understand that the so-called Archon Directorate hadn't really conquered humanity—it had tempted humanity with the tools to conquer itself.

Unregenerate greed, naked ambition, the monomania for power over others were the carrots snapped up by the predark decision makers. In order to survive, Balam and his folk had deceived humankind, but it was humanity's choice whether to live down to its worst impulses or rise above them.

Resurah led them to the top of the stairs, where they intersected with the first level of the ziggurat. The ramp stretched off and up to the right, climbing at an ever-increasing angle. Without pause, the masked priest began trudging across the terrace and up the next incline.

Grant dropped back and sidemouthed to Kane, "The padre is being suspiciously cooperative."

"You noticed that, too?" Kane whispered in reply. "Could be he just wants to impress the Archon of Destiny."

"Or," Grant rumbled, "he wants to trap the night demon and his friends inside a pyramid."

"Ziggurat," Kane corrected. "But that possibility *did* occur to me."

Grant nodded and with a faint whir and click, his Sin Eater slid from the holster beneath his right sleeve and slapped solidly into his hand. "Keep our triggers set."

Kane didn't unleather his own weapon, but he allowed Grant to precede him as he brought up the rear again, alert and aware. The fleecy clouds had dissipated from the face of the Moon, and enough light fell onto the structure so they could at least see where they were putting their feet. Kane was concerned that Grant might stumble and drop the interphaser, damaging it so they could not transit back to Cerberus. Although the device's carrying case was cushioned and insulated, he was still uncertain of just how delicate a mechanism it might be.

The decision to use the interphaser to make the transit to Iraq had been reached quickly. Balam scanned the Parallax Point coordinates in the database and selected one that he claimed correlated with the longitude and latitude of Nippur.

Although Lakesh wanted to accompany them, he saw the wisdom of not putting all of the key personnel, the command staff as it were, in jeopardy. Besides, he had the utmost faith in Kane, Brigid and Grant to handle anything they might encounter. Lakesh had once suggested that the trinity they formed when they worked in tandem seemed to exert an almost supernatural influence on the scales of chance, usually tipping them in their favor. The notion had both amused and repulsed Kane. He was too pragmatic to truly believe in such an esoteric concept, but not even he could deny that he and his two friends seemed to lead exceptionally charmed lives.

Still he felt a little guilty about leaving while Quavell was in labor, but Balam's insistence that time was critical overruled DeFore's protests. Although Kane hadn't discussed it with Grant and Brigid, he knew they shared his own distrust of Balam's story of the rebirth of the Annunaki overlords. That was the main reason Grant had refused Shizuka's offer to come along with them. He risked her ire to keep her as safe as he possibly could.

Not long ago the Cerberus warriors had been afforded a glimpse of their future, and it bore no relation to what Balam had described. According to the message conveyed to them from twenty-seven years hence, Sam ruled in a preeminent position of global power following a long conflict called the Consolidation War, but there had been no mention of Annunaki involvement.

However, the actions undertaken by Kane, Grant and Brigid to make sure such a future never came to pass could have shifted probabilities sufficiently to set in a motion an entirely new series of events, which in turn created a branching time line.

Or, he reflected bleakly, the rebirth of the Annunaki was always predestined—the future of the Consolidation War was the aberration, the accident. Something he had done or had yet to do—or not do—brought that alternate time line into existence.

Kane winced at a pinch of pain between his eyes. His brain wasn't flexible enough to deal with reality-bashing ideas like those, so instead he concentrated on scaling the ramp to the next terrace.

Although the surface of the ramp underfoot was smooth, it was also grainy and gritty, which made the upward progress slow and laborious. As one of his footfalls caused a section of the ramp to crack, Grant said dubiously, "How stable is this thing?"

"Compared to what?" Kane asked.

"To the pyramids, for example."

Brigid said, "The pyramids were built from enormous stones that often had to be transported for long distances. The Mesopotamian ziggurats were built from small mud bricks that were locally produced."

"Mud?" Grant's voice held a note of alarm.

"Don't worry," Brigid replied wryly. "I don't think it's going to rain any time soon."

A heap of debris that had fallen from a higher terrace formed a barrier the five people were forced to clamber over. Brigid lifted Balam atop the heap of rubble like a mother would a child. His rasped "Thank you" carried a hint of embarrassment in it.

Balam's endurance surprised Kane, since his spindly legs didn't appear to possess the muscle mass of an infant. Still, the entity trudged resolutely onward and upward at the dirt-crusted heels of Resurah.

Finally, the ramp opened onto the summit of the ziggurat, angling sharply into the open entrance of the flat-roofed shrine. Kane took a moment to catch his breath, glad for the fresh breeze blowing in off the desert. He looked toward the horizons and saw only rolling sand dunes stretching away like a brown ocean. The narrow ribbon of the Euphrates flowed into the darkness and distance.

Far below lay Nippur, its empty streets winding between ruins and sheared-off columns. Stepping up behind him, Brigid said quietly, almost sadly, "Nippur and her sister city-state, Ur, were the main centers of civilization and learning in this part of the world. They represented a highly advanced culture that predated pharonic Egypt by two thousand years."

"Yeah," Kane drawled bitterly. "Too bad it was built

to worship a bunch of scaly-assed aliens who thought
they were gods."

As he started to turn away, a flicker of light caught
his attention. Eyes narrowed, Kane moved closer to the
edge, gazing down at the colonnade. The eye in the center of the spiral mosaic sparkled dimly as if it reflected
an errant glitter of starlight.

"What is it?" Brigid asked.

Absently he replied, "I guess that depends on your
definition of 'what'—"

His spine stiffened in reaction to a sudden chill, as if
ice cubes had been dropped down his back. A fluttering
finger of incandescence stretched up from the glossy
surface of the mosaic's eye. Kane felt, rather than heard,
a pulsing vibration against his eardrums, as of the distant
beating of great wings. Then the mosaic and the entire
promenade erupted in a blinding explosion of white light.

Dazzled, Kane shielded his eyes with his hands,
aware of an undulating drone synchronized with almost
continuous bright bursts of energy stabbing at his optic
nerves. He heard Brigid cry out in surprise and dismay.

Vision swimming with flare-induced floaters, Kane
peered through watering eyes at the dark presences arrayed around the mosaic. Because of the swirling mass
of white energy surrounding the figures, finer details escaped him, but he guessed there were at least a dozen,
quite possibly more.

With each new flash of light, more figures seemed
to appear. He didn't back away from the edge despite
his point man's sense urging him to do so as quickly as
possible. Grant stepped up on his left side and grunted
wordlessly as he stared down.

Through the milky haze, they caught only fragmented glimpses of hairless heads scaled in vivid hues of green, crimsons and gold. They were crested with back curving spines. They couldn't make out individual features, but what they saw was enough to freeze them in place.

Balam's ghostly whisper broke the chains of their paralysis. "It appears the overlords and the Nephilim have arrived a bit ahead of schedule."

Chapter 14

The passageway curving through the interior of Ekur was as smooth as if the clay had been wax, pierced at a down-slanting angle by a red-hot needle. It wasn't completely dark inside the ziggurat. Both walls were paneled by cool blue squares that shed an eerie pellucid light. Grant, Kane and Brigid had seen the luminous panels before and knew they were of Archon manufacture.

The passage curved much like a gentle spiral, extending downward on an ever-steepening decline. Heart pounding, Kane called, "Balam! What's the damn drill?"

Balam's voice floated out of the blue shadows ahead of him. "Specify."

"Do we make a stand here and pick off the overlords as they come in?"

"That will not solve the problem of Tiamat. No, Enlil will seek out the Tablets of Destiny in the tabernacle. If he finds them, he will also find a portal by which he and the others will transport to the ship."

Brigid, striding behind a very apprehensive Resurah and Balam and trying to keep both of them within the field of her vision, inquired, "A portal? Do you mean a mat-trans unit?"

"Not precisely," Balam answered, his pale head reflecting the ectoplasmic light as if his flesh were phos-phorescent. "The Annunaki called them threshholds. They are to one of your gateway units as an ox-drawn cart is to a supersonic aircraft."

Grant grunted impatiently. "Sam—Enlil—used the Heart of the World to get him and the overlords here, so why would he need this threshold to transport to the spaceship?"

"Your question is its own answer," Balam replied. "The energies of the Heart of the World utilize natural geomagnetic streams and intersection points of the planet, much like your interphaser. Tiamat is patently not on the planet."

Kane dredged up an image from his memory, one that Balam had imparted to him during their telepathic exchange two years before. He recalled archways seem-ingly sheathed in flame. He asked, "The thresholds look like arches, right? That's how the early Annunaki col-onists came and went from Earth to Tiamat?"

"Yes."

Resuarah's bleating voices echoed hollowly within the passageway. "O, Balam of the Forty Legions—why do we flee instead of welcoming the assembly of the gods?"

Coldly, autocratically, Balam announced, "As the eyes of Enlil, he will see what I see. The tabernacle must be in order. If so, he will join us there and reward you for your diligence. If it is *not* in order—"

Balam didn't speak the rest, allowing the implica-tions hang in the air, knowing Resurah's imagination would conjure up far more terrifying threats than mere words could deliver.

Resurah quickened his pace, his sandaled feet making a continuous scuff-slap on the tunnel floor. In order to keep the old man in sight, Kane, Grant and Brigid slipped on night-vision glasses, the lenses of which were treated to amplify and enhance even the poorest light source. Balam didn't need an artificial aid to his vision, since his people's optic nerves operated far more effectively in murk than did theirs.

Resurah hustled through doorway after doorway. Brigid followed directly behind him, her right hand resting on the butt of the TP9 autopistol snugged into the holster attached by Velcro tabs at the small of her back. As the concourse curved ever downward, she repressed a shudder. Although she didn't frighten easily, plunging into the shadow-shrouded belly of the ancient temple awakened in her a lurking, atavistic fear, a rising sense she was rushing headlong into hell.

The angle of descent suddenly decreased. Almost as suddenly, the passageway opened into an immense chamber, like a vast hollow pyramid within the ziggurat. The ceiling was paneled by the blue light squares. The tiled floor gleamed with an elaborate multicolored mosaic, a much larger version of the one outside the ziggurat.

Four fluted pillars stood at equidistant points around the chamber, but their purpose seemed more for design than function. The floor area formed a perfect square, and Kane guessed the corners stretched a hundred feet from one another, extending 140 feet on the diagonal.

Dangling from the apex of the high ceiling, suspended by a web of wires, hung a gold-leaf stone sculpture fashioned into an exaggeratedly noble likeness of the crowned head of Enlil. It stared down with a fathomless gaze upon the massive altar. The lidless eyes were composed of the same luminous material as the light panels.

The altar itself was of simple construction, with heavy stone columns and the straight lines of a twenty-foot-long horizontal rock slab, supporting a fragment of pale blue crystal. Triangular in shape like the walls of the chamber itself, it reminded Brigid of a splinter of shattered glass. Nearly the height of Grant, the crystal glimmered as though cut from an enormous amethyst.

"This place is damn near as big as the outside," Grant remarked, staring around. "That means most of the building is hollow."

Her bright green eyes absorbing everything, Brigid said, "Ziggurats were said to house the divine source of light and energy as a living connection to the gods…sometimes even the house of the gods. They *had* to be big. Through the ziggurat, the gods could be close to humankind."

Brigid stepped up to the altar, staring at the shard of crystal in silence, one part of her mind noting clinically that the kaleidoscopic pattern of reflections within it had a slightly hypnotic effect. Another part of her mind listened to what seemed to be a chorus of faint, distant voices, thready and whispery tones that gently brushed and caressed the edges of her awareness.

She heard no words, only the murmuring song of a phantom choir, singing from a place and time so far in the dim past that no one should possibly be able to hear, much less understand them.

"What the hell is that?" Kane's question, spoken quietly into her right ear, caused her to jump and bite back a startled curse.

Shaking her head as though roused from a nap, she replied, "I think it's *shem-an-na*...the altar of the Star Fire."

"Oh, that explains a whole lot of...nothing," he retorted tersely, gazing around the chamber with alert eyes. His gaze swept over a free-standing archway of dull metal, positioned at the opposite side of the chamber from the altar. It reminded him of pix he had seen of the linteled door frames in predark cathedrals. In height and width, it looked to be an exact match for the fragment of blue crystal.

"The Star Fire," Brigid declared, "was a sacred crystal venerated by the ancient Sumerians and their descendants. Some scholars postulated it was the basis of the Philosopher's Stone used by alchemists. By staring into it long enough, it was reputed to heighten spiritual perception by imparting the arcane knowledge stored there by previous generations."

Kane's lips quirked in a crooked smile. "That old saw."

Testily, she countered, "The Tuatha de Danaan employed something like it. Remember the Speaking Stone of Cascorach?"

Morrigan, the blind telepath from Ireland's Priory of Awen, had told Brigid that ancient priesthoods knew stone and metal and crystalline things retained a memory. They could be charged with ancestral memories, like storage batteries.

Kane nodded distractedly, turning away. "I remember you talking about it."

Despite his dismissive response, Kane recollected everything they had ever learned of Annunaki mental abilities. Sumerian texts repeatedly asserted the Annunaki were all connected. No singularity existed among them. What one knew, all knew. A giant shard of crystal that stored the electromagnetic pattern of their mind energy, functioning like a database, didn't seem completely out of the realm of plausibility.

Grant stood at the entrance of the chamber, less interested in the interior of the tabernacle than the corridor they had just left. Sin Eater in hand, he peered into the gloom, saying, "It'll take them a while to get here."

"Yeah," Kane agreed, turning to face Balam. "And then what, O Master of the Forty Flatulencies?"

Balam made one of his diffident hand gestures. "When the Tablets of Destiny are retrieved by the overlords, you must appropriate them."

"Just like that?" Brigid challenged. "You make it sound like they'll be only too happy to give them up if we ask nicely enough."

Balam turned his black, penetrating stare on her. "I did not intend to convey that impression. There may be a struggle and if so, blood will most probably be spilled. But the tablets must not be damaged."

"How the hell do you even know they're in here?" Grant asked irritably.

Balam's response was simple. "Tradition."

Grant's slit-eyed gaze rested on Resurah. "What does he know about them?"

The old man had listened patiently to the exchange in a language he didn't understand. When Balam put a question to him in Arabic, the masked priest replied, "The Tablets of Destiny are here, where Enlil placed them for safekeeping over three thousand years ago. Only he may lay claim to them."

Resurah paused, and in a tone heavy with suspicion,

said, "As you should know if you serve him. Why do you come here?"

"We are the eyes of Enlil," Balam replied.

Resurah shook his head. "I do not believe you are. I believe you are enemies of the gods."

"You are mistaken. We came here at the summons of Enlil."

Resurah pondered Balam's rejoinder for a few seconds before saying, "It is strange that I, who am the ancestral high priest of Nippur, knows nothing of any summons. And if you are truly the eyes of Enlil, you should be leading his procession here, to the tabernacle."

Kane realized the old man was fast losing his sense of awe in the presence of the Archon of Destiny. Suspicion took its place. Grant made a casual but deliberate show of blocking the doorway, just in case Resurah tried to bolt.

"I shall be the judge of what I should do," Balam stated, an edge to his voice.

With his right hand, Resurah reached inside his robe as if to scratch at a louse bite. Then, with a speed surprising for a man of his years, he whipped out a leaf-shaped bronze-bladed knife. The engraved point touched Balam's short, slender neck. Grant took a half step forward, but stopped when Balam waved him back.

In a very unsteady voice, Resurah barked, "You are a demon and seek to deceive me, so I will betray my god."

"You are making a misjudgment," Balam replied blandly. "And perpetrating blasphemy."

Eyes flashing, Resurah shook his head fiercely. "You think me a fool? I know of the demon-spawn of the gods, how they repaid the gods' trust with treachery.

Your name was prominent on the tablets and scrolls I studied as a novitiate. Enlil will reward me for capturing you and your familiars. Do not resist—my knife has been blessed and inscribed with magic symbols. It will slash asunder all ensorcellments and witchcrafts."

Balam said idly. "I will not resist."

Tilting his head back, he studied the priest's half-concealed features as if he found them utterly fascinating. A choking cry burst from Resurah's lips. His lean body began shaking like a windblown leaf. The knife fell to the floor with a dull, discordant chime. Slowly, he sank to his knees, covering his face with trembling hands.

"The old Archon fear whammy," Kane commented with a grudging admiration. "That should keep him from warning the overlords…or doing much of anything."

"It is most effective on primitive minds," Balam said genially. "As you should know from experience."

A profane rebuttal leaped to Kane's tongue, but before it left his lips, Brigid Baptiste interjected hastily, "We've got to get him out sight."

She touched the priest on the shoulder, but he didn't react. Balam's telepathic infusion of fear had robbed the old man of his ability to think and act. Grant and Kane stepped over to him and latched on to an arm each. Heaving Resurah up from the floor, they dragged him into the narrow space between the rear of the altar and the wall.

Using cloth strips torn from his robe, the two men swiftly but expertly hog-tied him, binding his skinny ankles to his equally skinny wrists. Resurah's leather mask made an effective gag, jammed between his toothless jaws and kept in place by a rawhide lace from one of his sandals. Resurah didn't struggle or even give any indication he was aware of what was happening. He kept his eyes squeezed shut during the entire process, breathing fitfully through his nostrils.

When they were finished, Kane and Grant returned to the center of the chamber. "Now what?" Kane asked.

In an infuriatingly unperturbed voice, Balam said, "Now we must hide ourselves. The overlords come."

Chapter 15

The tramp of measured footfalls preceded their arrival, but the echoing acoustics of the passageway didn't carry voices. After straining his ears to catch even a mutter, Kane decided the silence was best.

Crouched in a wedge of shadow stretching between a pillar and the left-hand wall, Kane struggled to control his rising anxiety. The notion of lying in wait to ambush nine reborn Annunaki seemed worse than ill-conceived—in retrospect it fit the definition of insane. He wondered bleakly if Balam might not have exerted a more subtle form of mental manipulation on him and his friends to persuade them to agree to the plan.

He resisted the urge to peer around the pillar to make sure Grant and Brigid were both in their positions of choice, arranged to catch the overlords in a triangulated cross fire, if circumstances necessitated such a maneuver. Balam had joined Resurah behind the altar stone, presumably to keep him fearful and compliant.

"Status, Baptiste?" He subvocalized the call, relying on the cavernous room to make his whisper so faint as to be inaudible. He barely heard himself.

Her response was curt but immediate. "I'm set."

"Grant?"

"Set."

"Acknowledged." Because the Commtacts transmitted the electronic signals directly through the cranial bones, they could hear even the barest of whispers from one another.

The tramp of footfalls grew in volume and shadows flitted at the doorway. Kane pressed against the pillar, listening to his own pulse pounding in his temples. Adrenaline raced through his bloodstream. He took a deep breath and tried to concentrate. He told himself that whatever came through the door was mortal, not divine or demonic.

A tall figure swept into the tabernacle, striding with a ceremonial pomposity and an almost serpentine grace. Draped in a billowing robe of saffron hue, the creature bore no resemblance to Sam, nor to any of the barons he had ever seen. Still and all, Kane knew instantly he looked at Enlil.

Although his height was awesome, nearly seven feet, he was gaunt of physique. The scaled skin of his hairless head glistened in the pallid blue light shed by the eyes of the giant effigy suspended from the roof. Enlil's flesh glittered slightly, as if a pattern of metal were sewn into the flesh. The crest of spines curving back from the crown of his skull gleamed with a metallic luster, like wires made of burnished steel.

The resemblance to the preserved corpse of Enlil was superficial in the extreme—the figure marching imperiously into the chamber made the preserved body of the original creature seem like a crude plasticene sculpture by comparison. Kane remembered what Balam had once telepathically imparted to him: "The Enlil that was…is not the Enlil that now is."

At the time, Kane had not closely examined the meaning of Balam's cryptic comment. Now, finally he knew exactly what Balam meant.

A man a full head shorter flanked Enlil, wearing the tight-fitting jumpsuit of dark metallic weave favored by hybrids. However, he didn't look like a hybrid. His nose was short, his lips a thin slash above a blunt chin. High cheekbones and craggy brow ridges framed his most disturbing feature, his eyes. They were deep set, the irises as white as pearls. Like Enlil, he was hairless and his dark skin bore a pebbled pattern of scales.

Enlil and one of the Nephilim. The texture of Balam's telepathic insertion into his mind was at once familiar and unsettling. Kane had been in psychic communication with Balam before. He could only assume that after the first mind-to-mind channel was established, a semipermanent link had been forged.

Barons Cobalt and Sharpe arrive, Balam said. Two more figures entered the tabernacle, both of them wearing the ceremonial robes of the barons, but the pair didn't look anything like the individuals Kane had met in the past.

Now they remember who they were thousands of years ago, came Balam's mind-whisper. *Lords Marduk and Nergal.*

Kane had spent more time in the presence of Cobalt and Sharpe than any other members of the baronial oligarchy, but he saw almost no trace of the arrogant vengeance seeker or the half-mad trickster against whom he had contended on more than one occasion.

Although Marduk and Nergal were not identical to each other or to Enlil, they both shared the same protuberant bony ridges overhanging shadow-pooled eyes and scaled skin stretched tight over sharp-boned faces. The crests of spines sprouting from their skulls were not as long as Enlil's, and they shimmered iridescently with different colors; brick-red for Nergal and cobalt-blue for Marduk. Which, Kane reflected, was only appropriate.

As the other overlords marched in, Balam dutifully identified them: *Baron Mande...Lord Zu; Baron Palladium...Lord Dumuzi; Baron Thulia...Lord Shamash; Baron Snakefish...Lord Utu; Baron Samarium...Lord Ishkur.*

Just as dutifully, Kane repeated Balam's words, conveying them by whispers to Brigid and Grant over the Commtacts. Whatever their reactions, his friends kept them private.

Baroness Beausoliel stalked through the doorway last, the taut, scaled flesh of her proud face shining like polished amber. She moved with a liquid symmetry, a hip-swinging, swaggering superiority.

Lilitu, Balam's mind whispered. *The succubus of ancient legend, the seducer of man's dreams.*

Eight Nephilim accompanied the overlords. All were of the same height and general build, with the identical scaled skin, inhuman white eyes and blank expressions. They looked less like retainers to alien royalty than the walking dead.

Kane struggled to reconcile the sight of the tall, regal aristocrats striding into the tabernacle with the memories of the small, fragile creatures who had ruled the baronies from the shadows of their high, isolated aeries.

As the hybrid barons, they had been a beautiful folk and as the overlords they were still, but now there was something terrible, even revolting in their beauty. With their gracefully arrogant movements and glistening skins, they were like of a group of pampered, depraved children. Their fierce, lusting eyes put Kane in mind of overthrown monarchs who had long been held in captivity in filthy dungeons, but now had cast off their chains and climbed out of the pits to retake their thrones. Erica van Sloan's words ghosted through his consciousness: "The kings are returning to their kingdom."

Kane easily recalled the conditioning undergone by the Magistrates that instilled in them the belief the barons were kings, demigods, their personal deities and thus deserving of their unquestioning obedience. Even learning the barons were products of synthetic wombs and recombinant DNA hadn't completely stripped them of their semidivine mystique.

To see them now, transformed and evolved into creatures of myth, entities who had indeed behaved and been worshiped as gods, evoked emotions somewhere between terror and bleak resignation. But sparks of anger glowed in there, too, to be fanned into a full blaze. Kane hoped he would have the opportunity.

Enlil marched to the altar, the eight overlords gathering around him in a crescent. The eight Nephilim took up parade-rest positions on either side of the slab of stone, four to a corner.

Enlil began speaking in a fluid language Kane didn't understand, but guessed was the native tongue of Nibiru. The sound of his voice was other than he expected. It reminded him of the tolling of a gong he had heard recently in Angkor Thom—rich golden vibrations with dark notes underscoring it.

Light suddenly bloomed from within the shard of crystal, a flare of yellow radiance that lit up the area around the altar like the breaking of dawn. A low humming filled the chamber, and the light within the crystal grew brighter. Enlil continued to speak, lifting his voice in a song, cold and clear and of an inhuman sweetness. The overlords joined in, vocalizing a repetitive chant. The sound raised Kane's nape hairs. Somehow he knew it was an ancient hymn preserved from an age beyond human remembrance. The faces of the overlords were intent, their eyes eerily reflecting the glow from the crystal.

The light emitted by the Star Fire pulsed in rhythm with the song, increasing in brilliance until Kane had no choice but to remove his night-vision glasses or risk damage to his optic nerves. The crystal resonated with the chorus, its sharp edges humming like music heard only faintly when carried by the wind.

Grant's tension-drenched murmur of "What the hell is going on?" suddenly drowned out the song.

As if on cue, a prolonged grate of stone against stone echoed throughout the tabernacle. The shape of the altar shifted as a long section of the flat forepart rose on invisible pivots like a lid. On its underside multicolored lights blinked and flashed from within glass-encased readout screens. Nine metal cylinders gleaming as if made of polished chrome pushed their way upward. Four metal bands encircled each one.

Kane heard himself husk out, "A machine. Their altar is a machine."

Brigid's voice whispered in his head, "*Deus ex machina,* to quote an old bromide. Even the Annunaki made demigods of their machines. That's good to know."

"Why?" Grant asked.

"Behind all the ritual, there are some very basic scientific principles in operation. The altar is equipped with sound sensors. The overlords hit the right notes in the proper combination, like unlocking a safe. Gods wouldn't need such things."

Kane didn't contribute to the conversation. He fixed his attention on Enlil as he removed the metal bands from the chrome cylinders and passed them out among the overlords arrayed behind and around him. Each one of them took four of the circlets.

Moving with the same swift, sharp motions as if all of the overlords were mirror images of one another, they shrugged out of their robes, letting them drop to the tiled floor. They stood naked before the altar, bathed in the pulsating shimmer of the Star Fire, their sleek, sinuously muscled bodies seeming to ripple in the lambent aura. Only Enlil did not strip.

From their throats came a low chant, repeating three minor themes until they intermingled. With a studied, almost rehearsed synchronicity, the overlords snapped the bands of metal around the bases of their necks, their wrists and their ankles.

"What...?" came Grant's breathless growl of confusion. "They came all the way from their baronies to try on *jewelry?*"

From the circlets of alloy flowed sheaths of gleaming metal, writhing and sliding from their necks, down over their torsos, up their arms and legs. Like mercury, the liquid substance pouring from each of the bands joined in sections, then sculpted itself to conform to the shape of the individual body.

Within the space of a few heartbeats the material molded itself into a final form. As it solidified and metallicized, it acquired colors and detail. The armor encasing the bodies of each overlord glistened with a different tint that reflected the color of their skull crests. On the left pectoral the metal swirled to create a different cuneiform sigil for each one, the personal emblem of the overlord who wore it. The armor was obviously some kind of metal, but as pliable as stiff cloth.

With both arms, Enlil gestured imperiously to the Nephilim, who numbly and dumbly had observed the transformation process. One by one they shuffled forward, standing before Enlil with bowed heads.

From within the altar Enlil removed disk-shaped pods, approximately six inches in diameter, flat on one side, convex on the obverse. Each one was of a different color. He slapped the flat side of a red pod hard against the chest of the nearest Nephilim. With a soft click it adhered there magnetically, signifying it had locked into place. Spinning the man around, Enlil placed another disk on his back, between his shoulder blades.

From the outer edges of the pods sprang ribbons of liquid alloy, spreading swiftly over the dark mesh of the man's bodysuit, interacting with the garment, acquiring new shapes as the substance slid across his torso. The tendrils formed themselves into inch-thick reinforcing epaulets on his shoulders and then crept down the sleeves to sheath his hands and forearms in gauntlets.

Raised humps on both wrists gained dimension, and three short, hollow barrels protruded from them. Flexible conduits snaked out from cuffs, curving around to connect with the red pod attached to the man's back. Kane recognized a weapon when he saw one, but he had no idea of what kind it could be.

Another section of the red-tinted alloy shifted and elongated into a heavy collar encircling the base of the man's throat. A half ovoid shell sprouted from the rear, sweeping up to enclose the back and upper portion of his skull. From its underside hair-thin filaments extended down to pierce both sides of his hairless head. He winced slightly, then stepped aside, allowing another Nephilim to take his place.

Mouth filled with the bitter tang of fear, muscles quivering from barely leashed adrenaline, Kane heard himself whisper thinly, "Baptiste, what is all that?"

Her response was equally thin and fearful. "I don't have any idea. I never saw or heard of anything like it."

Balam's soothing mind energy calmed him somewhat. *It is not sorcery, Kane, but technology. You would call it a "smart metal," a liquid alloy that responds to a sequence of commands programmed into its extruder. A miniature cohesive binding field changes it from liquid to solid. The Nephilim are being outfitted in their traditional battle armor and personal weapons—directed energy emitters known as ASPs...accelerated stream of protons.*

Even Balam's assurance that they were not looking at magic didn't calm Kane He experienced a sensation of dread, a realization that the "smart metal" extruders were probably only the first of the terrifying traditional artifacts to be retrieved by the reborn Annunaki.

Kane whispered almost desperately, "What can we do against weapons like those?"

Follow my lead, Balam answered.

Chapter 16

Kane didn't know what Balam meant, but he resisted to the urge to ask for clarification. He repeated to Brigid and Grant what he had been told about the smart metal and the weaponry.

"What the hell are accelerated stream of proton emitters?" Grant demanded, his whisper so harsh that Kane felt his mastoid bone shiver in response. "Like the quartz cremators we found on the Moon base?"

"I sure as hell hope not," Kane replied, picturing the deadly pulse-plasma rifles and their sectionalized barrels that terminated in a long cylinders made of a crystalline substance. He also envisioned the manner in which bodies exploded from within when struck by the accelerated ion stream.

"I doubt they are," Brigid commented. "But that doesn't mean I want to face them without having some idea of what they can do."

They fell silent, watching as Enlil applied the pods to the Nephilim as they stepped forward, sheathing them in identical but differently colored armor and half helmets. After each one was equally attired and outfitted, Enlil returned his attention to the open altar stone. He gave the distinct impression of rummaging through a trunk.

Kane eased around the pillar in order to get a better look, Sin Eater held in both hands. Enlil's claw-tipped fingers removed flat square panels from narrow slots in the instrument board. They looked to be made of a dark, reflective, glassy substance, but he didn't handle them as if they were fragile. They were the same general shape and dimensions as oversize playing cards, and dots of colored lights played across their surfaces in nine ordered rows, like the beads on the strings of a Chinese abacus.

"Are those the Tablets of Destiny?" Kane asked.

When neither Balam, Brigid nor Grant offered a response, Kane decided not to repeat the question. He watched as Enlil touched a glowing dot on one of the panels with the tip of a finger, moving it across the surface. Somewhere a soft musical note sounded, and Enlil's eyes lost their focus, seemed to look inward.

Then he spoke, "Zu."

Armored in green, Lord Zu stepped forward and received the card from Enlil, holding it reverently in both hands. He bowed his crested head in acknowledgment or gratitude.

In a very unsteady voice, Brigid said, "I'd judge those are the tablets…just like I'd judge they're attuned to the individual overlord, either their genetic code or brain-wave frequency. Or both."

Kane's hand tightened around the butt of his Sin Eater. He guessed Enlil could somehow identify which tablet was attuned to what overlord and distribute them accordingly. Retrieving them from one hand would be easier than from eight.

The same thought had apparently occurred to Grant,

who demanded, "What the hell are we waiting for? Let's make a grab for the tablets."

"Negative," Kane replied. "Balam said to follow his lead."

"What lead?"

"I guess we'll know it when we see it."

The Commtact accurately transmitted Brigid's sudden sharp intake of breath. "I think we may be seeing it now."

From around the left end of the altar stone shuffled a robed, masked figure, fingers steepled together at his forehead.

"Resurah!" Kane was barely able to keep from blurting the priest's name. "Did Balam cut him loose?"

"I think so," Brigid answered in a thoughtful, musing tone he and Grant knew well. "But for his own purposes."

Resurah's eyes glittered with a hard, almost inner light. He swept Kane's hiding place with a swift dispassionate gaze and inclined his head in an almost imperceptible nod. When Kane met those dark eyes, he felt his flesh prickle despite having witnessed the phenomenon before.

"That's Balam," Kane managed to husk out. "He's using Resurah as a channel, like he did with Banks."

Grant and Brigid understood his reference. Twice before, Balam had used the psychic rapport he shared with Banks as a channel of communication, essentially possessing him.

Kane fancied he could glimpse Balam's huge, slanted black eyes superimposed over those of Resurah. He was overwhelmed once again by the knowledge that with Balam almost anything was possible—even mentally directing the body of the old priest like a puppet.

A Nephilim wearing purple-tinted armor caught sight
of the old man before any of the overlords. Instantly he
raised both arms, holding them straight out from the
shoulder, aligning the energy emitters mounted atop his
gauntlets with Resurah. Three flanges shaped like the
letter *S* cut in two sprang out with a flare of sparks and
a crackling hiss of energy. The metal curves were tipped
by the stylized heads of adders in postures of rearing
back for a strike, their mouths agape, red energy pulsing in their gullets. Kane understood why Balam had
called the weapons ASPs. The name wasn't so much an
acronym as it was an accurate description.

The priest continued walking slowly forward, taking
short, jerky steps as if his ankles were hobbled. Enlil
checked the Nephilim's movements with a sharp, sin-
gle-word command. Immediately the soldier dropped
his hands to his sides, the flanges clicking shut.

The eyes of all the overlords turned toward the
hunched figure of Resurah. He stutter-stepped up to
Enlil and bowed deeply from the waist, hands still
pressed together at his forehead. Then slowly he
dropped to his knees. Even Kane was impressed by the
sincere-seeming display of groveling.

Enlil stared down at him imperiously, then a slow, con-
descending smile tugged at the corners of his thin mouth.
Placing the tablets atop the altar, he spoke in a soft tone,
velvet yet sinister. Within the voice Kane detected a faint
undercurrent of Thrush's mocking, oily tones.

He spoke briefly, in a fluid language that meant nothing to Kane, but the other overlords laughed in appreciation. Reaching down, Enlil snatched the leather mask
from Resurah's head, revealing a bald, liver-spotted pate

surrounded by a fringe of gray hair. He examined the
mask, gingerly holding it by thumb and forefinger as if
it were a dirty diaper. His nostrils twitched in mock re-
pugnance and he flung the headgear aside. The overlords laughed again, their scaled faces split in grins of
delighted anticipation.

Resurah whispered a chant or a prayer. Kane wondered
if any of the reborn Annunaki overlords were impressed
that a human had tried to keep alive the ancient, muddled
religion that deified exploiters from another world.

Snorting impatiently, Enlil bent and secured a grip
on the collar of Resurah's robe. With one heave, he
jerked the old man to his feet, his molten gaze passing
with a detached, clinical measure over the priest's
browned, deeply seamed face. He shifted his grip from
the collar to the man's wattled throat. The priest lowered his hands from his forehead but still kept them
pressed together as he prayed.

Resurah's eyes were so liquid with adoration for an
instant Kane doubted his first assessment that Balam
controlled him. Then the old man's eyes became as hard
as chips of anthracite. Resurah's hands parted, and
cupped between them lay the bronze-bladed knife. For
an instant, the light shed from the Star Fire danced along
its edge. Then, with a swift, slashing motion he whipped
the knife toward the neck of Enlil.

The edge of the blade sawed for a microsecond
against the flesh beneath Enlil's left jaw hinge. With the
speed of a striking viper, Enlil's hand closed tightly
around Resurah's throat, thrusting him backward and
twisting simultaneously. The tabernacle echoed with
the crack of bones breaking, the mushy crunch of flesh

and muscle being crushed against vertebrae. The man's body hung limply in Enlil's grasp, his arms and legs shaking in a violent tremor. Life went out of his eyes with the suddenness of a candle being extinguished. The knife clinked dully on the floor.

Contemptuously, as if Resurah weighed no more than his robe, Enlil flung him away, hurling him bodily across the chamber. The back of his head struck the wall with a sound as of a melon being split by an ax. The priest bounced from the stone and fell facedown on the tiled floor, leaving a moist splotch of blood, brain matter and bone fragments on the wall to commemorate his impact.

Kane gaped in shock, not spying so much as a pinpoint of blood on Enlil's neck. He had no idea if the death of Resurah would adversely effect Balam's mental equilibrium, but at the moment he didn't consider the possibility very salient.

A white-hot torrent of loathing and hatred completely smothered the fear and awe the resurrected Enlil had evoked in him. All the repressed hatred and seething rage he felt for Thrush, for Sam, for each and every one of the barons roared out of the dark recesses of his mind and heart. It so consumed him he shivered as if with a chill.

The door-slamming bang of a gunshot startled him, made him jump. Then he realized he had squeezed off a round from his Sin Eater without knowing what he had done. Left hand cupping his right, finger hovering over the pistol's trigger stud, he saw Enlil clutch at his chest and stagger backward. Only the altar kept him from falling. Despite the long range, his shot had struck dead on target.

Kane felt almost as astonished as Brigid Baptiste, Grant and the assembled overlords. Their crested heads whipped around to stare at him in incredulous wonder, which was quickly replaced by raw fury. They may have been the Annunaki Supreme Council reborn, but they retained their memories as barons—and their hatred of him. He stared back, watching how Enlil's eyes narrowed with pain, with confusion. He waited for him to fall.

"Kane?" Brigid's whisper was quavery, brittle with fear. "What are—"

Lips peeling back over his teeth, Enlil pushed himself to his full height and dragged in a shuddery breath. With both hands he grasped his saffron robe at the collar and with one heaving motion, ripped it from his body. Snarling in wordless fury, he threw it from him, eyes fixed on Kane. They blazed with a pure, malign energy—and even a kind of savage satisfaction. He molded his snarl into a smirk of superiority.

Beneath the robe, Enlil's body was naked, but a glittering armor clothed his lean frame nevertheless. His neck, chest, arms and legs were coated with a pattern of tiny interlocking scales that resembled chain mail. Belly slipping sideways, Kane realized why Enlil hadn't put on the smart metal extruders. He didn't not need them, since an organic form of armor covered his body, more than likely a characteristic bestowed on him by the nanomachines he had controlled in his incarnations as Sam and Thrush. Three jointed metal spines curved out from his shoulder blades like the skeletons of wings.

Gazing unblinkingly at Kane, Enlil used the claw-tipped thumb and forefinger of his right hand to dig at his left pectoral. His smirk became a grimace of effort for a moment, then returned to a smirk as he plucked a little flattened cylinder of metal from his chest.

Flipping the bullet in the air like a coin, he caught it, hefted it on the palm of one hand and announced with an icy calm, "You only get one free shot, Kane."

Chapter 17

Enlil's proclamation was the signal for the overlords and the Nephilim to burst into a medley of angry yells and a confusing mill of rushing bodies. Grant interpreted it as a cue to lean out from his sheltering pillar and fire his Copperhead in a long staccato burst. Bright brass arced out of the smoking ejector port, tinkling down at his feet.

A blue-armored Nephilim was hammered off his feet, sparks flying from the multiple impact points. Howls and shrieks of fury erupted from the throats of the overlords, echoing and reechoing within the tabernacle. They dropped flat or took refuge behind the altar. The Nephilim took up protective positions around Enlil, enclosing him in a bastion of flesh and alloy.

One of the Nephilim, wearing purple armor, extended his arms, the viper heads snapping up on his gauntlets. Triple streams of eyeball-searing yellow light spit from the serpent mouths, joining together to form a coruscating globule of plasma that jetted toward Kane like a fireball launched from a catapult. He ducked back behind the pillar as a kaleidoscopic bolt of colors and energy splashed against the stone. Fist-sized chunks exploded from the column, and a wave of heat slapped at his exposed cheek.

More autofire from Grant's Copperhead rattled, weaving its stutter around single-shot cracks. A round from Brigid's TP9 drilled a hole through the jaw of one of the Nephilim, punching him backward with such force the back of his helmeted head hit the edge of the altar with a gonging chime. A scarlet geyser erupted from his mouth and a severed carotid artery. She felt a surge of elation that the pearl-eyed zombie was mortal, but just as quickly she felt regret that she had no choice but to kill the mind-controlled soldiers. She reminded herself that in legend, the Nephilim were the illegitimate children of fallen angels, wandering lost souls.

Brigid framed the Nephilim beside him in her sights and squeezed off a 3-round burst that pounded dents in his red armor, propelling him backward but not knocking him from his feet. He nearly went down, feet sliding and seeking purchase on the polished floor. Catching himself on the corner of the altar, he fired a stream of orange-cored energy from his left-hand ASP emitter.

Scrambling back to cover as the bolt of plasma lashed through the air a finger's width above her head, Brigid felt the flash of heat on her scalp and then the stink of scorched hair filled her nostrils. Desperately she patted the top of her head with her gloved hand, hoping to smother any flames that may have ignited in her mane of hair. She looked around for Kane and glimpsed him shoulder-rolling from behind his pillar. Enlil saw him, too, and he screamed orders to the Nephilim.

"Kane!" Brigid cried. "What the hell are you doing?"

Breathlessly he responded, "One of us is going to have to get the tablets—so cover me!"

Grant leaped out from behind his stone shelter, raised his Copperhead to his shoulder and raked the armored figures of the Nephilim with a deadly stream of auto-fire. The bullets struck sparks and bell-like chimes from their gleaming exoskeletons, bouncing off with angry, buzzing whines.

Only one of the Nephilim went down, clutching at his throat. Blood spilled between his alloy-coated fingers. His companions fired ASP bursts in Grant's direction. He backpedaled as fast as his legs would allow. A bolt of energy fanned a splash of scaldingly hot air on his face, and another brushed the collar of his coat, turning a spot of the fabric a charcoal gray. He didn't know if the Mag coat could turn an ASP blast, and he didn't care to find out. He bit out an obscenity and added, "Kane—think of something fast!"

Kane didn't bother to respond. From his prone position he took hasty aim with his Sin Eater and fired a burst at the four armored men still standing in front of Enlil. At the same time he heard Brigid open up with her own handblaster. A storm of rounds pounded into the Nephilim, jarring them, staggering them, but not penetrating their alloyed carapaces.

A flurry of ASP bolts lanced toward him, and Kane threw himself backward in a frantic somersault, trying to roll ahead of the deadly bursts of energy. They smashed into the floor within inches of his body, showering him with fragments of tile, peppering him with white-hot sparks.

Brigid dropped to a crouch with her back against the stone column, her TP9 held high. Carefully, she peered around the corner. Instantly the rock exploded under the impact of another ASP burst, scouring her left cheek with sharp bits of stone and grit. Only the hair screening the side of her face protected her eyes.

Easing down to one knee, Grant swiftly reached out around the column and kept the trigger of his subgun depressed, hosing down the area around the altar with a steady spray. Several rounds chopped fragments out of the edge of the crystal, and Enlil lifted his voice in a strident cry of warning, of anger. A Nephilim fired an ASP blast in his direction and he pulled back just as the bolt struck his shelter, dangerously close to his arm.

Coming out of his roll, Kane didn't hesitate to take advantage of the respite from the ASP barrage afforded him by Grant and Brigid Baptiste. Depressing the trigger stud of his Sin Eater, he emptied the entire magazine in a thundering drumroll and whine of ricochets. The Nephilim staggered and stumbled, colliding with one another.

When the firing pin of his handgun struck the empty chamber, Kane flexed his wrist tendons to retract the Sin Eater into the holster. At the same time he unclipped his Copperhead from beneath his coat. Bounding to his feet and placing the stock against his shoulder, he aligned Enlil's skull before the sights. The kill dot from the laser autotargeter shone like a pinpoint of blood against the dark gold scales on his forehead.

"Kane!"

The chord of recognition in the sharp voice so startled Kane, he didn't squeeze the subgun's trigger, but the edge of familiarity didn't warm his blood. He caught a shifting of shadows on the right side of the altar, and two figures emerged from behind it.

One was considerably taller than the other, his clawed hands tight around Balam's slender throat. Spur-tipped thumbs pricked the hinges of Balam's jaw. The crest of spines on the overlord's skull gleamed blue—a cobalt blue, as did his smart-metal armor. "Do you know me, Kane?"

Trying to suppress the tremor of fear and anger in his voice, Kane retorted, "I know who you used to be, Lord Baron Cobalt. But it's Marduk now, isn't it?"

A snarling laugh lurking at the back of his throat, he answered, "Marduk always, Kane. I just didn't realize it. I presume you know who I have here with me."

Balam's heavy-lidded eyes were half closed and his big head wobbled on his neck. Kane wondered if the overlords, several of whom had crept out from behind the altar, had abused him, or whether he suffered an aftereffect of psychically sharing Resurah's moment of death.

"What do you want us to do?" came Brigid's tense question into Kane's ear.

"Stay put for the time being," he whispered. "Wait and see what happens."

"What kind of strategy is that?" Grant demanded impatiently.

"A piss-poor one," Kane admitted. "But it's the only one I've got."

Enlil shouldered between two of the Nephilim, an unblinking gaze fixed on Kane, his eyes blazing with naked rage. In his right hand he held the tablets. In his left he gripped a multifaceted, fist-sized gem that throbbed with an eerie glow.

Marching over to Marduk, Enlil scowled down at

the groggy Balam. He spit a few words of incomprehensible Nibiruan, the tone of scorn unmistakable. Returning his hot aureate glare to Kane, he gestured to Balam and demanded, "He came to you, apprised you of how we had regained our true selves?"

"Him and your mom ratted you out," Kane replied, striving to sound confident and conversational, but still keeping the red pipper trained on Enlil's brow. "She thinks it's time for you to come home for dinner. She said you and your friends have played god long enough for one day."

To Kane's surprise, Enlil uttered a short laugh, but it held all the warmth of the hiss of a fer-de-lance. "My friends and I have several thousand years of playing god to make up for, Kane. You had best accustom yourself to the fact that there is a new order on Earth, an ancient empire reborn."

Kane snorted derisively. "All *nine* of you constitute an empire reborn? I guess that gives you lots of room for expansion."

Enlil bestowed a genial smile upon him. "All ten of us, actually. Or there soon will be ten…as you have reason to know."

Kane swallowed hard, but did not directly address the observation. "What about the pact with the Tuatha de Danaan? That was never rescinded or amended."

The overlords assembled around Enlil, flanked by the remaining Nephilim. "The Tuatha de Danaan?" Nergal echoed with mock incredulity. "I don't think any of the representatives are around to write up a violation of the treaty."

Probably not, Kane reflected sourly. As far as he

knew, the last of the Danaan lay buried under megatons of mile-high pyramid on Mars.

"The Danaan are gone," Enlil proclaimed. "Both of our races had peace forced upon us before we were ready for it. Afterward all we could do was dream of the past." He paused to take a breath, then shouted triumphantly, "We dream no more! We sleep no more! We have returned to claim, to conquer, to make what was ours once, ours again!"

Throwing back their crested heads, the overlords voiced an undulating howl so full of vicious, gloating victory that Kane felt his bowels loosen, his shoulders quaking in an involuntary shudder of loathing. Enlil smiled at him, eyes ablaze in his golden-scaled face.

While the echoes of the howl still chased themselves around the apex of the ceiling, Kane declared grimly, "And what do you think the rest of us will be doing while you try to remake Earth into Nibiru?"

Enlil tossed his head in arrogant dismissal. "As you should know by now, we place little value on humanity's actions or lack thereof, save as servants. If you oppose us, you will die swiftly. If you yield to us, you will live…at least as long as you prove useful. It is that simple."

"Actually," Kane stated coldly, "there's a tad more to it than that. Like—how many of you made-over monsters I can kill before I die swiftly."

Enlil shrugged. "If you feel that is something you should try to accomplish before you expire, by all means indulge yourself." He jerked his head toward Balam. "But of course he will die, too, as well as your friends who accompanied you here. And if you prevent me from uploading the Tablets of Destiny into Tiamat, every living thing on this planet will die, from the largest land mammal to the tiniest paramecium. You, your friends, Balam—all of us will precede them in death by only a few weeks."

Lilitu, attired in silver-blue armor, sidled up beside Enlil, her inhumanly beautiful face drawn in a troubled frown. She rested her head on his shoulder. "This is boring me, Enlil."

Grant's growl entered Kane's head, "Maybe I can amuse her with the point of my knife."

The corner of Kane's mouth quirked in a smile. "One of my friends would be glad to entertain you, Lady Lilitu…with his knife."

Toying idly with the mesh of scales on Enlil's chest, Lilitu said in a sibilant, almost coquettish croon, "By all means, let Mr. Grant try. For that matter, go ahead and shoot us all down if you think you can. Spare yourself a future battle that can only end in slaughter. Make the decision for all of humanity that extinction is preferable to our rule. Do as your heart tells you and we will all die. Do as your mind bids and you and your world will remain alive."

Kane met her gaze, sensing how a coldness of spirit radiated from her, from all of the overlords, like the dank breath from a glacial tomb. Slowly he lowered the Copperhead, letting it dangle at the end of his right arm. In a flat, dead voice, he intoned, "I'm used to ignoring what my heart tells me to do."

Enlil nodded graciously. "Which is why you have been a formidable enemy in the past, Kane. Clear reason guides your actions, and that I respect. One man or ten thousand, cannot arrest the tide that drives us forward."

Kane refused to respond to the comment. "Let Balam go."

Enlil shook his head. "He stays with us. You should understand why."

Kane snapped up the gun barrel. "I'm afraid I don't. He's not going with you."

Marduk removed his hands from Balam's neck and placed them on his narrow shoulders in a gesture Kane found unsettlingly paternal. "He is of no further use to you."

"Or to you," Kane shot back.

"Balam is of our blood," Zu announced stentoriously.

"And ours, too." Kane jammed the butt of the Copperhead against his hip. He ignored the imploring glance Balam cast toward him. "Let him go or we're back to where we started."

Enlil sighed in what sounded like genuine exasperation. "Kane, don't be a suicidal and ultimately genocidal fool."

"He stays." Kane bit out both words.

No.

Kane stiffened, but he didn't react to Balam's telepathic touch. *Kane, they have the advantage here. I am not a negotiation tool. They will not kill me. Do not fear, they will not sacrifice me in a needless fashion.*

Although he wanted to, Kane couldn't arrange his thoughts in a coherent enough way to question Balam, so he decided to trust him. Blowing out a resigned sigh, Kane lowered his Copperhead. "Take him, then."

Without another word, the Overlords and the surviving Nephilim marched across the tabernacle, Enlil herding Balam ahead of him like a recalcitrant child.

Stopping before the free-standing archway, Enlil passed the pulsing gem over its surface, uttering a guttural phrase as he did so.

The gem seemed to trace a glittering half circle of white fire that followed the lines of the archway. There was a low, soft thrumming sound like a plucked harp string. The crystalline shard of the Star Fire vibrated with the same semimusical note, and tiny lightnings played along its edges.

Within the frame of the threshold, variegated hues of color shifted and wavered. An image strobed, rippled, then coalesced. Beyond the portal lay the vista of a dark, twisting passageway. It was like looking through several feet of cloudy, disturbed water.

Before the overlords stepped through the arch, Enlil spoke to a green-armored Nephilim. Instantly he heeled around, extending both his arms upward. Buds of light burst from the ASP emitters and blazed upward.

Kane followed the bolts' flight with his eyes, watching first in confusion then alarm when the condensed proton blasts impacted against the cables suspending the sculpted effigy of Enlil. Smoke puffed and tongues of flame lapped up and down the length of the support cables. He heard several whiplike cracks right before the giant face plunged downward.

"Kane!" Brigid's scream of fear filled his head.

He was too busy diving for cover to respond. The chin of the face crashed onto the altar, striking the top edge of the Star Fire with a sound like a thousand glass panes shattering more or less simultaneously. Crystal and stone exploded with a cannonading, echoing boom! showering the tabernacle with a blizzard of razor-keen fragments and flinders of dried mud. An egg-sized chunk of rock fetched Kane a painful smack on the back of his head. The rolling echoes made a deafening, nerve-stinging cacophony.

Lying flat at the base of a pillar, Kane buried his face in his arms, protecting it from flying shards of crystal and sharp-edged stone. Even through his coat he felt his body being pelted. The shuddering crash of tumbling, rolling stone slowly faded, becoming a steady grind and grate. Carefully he raised his head and peered around.

A thick pall of dust filled the chamber, blotting out most of the light, coating Kane's tongue and stinging his eyes. Fanning the cloud away from his face, he staggered to his feet, dizzy from the blow to his head. The stone face, the altar and the crystal had joined to make a heap of settling rubble, burying the bodies of the two dead Nephilim. Splinters of the Star Fire glinted dully through the planes of pulverized grit.

Narrowing his watering eyes, he saw the last of the Nephilim disappear through the strange glowing portal. Beyond his armored form, he saw his brethren and the overlords standing in a dark, twisting corridor.

Brigid's faint whisper of "Come after us" entered his head.

Squinting through the streamers of dust, he glimpsed Brigid racing toward the archway, glowing brightly against the gloom. He cried out hoarsely, "Brigid—no!", stretching out an arm toward her. She bounded through the arch. Grant lurched from around a pillar, grabbing for her, a half second too late.

Even as he reached the portal, the glittering skein of fire flashed once and was gone. Grant plunged through the curving frame, rebounding from the stone wall of the tabernacle and staggering backward, uttering a bellow of frustrated fury.

Rubbing the lump swelling on the back of his head, Kane joined his partner at the empty archway. Both men walked around it, staring at it in baffled rage.

Clenching his teeth, then his fists, Grant growled, "That damn Star Fire crystal had something to do with powering this thing. Enlil destroyed it so we couldn't follow him."

Kane nodded grimly. "I know."

"What the *fuck* are we going to do now?" He snarled out the words.

Kane turned his head and spit out grit. "What Brigid said for us to do…go after her and Balam. I hope you remember how to work the interphaser."

Chapter 18

As Brigid raced toward the glowing arch, she cast one last glance behind her at the dust-thick tabernacle. She glimpsed the shadowy figure of Kane staggering erect and she whispered, "Come after us."

As she dived through the threshold, she thought she heard him cry out her name. Then he and the interior of the ziggurat vanished. Vertigo assailed her senses, as if she were tied to a giant centrifuge spinning so fast her mind didn't have time to record or measure the sensation. Her vision blurred and her stomach slipped sideways.

She was conscious of a split second of terrific, whirling speed, of a bone-numbing chill. Then she was on solid footing again, but her vision was blurred. She staggered drunkenly and would have fallen except for a pair of powerful hands closing around her upper arms. A cold arm encircled her neck from behind while a hand secured a painful grip around her right wrist. Another hand ripped away her pistol and holster with a crackle of Velcro.

She blinked her eyes repeatedly to clear them and saw that she stood in a wide, low-ceilinged corridor with the overlords and the Nephilim. The bulkhead and floor were featureless and gray, and the corridor curved off lazily to the right. At the end was a doorway, but the area beyond was cloaked in gloom.

Brigid strained briefly against the arms pinioning her, but the Nephilim tightened his grip on the high collar of her shadow suit, twisting it against her throat like a choke leash. She gagged, gasped briefly for air, stopped struggling and met Enlil's thoughtful stare with a challenging one of her own.

He strolled over to stare down at her, putting one hand on the dull metal arch of the threshold behind her. "Very courageous." He seemed genuinely impressed. "Very foolish."

Brigid felt Balam's stare on her, sensing it was full of reproach and even sadness. "I'm insatiably curious," she stated with a studied neutrality. "That sometimes makes me do very foolish things."

Enlil nodded as if sympathetic to a physical ailment she had just confessed to suffering from. "An inherent characteristic of humanity. I well remember how we tried to breed it out of you, but Enki claimed it was a function of the form."

At the mention of Enlil's half brother, whom she had seen vanish from his citadel on the moon, Brigid inhaled a sharp breath. Enlil noticed the reaction and he smiled. "The name means something to you?"

Brigid started to nod but the guard's hand tightened on her collar, making the motion painful. Enlil gestured to the Nephilim, and he relaxed his grip. "You will come with us."

"To where?" she asked.

Enlil heeled around and stalked down the passageway, his bare feet rasping on the floor plates like leather on glass. "To a place where even your insatiable curiosity may at last be satisfied…in a very final fashion. Besides, I find you charming."

Brigid's composed expression didn't alter. As an archivist in Cobaltville's Historical Division, she had spent years perfecting a poker face, hiding her feelings and innermost thoughts behind a pose of clinical, almost serene detachment. The overlords fell into step behind Enlil, flanked by the Nephilim, except for the one who kept a hand tight on Brigid's collar. She felt more in control now, despite playing the role of captive once again. The passage through the threshold hadn't been what she expected. The transit process wasn't as smooth as the interphaser, but it was far less stressful than traveling by the mat-trans units.

Balam dropped back to walk beside her. Softly yet severely he said, "You should not have come after me. I told Kane I was in no danger."

Her lips creased in a slight smile. "He failed to pass that on. But if it makes you feel any better, you were only part of the reason I jumped through the threshold."

"It does not."

"What does not what?"

"Make me feel any better. What was the main reason?"

She tried to shrug, but it wasn't easy with the hand grasping her collar. "I wanted to see Tiamat. It's not every day a human gets to crawl around inside of a creation goddess."

It was impossible for Balam's eyes to widen or for his face to express much emotion, but he conveyed a reaction of distinct discomfiture. Nergal cast an angry glare over his shoulder and hissed, "Silence. You blaspheme."

Brigid met his glare with an inoffensive stare. "You weren't this uptight when you answered to the name of Baron Sharpe."

"I was always Lord Nergal," he retorted a little sullenly. "Baron Sharpe was the masquerade."

"What about your high councilor, Crawler?" she pressed, referring to the crippled psi mutie who had served as Sharpe's confidante and adviser. "Does he know you were always Nergal—the god of the Sumerian underworld, of mass destruction and plague, consort of Ereshkigal? Before you abandoned him and your ville, did you tell poor Crawler how you were thrown out of heaven and then stormed the underworld with fourteen demons until Ereshkigal consented to marry you?"

She paused and allowed a slightly taunting smile to touch her lips. "Or if you want the demythologized version...out of all the Supreme Council, you lorded it over the worst, most infertile region. You tried to cozy up to Anu's daughter, Ereshkigal, so he would award you a more lucrative area, but your arrogance only angered the boss god and he banished you from your berth on Tiamat—heaven. So you threw a tantrum, killed a lot of native tribespeople and when Anu censured you for that, you staged a revolt. You held Ereshkigal hostage until Anu agreed to give you her hand in marriage...not to mention cut you in on a piece of the Nile Valley action. Of course that was such a long time ago, you might have forgotten some of the smaller details."

Nergal heeled around as if stung by an insect. Lips working, eyes hot with anger, he raised his right hand to strike Brigid. Balam slid between her and the overlord. He said nothing, made no gestures, but Nergal almost instantly turned away, a hissing growl humming in his throat. He quickened his pace, pushing past Lord Zu and a Nephilim.

"Thank you," Brigid said lowly to Balam. "I didn't know you had any kind of influence over them any longer."

"Very little," Balam admitted. "My influence with Nergal is familial, but of a very tenuous nature. The line of my father once served Nergal. We are related to the fourteen demons that you mentioned. However, you cannot rely on me to protect you from any of the others if you anger them, particularly Marduk or Lilitu. They still retain their personal baronial animosities toward you. It was your choice to come here—they did not force you."

Brigid tried to nod, but the Nephilim cinched her collar tight and she contented herself with murmuring, "So noted."

She allowed the guard to push her along the dimly lit hall. The air, though a bit cold and stale, was rich enough in oxygen that she didn't have to strain to breathe it. The gravity felt close to Earth normal, as well, perhaps slightly above. The narrow corridors she walked reminded her of passageways in ancient tombs, not those in a spaceship. The weight of centuries hung as palpable as dust. She received the same kind of shuddery impression as if she walked through a haunted castle.

As she walked, Brigid wondered about the impulse that had driven her to leap through the threshold. Curiosity had been part of her motivation to be sure, worry about Balam another, as well as the tactical need to learn as much as possible about the plans of the overlords. Regardless, such spur-of-the-moment actions weren't characteristic of her. They were more akin to Kane's reckless seat-of-the-pants strategies. She smiled wryly at the notion.

When she and Kane were first thrown together, their relationship had been volatile, marked by frequent quarrels, jealousies and resentments. The world in which she came of age was primarily quiet, focused on scholarly pursuits. Kane's was a world wherein he became accustomed to daily violence, supported by a belief system that demanded a ruthless single-mindedness to enforce baronial authority. Despite their differences, or perhaps because of them, the two people managed to forge the chains of partnership, linking them together through mutual respect and trust.

Only once had the links of that chain been stretched to a breaking point. Over a year before Kane had shot and killed a woman, a distant relative of Brigid's, whom he perceived as a threat to her life. It took her some time to realize that under the confusing circumstances, Kane had no choice but to make a snap judgment call. Making split-second, life-and-death decisions was part of his conditioning, his training in the Magistrate Division, as deeply ingrained as breathing.

What conflicted her during that time was not the slow process of forgiving him, but coming to terms with what he really was and accepting the reality rather than an illusion. Although his attitudes and perspectives had broadened since arriving at Cerberus, he was still primarily a soldier, not an explorer, not an academic, not an intellectual.

But the two people had long ago achieved a synthesis of attitudes and styles where they functioned as colleagues and teammates, extending to the other professional courtesies and respect. She also retained her utmost confidence and reliance in not only him but also Grant. She knew with an unshakable certainty that the two men would most definitely honor her request to come after her and Balam. She just hoped it would be soon, even though she had a tight grip on the fear swirling within her.

Over the past two years, Brigid had come to accept to risk as part of her chosen way of life, taking chances so that others might find the ground beneath their feet a little more secure. She didn't consider her attitude idealism but simple pragmatism, even though Kane might vociferously disagree with her.

There seemed to be little but shadows behind or ahead of them, but Brigid heard faint sounds and even felt rhythmic vibrations transmitted through the hull. The sounds hinted at operating machinery—or the metabolic processes of a giant living creature. Overhead were rows of the luminescent panels, the charges of most them long since depleted.

There were doors on either side of the corridor. Most of them were closed, but a few hung ajar and revealed rooms of varying sizes, crammed to capacity with artifacts and relics. The curiosity to break away from the procession and examine the items was almost unendurable. She realized the Annunaki had to have looted Nibiru, as well as their dead cities on Earth, before abandoning humankind.

She glimpsed art objects, statuary, tapestries, jewelry, musical instruments, pots, machines, scrolls and even toys—anything of Annunaki cultural influence had been hidden away in the belly of Tiamat. The history, the science, the art of a long vanished civilization survived in the vaults of the giant ship. They passed occasional wells with ladders stretching out of them and leading up through apertures in the ceiling.

Abruptly, the group came to a T-junction and turned down the left-hand corridor. The farther they progressed, the louder became the mechanical sounds and unidentifiable but disturbing noises—thumping, liquid gurgling, creaking and a faint but familiar drone. They walked past vents and what Brigid guessed to be utility boxes affixed to the bulkheads, some of them marked with unfamiliar cuneiform symbols—unfamiliar only to her, she corrected herself sourly.

Narrow trickles of liquid flowed through transparent conduits running the lengths of the walls. Some of them leaked, coating the deck below with a slick layer of grayish-green sludge. Somehow she knew the fluid was not water, and she repressed a shudder.

Mystified, Brigid couldn't help but ask Balam, "What is that stuff? A lubricant or coolant or something?"

Matter-of-factly, he answered, "Its composition would correspond more closely with hemoglobin."

"Hemoglobin?" she echoed. "The main constituent of red blood cells?"

Balam nodded, but didn't elaborate. Brigid had no reason to doubt his terse description. If Tiamat was indeed a blending of organic and inorganic materials, the ship would require some type of a circulatory system. Still, she really had no solid idea of the kind of biotechnology at work, or if a method of employing artificial intelligence had been perfected by the Annunaki. Although the wiring of the human brain and a computer shared many similarities, the crucial difference lay in the ability to learn new behaviors.

The factors that caused a neuron in the human brain to fire or not fire at its axon were much more complex that the simple binary combinations of a computer. A neuron learned to fire according to the patterns of its thousands of synapses. The ability to learn was controlled by a dominant, master synapse and as far as she knew, that ability had only been imitated by computer intelligences.

After marching along what seemed like miles of corridors and spending by her estimation two hours crossing one dark gallery after another, they approached a passageway that widened into another intersection. It became a circular catwalk surrounding a ten-foot-wide shaft. A staircase spiraled upward into murk. Far above glowed an oval of yellow light. Without hesitation, the overlords, Balam and the Nephilim began scaling it.

"The mighty chaosmother Tiamat doesn't have working elevators?" Brigid murmured with an edge of sarcasm in her voice.

Not surprisingly, her question wasn't answered.

As the staircase corkscrewed upward, they passed landings that led off to other passages. They kept climbing, over risers where the stairs were wet with the white slime. Liquid dripped down from an unseen source.

The stairs continued twisting up to meet another intersection, but Enlil pointed them upward again. Brigid's knees began to ache. The light grew brighter the higher they climbed, and finally they stepped onto a railed gallery. As they moved away from the stairway shaft, they walked into a courtyard—at least that was the first description that came to Brigid's mind. She froze, staring in wonder, feeling suddenly tiny and almost insignificant.

Above, looming tier by tier, rose a massive metal edifice gleaming brightly under the glare of banks of ceiling lights, blazing like miniature but incandescent suns. A forest of black support pylons soared all around the base of it, and from within each one came a gurgling, liquid sound as of running water. The chamber was enormous, holding bank after bank, chassis after chassis of computer stations, viewscreens and instrument panels.

The high-tech furnishings contrasted sharply with anachronistic tripod-supported braziers, colorful tapestries and bas-relief carvings on the walls. They depicted sharp cameos of man-shaped figures engaged in mysterious activities. She had seen similar carvings before, in the Annunaki catacombs deep beneath the Moon. Covering the far bulkheads was a pair of side-by-side rectangular crystal-fronted screens, stretching from the deck halfway to the ceiling.

"This is the control nexus of Tiamat," Balam told Brigid quietly. "What you would call the main bridge—" he nodded toward the multitiered metal structure "—or her cerebral cortex."

She felt as if she stood before a temple, a smaller version of the Ekur ziggurat, but one wrought in plates made of some dully gleaming alloy. As if from a great distance, she heard a rhythmic, familiar drone. Following the sound with her eyes, she saw what she expected—enclosed within slabs of transparent armaglass stood a fusion generator, only this one was twice the size of the versions she had seen before. More than twenty feet tall, it resembled two solid black cubes, a slightly smaller one balanced atop the other. The top cube rotated slowly, producing the steady drone.

Brigid had seen generators of that type before in various and unlikely places around the world. Lakesh had put forth the initial speculation they were fusion reactors, the energy output held in a delicately balanced magnetic matrix within the cubes. When the matrix was breached, an explosion of apocalyptic proportions resulted, which was what caused the destruction of the Archuleta Mesa installation.

Massive wedge-shaped ribs of metal supported the roof and curving walls of the bridge. The huge arching girders bore cuneiform markings and hieroglyphs, arranged in neat, compact vertical rows. She had seen identical symbols before, as well as a very similar layout, but on a smaller scale.

Years before she had explored a crashed spaceship, buried deep beneath the ancient city of Kharo-Khoto in Mongolia. She had always assumed the vessel had been built by the Archons because of the mummified corpse of one she found lying within a dysfunctional stasis unit. Now she realized the ship had been of Annunaki design and manufacture, perhaps a scout ship dispatched by Tiamat herself and appropriated by Balam's people.

Like the interior of the ship beneath the Black Gobi, the lines of the vast bridge were deceptively simple, but when she tried to follow the curves and angles, she found her head swimming and her eyes stinging. There was a quality to the architecture that eluded the human mind, as though it had been designed on geometric principles just slightly at a tangent from the brain's capacity to absorb it.

A horseshoe-curved console faced the pair of screens. From the center of the inside curve rose a high-backed chair. Ornately sculpted and glittering with all variety of precious gems, she knew it was more of a throne than a command chair. Directly above it hung a solid gold disk six feet in diameter, embossed on one side with the bas-relief image of a winged dragon. The obverse bore the likeness of a beautiful, majestic woman, yet she exuded a matronly air. The images were stylized representations of the two aspects of Tiamat, the destroyer and the mother goddess.

The overlords followed Enlil to the console, arranging themselves in a crescent formation just outside the curve. When Brigid made a move to follow them, her guard jerked her to a very ungentle stop. She gritted her teeth on a cry of anger and pain. With Balam standing beside her and bracketed by two pairs of Nephilim, she watched Enlil stroll to the throne and lift up its cushioned seat. From a recessed square, he removed several boxes.

A gold-armored Nephilim stepped inside the console, opening the boxes and taking items of clothing and jewelry from it. He attached a glittering collar of beaten gold around the base of Enlil's neck, draped a floor-length brocaded tabard of purple satin and silver embroidery over his broad shoulders, and wrapped his waist with a white kilt worked in gold thread.

Enlil extended his arms and hands and the Nephilim

adorned his fingers and wrists with jeweled rings and heavy bracelets. Dropping to his knees, the attendant laced up a pair of sandals attached to shin guards inscribed with cuneiform symbols.

The assembled overlords watched the procedure silently. Brigid realized the air of ceremony, of pomp and circumstance, wasn't accidental or contrived. The donning of royal raiment was part of an ancient ritual. The kings were returning to their kingdoms....

The Nephilim rose and reached into the hollow seat of the throne again. Reverently, holding it in both hands, he brought forth a headdress, a crown. He handed it to Enlil, who swept everyone present with an unblinking stare of awesome haughty challenge, as if daring any of the overlords to speak or object.

When none did, he slowly and majestically placed the tall, flat-topped crown upon his head. It gleamed brightly, inlaid with jewels, ingots of silver, gold and even platinum. The forepiece depicted a serpent writhing upward, a pair of batlike wings outspread from the scaled body.

No cheers or accolades were offered by the overlords, only a quiet, almost resigned attitude of accepting the inevitable. They gazed at Enlil expectantly, silently.

Taking the Tablets of Destiny in hand once more as he had in the ziggurat, Enlil moved the glowing beads of light on each one with a fingertip until a semimusical note sounded. He spoke a name—Shamash—and handed the tablet to the appropriate overlord.

Enlil repeated the process with each glassine square, and each tablet emitted a slightly different note. After he had attuned and handed over all the tablets—save for one—the overlords moved in a single file to small metal-walled box at the far end of the curving console.

One by one they inserted the tablets into an input port atop it. As each of the squares slid into the slot, the eyes of the dragon image of Tiamat hanging over the throne flashed, glowing progressively brighter. The entire disk slowly exuded a borealis-like shimmer around its rim.

Brigid could only speculate that as the Tablets of Destiny were loaded into a CPU, they were scanned, verified, accepted and absorbed into Tiamat's neural networks.

A stuttering sound, like the dots and dashes of Morse code amplified a hundredfold, suddenly thundered throughout the vast bridge. They were so loud Brigid winced and covered her ears with both hands. She could feel corresponding vibrations in her bones. Ribbons of multicolored light streaked across consoles, like tiny self-contained rainbows. All the indicator lights on the instrument boards flashed to life. Fires suddenly blazed up in the braziers, and the huge room filled with the cloying odor of incense. As the thunder of the code subsided, the suspended disk depicting Tiamat emitted a thin, high-pitched signal. It lasted only a moment.

When the signal ended, Enlil sat on the throne with a measured deliberation. Although his face remained a mask of indifference, his attitude was one of smug satisfaction, of finally reaching a long-sought-after goal. Propping his elbows on the armrests, beringed fingers steepled at his chin, he spoke a few words of terse Nibiruan.

Round apertures opened in the deck within the curve

of the control console. Smaller versions of his chair rose from them. The overlords all took seats, the arrangement in accordance to some ancient tradition. One chair remained empty.

The two giant screens on the far bulkhead flickered simultaneously, images wavering across them. Within seconds they sharpened to display twin slice-views of Earth, the blue-green orb dominating most of the image area. Only narrow, arching span of starfields were visible above the globes.

Brigid assumed the location of the viewscreens formed the exterior "eyes" of the ship's dragon prow. Although she experienced a keen sense of fascination, of being utterly enthralled by the very concept of a living ship, fear and confusion steadily gnawed away at her emotional equilibrium.

As quietly as she could, not wanting to alarm the Nephilim guard, she asked, "Balam—can you tell me what's going on?"

"I thought that would be obvious," Balam replied just as quietly, but with a hint of bitterness to his voice. "What I had enlisted your aid to prevent from coming to pass is 'going on.' The overlords, all of the Annunaki for that matter, are genetically connected to Tiamat. The tablets are rebooting Tiamat's parallel processors. All of her major systems and subroutines are even now restoring her to full power. Once the data banks are back online, Enlil will have unrestricted access to the minds, the knowledge of the entire Annunaki pantheon."

Startled, Brigid demanded, "How? They're dead!"

Balam's calm reply chilled her blood. "Only their bodies."

The memory of the mausoleum of the Annunaki she, Grant and Kane had entered beneath the Moon's surface leaped to the forefront of her mind. She had no problem remembering how the creatures looked like hideous travesties of humanity. They were taller than Grant, leaner by far than Kane, and she had passed between double rows of the lizard-things propped upright on thrones, their bowed, powerful legs tucked beneath them. The three of them had stared wide-eyed, stunned, shocked, awed and in her case— terrified.

The Serpent Kings had been buried royally, each one carefully embalmed and positioned upright on a funerary throne, wearing all the trappings of the godhood they had assumed upon Earth. The beautifully polished stone of the ceilings and walls had been carved in reliefs showing events in the lives of the various Annunaki who sat stiffly all down the length of the great hall.

Brigid had easily imagined carpets on the cold floor and a great deal of ornate furnishings. But all of that ancient splendor was long gone. The excavations of the human explorers from the Manitius base had caved in the rock-cut chambers, and the explorers themselves had taken all the funeral finery. Only the thrones and the Serpent Kings remained, shriveled corpses staring into nothingness.

Balam's voice brought her out of her reverie. "When their biological functions ceased, their mind energy was converted to digital information and stored within Tiamat's database."

Brigid felt a cold fist of dread knot in her belly. "Not too long ago on the Moon, I saw Enki assume a noncorporeal form and seem to be drawn into another state of existence—or dimension."

Balam inclined his head slightly. "His physical form was converted into energy, and the electromagnetic pattern that constituted his mind was removed from the organic, synaptic structure of the brain and transmitted to Tiamat's database."

Mentally replaying what she and Brewster Philboyd had witnessed that night in Enki's Lunar citadel, Brigid realized Balam's abridged version fit the facts as they saw them. From a transmission tower, a tiny spark of energy had leaped onto Enki's head and spread over his body like a cocoon of wildfire. She easily recollected how she sensed the approach of other presences, other minds, grave and powerful but stricken with sorrow.

Enki spoke to those other presences. Brigid couldn't understand his words, but she recognized he asked for forgiveness—and a desperate plea to join them. The glowing witchfire covering Enki's body was suddenly drawn toward the shaft, as if it were a sponge absorbing the energies. It leaped back to the metal, and Enki seemed to go with it. One instant he was there, and in the next the last of the living Serpent Kings, the Dragon Lords, was gone.

Now it all made sense, but Brigid took no comfort in the resolution of a mystery. Enki, like all the other Annunaki, had joined with Tiamat and now they were but bytes and bits of disembodied, digitized information, either awaiting access or rebirth into a new organic body.

"Are those minds conscious?" Brigid wanted to know.

"Specify."

"Are they aware of what has happened to them, where they are? For example, if I wished to communicate only with Enki's mind-energy would I be able to do it? Would he remember me?"

Balam made one of his negligent hand gestures. "I have no way of knowing. I can only speculate that Tiamat has yet to activate the neural network that contains their mental imprints. She has other concerns at the moment."

"Like what?" Brigid asked.

"Locating all of the Nephilim on Earth," Balam answered bleakly. "Once they have been found, they will be outfitted and assigned an overlord to serve."

"How many are there?"

"I could not say. Perhaps no more than two hundred. But the overlords will not tarry in recruiting others."

"That doesn't seem likely," she commented dubiously. "Even if the genetic engineering section of Dreamland was up and running at full capacity, they can't create an entire army overnight."

Balam glanced up at her, sorrow seeming to shine in his eyes. "They will not need to. The Magistrates of the different villes will still need a baron to serve, will they not? And do not forget that Tiamat is revered as the mother goddess of the Annunaki. "

Brigid began to ask for clarification, but Enlil's sharp, commanding voice drew her attention. He leaned forward intently in his chair, stabbing a finger at the monitor screens. At first she saw nothing but the partial views of Earth. Then she glimpsed two specks flickering at the uppermost edge of the screens, only slightly larger than the stars. All of the overlords shifted position to stare and mutter among themselves in their own language.

Brigid couldn't completely suppress a chuckle, which spurred Balam to voice a mutter himself, "Something amuses you, Brigid Baptiste?"

Not taking her eyes off the screen, she said softly, "I forgot you owned up to not being omnipotent."

"How is that salient?" he asked peevishly.

"I guess no one briefed you about the recent additions to Cerberus ordnance."

"Which are?" His tone was testy, almost petulant.

Brigid gestured toward the screens. "You have eyes, Balam. Very big ones, in fact. See for yourself."

Chapter 19

Kane stared at the blazing starfields all around him, as if he could somehow find with the unaided eye in all the velvet-dark immensity the one gleaming speck that was Tiamat. He knew the Transatmospheric Vehicle's on-board sensors would detect the ship long before his eyes.

The two TAVs he and Grant piloted held the general shape and configuration of seagoing manta rays, and as such they were little more than flattened wedges with wings. They were sheathed in bronze-hued metal, and intricate geometric designs covered almost the entire exterior surface. Deeply inscribed into the hull were interlocking swirling glyphs, cup-and-spiral symbols and even elaborate cuneiform markings. The composition of the hull, although it appeared to be of a burnished bronze alloy, was a material far tougher and more resilient.

The craft had no any external apparatus at all, no ailerons, no fins and no airfoils. The cockpits were almost invisible, little more than elongated symmetrical oval humps in the exact center of the sleek topside fuselages. The Manta's wingspans measured out to twenty years from tip to tip and the fuselage was around fifteen feet long.

Inside the cockpit, Kane wore his shadow suit and a bronze-colored helmet with a full-face visor. The helmet itself attached to the headrest of the pilot's chair. A pair of tubes stretched from the rear to an oxygen tank at the back of the ejection seat. The helmet and chair were of one piece, a self-contained unit.

The instrument panel was almost comical in its simplicity. The controls consisted primarily of a joystick, altimeter and fuel gauges. All the labeling was in English, squares of paper glued to the appropriate controls. But the interior curve of the helmet's visor swarmed with CGI icons of sensor scopes, range finders and various indicators.

Of Annunaki manufacture, the Mantas were in pristine condition, despite their great age. Powered by two different kinds of engines, a ramjet and solid-fuel pulse detonation air spikes, the Manta ships could fly in both a vacuum and in an atmosphere. The Manta transatmospheric plane wasn't an experimental craft, but an example of a technology that was mastered by a race when humanity still cowered in trees from saber-toothed tigers. Metallurgical analysis had suggested that the ships were a minimum of ten thousand years old.

Grant and Kane had easily learned to pilot the craft in the atmosphere, since they handled superficially like the Deathbirds the two men had flown when they were Cobaltville Magistrates. But when they first flew two of the TAVs down from the Moon where they had been found, there came the unsettling realization that the ships couldn't be piloted like winged aircraft while in space.

A pilot could select velocity, angle, attitude and other complex factors dictated by standard avionics, but space flight relied on a completely different set of principles. It called for the maximum manipulation of gravity, tra-

jectory, relative velocities and plain old luck. Despite all
the computer-calculated course programming, both men
learned quickly that successfully piloting the TAV
through space was more by God than by grace. The
technique for intercepting another space-based object
had yet to be tested by either of them, even in simula-
tion. So far, the Mantas had proved to be trustworthy in
all maneuvers.

He still felt a slight sense of surprise by how quickly
he, Grant, Philboyd and a couple of other Manitius techs
were able to prep the Mantas and get them airborne. He
and Grant had returned to Cerberus a little over two
hours before. As both men had hoped—and secretly
prayed—the interphaser reactivated the same vortex
node through which they had traveled. They rematerated-
alized safely in the redoubt's gateway unit.

They didn't spend much time briefing Lakesh or
even answering the barrage of questions put to them
by Philboyd and Bry as to the whereabouts of Brigid
and Balam.

To Grant's combined relief and upset, Shizuka and
her samurai had elected to remain at Cerberus until they
returned from Iraq. Her first flush of happiness upon
seeing him whole and unharmed dissolved into worry
when he told her what he and Kane had planned with
the Mantas.

Actually, to call it a plan was to be charitable—flying
the TAVs to intercept Tiamat was the only available option. Over the past couple of weeks all four of the Mantas
remaining on the Moon base had been brought down. Unlike a recent mission, there was no discord between Kane
and Grant about who would fly and who stayed dirtside.

Philboyd lodged a few objections about being grounded since he considered himself an accomplished pilot of the craft. But he dropped the argument when Kane reminded him that when he went on missions he usually made a better prisoner than a fighter. The astrophysicist knew he really couldn't refute those statements and graciously volunteered to make sure both ships were flight-ready.

Reba DeFore, on the other hand, was grim and resentful when Kane stopped by the infirmary to check on Quavell. Her condition was grave. She had lapsed into unconsciousness, despite the contractions. The medic's prognosis about the health of the child was no less pessimistic, even with Domi standing by to perform midwife duties. Leaving the redoubt again was almost a relief, despite the anxiety and discomfort of the launch.

The g-forces built steadily as the TAVs accelerated, reaching escape velocity by degrees. When the HUDs registered 100 percent power on the ramjets, the g-forces slammed Grant and Kane into their chairs and kept them there all through the bumpy, teeth-rattling ride through the atmospheric layers.

As the Mantas broke through the exosphere and jetted free of Earth's gravity well, Kane glanced around at the vast wilderness of stars ahead of him—remote, diamond bright and beautiful. For an instant he was almost overwhelmed by the desire to kick in the Manta's pulse detonation engines and fly among their splendor, giving vent to an eagle scream of defiant freedom, leaving behind all of his responsibilities on Earth.

Instead, he glanced over at Grant's Manta, some one hundred years off his starboard wing. He took care not to turn his helmet directly toward Sol. The visor was designed to react to its radiation, instantly polarizing to filter out the dangerous glare. But the process required a couple of seconds and he didn't want to risk impairing his vision as he flew wing to wing with Grant. The slightest variation in course could cause a collision before he could make a correction.

The two men input the coordinates of the last recorded position of Tiamat into the navigational computers and sat back, trying to relax, but knowing they couldn't. Although Kane wasn't surprised that Grant had unquestioningly accompanied him on the space flight, he was grateful nonetheless, particularly since he knew the man's choice might cause friction between him and Shizuka.

Unlike him, Grant hadn't freely chosen the life of an exile, an insurrectionist. He had sacrificed everything that gave his life a degree of purpose to help Kane and Brigid escape from Cobaltville. Even after all the time that had elapsed since that day, now feeling like a very long time ago, Kane still felt responsible for what the man had given up and what he had suffered since then in the war against the hybrid barons.

But old habits died very hard. Kane and Grant had been partners for nearly fifteen years, and it was part and parcel of Magistrate Division conditioning to always back a partner's play.

The Magistrate Divisions of the villes were formed as a complex police machine that demanded instant obedience to its edicts and to which there was no possible protest. Magistrates were a highly conservative, duty-bound group. The customs of enforcing the law and obeying orders were ingrained almost from birth.

The Magistrates submitted themselves to a grim and unyielding discipline because they believed it was necessary to reverse the floodtide of chaos and restore order to postholocaust America. As Magistrates, the courses their lives followed had been charted before their births. They had exchanged personal hopes, dreams and desires for a life of service. They were destined to live, fight and die, usually violently.

All Magistrates followed a patrilineal tradition, assuming the duties and positions of their fathers. They didn't have given names, rather, each took the surname of the father, as though the first Magistrate to bear the name were the same man as the last.

The originators of the Magistrate Divisions had believed that only surnames, family names, engendered a sense of obligation to the duties of their ancestors' office, insuring that subsequent generations never lost touch with their hereditary roles as enforcers. Last names became badges of social distinction, almost titles.

Over the past ninety years, both the oligarchy of barons and the Mags that served them had taken on a fearful, almost legendary aspect. For most of their adult lives, both Kane and Grant had been part of that legend, cogs in a merciless machine. They had been through the dehumanizing cruelty of Magistrate training yet had somehow, almost miraculously, managed to retain their humanity.

When faced with the choice of bleak acceptance of the reality in which humans were little more than chattel, living on the sufferance of the barons or a faint chance of salvaging humanity's future, they chose the faint chance.

Kane, Brigid, Grant and the Cerberus exiles declared war on the dark forces devoted to maintaining the yoke of slavery around the collective necks of humankind. It was a struggle not just for the physical survival of humanity, but for the human spirit, the soul of an entire race.

Over the past two years, they scored many victories, defeated many enemies and solved mysteries of the past that molded the present and affected the future. More importantly, they began to rekindle of the spark of hope within the breasts of the disenfranchised fighting to survive in the Outlands.

Victory, if not within their grasp, at least had no longer seemed an unattainable dream. But with the transformation of the barons into the overlords, Kane wondered if the war was now over—or if it had ever actually been waged at all. He was beginning to suspect that everything he and his friends had experienced and endured so far had only been minor skirmishes, a mere prologue to the true conflict.

"Won't be long now," Grant said casually over the intraship com link. "We ought to spot the damn thing any minute."

"Even if it's not long," Kane replied, striving to sound just as casual, "have you thought about what we're going to do once we see it?"

After a long moment, Grant admitted, "I've thought about it. That's about as far as it went. You?"

"The same." He paused, took a breath and said, "There might not be anything we *can* do…except…" His words trailed off.

"Except what?" Grant's flat tone indicated he knew exactly to what course of action Kane alluded.

"If we can't get aboard the ship, then we may have no choice but to destroy it. And we may not be able to do that unless we're willing to go out with it."

Grant didn't reply for a long, stretched-out tick of time. When he did, he said quietly, "I thought the same thing, to tell you the truth."

Kane gusted out a sigh. "Well, in that case—"

His ears suddenly started buzzing, and he jumped in his seat and swore. It required a second for him to recognize the sound as the radar lock-on warning, piped from the Manta's forward sensor array into his helmet. "I've got a hit."

"Roger that," Grant replied crisply. "Make the course adjustments."

"Complying." Kane did so and began scanning ahead. The HUD showed him a dark spot in the center of a CGI grid, nearly invisible. The spot glowed red with internally radiated heat. The spot was thirty miles off the Manta's portside bow. He and Grant remained silent as their TAVs approached at 200 mph, almost as if they were afraid that by talking they would scare off their quarry.

When the two men received their first look at Tiamat, they realized there was little or no chance of that happening.

Tiamat was massive, thick and broad and long. Illuminated by the Sun, she had the solidity of a battleship covered in thick, dark armor, scarred and pocked here and there from battles dimmed by time. All of the moisture in Grant's mouth dried up as he stared at the sleek lines of a vessel that had sailed the spaceways before Earth's continents had settled into their final forms.

Kane gazed in unblinking awe at Tiamat through his Manta's canopy. Even bathed in bright sunlight, the dark hull remained shadowy and dim. The ship was so vast that he felt like a dragonfly approaching a giant crocodile sunning itself on the bank of a river. The prow, fashioned to suggest a ferocious dragon's head, as well as the overlapping plates of armor, awakened an almost superstitious dread within him. He couldn't recall the last time his heart had pounded so hard and fast within his chest. Mustering all his self-control, he began paying attention to the numbers and symbols scrolling across the inner curve of his helmet's visor.

The sensors reported that Tiamat measured out to be one mile long and was just under one mile broad at its widest point, its mass was two million metric tons. Its orbit was still geosynchronous, twelve hundred miles above the Xian pyramid, give or take a few feet.

"Grant," he said as calmly as he could, "you still with me?"

"Where else would I be?" came the annoyed reply.

"It's a goddamn big ship," Kane pointed out unnecessarily.

"It's a *triple*-goddamn big ship," Grant agreed. "But it's still just a ship, not a real dragon. Let's see if we can find a way in."

Kane and Grant made several passes at a distance of a few miles before engaging intercept maneuvers, using only the station-keeping thrusters. They alternated the burn times of their port and starboard steering jets to ease up from beneath Tiamat. The Mantas onboard computers could have probably carried out the operation, but both Grant and Kane preferred to control their vessels themselves. As experienced pilots, both of them knew on an intuitive level that in case of a sudden crisis they would rather rely on their own reflexes than those of a machine.

The Mantas edged cautiously toward the gargantuan ship. Even at a range of two hundred yards, the dragon-shaped vessel completely filled their visors and kept expanding as they approached. They throttled back the thrusters, reducing the burn time to half a second.

"Think they know we're here?" Kane inquired softly, unconsciously lowering his voice.

"Yes," Grant intoned. "Yes, I do. And I also think if they wanted to blow us out of space, there's not a damn thing we could do about it."

"Fatalistic no matter the weather," Kane murmured. "That's why you're so much fun to hang with."

The two Mantas continued to drift alongside Tiamat at a distance of twenty yards, studying the details of the hull. Starboard-side aft they saw a wide hexagon inset deeply into the hull of the vessel, like a steel-rimmed well. It was about sixty yards in diameter, large enough to accommodate both Mantas at the same time. It was sealed by a black, reflective material that at first glance was glass, but was completely opaque.

"Air lock," Grant announced confidently. "Or a hangar entry port."

"You hope," Kane countered. "It could be the septic tank. But even if it's not, how do you figure to get it open? Missiles?"

"Maybe," Grant answered doubtfully. "Maybe if we look closer we can find some sort of controls or—"

On the outer rim of the hexagon, two lights flashed

green. The black glass portal split down the center and the two halves slid smoothly into a pair of recessed slots. There were no puffs of escaping frozen atmosphere, which both men knew meant the interior had been depressurized.

"Or," Kane finished in a bland tone, "somebody might decide to open the door for us."

Chapter 20

Kane eyed the HUD flashing sensor icons and inter-preted the symbols and scrolling digits to mean no atmosphere or biosigns awaited them in the hangar. Nor were there lights. It was totally black within. The land-ing spots from the TAVs pierced the darkness with rods of brilliance, but they still couldn't see much.

"Do you think we tripped an automatic sensor?" Grant ventured. "One that opened up the hangar for us when it recognized some kind of signature of these ships?"

Kane considered the likelihood for a few seconds, then answered, "It's possible, but that doesn't really track. I think it's more probable that they just opened the door so we couldn't make any mischief outside and maybe damage Tiamat."

Grant sighed. "That's what I thought you'd say."

"You did? Why?"

"Because that's what I would've said if you'd asked me the same question."

Once within the hangar bay, Grant and Kane turned the Mantas, revolving them so the bows faced the hex-agonal opening. Engaging the vectored vertical landing jets, they dropped their ships straight down to the deck and gracefully brought them to rest on the extended tri-pod landing gear.

They cut the engines and almost immediately the sections of the bay door slid shut, joining with a nearly imperceptible seam down the middle. The two men sat in the cockpits, eyeing the HUD readouts fed from the external scanners. Within moments they began registering an influx of oxygen, nitrogen and a mixture of trace elements. Simultaneously, their bodies experienced a sensation of being draped in layer after layer of heavy fabric. According to the HUD, a gravity of 1.2 g's spread across the hangar interior.

"Somebody's making it comfortable for us," Kane commented.

Grant grunted skeptically. "Tolerable, maybe. I wouldn't count on comfortable."

Carefully, the two men opened the seals of their helmets, pushed them off and unlatched the cockpit canopies. Sliding them back, they climbed out on the wings of the TAVs and dropped down to the hangar deck.

Grant and Kane carried their reliable Sin Eaters strapped around their forearms, and their war-bags were full of assorted odds and ends, some brought along due to their maximum destructive capabilities and others that served altogether different functions. They were experienced enough to know they couldn't plan for all contingencies.

Despite the thermal-control circuitry in their shadow suits, the temperature felt uncomfortably low, below freezing. The air smelled stale and even a little musty. Kane swept the gloom with a wide-angle flash beam taken from his war bag. It illuminated only their immediate area—they saw no walls and certainly no doors.

Activating his Commtact, Kane called Brigid, but

received nothing but a hash of static. He guessed that an energy field exuded by Tiamat interfered with the carrier wave—at least, he hoped that was the explanation. He refused to consider any other possibility.

Kane had yet to devote much thought to why Brigid had gone leaping through the threshold. Presumably her reasons stemmed from a genuine concern for Balam's safety, not to mention an abhorrence of allowing the overlords to put their plans into motion without knowing what they were. However, he knew curiosity played just as large a role in her motives. He tried to convince himself that even had she not done what she did, the strategy he and Grant embarked upon would still be the same.

Touching his Commtact, Grant whispered, "I just tried raising Brigid—"

Kane's ears caught a faint clicking, and he hushed Grant into silence. They listened intently as the clicking was repeated. The sound was definitely mechanical in nature, like switches being thrown. On the ceiling at least fifty feet above them, crescent-shaped light fixtures flickered, then shed a wavery, watery illumination.

Kane and Grant blinked up at them, as in a staggered sequence, lights flashed on along the length of the hangar's ceiling. The dim, suffuse illumination produced by the crescents wasn't bright enough to dazzle them, but they could at least see what lay ahead of them and to either side.

The view was unimpressive—a long expanse of featureless bulkhead and deck made of smooth, dull gray alloy. The ceiling lights led to a set of double doors at least one hundred yards away. Kane switched off the flashlight as he and Grant began walking, their boot heels ringing dull chimes from the floor plates.

They walked past a wide railed gallery that overlooked a big, hollow chamber. Looking through a transparent ob port, they saw nestled inside cradles of massive clamps dozens of disk-shaped objects, perhaps twenty feet in diameter. They had a silvery, metallic appearance, as bright as a newly minted coin. The alloyed skins were perfectly smooth and seamless, with no surface protuberances of any kind.

Arranged in three orderly rows, the disks led to a great empty space, as if a much larger object had once occupied the area. Beyond it they saw stars, glittering through a hexagonal opening in the vessel's hull. It was some eighty or ninety yards across. Four metal tracks in the center of the floor ran straight to the portal. The metal edges of the hull were bent outward, as if a very large and exceptionally heavy object had crashed its way out of the hangar.

Contemplatively, Kane asked, "Remember that spaceship we found buried in Mongolia?"

"I'm not likely to forget it," Grant retorted dryly. "Me, you and Brigid all nearly died inside of it."

"I'm thinking it was a scout ship from Tiamat, a secondary vessel." He gestured to the empty floor area. "Those dimensions seem about right and those tracks are for moving heavy machinery. This ship is too big to ever land and take off again. Brigid also said she saw a little silver saucer craft like those aboard it. They might be escape pods."

Grant nodded. "Could be. Balam claimed that Tiamat could launch smaller ships. That thing was big, but nowhere as big as this."

The two men moved on, walking toward the distant set of doors. When they reached them, they scanned the surface and bulkheads. They saw no electronic switch or keypads, but a two-pronged handle jutted out from a metal square in the center of both doors. After a moment of silent examination, Grant grasped the handle and turned it clockwise. It resisted for a couple of seconds, then with a faint creak, lock solenoids snapped open. He and Kane exchanged a quizzical glance.

"Go ahead." Kane flexed his wrist tendons and with the faint drone of the tiny electric motor his Sin Eater slid into his hand.

Grant pushed against the right-hand door but it didn't move. He put his shoulder against it and shoved. Hinges squealed in protest, but the door slowly swung open. Kane peered quickly around the edge while Grant hung back, unleathering his own pistol.

Three passages forked off in different, dark directions. A weak illumination filtered down from light panels inset in the ceiling. Kane and Grant hand signaled each other and slipped on their dark-vision glasses. After a swift game of rock-paper-scissors, they chose the left-hand corridor.

Kane took the point, walking down the center while Grant sidled along the right wall. They passed several sealed doors on both sides of the corridor, but they didn't try to open them. The passageway doglegged to the right.

A wide, arched doorway led into an adjoining antechamber. Artifacts of glistening metal and crystal were arrayed on shelves. Neither man paused to examine them. Chamber followed chamber in a straight line.

At the terminus, Kane and Grant entered a large vault-walled room. Wide with a high ceiling, there were alcoves on either side that could have served as storage bins, but were empty niches now, holding only shadows.

The far wall consisted of a thick metal door upon which was imprinted several cuneiform symbols. Kane ran his hands over the door and its rivet-studded frame, fingers seeking a hidden latch. When he found nothing, he fetched it a frustrated kick. To his and Grant's astonishment, the door slid aside with a squeaking whoosh of pneumatics.

"That's one way to do it," Grant muttered.

In the same low tone, Kane responded, "I don't think I did."

When he heard the footfall just outside the door, he silently amended his remark to *knowing* he didn't do it. Flattening against the wall beside the door, he listened to the deliberate, measured tread and lifted his pistol, finger hovering over the trigger stud.

The footfalls stopped and Balam's voice rasped, "Gentlemen, I've been sent to fetch you. You could wander these decks for weeks, if not months."

HANDS CLASPED behind his back, Balam gazed up at them placidly.

"Who sent you to fetch us?" Grant snapped suspiciously. "Sam—Enlil—himself?"

"None other."

"Why didn't he just blast us to scrap metal while we were in space?"

Balam shook his head. "I am not sure. I speculate that the proper weapons system for that function is not back online."

Kane felt a brief surge of hope. "Tiamat is not operational?"

"Not completely." Balam paused, then added ominously, "But that will change."

"Is Brigid with you?" Grant asked.

"She is and she is quite safe." He inclined his head toward the corridor. "If you please—"

Both men exchanged a quizzical glance, then eyed Balam distrustfully. "Why send you and not one of the Nephilim?" Kane wanted to know.

"Enlil does not want active hostilities to break out here. It would be disrespectful."

"To who?" Grant asked.

"Tiamat." With that, Balam turned on his heel and strode down the companionway.

After a moment of indecision, the two men fell in behind him, gun barrels questing for targets in the gloom. Balam said, "You might as well put those away, gentlemen. They will not do you any good under these circumstances."

"And what exactly are the circumstances?" Kane inquired sardonically.

"Have you sold us out—again?" Grant growled.

Balam uttered a sound shockingly like a sob, quickly swallowed. "Forces have been unleashed you do not understand. Destinies of three peoples have been tampered with. Due to a debt incurred by my forebears, I have brought great grief upon the Earth. How can you even imply that I would betray you now?"

Kane stared at him, shocked into speechlessness by the note of deep sadness, even guilt in Balam's tone. He glanced over at Grant, raised an eyebrow and both of them retracted their Sin Eaters into the forearm holsters. They took positions on either side of him.

"What debt?" Kane asked.

"My people, the First Folk, the custodians of humanity, sought to strike off the chains that the root races had bound your kind with. In doing so, they set into motion events far more destructive than the deluge engineered by Enlil centuries before."

Kane remembered what they had learned of the root races, the Annunaki the Tuatha de Danaan and their pact to leave Earth after turning the reins of stewardship over to the forebears of Balam's people. When the First Folk rebelled directly against the Annunaki and the Danaan edicts to curtail human development, the backlash of the weapon they utilized shifted the magnetic poles of Earth—vast portions of the ocean floor rose, while equally vast landmasses sank beneath the waves, the continent of Atlantis among them.

Convulsions shook mountains, the nights blazed with flame-spouting volcanoes. Earthquakes shook the walls and towers of the First Folk's cities. Their proud, thousand-year-old civilization crashed into ruins within a day. Many of the Folk died quickly, while others lingered in a state of near-death for years. The vast knowledge of their ancestors, the technical achievements bequeathed to them, became their only means of survival.

They had no choice but to change themselves with the world, to alter their physiologies. Using ancient techniques, the race transformed itself in order to survive. Their need for sustenance veered away from the near-depleted resources of their environment. They

found new means of nourishment other than the inges-
tion of bulk matter.

Only a handful of the Folk remained among the lichen-
covered stone walls of their once proud city. The new generations born to them were distortions of what they had
been. The weak died before they could produce offspring,
and the infant-mortality rate was frightful for a thousand
years. They didn't leave the ruins to find out how humanity had fared in the aftermath of the catastrophes.

Humankind adapted much faster to the postcata-
strophic world, and new generations began to explore,
to conquer. They brought war to the stunted survivors
of the catastrophes, viewing the descendents of the First
Folk not as semidivine oracles, but as *things*—neither
man, beast nor demon, but imbued with characteristics
superior and inferior to all three.

The First Folk knew they couldn't hope to contain
humankind, but they determined to guide them. If nothing else, they still possessed the monumental pride of
their race and devotion to the continuity of their people.
To accomplish that, they knew they had to retreat even
further, which they did into the subterranean kingdom
exalted in Tibetan legend as Agartha.

Lam, Balam's father, was the last of the pure-blooded
First Folk. He rallied his people, becoming a spiritual
leader, a general and a mentor. He knew his folk couldn't
stay hidden forever, nor did they care to do so. The human
race couldn't be influenced without interaction.

Under Lam's guidance, he and some of his people ascended again into the world of men, to influence the
Phoenicians, the Romans, the Sumerians, the Egyp-
tians, the Aztecs. Lam was known throughout human

historical epochs, but by names such as Osiris, Quetza-coatal, Nyarlthotep, Tsong Kaba and many others.

In the centuries following the catastrophe, Lam and his people continued to interact and influence human affairs, from the economic to the spiritual. They allowed things to happen they could have stopped, or nudged events in another direction.

"So what are you saying?" Grant asked. "That when your people tried to free man, you only decimated humanity, the Annunaki and the Danaan? Is that the debt?"

As they continued down the long stretch of empty, dimly lit corridor past cross-branches stretching into blackness, Balam said quietly, "Yes. To pay for that sin, we whom you called Archons were charged to set the stage for the eventual return of the overlords."

They came to an elevator shaft. It stretched upward, disappearing into a gray blur far above. The three of them boarded. The car was like a glass tube, the walls, floor and ceiling all transparent. As it rose, they were given quick, tantalizing glimpses into each of the levels as they passed them. The lighting was too poor to give them more than fleeting impressions of great chambers swathed in deep shadows. Despite the dim light, they saw objects looming in the murk. They were intricately fashioned out of complicated angles and curves of metal, instruments or devices of unguessable purpose.

Balam went on. " To that end I have labored almost all of my life, over fifteen hundred years of it. As the priest Resurah felt compelled to rebuild Enlil's holy city of Nippur, I and my kind were compelled to reshape the entire world, to recast it into a form fitting for their return. I watched all of my own people perish as we labored to pay the debt of our parents, and at last we succeeded. Earth is now much like it was at the height of the Annunaki empire, twenty thousand years ago. We have paid for a great sin with a far greater sin."

Harshly, bitterly Grant said, "What are you so broken up about? You're on the winning team. Like one of those overlords said, you're of their blood."

"And like Kane said," Balam retorted, "I am also of human blood. It is that heritage I choose to stand beside. If the overlords once more enslave humanity, I will bend my neck to them, as well."

Kane chuckled mirthlessly. "Will putting on shackles buy off your guilt?"

"No," Balam answered quietly. "But at least if I die in bondage along with the rest of humanity, I will know that I have not, as Grant said, 'sold you out.'"

"Nobody is going to die in bondage at the hands of inhuman masters ever again," Grant growled grimly.

"Or human ones," Kane put in.

Balam nodded graciously. "We shall see, gentlemen. We shall see."

The elevator stopped.

Chapter 21

An even dozen metal snake heads reared back, open jaws crackling and emitting tiny sparks. The armor-sheathed arms of three Nephilim were attached to them. They stood outside the elevator car in a semicircle, arms extended, faces impassive, white eyes unblinking.

Grant and Kane managed to keep their own expressions composed if not impassive, but they didn't raise their hands. The armored men paid no attention to Balam as he walked past them into the vast chamber.

"Come in, gentlemen," Enlil's hollow voice boomed. "Welcome to the bridge of Tiamat. I hope you understand why none of us was on hand to greet you. Royal protocol must be observed even at this early stage in our reign."

The two men looked beyond the Nephilim and the ASPs inches from their faces and saw Enlil lolling on a chair that was, for all intents and purposes, a throne. The other overlords were arrayed in chairs on either side of him. They sat brooding and silent. Brigid stood beside Enlil, and his right hand idly fondled her fall of hair. Her face was a blank mask, revealing nothing, but her eyes glinted emerald hard, jade bright.

The Nephilim marched Kane and Grant across the huge chamber. They couldn't help but glance around in awe at the controls, the huge viewscreens and the droning fusion reactor. The science and technology of Tiamat, of the Annunaki, was like a suffocating weight on their chests, slowly crushing out all their pride and confidence.

Almost apologetically, Enlil said, "I really should have realized that while Brigid Baptiste is in my custody you two would arrive in very short order. I still retain my memories of my guises as Sam and Thrush. You might be surprised by how many of them deal with incidents of the three of you vexing me nearly to madness."

"Funny," Kane commented, relieved by how steady his voice sounded. "I could say the same thing about my memories of you as Sam and Thrush."

The Nephilim escorted the two men to the opening between the two ends of the curving horseshoe console. They weren't disarmed, but the guards kept the ASP emitters trained on them. Grant and Kane knew that no matter how fast they could unleather their Sin Eaters, the ASPs were considerably faster.

Kane noticed Balam drifting off to one side, but he fixed his gaze on Brigid. "Are you all right?"

She shrugged. "They haven't harmed me."

"Yet," Lilitu interjected, her eyes glittering with malice.

Enlil regarded both men speculatively, then gestured with one hand toward the images of Earth displayed on the huge viewscreens. A pattern of tiny sparks glittered in various areas over the landmasses and even the seas. "It's really not a very big planet, you know. Quite a bit smaller than Nibiru."

Grant asked flatly, "Is that why you left it to come here? You had so much room you didn't know how to decorate it?"

Marduk hissed angrily, "Silence, Grant. Do not seek to mock us."

Kane gave the former Baron Cobalt a wide-eyed look of innocent reproach. "Gee, why wouldn't we want to do that? If we don't tease you just a little, you might get the ridiculous idea we're afraid of you."

Snorting out a laugh, Enlil hitched around in his chair, drawing Brigid toward him by a wrist. She resisted, but he was too strong and so she resigned herself to being pulled onto his lap. Absently caressing her thigh, he asked, "Are you afraid?"

"I'd be lying if I said I wasn't," she replied curtly. "But fear doesn't control me."

Enlil nodded as if he had expected the answer. Addressing all three of the outlanders, he stated, "While fear and force bring immediate results, belief in myth, faith and devotion to deities insures far more stable and longer lasting control conditions. Fear has its upper limits where it can no longer be a useful deterrent."

"You sound like you're speaking from experience," Grant rumbled.

Enlil hooded his eyes for a moment like a hawk, as if he stared into ages past. "My people in the early days of space-faring knew fear when encountering alien cultures for the first time."

"*Alien?*" Kane echoed, with a heavy ironic emphasis on the word. "Look who's talking." He shut off the part of emotions that raged against the overlord's touch on Brigid. He couldn't help but remember the tales of his activities as Samyaza or how in his previous incarnation, his last physical act had been to rape a human woman.

Enlil flashed his teeth in an appreciative grin. "Of

course, to you the Annunaki are alien. But to us *you* were—as was the other species we found evidence of on Earth."

Brigid stiffened, grasping his groping hand to keep it immobile. "The other alien species?"

"Surely you don't think the Annunaki were the first space travelers to visit Earth," Shamash stated patronizingly.

Ishkur explained, "We came across traces of a star-roving, nonhuman culture on several planets in the solar system. Very ancient and very much long-dead. Enki speculated they might be our ancestors. A few human religious texts called them the Old Ones."

"Regardless," Enlil continued, "when we did not find a race greater than our own, we lost our fear of all things."

"What about the Danaan?" Brigid asked.

Coldly, Enki retorted, "They were not greater. We met them when our empire was on the wane, after we had been weakened by endless internecine strife and liberal policies toward humankind."

"Policies advocated by Enki?" Brigid asked calmly. "You feared him, didn't you?"

Enlil narrowed his eyes, pursed his lips musingly as if he pondered Brigid's question. Then the hand that been stroking her as if she were a pet darted up and closed in the long hair at her nape. Springing out of his throne, Enlil shook her viciously by the hair, snarling out words in liquid Nibiruan. Brigid cried out in pain as she reached up behind her to clutch at his wrist.

Kane lunged forward, but a numbing blow landed on the back of his head, delivered with savage accuracy and

economy by a gold-armored Nephilim. A bomb seemed
to go off in his skull, and he was dimly aware of falling. He tried to catch himself by his hands, but they
didn't seem to be there anymore.

He didn't lose consciousness, but he hovered at its
brink for what seemed like a very long time. His dazed
brain replayed the fragmented glimpse of an alloy-
sheathed forearm hammering him off his feet. He tried
to get up, but a boot sole slammed against his neck,
mashing his face into the cold deck. Hands groped all
over him, snatching away his war bag and his Sin Eater.
He thought he heard Grant shout something. The words
were indistinct through the roaring waterfall in his head,
but the tone was angry.

He had no trouble hearing Enlil's maddened roar. "I
do all of you a great honor and you return it with disre-
spect! In the old days of my reign, very few of your race
ever saw my true face and lived!"

The pressure of the foot was removed, and Kane
slowly pushed himself up to all fours. Two of the Nephilim stood on either side of Grant, ASPs pointed at his
head. His Sin Eater was missing from his right forearm.
Brigid had been forced to her knees by Enlil, his hand
still tangled in her hair, wrenching her head back at a
brutal angle. Although her eyes were squeezed shut
against the pain, she made no outcry, nor did she try to
wrest away the overlord's fingers.

Kane's rage was somewhat cooled by the blood
freezing in his veins. The spectacle of the concentrated
Satanic fury blazing in Enlil's eyes drove all thoughts
of violence from his mind.

"Do you think I care anything for humanity?" Enlil

bellowed. "You were the slaves of my race and we were your *gods*. You will worship us as your gods again, and you will gladly be our tools to rebuild the empire of the Annunaki."

As Kane climbed back to his feet, Enlil released Brigid with a forceful flourish, and she fell heavily onto her right side. She began to push herself up to her hands and knees, but Enlil planted a foot between her shoulder blades and slammed her down to the deck again. "As we are restored, humanity is now returned to its rightful place—crawling on their bellies at our feet!"

The overlords laughed in cruel appreciation. As if playing to the crowd, Enlil kept his foot on Brigid and spread his arms wide, shouting, "And you apelings who defied my race and me—you were justly punished for your arrogance. You have been reduced to the ape again, by own your savage impulses. And now the Annunaki are ascendant once more."

He turned, thrusting both arms toward the viewscreens and the glittering pinpoints of light dotting the landmasses and oceans. "We will seek out the sites of our old cities, of our ancient ports and vaults. Oceans and barbarian tribes might have swept over them, and some lie beneath barren deserts, but we will uncover them, resurrect them, bring them forth into the dawning of this new age."

As he ranted, a green-armored Nephilim opened the war bags and dumped their contents onto the floor, a scattering of ammo clips, gas grenades, trans-comm units, batteries, blocks of plastic explosive, flashlights and the little electronic lock decrypters called Mnemosynes. Some of the smaller items clattered and rolled toward overlords.

Enlil peered over at the items, amused, and lifted his foot from Brigid. "Rise."

Face not showing her anger or humiliation, Brigid carefully climbed to her feet, brushing aside some of the loose odds and ends from the war bags in the process. She joined Grant and Kane, unconsciously stepping between the two men to stand shoulder to shoulder. In a calm, clear voice Brigid asked, "Is there any point in asking why you would do such things instead of starting fresh?"

Enlil reacted with mild surprise at the question. "You still do not fully understand, do you? None of you?"

Not waiting for an answer, Enlil declared, "*We* created human culture on Earth. All of your languages, your arts, your aspirations, all derive from Nibiru."

He slapped his chest, then gestured to the seated overlords. "*We* did it. It was by our hands that we raised your barbaric race from the mire of apedom. You advanced far and quickly and then turned treacherously upon those who ruled the world."

Lips curling in a sneer, Zu announced, "All that men know or have ever known is like a grain of sand beside a mountain compared to our knowledge, our science. Our hands lifted you from the muck and those same hands will cast you down into a Hell far more horrifying than your holy men ever envisioned."

Enlil showed the edges of his teeth in a cold, taunting grin. He swept a hand toward the multitiered edifice. "All during the rise of your planet's civilizations, humanity's ancient masters slept there, slumbering through the lost ages as mere minutes, awaiting the day of final awakening. There were some among your kind, special ones whom we anointed either with our blood or our dreams, who foresaw the day when your own self-hatred would scorch clean the face of the world and make ready for our return."

Kane's stomach muscles fluttered in adrenaline-fueled spasms. He struggled to tamp down the insane fury flooding through him, clouding his reason. During his encounters with the Thrush entity, he had found it difficult to hate a creature who didn't truly live. It was only during his final confrontation with Thrush on the third parallel casement that he realized the absolutely soul-deep hatred he felt toward the being

He saw him not as a man but as what he really was, an ancient evil thing that crept among the primordial grasses, apart from human life, but watching it with eyes of cold wisdom, offering a silent laugh of superiority, giving away nothing but bitterness.

He had the name of a bird and the appearance of a man, but his brain was that of the serpent. Kane had been overwhelmed with a hate-fueled rage to crush what passed for life out of him. Intermittently over the past two years, Kane had jerked awake from slumber, sweat-drenched and shaking, as his sleeping mind dredged up with terrifying clarity the words Thrush had once psionically impressed into his memory: "You will know my presence in your own casement soon enough. By then, I hope you will have resigned yourself to what cannot be changed. Do not fight any more. There is no use in it."

He understood now that on a visceral, subliminal level he had always realized the Thrush entity was something far worse, far more ancient and evil than a hybrid blending of machine, human and Annunaki genetic material.

"Do any of these special ones still exist?" Brigid asked. "Can you exert control over every creature that shares Annunaki genes?"

Kane's throat constricted as he grasped the ugly implications of her question. Years before, the preserved body of Enlil had been in the possession of the self-appointed ruler of Britain, a man calling himself Lord Strongbow. All of them had seen the corpse in Strongbow's fortress in New London.

Strongbow had admitted to using Enlil's genetic material to mutagenically modify himself and his shock troops, the Imperial Dragoons. Furthermore, he had arranged the creation of a hybrid mixture of three races— human, Tuatha de Danaan and Annunaki. Enlil died after impregnating a young woman who carried Danaan blood.

Lord Strongbow had made arrangements for both himself and the pregnant woman to be placed in cryonic suspension for nearly a century and a half. They had revived nearly thirty years before, but the woman escaped from Strongbow to Ireland and gave birth to an infant possessing the mixed blood of all three races.

The hybrid infant had grown into the beautiful demigoddess Sister Fand, whom he, Grant and Brigid had encountered on a couple of occasions. She had been instrumental in overthrowing Strongbow's Imperium Britannia. He wondered if the resurrected Enlil remembered the last act of his former incarnation—and if even now he influenced Fand and the remnants of the Dragoons from orbit.

He managed to keep the relief surging through him from showing on his face when Enlil answered disparagingly, "That would be quite impossible. The Nephilim are a different matter, since they were specifically engineered to be linked with Tiamat—and the overlords." His grin widened. "As is the girl-child that the female Quavell will soon bring into the world."

Kane felt his eyes widen, the wave of surprised apprehension making him forget about the throbbing pain in his skull. "How do you know it's a girl-child?"

Enlil chuckled, a sinister, slithery rustle like the shifting of distant bat wings. He tapped his temple with a forefinger. "I have always enjoyed a special rapport with my wife...Ninlil."

Both Grant and Kane were too stunned to reply, but Brigid startled everyone by uttering a sound of disdain. "Yes...Ninlil. The female with whom your reputation as a rapist was cemented. If I recall the legend aright, you followed her to the banks of the Id-nunbir-tum River, where she often went to bathe. It was there you attacked her and impregnated her."

As she spoke, Enlil's finger slid from his temple to his chin, where he tapped it contemplatively. "You recall the legend accurately. But it is only a legend, not quite the truth...nor yet a complete falsehood."

Kane felt as if he were trying to fight his way out of a bad dream. He stopped short of shaking his head, but he asked incredulously, "How could Quavell possibly give birth to your *wife?*"

"Of course she isn't," Enlil said impatiently. "She is giving birth to what you might call a blank slate, a tabula rasa... an empty vessel waiting to be filled. Although she carries the Annunaki genetic profile, the child is in an intermediate form of development...certain segments of her DNA, strands of her genetic material can be encoded after the fact."

With his right hand he made a flourishing gesture, like a conjurer performing a card trick, and a Tablet of Destiny glinted between his thumb and forefinger. "She will be brought here to be properly imprinted, both mentally and biologically. Her tablet will be downloaded and then the Supreme Council will be complete. After that, Tiamat will prepare to give birth—rebirth—to the entire Annunaki pantheon."

"Maybe that can be done," Grant said doubtfully, "and maybe it can't. Either way...won't you be taking the concept of cradle-robbing to a whole new level? Unless you plan to wait until she comes of age and I don't see you as a particularly patient snake-face."

"If we can extend our lives through genetic manipulation," Lilitu said scornfully but with a detectable note of jealousy, "doesn't that suggest we can effect changes upon the aging process?"

Grant did not answer, but Kane recalled how months earlier DeFore expressed concern over the irregularities in the genetic sequencing of Quavell's fetus. Her fears that the condition might result in either a birth defect or a miscarriage now seemed almost laughable.

"How do you plan to get the baby up here for the treatment?" Brigid asked.

Marduk brayed out a scornful laugh. "We'll go and fetch her, what do you think? Personally, I've waited long enough to get a look at that mountaintop rat hole of yours."

Kane uttered an equally scornful laugh. "Do you honestly think the people in Cerberus will turn her over to you just like that?"

Enlil sighed as if he found the query almost too absurd to address. "Kane, if there is one thing I am sure about your race—when faced with certain annihilation, you'll turn over anything, even your sense of self and identity, just so you can draw breath for one more day. Regardless of a superficial devotion to ideals, humankind are the ultimate pragmatists when the issues are your own lives...or deaths."

A voice wafted through the bridge. Although it held a whispery quality, their ears had no trouble registering it. "Even in a new form, you allow the same old blinding arrogance, the same overweening hubris to motivate your actions. I had hoped it might be otherwise."

Enlil and the overlords swung their heads up and around, goggling in shock toward the metal-walled structure rising from the deck. Balam stood on the middle tier, some fifty feet above them staring down with obsidian-eyed impassivity. Enlil shouted in furious Nibiruan, pointing first at the three outlanders then up at him with an accusatory, beringed forefinger. His tone held notes of a threat, a command and an ultimatum.

When the tirade ended, Balam stated quietly and calmly in English, "I beg to differ. The final destiny of the human race is not out of their reach. But if you are not opposed, humanity will slide back, degenerate into a condition far worse than its preflood state of slavery. You would work toward debasing an intelligent species to the level of animals that will scrabble and fight to survive at your whim. I will not help you in such an endeavor."

He paused, inhaled a short breath and said, "My blood flows with human and Annunaki qualities, true enough.

Far too long have I allowed myself to be guided my Annunaki heritage. It ends today, this very moment."

Enlil barked out another stream of Nibiruan invective. Balam replied smoothly, "I had assumed you would have guessed. I've opened an interface to the database and have singled out one mental signature in the neural net. I imagine you can guess the identity of that signature."

Enlil's reaction was swift and violent. He whirled toward the Nephilim standing guard around Kane, Brigid and Grant and snarled out a command. Sparks flared in the ASP emitters trained on them.

Brigid Baptiste exploded into motion, whipping her right arm up and around, balancing herself on the balls of her feet. A short, thick metal cylinder extended from her fist. A stream of white liquid sprayed from it, splashing against the unprotected faces of two of the Nephilim.

They didn't cry out, but the neurotoxin triggered almost instant convulsions.

Chapter 22

Both Grant and Kane recognized the canister and the effects of the nerve toxin it dispensed. The chemical was absorbed through the pores of the skin and disrupted the central nervous system for a short time. Grant had thought to bring the spray in his war bag, but neither he nor Kane had seen Brigid palm it.

Kane moved with the eye-blurring speed and explosion of near superhuman reflexes that had made him something of a legend in the Cobaltville Magistrate Division. Hurling himself forward, he shoulder-rolled between the pair of spasming Nephilim and snatched up his Sin Eater from the floor. As he rolled back up on the balls of his feet, he turned to see three Nephilim rushing to surround him and his friends.

The Sin Eater popped free of the holster into his hand. His first two shots struck a yellow-armored Nephilim full in his expressionless face, turning his features into a red-jelly smear. Pointing his pistol in the direction of the overlords, he continued firing, keeping the trigger pressed down. The subsonic 9 mm rounds ripped through the air, ricocheting off consoles with flares of blue sparks and keening whines. Bleating in angry fear, the overlords took cover behind their chairs, even though no rounds came very close to them.

Kane scooped up Grant's pistol and tossed it to him. Grant fired a 3-round burst as soon as the weapon was out of the holster and in his hand, bowling a Nephilim off his feet. Enlil shouted stridently over the racket of gunshots. An ASP bolt fired by a purple-armored man scorched the air very close to Grant's face.

Cursing, he grabbed one of the disabled Nephilim, grappling with him, using him as a shield. It was like wrestling with a human-sized dummy filled with molten lead, his arms hanging slack, his legs rubbery. An ASP blast struck him square in the chest, the energy interacting violently with the alloy of the armor. Sparks showered in an eye-hurting display of pyrotechnics, and the kinetic force sent Grant staggering backward several feet. Pain shivered through him. He would have fallen if not for one of the black pillars at his back.

"This way!" Brigid shouted, racing toward the metal ziggurat, using the pylons as cover.

Grant dropped the dead man, the smoke pouring from his slagged breastplate burning his nostrils. He and Kane followed Brigid. Grant brought up the rear, snapping off a few shots to discourage pursuit. There was no answering fire.

They wended their way among the dark pylons. Brigid reached the foot of the metal staircase that led to up the different tiers. The three of them sprinted up the stairs, two steps at a time. The stairway wound around the tower, hugging the lines of the exterior. From within it they heard the droning susuruss of power.

When they reached the catwalk that composed the first tier, they paused to catch their breaths. Crouching peering at the deck through the pillars, Kane said, "Swift move, Baptiste. I didn't even see you reach for the nerve spray much less grab it."

Brigid smiled wryly and shook the canister. "I was counting on all eyes being on Enlil as he strutted his stuff."

"No one seems to be following us," Grant commented uneasily.

Craning her neck, looking up and around, Brigid replied, "I'm not surprised. According to Balam, this is the main memory nexus of Tiamat. All those pipes supply the synthetic equivalent of blood and cerebral-spinal fluid to it. Not even an egotist like Enlil would want to risk damaging it—her. Not to mention, there might some pretty deadly self-defense systems built into it—her."

"Then why are we climbing around it—her?" Grant asked, alarmed.

"We aren't threatening her...yet."

Kane looked up, shading his eyes from the glare cast by the battery of ceiling lights. "Balam!" he called. "Do you want us to come to you or what?"

After a moment, his raspy voice responded faintly, "Join me on the third level—with alacrity if you please. I fear that Enlil knows my intentions and is taking action to stop me."

The Cerberus warriors started climbing again, bounding from step to step. Kane assumed the point man's position, alternating his attention from what lay ahead to the activities below. He caught only glimpses of armored figures flitting among the black columns surrounding the ziggurat.

"I don't think we're being followed," Grant panted as he brought up the rear.

Kane didn't reply, too occupied with maintaining a steady run-leap-run gait. When the risers ended abruptly on a ledge, he nearly pitched headlong over the rail trying to avoid a collision with Balam.

The Archon stood before a small computer terminal—at least, a winded Kane assumed it was a computer terminal. Instead of a conventional monitor screen, a series of crystals rose from within a glass-walled box. Several were shards much like smaller versions of the Star Fire, and others were sculpted cylinders, prisms and geometric shapes. A semitransparent crystal in the shape of a life-sized grinning skull rose above the rest.

Balam's long bony fingers manipulated tiny colored tiles over a flat surface that reminded Kane of a chessboard. As he slid the tiles from one section of the board to the other, the crystals shimmered with different colors and emitted semi-musical notes.

As Grant and Brigid pounded up, Kane wheezed, "You're not playing the Annunaki version of chess, I hope."

Balam didn't answer for a moment, intent on manipulating the little squares. At length he said, "After a fashion, I am indeed. What I am doing is complicated, but the closest analog in your frame of reference would be that I am attempting to infect Tiamat's data storage banks with a virus. Or to be more precise, convince a specific neural pattern within the database to act as one."

Kane and Grant only blinked at him. The two men were moderately familiar with computers. To them, they were simply sometimes useful machines, and their more arcane workings held little interest. Besides, there were plenty of people in the redoubt to perform the comp work if they needed it.

Brigid stepped close to Balam, her enthralled gaze passing over the sculpted crystals and Balam's long fingers moving the tiles this way and that. "This is a direct interface with Tiamat's database?" she asked.

Balam nodded. "I am circumventing her internal main memory core and entering through a back door—to once again employ your vernacular."

"Why?" Grant demanded impatiently, casting an apprehensive glance over his shoulder, down the stairs.

Balam flicked his eyes in his direction. "Do you know what a computer virus is or what it does?"

Grant's eyebrows lowered in a scowl. "To be frank," he said bluntly, "I don't. And I don't give a shit, either."

Balam uttered a strange noise, either an amused chuckle or exasperated sigh or a cross between the two. "You might give a shit about this one. A computer virus in the form of a hidden code infects a database. It can wipe out whole megafiles of memory. The main memory core is responsible in some way for the operation of virtually every other system of this vessel."

Grant grunted. "So it's like giving the machine a lobotomy."

Balam shook his head and said in a weary, patronizing tone, "If that description helps you to visualize it, then yes. It's like giving the machine a lobotomy."

"But you said you were trying to convince a certain neural pattern to act as a virus," Brigid stated.

"So I did. And that pattern belongs to Enki."

Kane shot him a startled stare. "Enlil's half brother? Why?"

The corners of Brigid's lips quirked in a smile. "I think I know. And it makes perfect sense."

From the photosensitive plate of her eidetic memory, Brigid retrieved the exchange between her, Brewster Philboyd and Enki in the Lunar citadel nearly six months before. The last living full-blooded Annunaki had told them how his people had factionalized violently over the issue of humankind's fate. The decision was reached to go along with Enlil's plan to drown humanity, return to Nibiru and then return to Earth after an appropriate period of time.

Although Enki took covert steps to insure there would be human survivors of the catastrophe, he had no choice but to leave Earth with the rest of his brethren. Enki and a small group of supporters had become attached to Earth and its inhabitants and were overwhelmed with guilt and remorse. They couldn't return to Nibiru or any of their outposts on the other planets in the solar system. They couldn't conceive of living in peace with Enlil and the others of the Supreme Council who had approved and engineered the near genocide of humankind.

Over the course of centuries on Earth, the perceptions of these few Annunaki about life had changed. They acquired a new need, a new passion that sent groups of them across the widest gulfs of space. They had stopped seeking power and even knowledge, and found themselves driven by a motivation grander than the simple survival of their race—a motivation to aid the development and fulfillment of all sentient life.

Because Enki and his faction couldn't undo what had been done to humanity, they sought to share Annunaki achievements with other races. They thought of life-forms springing into existence all over the universe, evolving races that needed their knowledge. Having acquired all the skills and technology that they were capable of acquiring, they spread across the galaxy, driven by a need to rectify their crime against humanity.

Although the main force of the Annunaki returned to Nibiru, Enki and many others did not. They became explorers, not exploiters. They learned that all life was growing. There was no limit to what life could be. Individuals and races had their limits, of course, but the process of life itself was unlimited. They came to the understanding that every living, sentient creature could contribute to its growth. Individuals and even races might perish, might be forgotten, but what they had accomplished could never be extinguished. It would echo for eternity because it had become part of the evolution of all life.

In the infinity of possibilities, there was only one restriction—no race could know the potential of another race and therefore could not pass judgment on its inherent worth. Hard as it was to realize, the older races had to allow the younger races to develop on their own, make their mistakes and not interfere. This epiphany was what Enlil could not accept.

"What makes perfect sense?" Grant asked. "And more importantly—why?"

Kane grinned. "I get it. Balam is trying to single Enki's consciousness out of all the pantheon that have been digitized and stored. He'll convince him to interfere with whatever Enlil programs this ship to do."

"You are essentially correct," Balam stated grimly,

"but it is not as easy as your facile description makes it sound. The sum total of data in Tiamat's memory tanks is so vast, that even the index is beyond the capacity of your life span to read. "

Kane angled an eyebrow at him, then said simply, "Oh."

"Trying to isolate Enki's specific signature among all the interconnected pathways," Balam continued, "is tantamount isolating a specific grain of sand with a certain silicon content in the Sahara."

After thoughtful moment, Kane again said, "Oh."

"Have you ever done anything like this before?" Grant asked.

"Never," Balam responded crisply. "Nor have I ever heard of it being attempted, much less accomplished. Brigid Baptiste gave me the idea when she inquired as to the self-aware states of the minds within the neural matrix. Unfortunately, I do not know if I am even on the proper track, or if I am, whether I can succeed in convincing Enki and those of his faction to act as viruses."

Kane gestured to the crystals. "What's with the one shaped like a skull?"

"It would correspond to a memory buffer in one of your computers," Balam answered.

Brigid combed her fingers through her hair. "That makes sense. Crystal skulls turned up at various archaeological sites during the nineteenth and twentieth centuries. There are legends that indigenous peoples have crystal skulls that they keep secretly hidden from the rest of the world."

"Why?" Grant asked.

Brigid shrugged. "They supposedly contain encoded

information. The public first became aware of the crystal skulls during the later part of the nineteenth century. At that time, many museums of the world became interested in displaying antiquities from past civilizations—Egypt, Greece, Meso-America. By the 1870s, the Museum of Man in Paris and the Museum of Man of London each had a clear quartz crystal skull on display."

"Where'd they come from?" Kane inquired, interested in spite of the tense circumstances.

"Both were discovered in the 1860s, during the French occupation of Mexico, purportedly found in Mayan sites."

Grant eyed her skeptically. "So the crystal skulls found there are the same thing as an Annunaki computer's memory buffer?"

Before Brigid could answer, Balam slapped the colored tiles with a frustrated flourish. "It is of no use. I do not know if Enlil is at another interface disrupting my efforts, or if my plan simply could not be implemented."

Kane frowned at him. "Do you usually give up this easy?"

Brigid stepped forward to stand beside Balam. She opened the seals at the sleeves of her shadow suit and peeled back her gloves. Bare-handed, she reached for the tiles. "Let me try."

Balam gazed up at her, his attitude, if not his expression, conveying disbelief and even annoyance. Superciliously he said, "Although your abilities are intriguing, as is your font of knowledge, you do not have the skills nor the necessary mind-energy signature to perform this function. As I informed you, Tiamat is a living ship, a blending of organic and inorganic. Her organic elements are, of course, derived from the DNA of the royal family. In order to even access the computer core, much less interact with it, Tiamat will need to recognize both your genetic code and your EEG pattern."

Even as he spoke, Brigid's fingers were sliding the tiles around the board, tentatively at first, gauging the reaction her movements received from the crystal sculptures. They flashed with different hues and sang with thready tones, like the prolonged sighing of distant violin strings.

"Did you not hear me?" Balam asked a little peevishly.

"I heard you fine," she responded, a line of concentration appearing between her eyes. "There's nothing to lose by my trying. Like you said...you're not omnipotent."

Kane didn't even bother repressing a laugh. He peered over the railing down into the bridge below. He saw none of the overlords or the Nephilim, but he wasn't comforted.

Eyeing the metal wall of the ziggurat speculatively, Grant asked, "Is there some reason we don't do this the old-fashioned way?"

"As in?" Kane inquired.

Grant tapped the exterior with the barrel of his Sin Eater and raised an eyebrow meaningfully. "If the objective is to take out the brain of this thing, why not just shoot it or find a way to pull the plug?"

Balam uttered a short exclamation of shock. "Impossible."

Grant speared him with a frosty glare. "Why?"

"Tiamat is sentient, even if she does obey a set of programs."

"She also presents a very clear threat to Earth," Kane argued.

"She cannot be held responsible for that," Balam retorted plaintively. "You can no more hold her personally responsible for what destruction she may wreak than you can blame a hurricane or an earthquake."

"Even forces of nature have countermeasures taken against them," Grant pointed out.

If Balam had a reply, it was lost in a warbling whine from the crystals. Whorls and waves of color passed through them, swirling the most intensely within the skull.

Brigid uttered a hoarse "Whoa" of uncertainty and surprise.

"What have you done?" Balam demanded.

Still sliding the tiles around, but this time with far more assured motions, Brigid answered distractedly, "You said Tiamat would need to recognize my genetic and EEG signature...but I wasn't trying to make her acquaintance."

"I still don't understand."

"You never met Enki, did you?"

After a thoughtful pause, Balam admitted, "No."

"Well, I have. It was recognition from him I was trying to elicit, and I think I've succeeded."

Balam came as close to gaping in astonishment as it was possible for the structure of his features to allow.

From the skull piped a series of signals, musical notes that seemed to weave and intertwine. They ran up the register from little high-pitched chirpings to deep bass throbbings.

Brigid Baptiste removed her fingers from the tiles, straightened and announced, "Hello, Enki."

Chapter 23

Balam placed his fingers on the tiles but didn't manipulate them. The colors shifting through the crystal skull cast multihued highlights over his pale face. His huge black eyes reflected them like miniature rainbows. He gazed intently at the crystals for a long, silent moment, then peered up at Brigid.

"It *is* Enki." His voice was softened to a whisper by surprise, even a hint of awe. "I must confess I don't quite understand how you managed this."

With an exaggerated air of being aggrieved, Kane intoned, "I must confess I don't quite understand *any* of this."

"The way I figured it," Brigid replied, gesturing to the tiles, "is that those little sensors read your DNA and EEG signature. If they're on file in the database, you can access the memory banks."

"Yeah," Grant rumbled, his brow furrowed. "But why would your DNA and EEG codes be on file in a Annunaki computer system?"

"They're not," she answered. "If Balam had the interface set for standard network access, nothing would have happened. I would not have been able to evoke any kind of response at all. But, as he said, he was entering the system through a back door. And that door bypassed all of Tiamat's security lockouts and led to a direct link with the mind energy of the pantheon in the matrix."

"From what you're saying," Grant said slowly, "it sounds like you basically just yelled 'Hey, Enki' in a crowded room and hoped he'd hear you."

Brigid chuckled. "That's about the cyber-equivalent. If Enki is only one tiny facet of Tiamat's colossal data storage capacity, then trying to reach him through a conventional access process is futile. I guessed that most of Tiamat's memory is based on the MOE model."

"The what?" Kane asked, arching an eyebrow.

"Memory Of Experience. Whatever Tiamat has experienced in her long existence, she remembers without it having to be specifically downloaded into her. I'm sure the same applies for her component subroutine modules, if they still possess any degree of independent data processing and function."

Balam nodded in comprehension. "Enki has no memory of me, but he has one of you—"

"And therefore he responded. I don't know if I can interact with him through this terminal, but at least he's acknowledged me. Or I think he has."

Balam, still sounding slightly incredulous, if not bewildered, said, "Enki recognized your unique imprint. He does indeed remember you and is exceptionally curious about your presence."

Brigid smiled wryly. "You'll explain it to him, won't you?"

"Why can't you do it directly?" Kane wanted to know.

She tapped her temple. "As biologically similar as we and the Annunaki are in most ways, the synaptic structures of our brains differ considerably. But Balam's people, the Archons, are probably identical."

"The differences are negligible," Balam agreed, big eyes fixed on the pattern of colors streaming through the crystal skull. "Our minds are in communication."

The chiming tones sounded like Morse code as tapped out on tiny tinkling bells. Balam slid the tiles swiftly to and fro, his expression and body language conveying complete concentration. From somewhere down below in the bridge echoed a cry of outrage and frustration.

Brigid glanced over the guardrail, then met Kane's and Grant's questioning looks with raised eyebrows. "I'm only guessing, but I think whatever Enlil was trying to pull with Tiamat's system has just been stymied by Enki."

The array of overhead lights suddenly flickered, dimmed and then began strobing in a strange sequence. Balam paid no attention, his long fingers sliding the tiles purposefully into positions on the board.

"I wish I knew if that was good or bad," Kane murmured, squinting up at the lights.

Static hissed in their heads, as well as the beeping signal that indicated the Commtact channels were open. Brigid said, "Good, I'd say. Enki has closed the dampening umbrella so our comms can function again."

Suddenly the catwalk shuddered beneath their feet and all of them experienced, for only a fraction of an instant, a lifting sensation in their stomachs, as if they were floating upward. Their own brief cries of surprise were mimicked by ones from the deck below.

"The synthetic gravity field fluctuated," Brigid declared. "Enki and maybe other minds of his former faction are affecting Tiamat's internal systems."

"Why?" Grant demanded, clutching the handrail just in case the gravity disappeared altogether.

"To prove to Enlil and the overlords what they can do," Balam answered, turning away from the terminal. "I have communicated to Enki all that I know of Enlil's intentions and how he will most probably use Tiamat to further them."

"So," Kane ventured hopefully, "he'll stop them?"

Balam closed his eyes as if in sadness. "That he cannot do. Enki may be a part of Tiamat, but only a small part, a fraction of a fraction of her overall systems. Yes, he can perform a few functions that are similar to a computer virus, but the effect is only temporary and impacts only on a few of her subroutines that have yet to be brought completely online."

"So what the hell *can* he do?" Grant demanded harshly, not releasing his grip on the rail. "Annoy the overlords by playing with the light switches?"

Balam opened his eyes again, staring solemnly at Grant. "At the moment, the action he takes may save our lives. Enlil does not know the extent of Enki's interference with Tiamat's central computer core. As far as he knows, Enki could have reprogrammed her self-destruct code and she is even now counting down to detonation."

"As far as he knows," Kane repeated sarcastically, "Enki is just bluffing, right?"

Balam nodded. "Precisely."

Enlil's voice, raised in an infuriated bellow, blared up the stairwell. He spoke in Nibiruan, which their Commtacts translated as gibberish.

Balam responded in English. "Yes, it is my doing. I have informed Enki of your plans. Much as it was thousands of years ago, he finds fault with them."

Enlil began a roaring reply, but Kane shouted, "Speekee the English!"

A noise very much like Enlil clearing his throat and hawking reached their ears. Then he snarled, "Enki has taken control of the critical environmental systems!"

"And the weapons," Balam replied blandly. He glanced over at Brigid and squeezed one eye shut in a conspiratorial wink.

"How long do you think he can maintain this kind of interdiction?" Enlil didn't give Balam the opportunity to respond. He answered his own question by roaring, "Not very long, I can promise you! I will turn every program, every function of every shipboard system against him and whoever else is aiding and abetting him!"

Unruffled, Balam declared, "Of that I have no doubt. But by the time you are able to implement such action, the damage he has wreaked may very well be incalculable, irreparable. Tiamat will be rendered uninhabitable for an indeterminate length of time. More than likely, a great deal of reprogramming of basic functions will be necessitated. Your reign will be over before it begins."

Outraged, scandalized, shocked, Enlil screeched, "You would dare do this to Tiamat?"

His calm, unperturbed tone a direct counterpoint to Enlil's stressed-out shriek, Balam answered, "She is not *my* mother."

Kane was so startled he nearly burst into a peal of laughter, but he repressed it, exchanging grins with Grant and Brigid.

Enlil sighed heavily. In a very doleful, flat voice, he asked, "What do you want?"

"Safe passage for my friends. Allow them to leave unmolested."

"You, too," Kane whispered. "We installed jump seats and auxiliary life-support gear in the Mantas. They can carry one passenger apiece. You don't need to stay behind."

Balam called down. "I will leave with them, via their transatmospheric craft."

Enlil echoed scornfully, *"Their* transatmospheric craft?" After a few seconds he said, "I agree under one condition. You will permit me to access the terminal that you used to interface with Enki. That way I may begin the process of undoing the damage."

Balam eyed the three people questioningly. "I am uncomfortable with granting him that condition."

"So am I," Brigid stated grimly. "It could take him only seconds to find out that Enki's effects on the systems are superficial and activate a general override."

"Well?" Enlil sounded impatient and a trifle suspicious.

Kane said quietly, "Let's agree to it—under a condition of our own."

"Which is what?" Grant asked.

"I'll stay behind to make sure Enlil doesn't touch the interface until at least two of you have launched."

Balam's slit of mouth compressed as if he tasted something sour. "I am qualified to pilot the craft. I suggest Grant return to Earth with Brigid Baptiste. I will wait for you, Kane, in the other ship."

Both Brigid and Grant opened their mouths to protest, but Kane called down, "Enlil—we accept your condition if you agree to one of ours. I'll hang with you up here until my friends are safely away. Once they are, you can have carte blanche to undo what Enki has done."

For a long, tense tick of time they heard nothing. Then Enlil snapped angrily, "Agreed."

Kane shouted, "Clear the bridge and the way to the hangar of all unsightly fin-heads and white eyes."

The second "Agreed" from Enlil sounded far angrier than the first. They heard Enlil barking commands in Nibiruan. After a couple of minutes of foot shuffling and resentful muttering, there was only silence. Then Enlil called up, "I have met your terms. It is time to abide by mine."

"Come on up," Kane retorted.

They heard the measured tread of feet on the risers, then Enlil strode onto the tier, eyeing them all with a cold loathing and disdain. He waved sharply, dismissively, with the ring-glittering fingers of his right hand. "You may go now. To tarry will give my brethren the chance to change their minds. Not all of them agree with allowing you to escape. Only their concern for Tiamat's well-being stays their hands."

"And is she not immortal?" Brigid asked sarcastically. "How could we apekin possibly hurt her?"

"She exists," Enlil retorted, his face an aloof mask. "She exists just as the fathomless void of space, of the universe exists. She can no more die than the universe can perish. She but dreams, asleep above the surface of Earth, but still strong, potent, dangerous and very, very real. Now, be off before she takes notice and decides to keep you here in her belly."

Brigid and Grant hesitated for a moment, but Kane

hefted his Sin Eater suggestively. "If he misbehaves, we'll find out how bulletproof that new hide of his might be at point-blank range."

Grant's lips twitched under his mustache. "That's almost worth staying around to see."

Enlil sniffed haughtily, then stared down at Balam. "You are repeating and perpetuating the same tragic error in judgment of your forebears. We forgave your folk's treachery once before. We will not do so a second time."

Balam met his imperious gaze unblinkingly, defiantly. "I trust," he said in a soft whisper, "that you are aware of the reverse."

Then he, Grant and Brigid walked past Enlil to the stairway. Brigid paused and tapped the Commtact behind her ear. "We'll let you know when we're aboard."

Kane nodded. "I'll be along directly."

Grant touched his right index finger to his nose and snapped it away in the wry "one percent" salute. It was a private gesture he and Kane had developed during their years as hard-contact Magistrates and reserved for high-risk undertakings with small ratios of success. Their half-serious belief was that ninety-nine percent of situations that went awry could be predicted and compensated for in advance. But there was always a one-percent margin of error, and playing against that percentage could have lethal consequences.

Kane returned the salute gravely.

As the sound of their descent down the stairs faded, Enlil folded his arms over his chest and regarded Kane with a predatory smile. Kane responded with a wintry one of his own, crossing his arms over his chest, resting the barrel of the Sin Eater on the crook of his left elbow, the bore more or less aligned with the overlord's head.

Without preamble, Enlil said, "Balam's people became weakened by their time among you apekin. I had hoped that he would have recognized the inherent catastrophic consequences of championing your kind as his father had done. Now he will die with you. It is a tragedy…the last of his kind, dying among savages."

Kane shrugged. "Seems to me that some of your own kind championed the cause of us apekin. That's sort of the reason you and I are even standing here right now." He nodded toward the computer terminal.

Enlil's eyes narrowed. "They did not see you as the rest of us did."

"As apelings?"

"Worse. As animals who love to kill one another, to make your brother and sister apelings suffer. You are happiest when covered with the blood of your own kind."

Kane nodded. "I've heard that. Just like I've heard about all the wars you superior snake-faces waged among yourselves. I can't disagree that humanity seems to have a taste for violence and bloodshed. But the funny thing is, whenever you start going back through history, looking for the source of humans warring on humans, there always seems to be a superior-acting snake-face at the bottom of it. Lots of different names in different places and times, but the MO is always the same."

Enlil made a spitting sound of contempt. "We merely channeled your inborn natural aggression and taste for blood so you would thin your own herd with the least amount of bother to us. And, of course, war is a sometimes beneficial commodity. Engendering it is an effective tool for maintaining control over an unstable population."

"Yeah, you took a personal hand with that tactic from what I've heard. Samyaza, Asmodeus, Thrush and God knows how many other aliases. You never could get it right, could you? You always underestimated the apelings."

Enlil's lips stretched away from his teeth in a taunting grin. "Actually, we always found your behaviors and attitudes very predictable."

His silky tone of menace raised Kane's nape hairs, but he maintained a neutral expression.

"For example," Enlil continued, "did you honestly believe that I would allow you, Balam and your two friends to get off this ship alive?"

Kane's head suddenly filled with a surge of static. His shoulders stiffened. Noting the reaction, Enlil uttered a low, guttural chuckle of triumph. "The dampening field is now back online, due to the efforts of Lord Utu. A self-indulgent voluptuary he may be, but he is also gifted in all things electronic."

He reached out for the colored tiles on the board and Kane leveled the Sin Eater, on a direct line with his head. Enlil regarded him with an emotion akin to pity. "You already know how ineffectual your weapon is against me, Kane. The projectiles certainly hurt, but they can't kill me—certainly not before I pluck out both your eyes and stuff them in your mouth."

When Kane didn't reply, Enlil lowered his voice and said in an almost sympathetic croon, "You may recall the counsel I offered you before, when I wore a different face and different name—resign yourself to what cannot be changed. Do not fight anymore. There is no use it."

"I remember," Kane replied in the same low tone. "And I also remembered how I took that advice to heart."

Swinging the Sin Eater toward the terminal, he depressed the trigger stud, firing through all the rounds remaining in the magazine in one long stuttering roar. Bright brass arcing from the ejector port mixed with flying splinters of crystal. The translucent skull dissolved in a spray of glittering fragments.

When the firing pin struck the empty chamber, Kane matter-of-factly returned the pistol to its holster and met Enlil's shocked gaze with an unemotional one of his own.

"Sort of like *that,* as I recall."

Chapter 24

The sudden squall of static from the Commtacts distracted Grant and Brigid Baptiste long enough for the pair of Nephilim to get the drop on them.

Brigid had taken only a few steps into the corridor leading to the hangar bay when the gray-armored man lunged from an open doorway and snatched her up in his arms, using her as a shield against Grant.

The big man was too occupied with fending off a Nephilim in red armor. He body-blocked Grant, driving him backward, reaching out for a scuttling Balam at the same time.

Raising her boot, Brigid stamped down hard on her captor's instep, raking the edge of her heel down his shin. It was a move she'd learned from Grant and Kane, but it was completely futile due to his alloy-shod limbs. Her next tactic was to butt the Nephilim with the back of her head. This move was marginally more effective.

The man grunted in pained surprise and loosened his grip. Taking advantage of the shift in his weight, Brigid secured a tight double-handed hold on his right arm and bent it forward, slamming her rear end into his lower belly. She put all of her strength in the move. The man came over her back, and she maintained the grip on his forearm as she dropped him to the deck, bringing him down with a loud clatter.

The breath left him in a whoosh. Without hesitation, Brigid kicked him in the temple as hard as she could. He groaned in pain and started trying to claw his way up from the floor. She kicked him in the face, splitting his lower lip, then again in the temple. The toe of her boot ripped away the filaments extending from the half helmet into his flesh. Little pinpoints of crimson bloomed on his skin, and the man stopped moving, frozen in place, his mouth half-open, blood trickling from his lacerated lip.

Staring at him nonplussed, Brigid carefully released her hold on his arm and stepped back. The Nephilim didn't move. He remained in the semiprone position, arm raised as if reaching for something.

At the same time, Grant opened up with his Sin Eater against the red-armored Nephilim who was intent on capturing Balam. The echoes of the Sin Eater's fusillade rolled and rang as Grant marched forward, arm extended straight out, the pistol at the end of it spitting fire and lead.

The Nephilim careened away from the 9 mm barrage, body jerking and twitching under the multiple impacts against his armor-encased torso. The corridor filled with a jackhammering racket, as of a blacksmith pounding an anvil in a crazed tempo. His feet slid and rasped on the floor as the bullets directed the Nephilim back into the open door of the chamber from which he had lunged. Heels catching on the edge of the raised floor, he fell unceremoniously onto his back, legs kicking furiously. One round punched a hole through his forehead, but he managed to fire one last ASP blast.

The bolt of flaming energy brushed the barrel of Grant's Sin Eater. For an instant, the gun was enclosed within a cocoon of blinding energy. The cocoon burst, and the Sin Eater exploded with it. Crying out in surprise and pain, Grant staggered the width of the corridor and fell heavily against the opposite wall. Both Brigid and Balam rushed to him. Lips compressed tightly, Grant gripped his right wrist with his left hand.

A halo of smoke surrounded what was left of his Sin Eater. His gloved hand still gripped the butt, but the rest of pistol was gone, blasted away by the proton plasma. Little blobs of semislagged steel clung to the sleeve of his shadow suit. He worked at the tabs and straps of the holster, finally just ripping it away and letting it drop to smolder on the deck.

Brigid reached out for his hand, but Grant pulled away. Grabbing him by the bicep, she said curtly, "Let me look at it."

"There's nothing to see," he bit out. Experimentally, he flexed his fingers. They stirred feebly. They were numb, feeling as large as cucumbers. "I'm all right, I think."

Balam regarded him searchingly, then gingerly touched his hand with one long finger, tracing a line from the knuckles to the wrist. After a moment, he said, "No serious damage. If not for your glove, you could have easily lost your hand."

"Feels like I have already," he snapped. "I hope I can still pilot us out of here."

"That may not be an option now," Brigid said grimly, tapping her Commtact. "The dampening umbrella is open again. I don't know if that means control of the computer has been taken back from Enki or if Kane is…"

She didn't finish, refusing to utter the possibility.

Balam narrowed his big eyes and turned his head this way and that, like a foxhound casting for a scent on the wind. He announced flatly, "He is not dead, but his thoughts are a chaotic jumble, far more extreme than is usual for him."

"Is he in trouble?" Grant demanded.

Balam nodded. "I believe so."

Grant stepped over to the Nephilim frozen on the deck and gingerly prodded him with the toe of his boot. The man fell over, his arms and legs barely moving as if he were a mannequin that had somehow dropped on the floor.

"What the hell is going on here?" he asked, mystified. "He's paralyzed or something."

"The control circuit was interrupted," Balam said, gesturing to the filaments hanging like loose threads from the underside of the helmet.

Grant's face twisted in disgust. "You mean the Nephilim don't possess the means for independent thought?"

Balam's thin mouth pursed. "That would depend greatly on what overlord they serve. This one belongs to Lord Nergal."

"Is there another access terminal anywhere nearby?" Brigid asked, eyes bright with worry and tension.

Balam surveyed the corridor, then started off quickly toward the double doors at the end of the passage. "Logic suggests there should be one right outside the launch bay."

Grant and Brigid started off after him. "Why do you say that?" Grant inquired, still cradling his injured hand.

"Annunaki engineers were notoriously efficient

about designing redundancies into their systems. If for some reason the hangar deck could not be depressurized or the exterior airlock doors opened or closed, a direct data feed to the appropriate control mechanism would overcome a number of problems."

On the bulkhead beside the right-hand door, Balam ran his fingers over the metal. A shutter opened, revealing a two-by-two-foot square made up of crystal points throbbing and pulsing with multihued light. Like a drawer, the board containing the colored tiles popped out. Immediately, Balam began manipulating the little squares, deftly sliding them from one position to another.

The lights changed color, shifted through different spectra, and Balam declared with relief, "Reactivating the jamming field apparently was the limit of the overlords' interference with Enki. The hangar deck operational systems are still open. We can depart at any time."

Grant and Brigid raised questioning eyebrows at each other. Grant wiggled his fingers and uttered a short hiss of pain. "I think it'd be best to wait for Kane."

Balam regarded him soberly. "Those were not his instructions."

Brigid shrugged. "He's not the boss of us."

"I understand," Balam retorted, "but it might be a very unwise tactic to wait for him indefinitely. We should set a time limit for him to join us here."

"What if he doesn't make it by then?" Grant challenged.

Balam blinked but said nothing.

Quietly, Brigid said, "If he's not back here in let's say

fifteen minutes, then you and Balam can fly back to Cerberus."

Balam swiveled his head toward her. "What will you do?"

"Go and find him and bring him back." Brigid's tone was cool, almost detached but very confident. "What else?"

Grant pulled in a long breath and released it slowly. "Why am I not surprised?"

ENLIL'S ASTOUNDED EYES darted from the shambles of the computer terminal to Kane's face. His lips worked, but no sound came forth. Kane guessed what he was trying to say.

"Yeah, yeah, I know," he stated with studied nonchalance. "I only bought me and my friends some time. There are plenty of other interfaces around this hulk. But this was the only one that had a direct link to Enki. Without it, you'll have to hunt and peck looking for him through all those data streams, all those digital impulses, and all those confusing neural networks. By the time you find him, we'll have forced you to live up to your end of the bargain."

He started to step past Enlil, but the consternation in the overlord's eyes was instantly replaced by fury. He reached out to push Kane back, and Kane slapped his hand away as hard as he could. A pair of rings flew from his fingers, clinking to the catwalk.

"Get out of my way," Kane said between clenched teeth. "I may not have been able to kill you as either Thrush or Sam, but if you don't step aside, I'll be scraping you off the bottom of my boot in about five minutes."

Enlil didn't reply in words. He took a long step backward, moving his arms in slow, sweeping arcs in accordance with an arcane school of martial arts. He growled a wordless challenge from deep in his throat. Kane assumed that the overlord expected the primitive sound to make him pause.

Instead he leaped to the attack, falling forward to deliver a swift roundhouse kick to his belly. He let the momentum carry him all the way around to drive a stab kick at the back of Enlil's right knee.

Enlil's leg buckled, but he didn't fall. He staggered, caught himself on the top rail and whirled to face his black-clad opponent, his eyes bright with kill lust. Kane assumed a combat posture, reservoirs of adrenaline pumping through his system.

In a deliberately theatrical, challenging move, he swept his arms up and around, locking them in positions diagonal to his torso. Allowing a cold, taunting smile to play over his face, he beckoned to Enlil with a forefinger and whispered, "Here endeth your reign, Sammy."

Roaring in fury, Enlil bounded toward him, swinging his clawed hands in strange, intricate, crisscrossing motions. Kane backed away from a slashing right hand, ducked to the left and leaped forward, throwing his fists in a one-two jab at Enlil's face with every ounce of his weight behind them.

Enlil evaded the both punches with lightning-swift moves of his head. He swung his left hand viciously in return, fingers bent into hooks. His claws struck Kane across the ribs and the impact numbed his left side. If not for the shadow suit, he had no doubt the raking blow would have disemboweled him. For a long moment they stood toe to toe and exchanged a flurry of blows and blocks. Kane landed a wicked uppercut, but then took a punishing right hook to the belly.

He nearly doubled over as streaks of pain lanced through his solar plexus, but he managed to shift aside and stay upright. He estimated that Enlil's strength was at least twice his own. His expression had to have betrayed that realization to Enlil.

Snarling out a laugh, Enlil closed in. Kane stood his ground and pumped both fists into Enlil's face in short pistoning motions. The overlord staggered, blood springing from his lips, but he didn't fall. He lunged forward again, long arms swinging wide. Kane used his left forearm to shunt aside a clawed hand driving toward his face. Following through, he delivered a backhanded ram's-head jab between Enlil's eyes. It was like backhanding a statue. Pain flared in his wrist, halfway up to his elbow.

Enlil stumbled back a pace, glared at Kane with a combination of rage and disbelief and then charged forward, sweeping him up in a vicious embrace. Kane tried to fight his way out of the hug, knowing close quarters would be fatal. He wasn't able to deflect Enlil's arms.

Close locked, Kane and Enlil wrestled and struggled, staggering on hard-braced legs, slamming against the metal wall of the ziggurat. Purple silk sleeves ripped. Enlil's arms encircled Kane's body and they tightened across his spine. He heard the creaking of cartilage, and his breath blew out of his mouth in a hoarse cry.

Enlil chuckled thickly. "Do you know what that sound signifies to me, Kane? It is the sound of your kind's extinction. A tiny whimper of resignation, not a roar of defiance."

Enlil cinched down tighter, and Kane knew his adversary's greater strength could break his back like latticework. Instead of trying to fight his way out of the hug, Kane drove the crown of his head against Enlil's chin. His jaws closed with a clack. Kane butted him again, this time flattening his nose. The overlord's head snapped back, the luster of his scales dimmed by a spattering of blood.

With a croaking bellow, Enlil flung Kane away from him. He fell heavily, the impact with the catwalk nearly driving all the air from his lungs. He rose as quickly as he could, a sick dizziness assailing him.

Enlil uncoiled into a spinning back-fist, pivoting from the waist, arms at full extension. Before Kane could move, the ring-weighted blow exploded against the right side of his jaw. Agony threaded through his consciousness. Instinctively, he turned with the punch, then dropped down to the floor to avoid his opponent's other hand. He swept Enlil's feet out from under him with a leg-scythe. His side and lower back felt as if they were on fire, taking his breath away, but he forced himself to his feet, achieving a standing posture before Enlil got to his knees.

Kane launched a front stab kick that caught Enlil in the chest. Enlil nearly went down again, but then set his knees and feet and sprang upward, his clawed hands whipping around in a blur.

Staying loose, bouncing on the balls of his feet, his breath ragged in his own ears, Kane danced away from the ivory talons slashing by his face, missing his eyes by a scant fraction of an inch. Perspiration beaded his forehead. Snarling, Enlil brought his left hand down in a vicious overhand loop. Kane sidestepped, using all of his Mag skills and experience to avoid the overlord's punch. Enlil stumbled, off balance from the force of his unconnected blow.

Instantly, Kane leaned back in, closing his hand around Enlil's left wrist. He slipped his forearm in front of Enlil's wrist, concentrating on keeping his opponent's limb locked down. He brought a knee up and slammed Enlil in the groin, having no idea if striking him in such an area would inflict any damage.

Enlil's reaction, if any, was minimal. Growling like an animal, Enlil twisted in Kane's grip, and with his free arm, Kane pounded three elbow strikes against the overlord's side and stomach. As Enlil continued twisting, the strange spiny growths from his shoulder ripped through the silk tabard, slashing at Kane's face. He released the arm-lock, but the tip of a spine sliced a thin, shallow furrow along his right temple.

Kane felt the flow of blood running down the side of his face and his neck. Putting his back to the metal rail of the catwalk, he watched Enlil approach him slowly, wiping the scarlet spatters from his face with the back of one hand.

Baring red-filmed teeth in either a grin or a grimace, Enlil intoned breathlessly, "Even if you escape Tiamat, you will not escape me. I will still come down to your stronghold and take my mate."

"You can try," Kane husked out. "We won't treat invaders mercifully."

"You dare speak of invasion?" Enlil's eyes blazed bright with fury as he swept his arms around. "You have invaded the holiest of holies, the most revered artifact

of my race and use her like a pawn in a cheap gambit?
I will not forget this blasphemy, Kane. Nor shall she."

Kane met Enlil's gaze unblinkingly. Then he feinted
toward him, turned and raced up to the uppermost level,
three risers at a time. When he reached the very top, he
realized he had made a serious mistake. He had run
himself into a trap, a cul de sac. There was no way up
or down except along the same stairway—and Enlil
was now climbing it, both hands on the rails.

He looked up at the array of lights on the ceiling, attached to a complicated framework. They were too high
to reach. Kane took a deep breath, crouched and set himself, eyes fixed on the head of the stairs. He strained his
ears, listening to the tramping sounds of Enlil's steady
ascent.

When his head and shoulders appeared, Kane sank
in almost a prone position, balancing himself on the ball
of his right foot and the flat of his left hand. Enlil's torso
rose and Kane launched himself into a spinning *tobi-
geri* flying kick. As he whirled, he slammed Enlil on the
side of his head with his extended left foot and smashed
his right heel into his jaw.

Kane's ferocious double kick drew a gargling cry
from Enlil. He tottered on the riser, arms windmilling
wildly. His left hand desperately closed around Kane's
right ankle as he toppled backward. He hung on to him
as he crashed down the stairs. Together they tumbled
headlong down the stairway locked in each other's arms,
tearing at each other. The brain-jarring impacts of hitting the risers caused Kane's surroundings to wink out
for an instant.

He relaxed his body, allowing it to go in the direction gravity pulled it. He used his legs as clubs, his head as a battering ram, smashing them against Enlil repeatedly as they rolled.

Moving with ophidian fluidity, Enlil twisted his body to one side when they hit the landing. Kane struck the floor grille on his left shoulder, and he bounced toward the edge of the tier.

Dazed, he tried to ignore the knives of pain stabbing through him as he hauled himself to his feet by the guardrail. Enlil, bleeding from a laceration on his scalp, bounded at him in a smashing attack, bending him back over the rail. His teeth gleamed in a snarl, and he sank steely fingers into the muscles of Kane's throat.

Only the high collar of his shadow suit kept Enlil's sharp nails from puncturing the flesh beneath. Kane hit him with all the strength he could muster, connecting with the heel of his left hand under his chin. Although Enlil's head snapped back amid a spray of crimson droplets, he only bore down on the stranglehold.

His hands cinched tighter around Kane's throat, cutting off his ability to breathe, to think. Enlil's face tilted crazily above him, swimming off into a blurry fog at the edges. Distantly a with a rather detached sense of horror, he heard the strange, dry sound of cracking vertebrae.

Fighting for air, Kane raised both hands above his head, clasping them together. Pivoting violently to the left from the waist, he used the well-developed wing muscle at the base of his shoulder socket as a fulcrum, prying away Enlil's stranglehold.

The overlord snarled as his hands lost their grip, and a gasping Kane lashed out with his leg, a blind flailing rather than a well-aimed or -timed kick. Still, Enlil stumbled backward a few paces as Kane sagged against the railing, tasting blood, breath coming in strangled rasps.

Enlil voiced a harsh, angry laugh, then rushed him. Clutching the rail with both hands, Kane kicked himself off the platform and closed his legs around Enlil's waist in a scissor-lock. Tightening his body like a bowstring, he allowed the momentum of the overlord's attack to lever him up and over.

Enlil, feeling himself anchored at the waist by lithe legs, cried out in alarm. Kane back somersaulted over the rail, his hands maintaining their grasp. However, he relaxed his legs' grip around the overlord.

Enlil had time only for one cry, more of anger and astonishment than fear, before he plummeted straight down to the deck fifty-plus feet below, the sleeves of his tabard flapping like wings. The hollow thud came up as faintly as the distant thump of a footfall. Still dangling from the rail, shoulder sockets burning with a deep, piercing pain as they supporting all of his weight, Kane twisted around and looked down past his feet. Enlil lay sprawled out, motionless, near the base of a black pylon. Even as he stared, Kane saw a dark red puddle edging out from beneath his body.

Clenching his teeth, Kane hauled himself back up to the tier, a fine sheen of moisture dampening his body, mixing with the blood trickling from the claw-inflicted wound on his temple. He felt justified in taking a moment to catch his breath and take stock of himself. His arms and legs ached and his rib cage felt sore and bruised. As he started down the stairs, a sharp pain drove its hot knife into his right thigh, letting him know he had torn or strained a ligament somewhere. He had gotten off lucky, though—or so he tried to tell himself as he used both metal banisters for support.

By the time he had reached the foot of the stairs, Kane leaned against only one of the rails. He hobbled among the pylons, making his way over to Enlil's body. When he couldn't find it, he at first hoped he had made a mistake as to where it was positioned. That hope lasted for less than twenty seconds. He came across a fresh smear of blood glistening on the deck, a scrap of purple silk, but no sign of Enlil.

Exhaling wearily, Kane put his back to one of the black pillars and murmured under his breath, "Why am I not surprised."

After a long moment of gathering his strength and massaging his sore muscles, he pushed himself away from the pylon , hobbling in the direction of the elevator. He had gone only a few steps when the gold-armored Nephilim, Enlil's personal attendant, stepped out from behind a pillar to block his way.

Kane stared into the man's white, blank eyes and intoned, "Get the fuck out of my way."

To his surprise, the Nephilim did just that.

Chapter 25

Most of the people who lived in the Cerberus redoubt acted in the capacity of support personnel, regardless of their specialized individual skills or training. They worked rotating shifts, eight hours a day, seven days a week. Primarily, their work was the routine maintenance and monitoring of the installation's environmental systems, the satellite data feed and the security network.

However, everyone was given at least a superficial understanding of all the redoubt's systems so anyone could pinch-hit in times of emergency. Fortunately, only once had such a time arrived. Afterward Lakesh felt completely justified in his insistence that everyone have a working knowledge of the inner systems so as to keep the redoubt operational.

Grant and Kane were exempt from this cross-training inasmuch as they served as the exploratory and enforcement arm of Cerberus and undertook far and away the lion's share of the risks. On their downtime between missions they made sure all the ordnance in the armory was in good condition and occasionally tuned up the vehicles in the depot.

Brigid Baptiste, due to her eidetic memory, was the most exemplary member of the redoubt's permanent staff, since she could step into any vacancy. However, her gifts were a two-edged sword, inasmuch as those selfsame polymathic skills made her an indispensable addition to away missions.

However one of the infrequent tasks that did not fall onto the shoulders of any one person was grave digging, although Farrell had been pressed into service more than once to fabricate gravestones in the redoubt's workshop.

Wegmann leaned on the handle of his shovel and looked at the row of headstones at the foot of the slope bordering the plateau. The small white cubes bore only engraved last names: Cotta, Rouch, Adrian, Davis and seven others. There were no other inscriptions, no birth or death dates on the austere markers.

Wegmann wondered idly if Farrell would have to fashion the headstones for Kane, Brigid and Grant before too much longer. If so, he would not volunteer to dig their graves.

He glanced up into the leaden, midmorning sky. The wind, which had been gusting around the mountain peak for the past hour, had grown progressively colder. Indian summer felt as if it had come to a decisive end, and the overcast day was perfect backdrop to his task.

A balding, sharp-featured, slightly built man under medium height, Wegmann served as the Cerberus redoubt's engineer, tending to the nuclear generators and the reactor buried deep within the stony bosom of the mountain. This day he had volunteered for the grave-digging duty for reasons that were murky even to him. He didn't mind the ache settling into his lower back or the slight sting of blisters forming on his hands.

The pain kept his mind from dwelling on far more

anguishing memories, the least of which was the unpleasant recollections the sight of Rouch's grave marker evoked in him.

Beth-Li Rouch's headstone was the grim symbol of what had become of Lakesh's abortive plan to turn Cerberus from a sanctuary to a colony. The man had wanted babies to be born, but only ones with superior genes so they would grow into adulthood as warriors against the barons.

Making a unilateral decision, Lakesh arranged for a woman named Beth-Li Rouch to be brought into the redoubt from one of the baronies to mate with Kane, to insure that his superior abilities were passed on to offspring.

Without access to the techniques of fetal development outside the womb that were practiced in the villes, the conventional means of procreation was the only option. And that meant sex and passion and the fury of a woman scorned.

Although Wegmann wasn't sure of all the details, he knew Kane had refused to cooperate for a variety of reasons, primarily because he felt the plan was a continuation of sinister, manipulative elements that had brought about the nukecaust and the tyranny of the villes. His refusal had tragic consequences. Only a thirst for revenge and a conspiracy to murder had been birthed within the walls of the redoubt, not children.

Wegmann sighed sadly. The beautiful Beth-Li had tried to seduce him, set him up as the assassin of Kane, Grant and Brigid Baptiste. Instead, he had set her up but he hadn't foreseen she would be killed by Domi and buried in a simple grave out on the hillside.

Suddenly, at the far edge of audibility he heard a faint, keening whine. Looking up, he scanning the overcast sky as the whines grew in volume. The familiar winged outlines of two of the Manta TAVs appeared overhead.

Engaging the vectored-thrust ramjets, the Mantas dropped straight down and gracefully came to rest on the extended landing gear, on either side of the other pair of ships covered by camouflage netting. Fine clouds of dust puffed up all around, and Wegmann squinted away from the grit, shielding his eyes.

When the throb of the engines cycled down to a whine, he looked toward the craft again. The canopies were opaque so it was impossible to see who sat within the cockpits.

With a click of solenoids and a hiss of seals releasing, the canopy of the Manta nearest him popped open and slid back. Silently, he watched Kane heave himself out of the pilot's seat and stand on the wing. He extended a hand into the cockpit and when the sunset hue of Brigid Baptiste's hair came into view, Wegmann experienced a wave of relief so intense his knees went momentarily weak.

His relief wasn't quite as pronounced when he saw Grant and Balam climb out of the second Manta. He held no onus against Grant, since the big man had always treated him cordially, but the sight of the big-headed, big-eyed Balam still gave him the shivers.

Wegmann didn't show his apprehension of the Archon. He continued to lean on the shovel as the four figures approached. He took note of the dried blood streaking the right side of Kane's face and how he walked stiffly, as if his legs pained him. The others appeared to be uninjured, but they didn't seem very happy to be back at Cerberus, either.

When they caught sight of him standing at the bottom of the half-dug grave, all of their faces registered emotion of differing degrees. Wegmann fancied that even Balam's face twitched in reaction.

Standing at the head of the grave site, Kane asked, "When?" His voice was little more than a rustling whisper.

"Around daybreak," Wegmann answered matter-of-factly.

Brigid swallowed hard before asking, "And the baby?"

"She gave birth to a little girl—that's all I know." He tightened his hands around the shovel's handle and the wood creaked. "As far as I know, she was born perfectly healthy. Domi is looking after her—"

Wegmann's business-like demeanor cracked, and he squeezed his eyes shut against the hot sting of tears. "She was always nice to me. I liked her. Respected her."

"We know," Brigid said softly, the breeze stirring her hair. "She felt the same way about you."

Wegmann took a steadying breath, then plunged the shovel blade into the ground. "DeFore said she died of eclampsia, but I think she only said that for our benefit…maybe hers, too. I don't think she really knows what killed her."

Quietly, Grant stated, "You may want to put that off for a bit. We're expecting company."

Wegmann affected not to have heard him, levering up a shovel full of loose earth and dumping it on the pile to his left.

"When they come," Grant continued, raising his voice a trifle, "they're not coming for us but for Qua-vell's baby."

Wegmann looked up at him. "Who is?"

"We're convening a redoubt-wide briefing," Kane answered flatly. "We'll explain then."

Wegmann started shoveling again. "Fetch me then."

Brigid reached down and laid a hand on the back of his head, where his gray-threaded brown hair was tied back in a knot. In a remarkably gentle tone, she said, "We're calling it now. We don't have much time to pre-pare. As hard-hearted as this sounds, if we don't make ready as soon as possible, then you'll find yourself dig-ging a lot more graves."

Wegmann paused, pondering, not looking at her. Then he shot an inquisitive glance up at Brigid, then over at Kane and Grant. They met his gaze sympathet-ically. None of them took his misanthropic tendencies seriously, not since he had risked his own life to save theirs from Beth-Li's machinations. Brigid extended her hand to him.

With a profanity-seasoned sigh, Wegmann jammed the blade of the shovel into the loose dirt and took Brigid's hand. "I'm getting blisters anyway."

THEY WASTED NO TIME with explanations on anyone, even an agitated Lakesh, whom they found in the oper-ations center. Brigid announced a meeting in the third-level briefing room in ten minutes. They didn't see DeFore or Domi, and Kane wasn't inclined to seek ei-ther of them out.

During times of crisis, he could essentially turn his

emotions off or at the very least shove them into a dark corner of his psyche. As hot as his anger could burn, he could also make himself glacially cold if circumstances warranted. The circumstances definitely warranted, as far as he and his friends were concerned.

The miniauditorium hadn't been used for its official function since its first installation-wide briefing a few months before. Generally, the big room served as a theater where the personnel watched old movies on DVD and laser disks found in storage.

Kane mounted the stage a precise ten minutes after Brigid had made the announcement, and like the previous incident, she and Grant flanked him as he faced the seventy-plus members of the Cerberus staff who had sat in the auditorium.

Once again he was struck by the number of people who had made the redoubt their home over the past five months. When he, Grant, Domi and Brigid had arrived at the installation more than two years before, there had been only a dozen permanent residents. Like them, they were all exiles from the villes, but unlike them, the others had been brought there by Lakesh because of their training and abilities. For a long time, the Cerberus personnel were outnumbered by shadowed corridors, empty rooms and sepulchral silences.

As the three people stood shoulder to shoulder on the stage, they took full advantage of their reputations among the Moon base émigrés. Kane had deliberately refrained from cleaning the dried blood from his face. Even if their warrior mystique had lost some of its luster due to familiarity, the three of them still symbolized the heroic trinity that had freed the inhabitants of Manitius from lives of unending terror and offered them an alternative to dying unknown and unmourned on Luna.

The sounds of murmuring and shuffling feet faded away as the three people stood at the podium and looked out over the faces they recognized and the many they didn't. They saw Auerbach, Farrell, Wegmann and Lakesh scattered among the Moon base evacuees. They spotted Shizuka, Philboyd and the Tigers of Heaven sitting together. To Kane's surprise he saw Erica van Sloan sitting in the rear. He had thought she would have returned to Xian long before.

Neither Bry nor Balam was in attendance. Bry was absent because Brigid had asked him to keep tracking Tiamat. They had decided Balam's presence would excite the wrong kind of emotion.

When silence fell over the room, Kane said without any form of introduction, "We called all of you here to let you know that in a short time, Cerberus will most likely be under attack…not from Mags or barons but from the bastards who've been pulling their strings for the last few thousand years."

The acoustics in the miniauditorium were such he didn't need to use the public-address system. Everyone heard him perfectly and they didn't like what they heard.

"Those of you who lived on the Moon base already know about the reality of the Annunaki," Brigid declared in a strong, clear voice. "We don't have to convince you about the fact of their existence. You know they used Luna as their cemetery, their crypts and mausoleums. Some of you may have even seen their bodies in the tombs. But it was *only* their bodies that died. Their minds lived on."

Without waiting for the surge of apprehensive murmuring to ebb, Brigid explained in terse, unprettied language all that they learned about the Supreme Council of Overlords, Tiamat and the events they had witnessed aboard her.

"We don't know the full extent of the interference with the ship's onboard computer systems," Kane interjected. "But we have it on fairly reliable authority that Tiamat can launch small ships against us."

The remark drew a collective moan of dismay from the assemblage. Philboyd called up, "Why would they bother to do that? Once Tiamat's systems are back online and fully restored, why can't they just assume a geosynchronous orbit over Cerberus and blow the whole damn mountain to gravel?"

Another voice, quavering with panic shouted, "We can't make a fight against something like that!"

People fearfully shouted their querulous agreement with the sentiment, several voices clamoring at once.

"They won't do that!" Grant had to bellow in order to be heard over the frightened babbling. "We've got something they want!"

His pronouncement shut everyone up for a moment. From the front row, Avery demanded, "Like what? What the hell do we have that gods care about it?"

"They're a bunch of jumped-up half-alien egomaniacs who got used to being treated like gods," Kane snapped. "They got so used to it, they couldn't give it up, not even when they died. Just because a bunch of desert tribespeople kissed their scaly asses twenty thousand years ago doesn't make them gods."

"What do we have they want?" Wegmann asked waspishly, shooting a cold, warning stare at Avery.

Kane glanced over at Lakesh, his elbow propped up on an armrest of his chair, fist under his chin. Judging by the grave expression on the scientist's face, Kane knew he had already reasoned it out.

"We have Enlil's wife," Brigid declared. "Quavell gave birth to her."

Stunned silence hung over the auditorium for a long moment as shocked, confused eyes fixed on her. Before questions about her veracity, sanity or lack of both qualities could be hurled her way, Brigid tersely repeated everything that Enlil had revealed to them aboard Tiamat.

"It sounds far-fetched, I know," she concluded. "Perhaps even mad. But we've seen extraordinary examples of Annunaki genetic engineering before. So, just like I have no doubt they can accomplish resurrecting Ninlil in such a fashion, I have no doubt that Enlil and the overlords *will* come here to fetch her."

"How the hell did you manage to escape?" Poltrino asked suspiciously from the front row.

"Sheer luck," Kane admitted. "That's all there was to it. We bluffed the overlords into fearing that if they didn't let us go, then Enki would instigate a system-wide shutdown of the entire ship."

"With all the power they have, they're coming here to abduct Quavell's baby?" Auerbach asked, puzzled. A burly man with a red buzz cut, he served as DeFore's medical aide.

"Abduct wouldn't be the right word," Brigid said curtly. "Enlil thinks he's just reclaiming her. He won't take no for an answer."

Poltrino stood up, but he turned his back on the stage and addressed the assembled people. "Why don't we give the overlords what they want? None of us has any reason to risk our lives for a mutant baby or alien or whatever the hell it is."

"'She,' not 'it,'" Brigid said with icy contempt. "From what I've heard."

Poltrino turned to face her, but he stabbed a finger at Kane. "Yeah? Well, from what *I've* heard, he's the only one with a connection to either the baby or the mother."

"You heard wrong," Kane bit out.

Poltrino affected not have heard. "Why don't you give yourself and the baby over to Enlil? It's you two he has the problem with."

Lakesh's voice came as sharp as a whip crack. "Shut up and sit down."

Poltrino regarded him with an over-the-shoulder scowl. "We should take a vote on this. If the majority decides that—"

Lakesh levered himself out his chair with both arms. "I told you to shut up and sit down, Mr. Poltrino. One more word and I'll have you sent back to Manitius—permanently."

The man thrust out his jaw in a feeble show of pugnacious defiance. "I'm not the only one here thinking this. Everybody knows Kane knocked up Quavell, right? He's the father, so why should we stick our necks out—?"

"Enough!" Lakesh lost his temper, pushing his way between the chairs. Grabbing a double handful of the man's bodysuit, he slammed him violently back into his seat.

"You execrable idiot!" His voice was a strident crash of fury, his blue eyes alight with it. "Kane is not the father of Quavell's baby, and it would not matter even if he were! Everyone in Cerberus owes him, Brigid and Grant their lives. In my case, several times over."

All eyes gazed with surprise at Lakesh's sudden and unexpected display of outrage. Normally, he presented a warm facade, the epitome of the absentminded but good-natured man of science. Now he seemed consumed by volcanic anger.

"Haven't you been listening?" he shouted. "If the Annunaki reassert their reign, rebuild their empire, there will be no such thing as free humans except as slaves to be pampered, tortured or otherwise subjected to the whims of their masters. As for this matter—the overlords would not spare us regardless of what we do to appease them. Their egos won't allow anyone here in the redoubt to live!"

Stepping to the edge of the stage, Brigid said, "Lakesh is right. Even as reborn Annunaki, they haven't forgotten anything of their lives as barons. More than a couple of them have personal scores to settle with us."

"Besides," Kane declared flatly, "there's nowhere to run. If any of you go back to the Moon, you'll only be returning to snake-face central. They'll be along directly to salvage what they left there, and they won't take kindly to squatters."

Grant nodded. "And settling in any of the ville territories is out of the question. Once word spreads that the barons are gone, most of the villes will tear themselves apart with civil war."

"That's already started in a couple of the baronies," Philboyd spoke up bleakly. "We've listened in on reports of riots and attempted coups. It didn't take long for factionalizing to begin, according to what we've heard."

Philboyd referred to the eavesdropping system Bry had established through the communications linkup with the Comsat satellite. It was the same system and same satellite used to track the subcutaneous transponder signals implanted within the Cerberus personnel.

Bry had worked on the system for a long time and had managed to develop an undetectable method of patching into the wireless communications channels of all the baronies in one form or another. The success rate wasn't one hundred percent, but Cerberus had been able to eavesdrop on a number of the villes and learn about baron-sanctioned operations in the Outlands. The different frequencies were monitored on a daily basis, at least part of the day by Philboyd.

"This place is defensible," Grant rumbled, raking the assembled personnel with a challenging, flinty stare. "We've got enough firepower here to overthrow a couple of villes ourselves."

"Do we get to use any of that firepower?" Reynolds asked with a feeble grin. "Or will you be handing out more pointy sticks?"

A ripple of nervous but appreciative laughter passed among the people. Kane chuckled, too, and he hoped it didn't sound too forced. "You can have your pick of the toys in the armory."

Sullenly, Poltrino asked, "You think any of your toys will do us any good in a fight against a mile-long spaceship and particle-beam weapons?"

A corner of Kane's mouth curved upward in an insolent half smirk. "I think that you can't always choose the winning side, Mr. Poltrino. And a lot of times, you shouldn't. I also think this is a fight that's been building for thousands of years. Make no mistake about this—the overlords won't operate the same way as the barons. They won't stake out small pieces of territory and be content to live within their boundaries."

"Hardly," Lakesh said with a hard edge of certainty. "All the former checks and balances that kept the barons behaving halfway civilly among one another have been flushed down the proverbial toilet. According to myth and history, the Annunaki royalty divided up entire countries, even continents among themselves."

"And," Brigid interjected, "they engaged in never-ending conflicts to take them away from one another, using humanity as both beasts of burden and cannon fodder. This is *not* a kinder or more enlightened Supreme Council. If anything, they'll be more ruthless than they were twenty thousand years ago. There is none of their own kind to stand up against their excesses."

Kane tapped his chest, gestured to Grant and Brigid and then to everyone in the briefing hall. "That's why it's up to us. We have to draw the line here and now— show them how far they can go and no farther. They've got to learn that there are some humans on Earth who won't be queuing up to kiss their scaly asses."

Bluntly, Grant said, "This isn't an army. None of you here are conscripts. We can't force you to fight. But if you don't come up with a workable alternative to fighting the overlords, then I suggest you gate out of here as soon as you can. I wouldn't count on being welcomed back, though."

Philboyd gazed up at him with troubled, surprised eyes. "That's a little hard-nosed, isn't it?"

"It's a *lot* hard-nosed," Grant conceded harshly. "But whatever happens, I don't want Cerberus to be supplying the first generation of new slaves to the overlords. Those of you who do elect stay, there's only two rules—you *will* fight and you won't quit."

Kane declared, "I can't even guess how this will end or even give you odds who'll come out of it alive. If it's any consolation at all, the Annunaki aren't ready to fight an all-out war yet...at least I don't think they are.

"All I really know is this—I'm no more eager to serve the overlords than I was the barons. I'm even less eager to see the Annunaki get a toehold on the Earth again. We may not be able to stop them from taking Quavell's baby, but we can sure as hell make it so difficult for them they'll have nightmares about it for the rest of their misbegotten lives."

He took a deep breath and then waved toward the door. "Let's start planning their welcome-home party."

None of the people cheered at the words, but they all seemed to accept the reality. There was no other option than to make a fight of it. They were not determined or inspired, they were simply resigned. They left the mini-auditorium to prepare. Although he looked for her, Kane did not see Erica leave.

Lakesh and Philboyd moved to the edge of the stage. "Very stirring, friend Kane," Lakesh said.

"Thanks," Kane replied dryly. "And thanks for standing up for me."

Lines of sadness deepened on either side of Lakesh's nose and furrowed his brow. "I fear I've had to do quite a bit of that over the last day or so. Our good doctor is very unhappy with you."

Kane nodded as if he expected to hear the observation. "I'll drop by the infirmary and try to make amends. But I'm not very happy with myself at the moment, either."

Brigid eyed him with surprise. "Why? What've you done?"

Kane turned away. "It's what I didn't get done. I didn't kill Enlil. I hope I get a second chance."

Chapter 26

The passage of time in Cerberus was measured by the controlled dimming and brightening of lights to simulate sunrise and sunset, and since most of the people there—with the exception of Domi—had lived for years in enclosed environments, they didn't mind the artificial changeover from day to dusk.

Kane wondered briefly about the shades of twilight inside the infirmary, a stark contrast with the bright lights gleaming on the vanadium-sheathed walls and floors of the main corridor. He stood in the doorway for a moment, allowing his eyes to adjust to the gloom.

The examination area was unoccupied, but he heard a faint murmuring from the laboratory. Soft-footing across the big room, he peered around the door frame and a fist seemed to knot painfully inside his chest. He saw a sheet-shrouded form lying on the table. He had no trouble recognizing Quavell's slight figure beneath the covering.

Her left hand was visible, only partially concealed. A wheeled tray of medical instruments had been pushed against the head of the bed, and Kane wondered if DeFore had performed an autopsy or was making preparations.

Shadows shifted on the far side of the room. It required a few seconds for him to realize that Balam sat in a chair cradling a tiny, blanket-swathed shape in his arms. Domi and DeFore stood watchfully on either side of him. Domi whispered something inaudible, and Balam replied in an equally low-pitched voice.

Very quietly, Kane asked, "May I come in?"

None of three reacted with much surprise to his voice or presence. Domi whispered, "She's sleeping, so try not to make any noise."

With exaggerated caution, Kane sidled over to the chair. Balam removed a plastic bottle from under a fold of blanket and lifted the fabric away. Because of the dim light, Kane couldn't quickly make out the small, round face topped by wispy dark hair. He gazed down at the sleeping baby, feeling slightly disoriented.

He had not really known what to expect, but the baby appeared so normal, his emotional equilibrium was tilted for a few seconds. The realization that Balam had been feeding the infant was also a difficult concept to quickly grasp.

"Is she all right?" he asked.

A bit stiffly, DeFore answered, "She's a little underweight, but that's not surprising. Otherwise, she's perfectly healthy and normal. No funny eyes, she has ten fingers and ten toes, there's no tail, no scales. Barring the results of a DNA examination, I'd judge she's completely human, genetically."

Kane declined to mention how Enlil had described her genetic structure. "Did Quavell see her before she died?"

Bitterly, eyes glistening like damp rubies, Domi said, "She did…but I don't think she knew little Quav was her baby."

"Little Quav?" Kane echoed.

DeFore shrugged. "It'll do until we come up with a real name for her."

As with the matter of the baby's DNA, Kane decided not mention that Enlil already had a name for her. "What happened to Quavell?"

"A few minutes after you and Grant took off in the Mantas," DeFore replied, "Quavell lapsed into a coma. She was in labor until about dawn. When she delivered the baby, she seemed to rouse. She didn't speak, but she looked straight at little Quav. Then she died. Just like that."

In a broken voice, Domi said, "Like a little bird I had once. She breathed her last, laid her head down and died. She just—"

Domi broke off and turned her face away, her shoulders quaking. Kane gazed at her, too surprised to speak. He had never seen Domi moved to tears before, not even when she learned her entire Outland settlement had been butchered. As it was, he had always been a little puzzled by her attachment to Quavell.

Like Kane, Domi had spent two weeks in captivity within the vast subterranean installation of Area 51. Both of them had been shown the end result of their war against the barons—dying hybrid infants.

Domi experienced profound horror at the sight, filled with guilt and remorse. Kane remembered how the very concept of hybrids once triggered a xenophobic madness in her, the overwhelming urge to kill them, as she had killed mutie borer beetles that sometimes infested the Outland settlement in which she had been born. But upon visiting the nursery-turned-morgue, she felt only a shame, as if the guilt of the entire human race were laid on her small shoulders.

When she was finally reunited with Kane, he reminded her how devoted she was to the war against the hybrid barons and he recalled with crystal clarity the furious, accusatory words she flung at him: "War isn't against babies, not even against hybrids. It's against the barons and against men like you and Grant! Men like you used to be. I wasn't afraid of hybrids in the Outlands. Didn't even know such as them existed. But I was sure as shit scared of the baron's sec men—the Mags. That's who was my enemy."

When Kane darkly observed that the words she spoke didn't sound in character, she retorted angrily, "You and Grant didn't stay what you were. I don't have to stay what I am. I'll forgive 'em for being born."

Recalling that incident, Kane struggled to speak around the hard lump swelling in his throat. "Was it eclampsia that killed her?"

DeFore pursed her lips. "Yes and no. Quavell definitely exhibited the symptoms, but I don't think she died of it. This might not sound very scientific, but I think on some basic, almost autonomic level, Quavell willed herself to die after she gave birth."

"Why would she do that?" Kane demanded suspiciously.

Balam spoke for the first time since Kane entered the room. "She willed herself to conceive a child by the man Maddock, did she not? She was aware of her mind and body's transformation, so I find it reasonable to believe she preferred death to living as a drone of the overlords."

"That's as sound a cause of death as eclampsia," DeFore declared sadly.

The baby stirred and whimpered slightly in Balam's arms. Kane glanced over at Quavell's body on the table. "You haven't done a postmortem?"

DeFore shook her head. "I intended to, but he—" she nodded toward Balam "—convinced me it was pointless. All I would be doing is putting myself and the people who cared about Quavell through needless emotional turmoil."

Kane met Balam's depthless obsidian gaze. "I agree."

Balam stated matter-of-factly, "I also explained to the doctor about the events in Nippur and aboard Tiamat...and the fate Enlil has in mind for the child."

"Yes," DeFore said absently. "You wouldn't have been much use here, Kane. Domi gave me all the support and assistance I needed. It sounds like it was pretty damn rough for you. Do you need any pain medication?"

"No, thanks. I can get by." Kane understood that Balam had exerted a mild psychic nudge on DeFore and probably Domi, to defuse their anger toward him and turn it to compassion.

He inclined his head toward Balam in a short nod of acknowledgment and asked, "Why are you holding little Quav?"

The question seemed to startle DeFore and Domi. Running a hand over her close-cropped white hair, Domi murmured, "Yeah, why are you? I was trying to feed her—"

"I informed you I had a great deal of experience in caring for infants," Balam said flatly, unemotionally. "You had encountered difficulty in persuading the child to take nourishment from the bottle, so I volunteered to try."

"Oh, yeah, right," Domi said vaguely. "Remember now."

Kane figured Balam had telepathically imparted a deftness at child care to the two women. He recalled meeting Balam's two sons in the subterranean city of Agartha in Tibet, so the experience he referred to had some basis in truth.

Stepping over to the table on which Quavell's body was laid out, Kane started to tug the sheet over her exposed hand. He paused, then lifted it, pressing it between both of his. It was like a child's hand, the scale-pebbled flesh clammy but still holding a trace of warmth. Clutched within it was the small figure of Bastet.

"I misjudged her," he said hoarsely.

"She understood why," Balam whispered. "And she did not hold your prejudices against you."

"I'm sorry," he murmured to the shrouded figure. "I shouldn't have been so judgmental, so distrustful of you and your kind."

Nor should she have been toward your kind. Balam didn't speak, but Kane heard him nonetheless. *She made amends, as do you.*

At the sound of footfalls, Kane looked up. Grant, Lakesh, Brigid and Shizuka stepped through the doorway. Softly, Grant said, "We came to pay our respects."

"And to see the baby," Brigid declared.

They clustered around the chair, and if any of them thought the sight of Balam holding a baby in his arms was a strange one, they kept their opinions to themselves.

"She's beautiful," Shizuka breathed.

Brigid lightly stroked the slumbering child's feathery hair. "And she looks completely human, which makes me wonder if Enlil's plans for her have any foundation in reality."

Grant grunted. "She doesn't look like she has even a microscopic dab of Annunaki blood in her."

Dolefully, Lakesh said, "If I recall the Sumerian myth of Ninlil and Enlil correctly, Ninlil was only of partial Annunaki ancestry. She was distantly related to the royal family, but her mother was a human woman."

Shizuka frowned. "How could that be?"

Brigid quoted quietly, "'And it came to pass when the children of men had multiplied, that in those days were born unto them beautiful and comely daughters. And the Watchers lusted after them, and Samyaza who was their leader, said unto them, 'Come, let us choose us wives from among the children of men and beget us children ourselves.'"

Lakesh did a poor job of repressing a shudder, but he said, "Apparently when the Annunaki royal family found a congenial genetic template among humans, they preferred to use it over and over again, with minor variations."

Grant threw him a slit-eyed stare. "In that case, we may not be helping little Quav—or Ninlil—at all. By keeping her away from the overlords, we may be preventing her from reaching her full potential."

Kane made a scoffing sound. "You don't really believe that."

"No, I don't," Grant agreed. "I just thought I'd throw it out there, since we're going to be fighting and possibly dying for her in the not too distant future."

Domi demanded hotly. "You want to give the baby up so a lizard-man can turn her into his bride?"

Lakesh interposed smoothly, "Friend Grant has a point, darlingest Domi, but it is not one we have the luxury of belaboring."

"Indeed not," Balam said. "*When,* not *if,* the overlords launch an assault, it will be a matter of great indifference to them whether you turn the child over to them willingly or they fight for her."

Brigid nodded in grim agreement. "That's how I see the scenario playing out."

Kane laid Quavell's hand down and covered it with the sheet. "Let's get ready for them, then."

Hesitantly, DeFore asked, "Shouldn't we have a memorial service or something for Quavell first?"

Kane's heart felt frozen within him, and it required great effort to turn around and face everyone. "It'll have to wait...otherwise Quavell will have a lot of company, and I don't think she'd want that."

IT SHOULD HAVE BEEN a simple operation, swiftly done, but the Manitius émigrés were unaccustomed to such unremitting physical labor and exertion.

Kane stood out on the plateau, watching from atop the same boulder he had stood upon less than two full days before. It felt like several lifetimes ago.

He oversaw the construction of breastworks and the building of a defensive perimeter all around the edge of the plateau. He gave instructions, offered suggestions and more than once employed insults and threats of violence. He knew the people did their best, but they had become irritable and sore footed, particularly the ones who had made a dozen back-and-forth trips from the armory to the plateau. Several arguments broke out among them, which Kane was forced to settle.

Weapons of all sorts were brought from the arsenal, ordnance that even Kane was somewhat surprised to see—various kinds of rocket launchers, multispigot PRB mortars, and heavy tripod-mounted machine guns that ran the gamut from M-60s to GEC miniguns.

The people running back and forth into the armory chose a variety of small arms for themselves, as well as body armor, helmets and Kevlar vests. Kane's fully loaded Sin Eater was secured to his right forearm and a brace of pistols was holstered at his hips—a trustworthy Colt 1911 A1 pistol and a smaller H&K VP-70.

Kane and Grant spent most of the afternoon trying to coordinate all of the ill-mated strategies and people. To their considerable surprise, Erica van Sloan had not fled the redoubt. In fact, the imperial trooper who had accompanied her busied himself hauling out and setting up weapons emplacements with considerably more efficiency than the Moon base émigrés.

The sky remained cloudy, and they labored beneath a canopy of pewter-colored clouds. The temperature continued to drop, and snow flurries dusted the tarmac. More than once, Kane caught the Manitius personnel looking at him, either for reassurance or orders. He could provide only the latter. For the people who couldn't handle the prospect of what was to come, nothing he could say would reassure them. As it was, there was no time to drill them.

Bry monitored the status of Tiamat throughout the early afternoon, but the ship had not moved from its position over China. Kane figured the vessel's apparent fondness for hovering over the Xian pyramid was one reason Erica had decided to linger in Montana.

He glanced up the slope, noting Grant's activities with a number of volunteers, hiding mortar launchers among the high grasses. Turning toward the point where the plateau narrowed down the road, he watched Lakesh and a couple of techs perform another test on their last line of defense—or the first, depending on from which direction the attack might come.

Lakesh thumbed a toggle on a remote-control box in his right hand, and a pair of metal cylinders, facing each other on opposite sides of road, rose quickly and smoothly from the ground. They towered twelve feet tall and were topped by squares of camouflaging turf. A series of round lights flashed in sequence on their alloyed skins.

Kane resisted the urge to call out a question to Lakesh. He had to presume that the man and the people he had chosen to assist him knew their jobs. Besides, his knowledge about the operation of an electronic force field, energized with particles of antimatter, was somewhat less than marginal.

In one way, the force field was the most recent addition to the Cerberus security systems, but in another way, one of the oldest. The plateau had originally been protected by the energy shield, but at some point over the past hundred years, it had become deactivated. With the help of Brewster Philboyd, the force-field emitter had been repaired and put back into service.

"Kane."

He turned his head and looked down at Brigid Baptiste, standing at the base of the boulder. Like him, she was still attired in the shadow suit, but unlike him, she was unarmed. "Don't you think you need to get heeled, Baptiste?"

She brushed a wind-tossed strand of hair away from her face. "Plenty of time. At last report, Tiamat's status was unchanged."

He jumped down from the rock. "We're not getting real-time telemetry, you know," he reminded her. "She could be on her way here right now."

She didn't respond to his comment, her green eyes never still for an instant, despite the placidity of her expression. Almost on impulse, she blurted, "We've got seventy-seven combat personnel."

"I know. I'll split them up between here and inside, a sixty-forty spread."

"We may want to think about reinforcements."

He angled a questioning eyebrow at her. "Do you have any suggestions?"

"Shizuka volunteered the entire contingent of the Tigers of Heaven, but I don't think *katanas* would do much good. What about Sky Dog?"

"If swords won't be much help, bows and arrows and tomahawks won't be, either. Besides, it would take too long to get word to him."

"We could send Domi down to his village with the baby, in a Sandcat," she ventured.

He shook his head. "You're talking a minimum of twenty hours turnaround time. We might not have twenty minutes."

"Domi and the baby would be safe, at least. Besides, Sky Dog owes you."

Nearly two years before, a squad of hard-contact

Mags from Cobaltville had made an incursion into the Bitterroot Range as part of a ville-wide cooperative effort. The squad's mission was to investigate the Cerberus redoubt and ascertain if it was playing host to three wanted seditionists—namely Kane, Grant and Brigid.

The Magistrates were stopped and soundly defeated by Sky Dog's band of Amerindians in the flatlands bordering the foothills. Grant and Kane were instrumental in the victory, although they managed to keep their involvement concealed from the invading Mags.

Since then, Kane would occasionally complain of suffering from redoubt fever and borrow one of the milspec vehicles in Cerberus to drive down the treacherous mountain road to the foothills where Sky Dog's band of Sioux and Cheyenne was permanently encamped.

No one asked what he did down there among the Amerindians, where he was known as Unktomi Shunkaha, Trickster Wolf, the name they had bestowed upon Kane. At first conceived as an insult, it became synonymous with cunning and courage, after he orchestrated the Indian's victory over the Magistrate assault force.

After remaining with the band for a few days, Kane would return to the redoubt, often times dirty and disheveled, but always relaxed. There was some speculation that Kane had a willing harem of Indian maidens who always looked forward to a visit from Unktomi Shunkaha, but no one ever inquired about it.

Lakesh shouted from the mouth of the road, "Has anyone seen Philboyd? We need his help on circuit rerouting."

"The last I saw," Brigid called in response, "he was down in the storage bays, salvaging."

"Salvaging what?" Lakesh asked impatiently.

She uttered a weary little laugh. "What there is to salvage, I guess. Want me to go and fetch him?"

"I do, indeed."

Kane said, "We'll both go. I'd like to get a bite to eat."

He climbed back atop the boulder and said loudly, "Everybody carry on."

When Kane received a chorus of "Yes, sirs!" his face twisted in annoyed embarrassment. He and Brigid crossed the tarmac and as they reached the open sec door, Brewster Philboyd bustled through. He carried a six-foot-long metal staff, the shaft of which was wrapped with brightly colored cloth. The pole was topped by a gold-colored eagle figurine, and Kane had to dodge aside to keep the beak from poking him in the nose.

"What the hell you got there, Brewster?" Kane demanded gruffly.

"A flag," Philboyd retorted. "Remember me telling you about all the military stuff in storage?"

As he spoke, he shook out the rectangle of white-and-red-striped broadcloth. Kane recognized the colors and the fifty white stars emblazoned on a dark blue background. He wasn't impressed.

"We need a hell of a lot more out here than old flags," he snapped.

Philboyd eyed him critically. "I don't think we do. To most of the people who'll be expected to do the fighting, this flag means a hell of a lot."

"It's the flag of a country that hasn't existed for two hundred years," Kane declared flatly.

Philboyd shook his head. "I beg to differ, Kane.

America—its ideals, its aspirations, even its mistakes—exists here." He tapped the side of his head. "And more importantly, here." He touched his chest.

"Whether you know it or not," he continued, "you, Brigid, Grant, Lakesh, even Domi have been fighting to restore those ideals to this country. It's not the same United States that I remember…maybe the flag itself means something different now. Instead of symbolizing one country, it represents what's left of a free humanity, regardless of nationality.

"Hell, you could look at it as the flag of all humankind, waving in the face of an oppressor who never gave a damn about the political differences among their slaves. Maybe it took all these years and all the postnuke horrors for us to finally realize, that as far the real tyrants are concerned, Republicans, Democrats, Communists are all the same—slaves to be harnessed or enemies to be destroyed."

Kane stared at him levelly for a long, silent moment. Then he asked, "You done?"

Philboyd sighed and nodded. "For the moment."

Kane jerked a thumb over his shoulder. "Find a place to set it up, then get back to building a perimeter."

The astrophysicist smiled slightly and snapped off a salute. "You got it, General."

Kane rolled his eyes and Brigid chuckled. As they entered the redoubt, Kane asked haughtily, "Do I amuse you, Baptiste?"

"More than you know."

They paused just inside the entrance and glanced at the lurid illustration of three-headed Cerberus painted on the wall. "I suppose we could make banners with him sewn on them," Brigid commented.

Kane smiled ruefully. "Something to think about…if we live through today."

Brigid eyed him keenly. He met her gaze and asked warily, "What?"

With a startling frankness she declared, "You've been a good friend, Kane. We've fought well together, and I've always hoped we'd see the end of the fighting together."

Kane found it difficult to keep his eyes locked on hers but he took a half step toward her. "We might yet."

Brigid Baptiste smiled at him, with tenderness and understanding. "I know this doesn't sound like me, but I think you were fated to lead us on this day. I'll obey your orders without question and argument—for this day only."

His eyes narrowed to suspicious slits. "What's the catch?"

"All I ask is for you not to waste yourself because of your anger against the overlords. Don't make a grand sacrifice and leave the rest of us to mourn. Deal?"

This time, she stepped up to him and Kane imagined he felt the heat of her through their shadow suits. He bent his head toward hers and she lifted her lips, whispering, "Deal?"

"Kane! Brigid!" Bry's agitated voice blared out over the public-address system. Both of them jumped and Kane bit back a profanity.

Bry sounded on the verge of hysterics. "Tiamat is finally moving! Direct heading with the North American continent! Picking up speed as she approaches, so I can't project an ETA, but it'll be soon!"

Brigid and Kane broke into side-by-side sprints for the op center. He bit out a single word. "Deal."

Chapter 27

"Incoming!"

As Bry's voice filtered into his head, Kane felt his temples begin to pound, his palms begin to sweat, his heart begin to race. It wasn't fear but anticipation—at least, mostly anticipation.

"Three—no, four hits," Bry continued. "Coming in north by northeast, altitude twenty-five hundred feet, distance fifteen nautical miles."

The radar array hidden within a cleft on the mountain peak looming above the plateau fed the hits to Bry in the op center and he, in turn, relayed the data to everyone wearing a Commtact.

Raising a pair of binoculars to his eyes, Kane scanned the sky with ruby-coated lenses. He didn't see much, nor had he expected to. The clouds had lowered around the Bitterroot Range, bringing veils of mist and a more persistent snowfall. Although little more than flurries, it still cut down on visibility as twilight deepened.

Sunsets were always spectacular in the Outlands, due to the pollutants and lingering radiation still in the upper atmosphere. Full night would fall swiftly, like the dropping of a curtain.

Suddenly, at the extreme limit of his enhanced vision, he caught the glint of reflected light, like the twinkling of the first stars of the evening. He counted four of the tiny pinpoints.

He announced loudly, "They're on their way, people. Keep your heads, count on the person next to you, and we'll get through this."

There was no response except for a shifting of feet and metallic clinkings of weapons being repositioned. In the chilly breeze, he heard the flap of the flag Philboyd had planted.

"Five miles," Bry said.

Still looking through the binoculars, Kane stated, "Grant."

From the ridgeline, Grant responded, "Here."

"Your crew on their toes?"

"It's dance time."

"Roger that. Lakesh, Baptiste, Philboyd?"

"We're at our stations," Brigid said, answering for all three of them. "How about you?"

"Affirmative. For what it's worth."

"Two miles," came Bry's voice. "Altitude dropping."

Squinting through the eyepieces, tightening the focus to bring distant details to clarity, Kane saw four disks swooping through the sky, the cloud cover turning their silvery hulls to a dull gray. They followed a straight, flat trajectory as he hoped. Either Tiamat's weapons systems were not online, or the overlords had determined that if they unleashed them against Cerberus they would only achieve half of what they wanted—the death of the people the redoubt, but the death also of the child who would be Enlil's queen.

Kane lowered the binoculars and surveyed the people and armament formed up for battle on the plateau.

They hunkered down behind breastworks made of sacks, logs and even crates stuffed with spare mattresses. It wasn't the best cover for an aerial assault, but everyone had apparently resigned themselves to this fact and made the best of it. Almost everyone holding a weapon wore helmets and vests made of Kevlar.

Kane had briefly considered suiting up in his Magistrate body armor, but decided he preferred the freedom of movement provided by the shadow suit and his long, Mag-issue coat. Besides, he seriously doubted his black polycarbonate armor would offer more protection from accelerated streams of protons than anything else he might wear.

He glanced over at the top of the slope and glimpsed the mortar crew scurrying about, loading, aiming and stabilizing the launchers. He hoped Grant could stabilize their nerves so they could fire off the high-explosive rounds with some degree of accuracy.

Tossing back the tails of his coat, he sat down behind the crosshair sight of the M168 minicannon emplacement and rested his hands lightly on the trigger switches.

"Quarter of a mile." Bry's voice now sounded eerily calm.

The saucer-shaped craft skimmed directly toward the plateau, flying in a reversed delta formation, as if they meant for the two arms of the V to catch the mountain peak in a pincer maneuver. Their configurations and smooth hulls reminded Kane of the throwing discus used by athletes—if the disks were twenty feet in diameter and coated with quicksilver. He wondered if the craft were personally piloted or remote controlled. He decided it made no difference.

"Make ready," Kane shouted at the top of his voice, even though the flying disks were silent.

The disks came to abrupt, simultaneous dead stops in midair. They hovered less than a hundred feet overhead. They gave the impression of searching for live targets. No one on the plateau spoke, or even so much as moved. All anyone heard was the hiss of the wind and the flap of the American flag. Then, one of the craft dropped away from the arms of the V, sliding sideways and down.

"Hit it!" Kane roared.

A long, ragged detonation, as of an enormous piece of canvas being torn lengthwise, ripped through the gathering dusk. The mortars on the ridgeline gouted smoke and flame, a sequenced volley that began with a launcher on one end and thudded back toward the far end.

Explosions mushroomed all over the hull of the saucer-ship, the reports pounding at everyone's ears. The craft shuddered and swayed like a toy dangling at the end of a string, pummeled by snowballs.

Kane swung the minicannon around in a tight arc and put the crosshairs over the disk-shaped craft. He checked the ammo belt, made sure the box was lined up so the feed wouldn't be interrupted and pulled back the trigger lever.

Tracer rounds burned white phosphorus threads in the dusk, and the electric-powered, flame-lipping barrels rotated in a blur, spitting out 20 mm rounds at a rate of 6000 rounds per minute. Kane adjusted his aim, hearing and seeing the machine guns manned by the defenders join in the jackhammering chorus. He kept the disk in his sights.

He hammered it unmercifully, striking sparks from the hull as the phosphorus tracers impacted and exploded in puffs of fire-laced smoke. Brass spun out in flashing arcs, spinning heat against his face. The rounds from the other automatic-weapon emplacements tracked the craft, the streams of fire crisscrossing, intersecting. Perforations appeared on the hull, then almost instantly disappeared.

From the underside of the disk streaked short pencils of light. Craters opened up in the asphalt, and Kane felt the concussions of the explosive impacts. Chunks of tarmac exploded in all directions. He adjusted his aim again, swinging the multiple barrels around on the gimbel. The ammo belt twisted and Kane reached down with onehand to shake out the knot, but he couldn't quite reach it. Suddenly Domi pulled herself up beside him and worked the belt feeds.

"Bullets just sink in damn ships!" she yelled over the drumming roar.

"I noticed that," Kane bit out. He didn't tell her that more than likely the hulls of the disks were made of the same kind of smart metal as the body armor of both the Nephilim and the overlords.

Even as the notion registered, the hull of the saucership shimmered and swirled. The rims on both sides stretched out to form flat glider wings, as it inscribed a parabolic course.

He squeezed the autocannon's trigger tight as the disk curved around. He targeted the six apertures on the underbelly. He assumed they were weapons ports. The heavy-caliber explosive shells pounded into three of them and sparks flared from within.

Suddenly, the disk slid sideways in the air, tipping over on its starboard side. The wings were retracted into its pulsating hull. Wobbling, it dropped out of sight behind a curve in the road. A moment later, blindingly intense light split the dusk. A funnel of orange flame streaked skyward.

Sporadic cheers broke out among the people on the plateau. The cheers almost instantly became screams as threads of white light lanced downward from one of the hovering disks, then another fusillade fired from the third disk. Kane thought of fire-arrows flying in downward arcs toward the battlements of a castle.

All frivolous thoughts vanished in the explosions that rocked the plateau, the concussions knocking people off their feet and pelting them with gravel. Kane felt his body jerk with the impact. He glimpsed two people tumbling violently end over end. Figures began rushing to and fro in a panic.

"Keep to your posts!" he yelled. "Keep to your posts!"

Not everyone obeyed, but the panic-stricken rush slowed and they directed their fire upward once more, although the M-16 autorifles didn't have the necessary muzzle velocity to do more than ding the hull of the sky-fliers.

"Hit 'em again!" Grant roared from the top of the ridge.

His men cut loose with another salvo of mortar fire, pounding a disk with a barrage of flame and ear-knocking explosions. The silver saucer struggled to stay aloft, but finally slipped toward the mountain peak. Its rim clipped a projecting finger of granite, then spun away and smashed against the crags on the northern hillside, but didn't break apart. The disk bounced, then lodged between two outcroppings. Hook-tipped tentacles of alloy slid out from underneath it and secured a grasp on the rock.

Muscling the M-61 back around, Kane took aim at one of the remaining disks. Tracers blazed through the night from the other machine-gun stations. The two craft instantly spread out in a wide six-o' clock formation, flying in an ever widening counterclockwise circle, orbiting the plateau. Plasma bursts ripped downward into the defender's ranks.

The mountain air filled with the hammer of raking autofire, as well as screams and yells, both of pain and fear. Bursts of flame and body parts rained all over the plateau.

Kane glimpsed Avery, crouched behind a BAR, clutch at the side of his face and slump down. Domi instantly scrambled the few yards to him and pulled his body away, taking his place. She swung the machine gun on its pintels in short, left-to-right arcs, a constant tongue of fire lipping from the long, perforated barrel.

The rounds struck the hull of a disk with semimusical clangs and little flaring sparks. Another streak and explosion of plasma energy slapped two men off their feet in tumbling, limb-twisting tangles. One of them fell almost atop Domi, but she paid no attention. The BAR continued with its jackhammer drumming, the cartridge belt writhing like a brass serpent, spent shell casings spewing from the ejector port in a glittering rain.

A Cerberus defender sprang from cover, the stock of his AR-18 jammed tight against his shoulder as he fired upward in a cursing frenzy. A glowing white line lanced down, slicing through his Kevlar-covered vest just below his collarbone and separating the upper part of his chest, neck and shoulders from the torso below. For an instant the lower body stood stock-still, blood showering all around him in a fountain, then his legs folded beneath him.

The return fire from the enraged and terrified defenders whiplashed up and knocked a constellation of sparks from both disks. The two silver craft responded with a spray of white pulses. The entire plateau lit up with the spattering, coruscating multiple flashes of explosions. The blasts sent bodies as limp as rag dolls flailing into the air, wreathing them in fire. Sizable portions of the plateau flew skyward, mixed in with weapon and body parts.

An eruption of flame dazzled Kane's eyes; a detonation nearly deafened him and scoured his face with grit. The concussion was like a battering ram of hot, almost solid air swatting him away from the autocannon. He cartwheeled head over heels and slammed down on the tarmac with a body-numbing jolt. He felt the sear of heat against his face.

Kane lay there for a moment, eyes stinging from smoke, the stink of scorched human hair and flesh thick in his nostrils. His stunned eardrums registered little more than a surflike throb. A fine rain of pulverized pebbles and asphalt drizzled on him.

Dizzy, ears ringing, Kane fought his way to his feet, clearing his vision with swipes of his hands. He peered through the scraps of smoke, settling dust and swirling snow flurries. The stretch of ground between him and the mouth of the road was perforated with smoking craters and carpeted with bodies, some moaning and trying to move, most motionless and leaking fluids. Smoke drifted in flat planes over them, blending with the snow to make an almost impenetrable haze.

The M-61 lay canted on its left side, the ammo belt twisted and looped, the electric motor whining impotently. He didn't see Domi. He glanced up toward the ridgeline just as flame and smoke spewed from the hollow bore of the Dragon rocket launcher Grant had lugged up there. Propelled by a wavering ribbon of vapor and sparks, the HEAT round leaped from the tube, accompanied by a ripping roar.

Small fins popped open on the tail of the rocket as it rotated, snaking upward in an arc. The warhead impacted on a disk's underbelly in an eruption of billowing orange-yellow flame.

The rocket didn't do any structural damage that Kane could see, but the impact knocked the ship out of control. For few seconds, it seemed the swerving, wheeling disk would crash, but it stabilized and hovered barely a half-score of feet above the mouth of the road.

Praying his Commtact hadn't been damaged, Kane roared at the top of his lungs, "Lakesh! Let 'er loose!"

Because of shifting dust, snow and smoke, Kane only caught a fragmented glimpse of Brigid, Lakesh and Philboyd tossing aside camouflage netting and leaping away from the roadside. Almost simultaneously, the twin towers of the force-field projector popped up from ground. Streams of fog jetted from either cylinder, but Kane knew it wasn't fog, but plasma wave forms.

The viscous vapor clung to the hull of the disk, shrouding it like a white blanket on either side. The craft rose vertically and the fog stretched with it, as if the disk were a fly trying to escape a spider web. Then the silver ship exploded.

To Kane's eyes, it appeared as if the craft vanished in a flowering blossom of intense white light. For an instant, the outline hung in the sky, like a flaming, lidless eye, then it ballooned outward. For a couple of seconds, the dusk-shadowed plateau became as bright as high noon on a cloudless summer's day.

A brutal shock wave, hard as steel, bowled Kane over. He was only dimly aware of other bodies tumbling all around him, as well as boxes, weapons and anything under one hundred pounds. The cataclysm of violent disintegration expanded like a rolling torrent of force. Compressed air smashed against him, seeming to crowd his eyeballs deep into their sockets, to rip the hair from his head, peel the flesh from his face.

Kane didn't completely lose consciousness, but even in a dazed state, he gained a total appreciation of the result of a meeting between matter and antimatter. He recalled Lakesh's warnings and realized now that for once the man had not been acting as an alarmist.

Slowly, he made himself sit up, squinting through the ghostly streamers of smoke and fog filling the sky. A fiery hue lit up the area around the force-field projectors. He couldn't see the cylinders through the haze. Bodies lay all around him, some stirring feebly, others sprawled and motionless, blood trickling from their nostrils. He saw Domi raising herself to all fours on trembling arms and legs, hanging her head, white hair full of dirt and debris.

Staggering to his feet, he helped Domi stand. She leaned into him, her ruby eyes unfocused. The entire surface of the plateau was covered by all manner of rubble. Only the flagpole on the far side remained somewhat upright, and it was almost in a U shape. More people began raising themselves stiffly from the tarmac, blinking around in amazement. Kane presumed they were surprised to find themselves alive. Two of them Kane recognized as Erica van Sloan and her trooper. She brushed herself off with a calm, collected dignity that was almost a parody.

"Brigid!" Kane called and then realized he hadn't addressed her by her last name, as was his habit.

"Right here."

Her voice wasn't transmitted over the Commtact but came from his left. She, Lakesh and Philboyd trudged through the rubble and the smoke. Their faces were dirty, clothes and hair disheveled. Philboyd had lost his glasses somewhere. All three of them looked profoundly shaken. In a trembling, quavery voice, he said, "Talk about the cure being worse than the disease…"

Brushing her mane of hair out of her eyes, Brigid said tremulously, "It was a good strategy, Kane. But there's only one problem with it."

Kane coughed and asked, "What?"

The last silver disk ship dropped straight down through the haze, landing gear sprouting from beneath it. It settled silently and gracefully on the plateau between them and the sec door.

"You can only do it once," Brigid stated hoarsely.

A circle of light sprang out from the hull of the ship and enveloped Kane and Domi, painting them in glaring relief. He shielded his eyes from the brightness but didn't move. There was nowhere to run even if he felt up to it, which he didn't.

"We are *so* screwed," Domi intoned flatly.

Chapter 28

A section of the hull split wide in a triangular shape, as if it were cloth slit open by an invisible blade. Kane resisted the urge to draw one of the three pistols on his person. Not only did he doubt they would do him or Domi any good, but also he was curious to see what would happen next.

A ramp extended outward, the smart metal of the ship forming a long walkway, as if the ship itself were sticking out its tongue.

"You smile in the face of certain death, Kane?" Enlil's enraged voice roared like a brass horn.

The spotlight dimmed, and Kane made out the overlord's lean silhouette standing in the hatchway. "Oh, was I smiling?" he asked, gently pushing Domi away from him. "I must have thought about something funny."

"I can kill you, kill everyone of you savage apekin within fifty meters, before you can draw one of your firearms." Enlil's warning dripped with contempt.

Kane shook his head. "I'm not going to try to outdraw you, Sammy. I think I—and all of us savage apekin within fifty meters—got our point across to you."

"Which was what?" Enlil stepped onto the ramp. He was no longer attired in the flowing purple tabard, but in elaborate body armor of the same tint, with flaring shoulder epaulets and iridescent gem-encrusted pectorals.

"You look ridiculous," Kane told him in a voice heavy with disgust. "Who the hell dresses you? Oh, that's right—a zombie in gold armor."

Enlil reached the end of the ramp, his teeth bared in an effort to suppress his fury. "What was that about a point?"

"Oh, right." Kane gestured to the debris and rubble all around. "This is just a sample of what you and the rest of your fashion-challenged family will run into next time. We cost you tonight, and we'll cost you a hell of a lot more if you show up here again."

Enlil snorted disdainfully. "You cost me a few attack pods and a couple of Nephilim. All are replaceable."

"But what about Ninlil?" Brigid asked as she stepped forward. "You can't find another one like her, can you?"

"Don't be so certain."

Lakesh declared matter-of-factly, "If you could find another one like her, I doubt you'd be embarking on these extreme lengths to claim her, your stratospheric ego notwithstanding."

Enlil's upper lip curled over his teeth in a sneer. "Lakesh, you are such a pompous fool. I almost wish now you had joined the imperator. I would've so enjoyed the look on your face when I made the change to my true form."

He gestured to Erica van Sloan, standing behind Philboyd. "Like that silly cow's expression. Priceless."

The woman's face remained a blank mask, drained of all color, but her violet eyes were hard and haunted. A big-bored pistol was suddenly in her hand. She pointed it at the end of her extended arm on a direct line with Enlil's face.

"Perhaps I'll enjoy the look on *your* face—right before I put a bullet in the middle of it." She spoke without heat, but with a grim certainty.

Enlil shrugged. "You and I both know you won't do that."

"And why not?"

"First of all, you don't have the courage. Second of all—"

"There is no need for it." Balam's voice ghosted out of the gloom.

All eyes turned toward him as he approached from the direction of the sec door, which was slightly open. Everyone looked at him and the gurgling, blanket-wrapped baby in his arms.

Enlil made a lunging motion for him, eyes shining raptorially, but a number of gun barrels swiveled in his direction, Erica's foremost among them.

"Don't be an idiot," he snapped, voice sharp with angry impatience. "You don't dare kill me. If you do, you unleash the full wrath of Tiamat."

Erica's lips creased in a cold smile. "Thanks for making that clear."

She shifted the barrel of her pistol, placing the bore almost against the baby's head. Enlil uttered a sound very much like a squawk of both shock and outrage.

"Erica—" Lakesh began.

"Shut up, Mohandas," she spit. "He's taken everything from me—my son, my position, my home, even my lover—" She clamped her lips tight on whatever else she meant to say and moved a step closer to Balam and the baby.

"If this newborn mutant means so much to the overlord of the Supreme Council, why shouldn't I make him pay for her?"

Enlil knotted his fists, the knuckles straining at the scaled flesh. In a voice pitched so low it was almost a guttural growl, he said, "I returned to you your youth and beauty... restored your legs. I cannot take them away from you now, so I would judge that it is you who owe me...Mother."

"Don't call me that." Her finger tightened around the trigger. "When you cast me aside after I served your purpose, that put paid to any debt. Besides, we're not discussing old transactions...it's the future. What do I get out of being tricked and manipulated into acting as your servant, your agent, your mother for all these months?"

Enlil sighed wearily. "Keep the pyramid and everything in it. Give me my mate, and I will find a place for you as a retainer in my retinue."

Hesitation flickered in Erica van Sloan's eyes. She opened her mouth to speak, then Grant's voice rumbled, "And I'll find a place for both of you—in doublecrosser's Hell."

Grant stood at the crest of the slope and even in the poor light, they saw the bulky Dragon rocket launcher resting on his right shoulder. Everyone gaped up at him in astonishment, including Kane.

Enlil snarled, "If I don't return to Tiamat, she will begin to destroy this world in twenty-four hours. That's all it will take."

"What a coincidence," Grant replied casually. "All I have to do is squeeze this little trigger doohickey. That's all it will take."

For a long, tense moment, the tableau held, everyone standing frozen, eyes darting from faces to guns to rocket launchers to trigger fingers. Very quietly, Balam said, "There is only one way to break this deadlock with no one else, particularly this child, losing their lives."

"We're listening," Enlil and Kane said in unison and then, in tandem, glared at each other.

"Enlil, would you entrust this child, who you believe is your wife, Ninlil, to the care of these humans?"

"Absolutely not," he barked, sounding scandalized by the very suggestion.

"And you," Balam said, surveying Kane, Lakesh and Brigid with his jet-black eyes, "will not permit Enlil to take her from you."

"Got that right, scrotum-head!" Domi blurted.

Balam didn't react to the epithet except to say, "Human and Annunaki, hating and distrusting each other once again. However, the blood of both human and Annunaki flows through me and that puts me in a unique position."

"How so?" Lakesh asked.

" I propose to take custody of the child until she reaches an age of emotional and mental maturity, to decide which aspect of her own heritage she wishes to explore."

"No!" Enlil shouted. "She is not your child!"

Balam regarded him with somber reproach. "Nor is she yours—nor yet your mate. As you said…she is a tabula rasa, a blank slate. She is not fully human nor fully Annunaki, just as I am neither. If I raise her in Agartha, she will not be the focal point of a conflict that will end in the deaths of millions."

Enlil speared Balam with a hate-filled glare, then swept his molten eyes over Kane as Balam continued, "The humans here at Cerberus cared for this child's mother for many months—therefore they will not allow you to take her baby for whatever reason. They will most certainly kill you to prevent you for doing so, and then Tiamat will most certainly lay waste to the world…in which case, the child will perish anyway. That does not seem like an equitable exchange."

The expression on Enlil's face was as if he tasted and smelled something exceptionally foul. Eyes still fixed unblinkingly on Kane, he demanded, "Are these terms acceptable to you?"

Kane lifted a shoulder in a shrug. "I like what I've heard so far…but what's to keep Tiamat from blowing up this mountain once little Quav—"

"Ninlil," Enlil barked.

"Whatever. What's to keep that ship and the rest of your nasty-ass family off our necks once the baby is tucked away safe in Agartha?"

Balam nodded approvingly. "Perceptive. A new pact will be established, one similar in spirit to the one the Annunaki and the Danaan abided by millennia ago."

Enlil's eyes burned hot with frustration. "What do you mean?"

"You and the overlords have no immediate concerns on this continent, do you?"

The question so startled Enlil his shoulders jerked

slightly. He pondered silently for a moment, then reluctantly shook his head. "No, not at this time. We have no holdings here—yet. Our goals are to reoccupy our former territories in Mesopotamia, Africa, the Sudan."

He paused, then added, "But that does not obviate our intention to establish our reign, build outposts of our empire on every continent, in every nation of the world."

"But that would not be for quite some time?" Balam pressed.

"True," Enlil admitted. "Quite some time."

"In the interim, you will agree not to molest the people here, not to interfere in their work."

Enlil snarled out an incredulous laugh. "And what about their interference with *my* work, as I attend to the fruition of the final destiny of the Annunaki, the true rulers of this world?"

"If they trespass in your territories," Balam answered smoothly, "then of course you cannot be expected to treat them as anything other than transgressors. However, as long as you do not initiate acts of aggression, covert or overt, against Cerberus or this country, then the pact will be inviolate."

Enlil's lips compressed in a straight line, like a razor slash. He stared hard at Balam, the baby in his arms, then passed his angry gaze over the faces of everyone standing in the vicinity. Finally, they locked on Kane again.

In a hoarse, husky whisper, full of barely repressed loathing, he asked, "You don't really think you can survive the Annunaki return to power, do you?"

Humanity could and did survive, Kane reflected. Humankind had survived ice ages, all manner of pestilences, global catastrophes and even the nukecaust.

They could survive Enlil and the overlords—again. The human will to live against all odds was nearly infinite.

Kane nodded. "I'm pretty confident we will. We survived your scaly asses the first time. "

A wind had come down from the mountain peak now and began sweeping the smoke and fog from the plateau. The damage and the bodies stood out clearly. At the sight of it, Kane felt a homicidal rage building within him. He struggled to tamp it down.

"However," he said acidly, "an all-out war would be a lot more welcome to me than a pact between us. But I can't think only of what *I* want." He nodded toward the baby now dozing in Balam's arms. "She could very well be the future of both our kind."

Enlil grinned, but there was no humor in it. "So are all parties agreed? Balam will take Ninlil to Agartha and hold her as hostage to fortune."

"Look at it as the purest form of détente." Brigid stated. "You don't have her, we don't have her."

There were murmurs of agreement all around. Kane waved for Grant to climb down from the slope and he did so, followed by his gunnery crew.

"How will you get to Agartha?" Enlil asked Balam.

"I have my own methods of travel," he answered. "And you will return to Tiamat?"

"For a short time only." He shifted his gaze from Balam to Kane. "You'll hear from me, from my brethren again, soon enough. And then what will you do?"

Kane said flatly, "First we'll take care of the dead and wounded. We'll hold a memorial service for those who perished opposing you, and we'll celebrate their lives and that of the brave woman who died giving birth to a child—a woman who preferred death to a future of serving you bastards."

It was impossible for Enlil to flush with anger, but Kane received the distinct impression the overlord was virtually boiling with mad rage. He was glad when Grant joined him, the rocket launcher still supported on a shoulder.

Enlil inhaled a long breath through his nostrils. He half turned toward his ship. "Then we are all agreed? A mutual pact of noninterference? It's settled?"

"As far as it goes," Kane answered. "Yes."

"Good."

Enlil whipped his long left arm around in blurring backhand. It caught Kane on the chin with a meaty impact, lifting him off his feet and dropping him on his back. Air was slammed from his lungs through his nose and mouth. It was an effort to think, to blink. Even the blood seemed to cease flowing through his body. Through the fog of pain swirling through his vision, he saw Enlil saunter up the ramp to the ship, carrying himself with the self-assured manner of a male lion that had established dominance over a rival.

Crying out in wordless anger, Domi aimed a pistol at his back, but Lakesh hastily pushed her arm down. He was still wrestling with the little albino when the ramp withdrew into the bottom of the disk and the opening in the hull sealed, leaving not so much as a seam.

Grant laid down the rocket launcher, and he managed to heave Kane to his feet. He tottered on unsteady legs as the silver craft shot straight up, as if propelled by a cannon. Within seconds, it was lost in the darkness. A moment later, the disk caught on the crags took flight, wobbling as it ascended in a reverse falling-leaf motion.

"Well," Kane said as he fingered blood away from his lip, "so much for that."

"Not really," Grant said grimly.

Kane glanced at the people standing around him. Through his mind passed a brief vision of humanity's experiences on a planet whose environment was often overtaken by natural disasters, ecological catastrophes, plagues, wars and would-be conquerors.

He scanned the faces of the people as they slowly began picking through the rubble and tending to the injured and the dead. They were good faces, strong faces, all different, showing age and wisdom, pain and determination, the courage of youth with a special kind of beauty and endurance. Human faces, once exiles and now explorers of a strange new world—the planet of their birth.

He looked up at the emerging stars, barely visible through the cloud cover. Brigid stepped up beside him, following his gaze. Her face was pale and tight.

"There's a lot of unfinished business ahead of us," she murmured wearily.

Kane managed a faint smile, despite the pain it caused in his lacerated lip. "We've faced the same problem before, haven't we?"

Together, they looked up toward the stars.

THE DESTROYER

DARK AGES

LONDON CALLING...

Knights rule—in England anyway, and ages ago they were really good in a crisis. Never mind that today's English knights are inbred earls, rock stars, American mayors and French Grand Prix winners. Under English law, they still totally *rock*. Which is why Sir James Wylings and his Knights Temporary are invading—in the name of Her Majesty.

Naturally, Remo is annoyed. He is from New Jersey. So when Parliament is finally forced to declare the Knight maneuvers illegal, he happily begins smashing kippers...knickers...whatever. Unfortunately, Sir James Wylings responds by unleashing his weapons of mass destruction—and only time will tell if the Destroyer will make history...or be history, by the time he's through.

TAKE 'EM FREE

2 action-packed novels plus a mystery bonus

NO RISK

NO OBLIGATION TO BUY